GUARDIAN OF WRATH

A NYX FORTUNA NOVEL

MICHELLE MANUS

Guardian of Wrath Copyright © August 2025 by Michelle Manus
ebook ISBN: 978-1-954400-38-2
Paperback ISBN: 978-1-954400-39-9
Publisher: Seclusion Publishing
Cover Design: Damonza.com

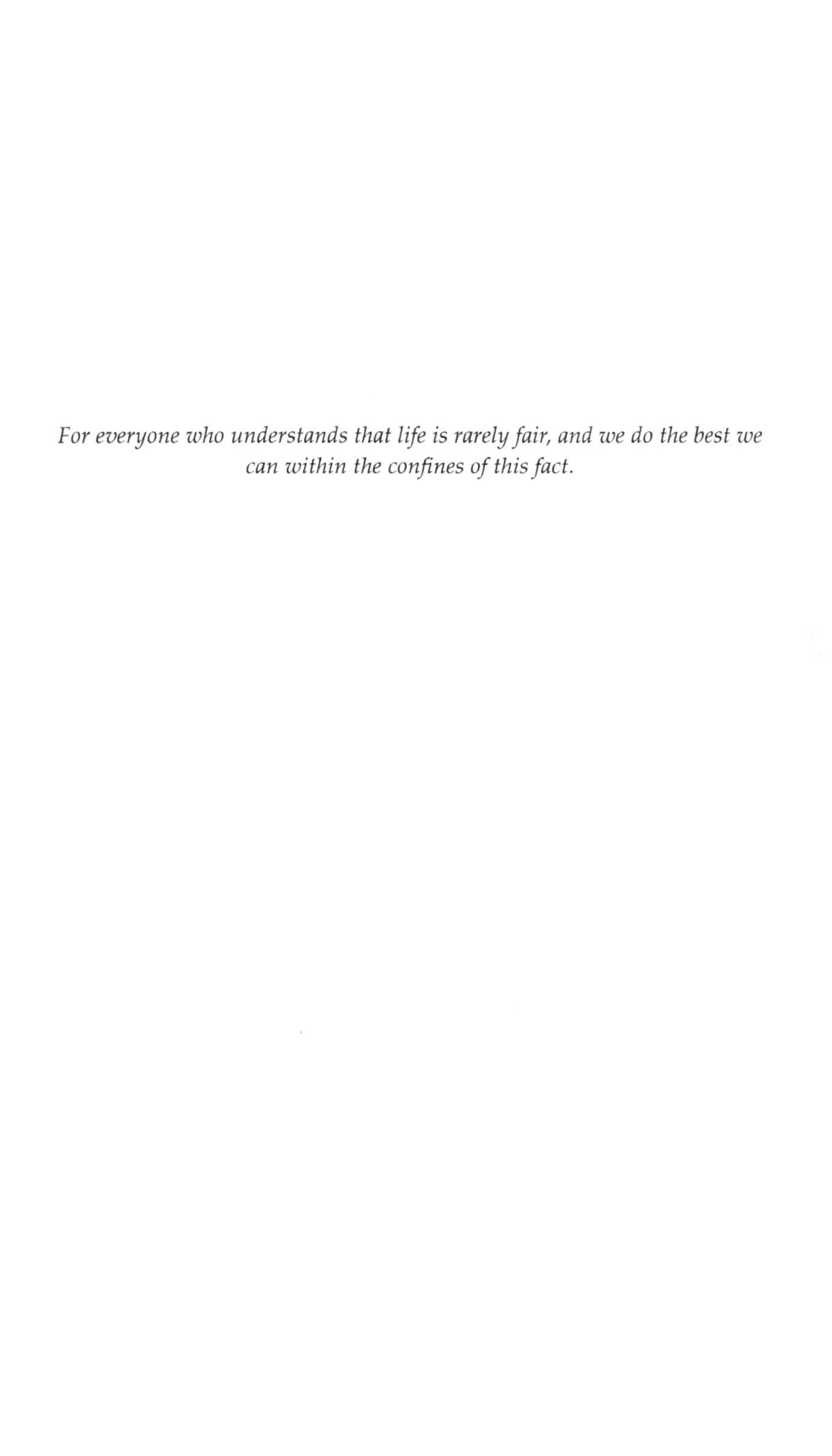

For everyone who understands that life is rarely fair, and we do the best we can within the confines of this fact.

1

Death, Nyx Fortuna had come to understand in the last six months, was a place inside herself. A place that could be found by searching for that darkness she had always known she possessed, but had never understood was a power rather than an impulse. She waited in that place now, perched on the very ledge of death, the power that had brought her here whipping around her in currents that tipped her body to one side of that ledge before catching her and tipping her to the other, swinging her back and forth like an upside-down pendulum.

"Stop that," Jevryn commanded. His voice was as cool and unflustered as ever, though Nyx had come to know the slight edge of tension it held when she put *him* on edge. She sighed and ceased her teeter-tottering. "Death," he intoned, "is not—"

"—a game," she finished for him, in a dry mimicry of a lecture she had probably heard a thousand times by now. "Death is not to be trifled with. Death is power and peace and protection. It is neither kind nor unkind, but it is unyielding and it is irrevocable."

It was that last word he'd sought to drill into her over and over, as if she didn't already *know*. The irrevocability of it all was the only thing she fully understood. She'd held the proof of it in her arms, after all, before Jevryn had turned that proof to ash and hardened it into a stone that now rested against the hollow of her throat.

Perhaps he sought to drive the message home because she

refused to talk about it, and he wasn't very good at attempting to encourage her to. Jevryn A-Morridahn was not kind and loving. He was not the type of man to invite confidences and inspire a person to spill their inner fears and insecurities to him. Not even if that person was his daughter.

A daughter he most assuredly did not trust, likely because he hadn't forgotten she possessed a certain magical object that another person had once committed atrocities with in the name of lost love. Nyx could have reassured him at any point that she was not Laiveran. That as much pain as she felt, as much as the empty chasm inside her where Seth had once been demanded that she do *something*, that something would never be using the Harvester in a misguided attempt to turn back time.

She could have reassured Jevryn of all that, but she did not. And because she did not, he wondered. It was cruel of her to let him wonder about something she would never do. She would give anything that was hers to give to bring Seth back, if such a thing were possible, but she would not give what wasn't hers. She would not become a devourer of worlds because she thought her own pain trumped the lives of others.

But she thought, now, that she finally understood how someone *could*. Because sometimes, late at night, when she couldn't hide from herself what was missing and the hurt blossomed all over again, she wished she was selfish enough to. Selfish enough to do it, and dumb enough to believe it would work. But loss had not fundamentally changed who she was. It had simply chained her to the ground.

"I think that is enough for tonight," Jevryn said. "Return."

Nyx didn't want to. Death was a peaceful place, all washed-out colors and stillness. There was a weightlessness there, a shrugging off of the body that felt like freedom. It was why, Jevryn had told her, the Salyrian word for it was A-Queltr, meaning "of peace".

"*Now.*" His voice cracked like a whip. If she didn't come back on her own, he would drag her back. He wouldn't do it gently, and it would hurt. Well, it would hurt more than it was already going to.

Jevryn had told her, when he'd begun teaching her about the power she'd inherited from him, that she would hate him quickly enough for that tutelage. That to never tip over the edge into death meant understanding every millimeter of its boundaries, and *that* meant spending time there. He'd said it would be painful, and she'd thought he'd meant it was time spent in A-Queltr that would hurt. But it was coming back to her body that caused pain, and the longer she stayed in A-Queltr, the more it hurt to come back to life.

She did so now with reluctance. The ceaseless black ocean of the void beneath her beckoned, enticing her to stay. Nothing truly mattered in this place. It was somewhere to be and yet not be, an escape where she could almost forget the pain of living.

But almost was not entirely, so she turned her gaze from the void. As soon as she did, a snow-covered mountainside appeared, bridging the primordial emptiness. She left the serenity of the ledge and stepped onto that mountainside, snow crunching beneath her bare feet. It was cold, but only because she imagined it to be so. The snow was not any more real than the mountain, and Nyx's physical body was not present in that make-believe place. This landscape was simply a piece of the path she had imagined into being in order to find her way to A-Queltr.

Jevryn had told her that everyone found their own way to A-Queltr, and everyone's path was different. That her own path might change over time, until it was unrecognizable from the original. Or it might stay exactly as it was now. She had asked him what his path was, even as she had recoiled at the idea of giving him any details of her own. She had felt a fierce possessiveness regarding her path, a need to keep it a secret all her own, as if it was sacred to her. This, he had told her, when he'd declined to share anything of his own path, was normal. The path, he'd said, reflected the person.

Nyx was not sure what hers said about her. It was not complex, but it was cold and harsh and barren, and coming to it felt like a stripping of her soul down to the essence. She did not particularly enjoy the experience, but it felt right, somehow. Fitting.

She walked across the snow-covered ground, feeling the crunch and compaction of the snow where her feet fell, the cold pushing between her toes. She walked until she came upon a spiral staircase and paused at the base. Sometimes, she could walk for miles before she found the staircase. The length seemed to correspond to her willingness to leave, and today the bite in Jevryn's voice when he'd ordered her to return meant her willingness, such as it was, was higher than usual.

Nyx placed her foot on the first stair and the mountains vanished, leaving her in an enclosed tower, going up and up and around and around. Her climb up the stairs, like the prior trek across the mountain, was of a variable distance. The number of stairs changed from day to day, depending on her mood. Today the twists were few, but it did not change the growing sense of distance between her and A-Queltr. Each time she left the serenity of that place, it was like winding back into herself, each step anchoring her once more in her physical body.

Jevryn claimed that to be fully in A-Queltr *and* fully aware of and in control of one's body was the truest test of an A-Morridahn's grasp of death. Nyx had yet to manage the feat. Possibly because she did not want to *be* in her physical body. The heaviness of her mortal coil grew with each stair, until she reached the top and the weight of herself was nearly unbearable. A door appeared in the otherwise nebulous space. As she always did, she considered not opening it. But if she didn't, Jevryn would tear through her temporary world and slam her back into reality.

So she pushed the door open and stepped through. The last remnants of peace and light were replaced by the turmoil of her mind and the heaviness of her body. Settling back into herself felt like pulling on an old coat, one she'd worn for years and never thought about, but which she had now become uncomfortably aware of and wasn't certain she liked anymore.

Reinhabiting her body produced a feeling not entirely unlike the pins and needles when her feet woke up after having fallen asleep. Except that instead of mild discomfort, it felt like her fingertips were splintering apart, and that fracture was traveling all the way through her body. She gritted her teeth and held perfectly still, despite the desire to move. Because also like a limb that had fallen asleep and was now waking, movement only made everything hurt more.

Every time she went through this process, every time she experienced the whole of her body splintering apart, she wondered if this was where Jevryn had learned his perfect control. Before, she'd assumed he'd come out of the womb with an aloof expression and a healthy disdain for everything and everyone around him. But she supposed doing *this* every day would have the same effect.

The pain, which had started in her toes and her fingertips, finally joined in the center of her body in a white-hot burst, and then it was over. She blinked her eyes open and found Jevryn staring intently at her. She sat across from him on the plush rug that covered his library floor, her legs crossed, hands resting on her knees. Jevryn mirrored her, the only difference between them that scrutinizing expression on his face.

"What?" she snapped. She had never particularly cared for being stared at. She cared for it a lot less now that everyone kept looking at her like they expected her to break at any moment. Considering "everyone" consisted of all of two people, and she couldn't even handle that, it didn't bode well for her reintroduction into the wider world. Something Jevryn's next words made clear he'd been considering as well, if not with the same pessimism as she.

"Have you given any thought to when you will return home?"

Nyx's heart squeezed in her chest. Sometimes, home was something she wanted so badly she didn't know how she stood being *here* a moment longer. Home was the embrace of Kaliaris's senses, the comfort and steadiness of Griff's acceptance, the warmth and laughter of Morgen and Evra.

But home was a place she couldn't go. "Not yet."

Jevryn exhaled softly. "It has been six months, *na'tria*."

He had never stopped calling her that. Sometimes it comforted her and sometimes it irritated her, and she could never decide which reaction was better. At the moment, it irritated. "And how long, in the expert opinion gained from your years of infinite wisdom, should it take?"

"You cannot hide yourself away from the world forever."

"Why not? You do."

He didn't deign to dignify that with an answer, merely held her gaze, his gray eyes cool and piercing. Hers were no longer that color. When she looked in mirrors these days, her irises were always the deepest indigo, a reminder that she might be up and walking and talking and doing things now, but inside, she was still curled beneath a tree in a maze. And Jevryn knew it.

"*You're* the one who brought me here," she pointed out. And for the last three weeks, there hadn't been a single day where he hadn't broached the subject of her returning to Earth.

"I never intended for this arrangement to be permanent."

"Tired of playing the concerned father already? I'm shocked." She wanted to take the words back as soon as she said them. She had always been sarcastic, always unable to filter the thoughts that popped into her mind and inevitably found their way out of her mouth. She had never been cruel. But lately, cruelty seemed to keep lashing out of her unexpectedly.

At first, a part of her had reveled in the biting comments. Jevryn, who had always been cold and aloof, had felt like a safe target for her need to vent the darkness in her. The only target, really, as the household's other resident was famed for his ability to go entire days without speaking, and Nyx rarely saw him, besides. She hadn't thought it would matter to Jevryn what she said, had not imagined she could actually hurt him.

In the first few weeks, that had certainly seemed true. But as time went on, the steel of his indifferent presentation began to crack, and she grew more and more certain that her words did affect him. That was when a small part of her, tucked away in the back of her mind, began trying to remind her that she had always wanted a father, and if this pain inside her ever ceased, she would regret alienating the one before her now.

And yet she couldn't stop herself from doing it, again and again.

Jevryn stood. His expression was, as ever, inscrutable. She couldn't tell if he was angry or hurt or annoyed. He didn't address her last remark. "I will tell Arradin, again, then, that you will not be returning home yet."

He waited a moment, as if hoping his mention of Griff would change her mind. When it didn't, he portaled from the room with so little warning that she barely had time to Hide a small pinch of the portal magic he drew from his bracelets and pull it to herself. She had started out siphoning even smaller pieces than the one she now held, her original thefts little more than specks of portal dust. Jevryn might not be able to feel the magic she stole, once it was Hidden, but he was exceptionally aware of how much magic it took him to perform any specific portaling task, and how much magic his bracelets held. If she took too much, he would notice, and so she had been very careful to take only the smallest of bits, and never steal more than twice from the same bracelet.

She added the small tuft to the little ball of portal magic, also Hidden, that was always stuffed into her pocket. Was it enough? Maybe. Probably. Did her hesitation stem from true uncertainty, or from how easy it was to remain here in this stasis?

She stood and wandered to the center of the room, to the black floor beneath which ran a river of portal magic. She couldn't feel it, couldn't reach it through the thalacite. Jevryn didn't trust her with portal magic. He'd taken all the empty bracelets she'd been wearing when he'd brought her here, and he had never once in her presence opened the floor to reveal the magic reservoir beneath it.

Though Nyx had looked for seams in the floor, or mechanisms by which it might be opened, she had never found any and wasn't surprised by her lack of success. She had looked for these markers out of a sense of obligation, not because she thought they actually existed. She had thought the home was a Station, despite Jevryn's assertion that it was not.

Oh, she hadn't expected an Arrival Room or a connection to the ley lines, but given this appeared to be where he spent most of his time, and he very obviously wasn't aging, she had assumed the building had to be a Nexus. She was pretty sure there was only one way of making those. Add in that the building rearranged itself on a whim to answer his requests, and it only made sense for it to be a Station.

Which meant the only way to access the reservoir of portal magic was to convince the building to access it for her. The only problem with that? Despite all evidence that pointed to *Station,* she was starting to think Jevryn had told the truth when he'd said it wasn't one. Given her bond to Kaliaris, Nyx was acutely aware of how Stations felt. Even ones she wasn't magically bonded to. She had spoken to Calista and Altiran, had felt a rush of connection to both of them that, while leagues paler than her connection to Kaliaris, was nonetheless marked.

She felt none of that here. As if this residence had no soul. Yet it rearranged itself at a whim to answer Jevryn's requests. Not only had she seen the floor move when he'd wished to access the well, but he had rearranged the interior of the building with barely a thought. Her room, once isolated save for access to a bathroom, was now a short hallway from this library, which in turn was another short hallway from the kitchen.

Jevryn had accomplished this change in the same manner she did when she rearranged the Station's interior to suit her whims. Yet she hadn't felt a presence akin to Kaliaris's even then, and she was certain she would have. She had tried to talk to it, as she had talked to Calista and Altiran, but if the building could hear her, it had given her no answer. That was the primary reason she was convinced the building was nothing more than a building. Because she knew which planetary soul Jevryn possessed and, having once swallowed a sliver of that soul, she also knew that Lethe-Alihana would love to talk with her.

Her biological father might have difficulty with her relationship to him, but the soul of the planet that had birthed his race had had no qualms about calling her "Daughter". The soul shard she had interacted with had not been particularly sane, cut off from the rest of the main body and used to animate a construct, but that piece of Lethe-Alihana had still recognized her instantly. She didn't know if they had liked her, but they had felt inherently possessive of her. They might not do what she asked of them, but if the opportunity was available, she was certain they would talk to her.

That her requests to speak to them had gone unanswered could only mean the building was just a building. Yet she stood here, staring at the floor because she couldn't fathom any other way to make it move. Gradually, she became aware of another presence in the room and looked up.

Kaden stood just inside the doorway, watching her. The first time Jevryn had put them in a room together, a mere two days after bringing her here, Nyx had lost it. She couldn't remember precisely what she'd said, but she could imagine, because she remembered how she'd felt in that moment. Like Jevryn thought if he threw Kaden at her, someone she'd once had a relationship with, that she would stop feeling the way she felt and move on to something—someone—else.

Calling her mood at that time livid grossly understated her reaction. The event had occurred in the kitchen and Nyx had broken every breakable item within reach by throwing them all at Jevryn's head. None of them had hit. As it turned out, he could draw his sword in less than a breath, and he'd cut everything she'd thrown at him to pieces.

When she'd finally raged herself out, the black in her veins fading, she'd realized that somewhere in between cutting down projectiles, Jevryn had portaled Kaden out of the room. He'd said only, "My prior experience with you led me to believe that, despite your obvious inheritance of the A-Morridahn temper, you were a reasonable person and I did not need to confine my other tenant to an entirely separate area of the home. I see that I was mistaken."

That was the point at which she'd realized Jevryn hadn't thrown them together at all. He'd simply brought her to the kitchen, and Kaden had happened to be there.

She'd never apologized. Her incessant need to say *I'm sorry* every time she felt bad, or was worried someone had misinterpreted something she'd said or done, had become muted beneath the anger that always simmered beneath her skin these days, ready to burst out at any moment. So she hadn't said the words. But she had, after a few days, told Jevryn he could arrange his house and his "tenants" however he wanted.

How much rearranging he'd done, she didn't entirely know, but she was vaguely aware that Kaden's room was somewhere on the other side of the kitchen, like Jevryn's was somewhere on another side of the library. He'd placed them all like spokes on a wheel, with the library and the kitchen at the heart, with the hallways being the spokes that led to different endpoints. There were other rooms, but they remained inaccessible unless Jevryn portaled her to them.

Nyx had gotten used to Kaden's presence, mostly because he spoke so little. For the first time in a long time, she appreciated his taciturn nature. For the most part, she never saw him, and after a while she had put together that he only appeared whenever Jevryn was gone. Not gone from the common spaces, but gone from the house entirely. Her father thought she needed a babysitter when he wasn't around, and he'd decided Kaden was the man for the job.

Nyx had spoken to Kaden precisely once, and only then because she'd needed something she hadn't thought Jevryn would give her without a lecture or an are-you-sure or a pitying glance. So she'd waited until he was gone, then taken Seth's raven-feather earring to Kaden and said, "I need my ear pierced." All Kaden had done was nod and come back two days later with a piercing needle, a starter earring, and some saline wash.

It had barely hurt, and when she had switched the starter earring out for the raven's feather far earlier than was advisable, Jevryn had had the good sense to not comment on the change. But he had left immediately after he'd seen it, and she had little doubt he'd gone straight to Earth Between, to the Station—*her* Station—and Griff. Because not long after, he'd started asking her when she wanted to return home. Something about wearing her dead boyfriend's earring had clearly worried both of her fathers, and made them reconsider if taking her to an isolated location was really the best choice for her.

That had been a month ago. Despite her having done nothing suspicious during any of Jevryn's absences, each time he left, Kaden still came out. Today he'd settled into one corner of the library, like he always did, where she could pretend he wasn't there, like *she* always did. She wasn't sure when she'd decided to hate him simply because he was alive and Seth wasn't. Maybe it was because she couldn't look at him without thinking of Seth. Or maybe it was because he had to know how she felt and he just…took it.

Nyx slipped her hand into her pocket, brushing her fingers against the portal magic there. Was it enough?

She didn't want to be here anymore. But she couldn't go *home*, either, because nothing had changed from when Jevryn had taken her away. *She* hadn't changed. She might be walking and talking, but inside she was still trapped in that moment of loss, and she didn't know if stopping Kiev A-Morridahn would fix it, but she did know someone had to. She knew *she* had to.

But if she was going to do it, she needed three things: portal magic, a container for it, and a way to find her uncle. There was no point in thinking about the third until she had the first two, and no point in amassing significant portal magic without the second.

Searching Jevryn's house for any spare portal magic bracelets he might have lying around was impossible, even when he was gone, because the only time Kaden let her out of his sight when he was on watchdog detail was when she went to the bathroom. If she decided to search Jevryn's rooms anyway, he might not prevent her—she really didn't know—but he would almost certainly tell Jevryn about it later. All of which meant she wouldn't be finding what she needed here. That was fine. She knew where else she could find it. She'd just needed enough magic to get there.

So did she have enough? It was time to find out.

She spun and made for her room. *Please don't follow me. Please don't—*

A chair creaked behind her as Kaden stood. She halted, looked over her shoulder, and snapped, "I don't need an escort."

"Where are you going?"

"To the one room at the end of this hallway," she bit off. "Obviously."

He shook his head. "Where are you *going*, Nyx?"

The ice of unease stole up her spine. "I don't know what you mean."

"You've been stealing portal magic from Jevryn for weeks."

The ice sprouted fingers that wrapped around her throat. She thought about denying it anyway, but what was the point? "Does he know?"

Kaden shook his head again. If Jevryn hadn't realized what she was doing, how had Kaden?

"You focus on him too intently when he portals out," he said in answer to her unasked question. "Where are you going?"

"It doesn't matter. I'll be back before he is."

"Nyx—"

"Are you going to tell him?"

He studied her for a long moment, a muscle feathering in his jaw. "No."

That answer took her off guard enough she almost asked him why not. She'd expected a *yes*. But she didn't want to invite further discussion, so she only said, "Good."

And before she could change her mind, before she could question herself, she grabbed hold of the magic and portaled.

2

Nyx hadn't portaled in six months, but it came to her easily. A quick search through the magic to her anchor point and then she was hooked, hurtling through the universe in a blink, landing next to a tree outside her Station. She reached up and brushed her fingers against the throwing star embedded in the trunk, fingers gliding along the smooth metal.

A flash of black hair, warm brown eyes, a perpetual smirk. She shoved the memory out before it could take root. If it did, she would stay there, wrapped in the warmth of it, until two words wormed their way through, like they always did: *her fault*. She'd been so insistent that she had to go to Kyvren, that no one else could possibly ensure the Meerkin were well. She'd let Kiev realize she could find Seth beneath the cloak of his illusion, when she'd yelled at him in the prisons of Eravendrin, so Kiev's phantom snakes wouldn't touch him. She'd looked for him after the battle, so foolishly naive in thinking Kiev had fled.

She knew what someone else would tell her, if she explained it that way. She knew what *she* would tell someone else in her place: *It isn't your fault.* She could tell herself that all she wanted, but the thing about being on the inside of the problem? What she told herself didn't change how she felt.

Her hand dropped from the throwing star and she approached the invisible boundary that demarcated the Station's grounds from the rest of Earth Between. The raven's feather dangling from her left ear fluttered in the light breeze. Now that she was here, she wished she hadn't come. In Jevryn's home, everything was muted: her emotions, her thoughts, her pain. Jevryn's home was quiet. Built as it was, from thick rock with no physical ingress or egress, precious little managed to find its way inside to *make* sound. No noises from the outside world filtered through the solid stone walls, no pets wandered the halls to demand food or attention, and no appliances hummed and whirred as they would in Dead Earth.

She would have once found it amusing that he'd ostensibly brought her to his residence to ensure she lived, when the place had the quiet and stillness of a mausoleum. That old sense of humor tried and failed to rise more than a scant millimeter in her chest. It was a brief curl of smoke, quickly dissipated by the unyielding wind of her indifference.

But beneath indifference, pain was unfurling from a long slumber, awakened by the noise of the world around her. The *life* of the world around her. It all felt so loud. The call and chatter of the birds, the scurrying of squirrels, the rustle of leaves in the wind. An assault of sounds and scents and textures that had been absent from her life, now all clambering for attention at once. She'd been in a deprivation chamber of sorts, she supposed, and now she'd thrust herself into normality with no care or preparation.

Far more than the world itself, though, looking at the Station hurt. She felt like someone who had been missing for years, only to claw their way back to their home and find themselves unable to go inside. Instead they stood out in the frigid cold, looking through a window into the warmth beyond, wondering if the people they'd left inside would even want them back. The boundary was her window, the Station was her home, and the people she couldn't see.

Was anyone even still inside, save for Griff? Kalvar was gone, Jevryn having informed her he'd passed the exams for entrance to the Governance Academy. Liya had returned to Alzherra with Valedan. That only left Evra and Morgen, and what reason would they have had to stay? Nyx closed her eyes, remembering that awful crack as Evra, thrown out of Nyx's room, had hit the wall.

Nyx hadn't meant to hurt her. She'd just wanted her to *stop*. Stop trying to make Nyx get up, stop trying to make her be normal. She hadn't been capable of normal—not even enough to apologize, to try to fix it—and Evra had left and hadn't come back. On Nyx's good days, she didn't blame Evra for that. On her bad days, she felt like everyone was happy to be rid of her. And while part of her wanted to apologize to Evra now, to fix things *now*, she wouldn't. She couldn't.

The only thing that got her out of bed in the mornings was a single thought: Kiev A-Morridahn had to pay. That thought, and the anger that burned behind it, was what had given her the patience to steal enough magic to bring herself here. She wasn't sure what was left of her outside of that desire. So she focused on what she needed now—the portal magic bracelets in her room, the ones still filled with magic, and which could be refilled again after they were used.

Despite Jevryn's belief that teaching her to "be an A-Morridahn" was just the thing to once again give meaning to her life, and despite her absorbing his lessons without complaint, he didn't trust her. It was a completely warranted distrust, but it made her life difficult. He wasn't going to hand her a wealth of portal magic without suspicion, and while he might be willing to return her to her life here at the Station, she didn't think Kaliaris would let her go again. Not for a long, long time.

The travel tattoo on her left hand had ticked down from a two to a one, and though Kaliaris had granted her an unlimited timeframe on this absence, she doubted they would do so a second time. If she walked through the Station doors and announced her presence, Kaliaris would keep her, and she couldn't stay. Not yet. Not until she finished this. And even then…

She swallowed. She would worry about *then* when—if—it came. All of which meant she needed to get into the Station, up to her room, without Griff or Kaliaris knowing she was there. So she could leave again without them ever knowing she had come.

She didn't know if that was actually possible. Seth, for all his brilliance with illusion, had never managed to go beneath the Station's notice. She could picture him in their room, whining about how he'd done everything right, covered all the senses, and yet she —through Kaliaris—could still always tell where he was within the Station.

The memory was a knife through her heart. It was exactly why she didn't want to be here. The quiet stillness of her rooms in Jevryn's home made her time there feel as if it was in stasis. As if time wasn't passing at all, as if the world didn't really exist. Nothing felt truly urgent within its walls, and it had always felt like she could emerge from them and find everything outside picking up at the moment Jevryn had carried her away from it all.

But however it might feel that way, time hadn't stopped in the rest of the world while she was gone. And she wasn't ready to face how everything had changed. She wasn't ready to face an actual life without Seth in it. She didn't know how to live that life.

So she shoved the memory of him—the memory of everyone—aside and focused on the cloak of Hiding woven around her. Despite how a Hiding could be used interchangeably with an illusion of invisibility, the two were not the same thing. An illusion masked a person's presence by mimicking the environment as it would be without the person in it, replacing the sights and sounds and touch of the person with the sights and sounds and textures of the ordinary environment.

Hidden magic did not work in the same way. When she Hid something from a person, she wasn't tricking the person's senses into believing that everything they saw and heard and felt was exactly as it would be without the object there. She was removing the idea of the thing from the fabric of their existence, and that was always a thing more easily done from a sideways approach.

Nyx *knew* she couldn't have Hidden herself from the Station while she was already on its grounds. She did not possess the amount of magic it would take to convince a being as immense as Kaliaris that she was no longer present when they knew she was. She didn't even think it would have worked before, if she'd left the Station for a few minutes and come back Hidden. She would still have been touching Kaliaris' ground, breathing their air. They would have been expecting her return, and they would recognize the ripple as she stepped beyond the boundary *as* her.

Now…now they still might. But now they were not expecting her. Now, if she walked in Hidden, her magic whispering that she wasn't there, they would have no reason to believe she *was*. No reason to fight against her magic in order to *continue* believing she was. And if they didn't do that, then the effort required to maintain the Hiding would not become so vast that she couldn't keep it going.

She couldn't know how it would turn out until she crossed the threshold. And yet she didn't want to take that first step. She glanced at her watch, the pang that went through her at seeing it muted by the number of times she'd felt it. Thirteen minutes, twenty-three seconds. That was how long she'd been standing here. Slightly less time than Jevryn had been gone. Sometimes, when he left, it was for twenty minutes. Sometimes it was half a day.

Nyx quit stalling and crossed the threshold. Instinctively, she wanted to reach for Kaliaris' senses, to sink into them, to come *home*. She shut them out ruthlessly, sinking deep into her Hiding, so far removed that she was a hairs-breadth from being lost inside herself, every iota of her magic whispering *Not here, not here, I'm not here.*

She waited, her breath caught in her chest. A slight ripple went through the Station. A light brush from Kaliaris, but it was pointed at the general area, not at her specifically, and so it slipped off the cloak of her Hiding. Another ripple traveled through the Station, a disappointed sigh, and her sense of Kaliaris' attention vanished.

Nyx exhaled. Not caught yet. On her left arm, Constance, which had foregone its usual bo-staff form in the last few months in favor of a more easily worn bracer, warmed gently, as if happy to be back within the Station's grounds. Nyx gave it an absent pat and jogged to the back porch, pausing at the closed door. If she opened it, Kaliaris would *feel* it open. Griff, through Kaliaris, would feel it open. With Nyx Hidden, there would be no easy explanation for *why* the door had opened, and if either Griff or Kaliaris noticed and focused their attention on the event, she might be caught. And yet the Station was a large place. Though it lacked the wealth of residents it had once had, there could still be enough going on that Griff and Kaliaris might miss that, to them, it would appear the door had opened unaided by human hands.

She was trying to decide if it was worth it or not when movement flashed on the other side of the glass. She moved back and to the side as the door slid open and Evra and Morgen stepped out.

Here. They were both still here. They hadn't left.

The relief that swelled in Nyx's chest at this simple fact almost made her miss her opportunity to slip inside, but she darted through the door just before Evra closed it. Nyx watched as the two of them moved away. Evra's gaze caught on the television mounted on the patio wall, a strange expression crossing her face. She said something to Morgen, but without tapping into Kaliaris's senses—

and thus alerting the Station to her presence—Nyx couldn't hear what it was. Morgen wrapped his arms around her, his lips moving as he responded. He looked a little hurt and a little angry—they both did, but not at each other.

Given where Evra had looked before she'd spoken—and the fact a glance at the weekday readout on Nyx's watch showed it was movie night—Nyx could guess what they were hurt and angry about: her. And yet Nyx was hurt and angry too. That they had—all of them—sent her away to be Jevryn's problem. She knew he visited the Station regularly, but had he ever returned with so much as a letter from any of them? No.

She shook off the confused tumult of her feelings and backed away from the door, heading for the spiral staircase that led up to her bedroom. She sprinted up the stairs and halted at the landing, not even breathing hard. If Jevryn was good for one thing other than teaching her about death magic, it was increasing her physical endurance. He'd taken one look at her swordsmanship, wrinkled his nose, and pronounced it "barely passable".

The sword had never been her favorite weapon. She had always, even in her youth, preferred non-bladed weapons or hand-to-hand, and she'd practiced with bladed weapons just enough to keep Viktor off her back. Since she'd decided to go after Kiev, it felt like an oversight, so she'd had Constance shift from staff to sword, and started going through forms.

That was how Jevryn had found her, in his gymnasium. Given that her technique was, apparently, an affront to nature, he'd taken it upon himself to correct it. After her first "lesson", he'd pointed at the wall, where a door had opened, leading to a circular track. Evra would be shocked to learn Nyx had been doing regular cardio of her own volition. She thought she finally understood the purpose—the hope that if she ran fast enough, for long enough, she could outrun the shadows chasing her.

But she never did.

She forced herself back to the present. The door to her bedroom was open, as if in anticipation of her return. Her bed was made. She doubted—knew—she hadn't left it that way, and she wondered at Griff tidying the space. If it had made him feel better to do it. If it had made him feel worse.

She set her teeth and strode in, ignoring the room and all the memories it held. She walked straight for the chest settled in a recessed portion of the wall, grateful that the fact it was already Hidden meant Kaliaris would not feel it open. She popped open the secret drawer at the bottom, looking at the options available to her. Only three bracelets were left. She'd been wearing all the others, and Jevryn had taken them back.

She swiped the three and clasped them around her right forearm, a tension she hadn't realized she'd carried dissipating at the familiar comfort of the magic. A survey of her remaining options told her she should have had Kaden pierce her right ear as well as her left. But she hadn't, and since she wasn't going to be removing the raven's feather earring she wore, she skipped over all of the earring options. It left her with a few necklaces, which she layered, and several rings, which she slid on to whichever fingers they would fit.

Closing the chest, she rose. She should leave. Get in, get out. That had been the plan. Instead, she found her feet carrying her, seemingly of their own accord, to Griff's room. She wasn't surprised to find Jevryn with him. She'd known exactly where her biological father was going when he'd left. She *was* surprised to find Griff looking as he had in the picture he'd once shown her. Tall, with warm brown skin and golden hair, those magnificent golden wings draped behind him.

Jevryn sat next to him, their hands lightly clasped, and something about the way they connected made Nyx think that keeping Griff in his current form required the physical touch between them. They were talking.

"—angry with me," Griff said. She saw the pain on his face, his expressions infinitely easier to interpret in his base Human form than in his griffin one.

"She is angry with the world," Jevryn responded. "Not *you.*"

Griff shook his head. "I asked you to take her. I *begged* you to take her. I accept full responsibility for that. I only wish she would stop punishing me for it."

Something squeezed in Nyx's chest. She *had* been angry with him. That he'd sent her away, that he'd sent her to Jevryn. She'd felt abandoned and betrayed. But once the rawness of her pain had eased, she'd understood why he'd done it. He'd been afraid for her, and yet…it still hurt.

But she wasn't refusing to come home in order to punish him.

Jevryn cupped Griff's face in his hand. "She *is* my daughter," he said softly. "There is much of me in her. And I can tell you that after I lost you—"

"Please don't." Griff's eyes fluttered closed.

Jevryn swallowed. "After I lost you," he repeated, "in the absence of any ability to free you, and with you not wanting me here, the only thing that mattered to me was revenge. I suspect that that is all that matters to *her* at this moment. She is not punishing you. She does not return because she does not want to risk that the Station will not allow her to leave again if she does."

Nyx had never once told Jevryn *why* she wouldn't go back. She had assumed he would think the worst of her—that she was being petulant and stubborn, simply to test him. She had never imagined he would understand so precisely where her refusal came from. Or rather, she had assumed that if he'd understood it, he would have forced her to come back here, where he could be certain she could not leave. Not for longer than a week, anyway.

She wondered why he hadn't.

Jevryn's hand fell from Griff's face and he stood, his other hand still clasped in Griff's. "I should return. It is cruel of me to leave her overlong under Kaden's watch. To both of them."

Griff's hand tightened on Jevryn's. "Could you stay? Only a few minutes longer. Please."

Nyx had not known Jevryn A-Morridahn was capable of softening until that moment—until she watched it happen.

"Of course."

Nyx backpedaled, suddenly very aware that she was intruding on a private moment. She didn't know if Griff wanted Jevryn to stay because he wanted more time in his true form, to feel like himself, or if he simply wanted more time with Jevryn. Either way, it was none of her business, and it hurt to see them that way. Together.

There was so much history between them, so much they had been through. Despite everything, they could still read each other the way she had once read Seth, and he her. And it filled her with an irrational jealousy to know that they had the possibility of repairing the divide between them. Someday, if she managed to break the bonds that held Griff here, if he was free, they had that chance.

She could never again have what she'd lost. She turned away, jogging down the stairs, into the storeroom where the bottle illusions Seth had made for Griff were stored. The ones that let her Avatar pose as Nyx during those times she was gone, the ones he must be relying on constantly now to take Arrivals and Departures.

The numbers were depleted, but there were still more than Griff could use in even a year's time. Seth had practically *dripped* illusion, the magic building up and needing constant use. He entertained with it, he played practical jokes with it, and when that was not enough, he stored it as bottle illusions for some future need.

Nyx's hand trembled as she reached for the bottles. She could feel the magic in them. She could feel *him* in them, and it almost broke her. But it couldn't because she'd broken the moment he'd died. The A-Morridahn motto was not, and never would be, hers. And she wondered how cold her ancestors had been, that they could claim it.

She swiped ten bottles, storing five in each side pocket of her cargo pants, and made her way outside, beyond the boundary before Kaliaris—or Griff—could notice that something had moved on a shelf where theoretically no one was. She doubted they *would* notice. It was such a small thing in the grand scheme of Kaliaris's senses, like a fly landing on the hide of an elephant, but it was better to be off the premises just in case.

And when, as she turned back for a final look at the Station, Jevryn came striding out, she knew it was good she hadn't lingered. A thin line of portal magic streamed to her fingertips in answer to her call, and she reached for the anchor left in her room in Jevryn's home. It was fortunate she could make anything into an anchor merely by Hiding it, because while she had the anchor Jevryn had given her to his library, she didn't know if he would be aware of it if she used it.

The portal spun open and she stepped through, into her room. She Hid the bottle illusions, shoved them into a dresser drawer, and dashed for the library. Kaden's eyebrows raised as she ran in. She threw herself onto the couch, grabbed the nearest book and opened it to a random page half a second before Jevryn blinked into the room.

He looked completely unruffled, but then, he always did around her. She suspected Griff was the only person he ever allowed himself to be vulnerable with, and she wasn't even sure if she would call what she'd witnessed between them in the Station vulnerability so much as honesty. Then again, maybe the two were the same thing.

He took a step away from her, then froze and turned back, a frown furrowing his brow. Her heart was a staccato beat in her chest as she checked the bracelets, the necklaces, the rings, looking for one she had somehow forgotten, but they were all Hidden. So what had caught his attention? Were there pine needles stuck in the tread of her boots, giving away the fact she'd left the house? Or was her guilt simply written all over her face?

"I had no idea your grasp of the Salyrian language had progressed to the point that you now find ancient philosophical tomes accessible," he said finally.

Nyx had to work to control a sigh of relief as she focused on the page before her. The book she'd grabbed must have been whatever Jevryn had been reading last, as the words were, in fact, impenetrable to her. He'd been trying to teach it to her, but it turned out both that he wasn't a very good teacher when it came to languages, and she wasn't a very good student. "It hasn't."

She flipped the book around, showing him a page covered in an illustration of a tree. It was full color, and resembled the very real tree growing in the middle of Jevryn's library, albeit in the illustration, the roots were manifold and gnarled, all tangled together. "I'm just looking at the pretty pictures."

"If there is reading material you would prefer, I am happy to—"

"I'm fine." He'd already brought her two full bookcases worth of books in English from the Station's library, without her asking. If he brought back any more, she would need a bigger room. On the days Jevryn was here, reading was the last thing on her mind. She trained —physically and with death magic—and the rest of the time she slept. She knew she slept too much, and that it worried him, but she couldn't seem to stop herself.

When he was gone, though, sometimes for days at a time, the doorways to all interesting areas of his home walled over with stone, she needed something to occupy her time. And it was just as well that Jevryn didn't know what she liked to read, and that the Station's library had expanded to encompass the tastes of its other residents, because she didn't think she could have read the types of books she used to, anymore.

He'd chosen titles at random and she read them at random, taking an odd comfort in the unfamiliar story structures of genres she didn't ordinarily delve into. It fed an ember deep inside her, that part of herself that craved novelty. That craved life. That part of her was trying desperately to come back *to* life, but the rest of her was firmly stuck right where she was, unwilling to fan the ember into flames, but also unwilling to snuff it out entirely.

Nyx flipped the book closed and set it aside, standing. "I'm tired. I think I'll turn in."

"You have not eaten," Jevryn objected.

"I'm not hungry."

"Nyx—"

She disappeared into her room, twitching the curtain that covered the opening to her room back into place behind her. She wasn't sure if Jevryn didn't believe in doors, or if he just didn't trust her. Or both. But, at least she had a curtain now.

She fell asleep that night running her hand over the portal magic bracelets, the rings. *I'll make him pay*, she promised. It wouldn't fix anything. She wasn't naive enough to expect it to. But she couldn't just let it go. Kiev had caused so much harm. He'd taken so much, had destroyed so many lives. And if he was left to his own devices, he would continue to harm and destroy.

She wanted vengeance, yes. But she also simply wanted an end to the blight that was Kiev A-Morridahn.

3

On mornings like this—meaning mornings when Jevryn was home—Nyx contemplated going back to the Station just so she wouldn't have to endure the cruelty of waking up at four in the morning. While she had no idea what planet Jevryn's home was on, or the length of its days and nights—the house had no windows or exterior doors—he kept their schedule on a twenty-four hour cycle. She suspected this was out of politeness to her, though why he could manage *that* politeness and not the one of letting her sleep in until, say, seven or eight, was a mystery.

She pulled on her workout clothes and stumbled out of her room. The library, perhaps because it had an actual live tree in it, had solar lighting that mimicked sunrise and sunset. It wasn't like there was an orange ball that rose and set, or anything like that, but the way the light moved over the room, growing more intense during the first half of the day and then waning in the second, reminded her of sunlight. It was one of the little mysteries of the place, like how the air never went stale when she couldn't find any openings that looked like ventilation. The rooms hadn't even had *doors*, each one entirely closed off to itself, until she'd insisted on connecting hallways and Jevryn had finally capitulated.

It all led her back to the question of Station or not-Station?

She walked by the tree in the library, absently stretching out a hand to brush against one of the indigo blooms as she passed. For a

long time, she had hoped that the flowers contained portal magic—
that the tree's placement above the reservoir and the color of the
leaves meant it drank portal magic like water. But if it did, she'd
never sensed the magic or been able to draw it out.

Not that it mattered, now she had her magic from another
source. And now that she did—now that steps one and two of her
very basic plan were checked off—it left her with the final problem:
Kiev. Finding him, yes, but more importantly outmaneuvering him.
Nyx had never been prone to hubris, which was why she knew
exactly where she stood against her uncle.

Viktor had taught her how to fight. In hand-to-hand, she was
good. Very good, because she'd found it fun, because she hadn't had
much else to occupy her time, and because Seth fighting dirty had
always made her have to work that little bit harder. The sword had
never been her favorite weapon, and while Jevryn might despair
over her technique and call it "atrocious", she could hold her own.
Better than in her childhood, even, despite the gap of time in Dead
Earth when she hadn't practiced, because sparring with Evra and
Morgen and Kalvar at the Station had exposed her to a wider range
of fighting styles and the minds behind them. She *was* good.

But compared to Jevryn? She might as well be a novice. His foot-
work was pure artistry, his speed and precision breathtaking, and he
didn't ever seem to think in a fight. He'd been practicing for nine
centuries, he didn't *have* to think. It was all just there, programmed
into his muscle memory. When they sparred, Nyx rarely scored a
hit. If they'd been fighting for real, she'd have been dead a few
hundred times by now.

Barring a stroke of blindingly good fortune, which was always a
possibility in any fight, no matter the skill of the opposing side, she
couldn't beat him. If she couldn't beat him, she couldn't beat Kiev.
She'd seen them fight on Kyvren. They'd been equally matched,
impossibly fast.

She could practice for years and never change the fact that she
didn't measure up. She certainly couldn't change it in the next few
days, or weeks, or even months. When she found Kiev, she would
not be his equal on this front. She needed another way, a different
approach, if she was going to defeat him.

She just didn't know what it was. However calming she might
find the landscape of death within her, the chances of her defeating

Kiev with it were slimmer than her chances with a blade. The black cloud of magic Kiev had unleashed upon her in Eravendrin's prison had been no true danger to her. Learning what she had—remembering how easily she had taken apart A-Lethe—she thought often about Jevryn stepping in front of her. About how, despite his own burgeoning belief that she had inherited the A-Morridahn magic, he had been unwilling to risk the possibility that she had not.

She should be nicer to him. Probably.

"You okay?"

The voice startled her, though not on a physical level—she didn't jump or otherwise outwardly react. It was more the surprise of realizing she'd arrived in the kitchen without noticing the fact. She'd been so deep in her head that her body had been moving of its own accord, following patterns, and she hadn't realized where she'd gone, or that someone else was in the space with her.

She offered a shrug in response to Kaden's inquiry and poured herself a cup of coffee from the French press sitting on the counter. Apparently Jevryn actually cared about his employee's happiness, because the French press—and the coffee that went with it—were Kaden's, and she'd never once seen her father partake. It didn't surprise her that Jevryn A-Morridahn hadn't come around to the wonders of morning caffeine. It might actually make him less severe and intimidating, and he certainly couldn't risk that.

She leaned back against the counter, holding the cup in both hands and blowing across the surface, Kaden's question repeating irritatingly in her head. *You okay?* What kind of question was that anyway? One she had probably asked someone else before and which didn't make any sense to her now. Asking it after someone had sustained a physical injury? Sure. Made sense. But asking it when you wanted to know about someone's mental state? What was the point?

When it came down to it, Kaden didn't want to hear how she felt. Not really. He felt obligated to ask and wanted to hear that she was fine in response, and she didn't want to be honest with him any more than *he* wanted her to be honest. She had no intention of opening up and crying on his—or anyone's—shoulder.

He looked as if he was about to speak again—she had no idea what she could have done to prompt more than a single sentence out of him in one morning—but just then Jevryn walked in. He frowned at her cup of coffee. "Is that all you are having?"

"Yep."

His frown deepened. "It is not an appropriate morning meal. It is not a meal at all, and you did not eat last night."

She took a long drink. The hot liquid had more bite than she usually liked. Part of that was because she was drinking it black now, and the other part was because Kaden was the one making it, and he made it strong. She didn't mind the kick. She took a perverse sort of satisfaction in something she'd once found comforting now being bracing.

She swallowed and looked at Jevryn. "And yet I find it so filling."

"You should ingest something of nutritional value."

Nyx was tired of this argument. She heard it a lot. Not *every* time she didn't eat breakfast, because she failed to eat it more often than she didn't, but enough that she was done with the same old back-and-forth. He didn't need to fuss over her like he cared. Like he had any right to care.

"I'm sorry," she said, lacing her voice with false sweetness, "did you raise me? Are things still all jumbled up in here"—she rapped her knuckles against her skull—"and I've just forgotten your loving presence throughout my childhood, during which time you instilled in me a firm belief about what was and was not an acceptable morning meal?" She paused for dramatic effect, letting her eyes widen in the temporary silence. "What's that? You didn't?"

The muscle beneath Jevryn's left eye twitched. "If you have so much energy without an appetite, you may burn it off in practice." He nodded in the direction of the gym. "Now."

Nyx knew from experience that if she didn't go *now* the next two seconds would find her coffee dumped out and the grounds for making more removed to some part of the house she couldn't access. Like her, Jevryn didn't appreciate being ignored.

"Fine." She drained the nearly full mug, her mouth twisting in distaste—coffee was meant to be savored, not downed like weak beer at a party—and slammed the cup down onto the counter beside her. "But you're lucky I'm in the mood for exercise."

"Your attitude is becoming exceedingly tiresome, *na'tria*."

"Thanks," she snapped back as they walked down the narrow hall to the gym. "I feel the same way about yours."

"I am trying to keep you alive, child." Frustration laced his voice.

"And I'm trying to endure your idea of parenting."

"Return to Arradin and you will no longer *have* to endure it."

"No."

He dropped without warning, spinning, foot snaking out to sweep her legs from beneath her. She jumped over the sweep, landing as he carried the spin into upward momentum and struck out with his fist. She blocked, caught his arm and drove it upward, then hammered her knee into his gut. Except he'd anticipated her, drawing his leg up to block.

As she stamped her foot back on solid ground he brought his hands together and struck her in the chest with the heels of his palms. A surge of unnatural strength laced the strike and she flew back six feet, through the opening into the gym. She tucked and rolled as she hit, but the impact jarred her and she was going to have a lovely bruise on her hip. She came up into a crouch, facing the doorway.

Jevryn strode through it, neither hurried nor slow, portaling his sword into his hand as he advanced. The sword he once carried had been similar in style to a katana. But as Nyx had favored the longsword, he'd traded his original blade for something more similar in size to an ōdachi, the Japanese great sword. He said his form suffered from the switch, for lack of regular practice with that blade. If that was the case, she couldn't tell.

She flicked her hand down. The bracer on her forearm melted without heat, Constance sliding liquid across her skin. The blade that formed in her hand was closer in style, if not size, to Jevryn's sword than the longsword she'd once favored. Since Jevryn had changed his weapon, Constance had begun subtly shifting their design each time she and Jevryn fought. It had thrown Nyx off-balance at first, the weight and angle of the blade shifting from where she expected it to be, but when Constance had eventually settled on a final form, Nyx couldn't deny that the end result fit her better.

The hilt materialized against her palm and she grasped it in both hands, swinging upward, Constance solidifying just as metal struck metal. Nyx gave everything she had to the fight. She'd learned quickly that Jevryn didn't pull his strikes, and though both his practice sword and Constance had blunted edges, a forceful hit still bruised like a bitch.

Her world narrowed to strike and parry, evade and cut in. She couldn't deny the thrill that ran through her veins, couldn't deny that these moments were the only ones in which she truly felt alive anymore. That space inside her where death resided was too calm, the rest of this house too numb. Here—fighting an opponent who was better than her, who she probably had no chance of besting without years of practice—was where she lived. Sometimes she wondered if that was where this sustained desire to find Kiev came from—a desperate need to feel alive one last time before she inevitably failed.

But there was something about that thought—not the failure, but the dedication, the practice it would take to defeat Jevryn—that made the gears in her brain start turning. A fight—any fight—was never purely physical. Because there were people behind the clash of weapons, the dance of bodies, the strategy of where and when and how to strike. And people were emotional. Some hid it better than others. Most sought to turn it off entirely when locked in a fight. But a smart fighter looked for some way to turn that emotion back on. To unbalance their opponent.

Even so, the idea of emotionally unbalancing Jevryn seemed impossible. But she knew him, now, if only a little. If she couldn't manage it with him, she couldn't hope to succeed with Kiev. Yet she wasn't sure where her opening would be. They rarely talked when sparring, save for Jevryn's frequent corrections to her technique, her speed, her choice of this or that block or parry, which he somehow managed to deliver without ever missing a step or strike of his own in the delivery.

But there was something different in his face today, as there had been something different in the savagery with which he'd begun this match, and in the end it was he who gave her the opening when he demanded to know, "Why will you not return home, *na'tria?*"

She had a split second to consider her response. She didn't think asking him if he was eager to be rid of her would have the desired effect. He was too accustomed to her taunts on that front. So she went with the one thing she had never brought up, had never indicated to him that she understood the meaning of. "Maybe I'm punishing you for always calling me *na'tria*. Do you think I don't know what it means? Do you think I don't understand your constant reminder that I've irrevocably ruined your life? Do you think I don't wonder, every time we spar, if today might be the day you 'slip' and I find myself on the end of a sharp blade instead of a dull one?"

He faltered as their next strikes connected and they hit a bind. It was less than a second, but he faltered. Apparently, suggesting to her father that he might be harboring murderous fantasies regarding his daughter was, in fact, the right lever to pull. She took the opening, pushing forward and inverting her blade, rotating the hilt toward Jevryn. At the same time, she drew her left hand from the hilt to clamp the two blades together. Her right hand drove the hilt of her own sword beneath Jevryn's wrists, their blades coming almost parallel, and then she wrenched her hilt up and back in a tight clockwise motion that broke Jevryn's sword free of his hands.

It was a classic longsword-taking technique, which should have been followed with her passing backward and bringing the points of both swords forward defensively. But as she passed backward, the edges of Jevryn's sword suddenly sharpened. As if, now out of his direct control, the blade no longer felt inspired to be dull.

She dropped it out of surprise more than injury, the edge slicing no deeper than a paper-cut on one finger before she let go. The sword hit the ground, but Jevryn made no move to retrieve it. His gaze was intent upon her, the irises darkened to a deep, bruised purple. "Is this truly what you think of me? That I am the kind of man who would murder his own daughter?"

Tell him no. *Reassure him.* Six months ago, she would have. But she *hurt* and there was something comforting—something not alone —about another person hurting with her, even if for different reasons.

She gave him no answer. He made no move to retrieve his sword, and she wanted him to. Her blood pulsed hotly in her veins, wanting the fight to continue. So she shifted Constance to her left hand and retrieved his sword with her right, intending to return it to him.

But as soon as she grasped the hilt, a sense of peace washed over her, as it had when she'd lifted his previous sword months ago in the Station. While this blade was different—different type and length and weight and balance—the way it made her feel was identical.

Then, she had assumed—and he had allowed her to believe—that it was imbued with death magic. And it was. But it was not *only* death magic running through the blade. Now that she understood fully what that magic felt like, she could say this for certain. What she felt coursing through her now was something more. Something that had come before the magic. Something that felt like A-Queltr, something she had glimpsed a sliver of when she had swallowed a death and the soul-shard that fueled it.

Lethe-Alihana? She asked the question silently, directing it to the blade in her hand. No response. But she knew—she *knew*—what she held. And it made her angry, that they ignored her. The veins beneath her hands darkened to black as she squeezed the hilt. *Answer me.*

She felt an annoyed submission to the request. *Hello, Nyx Ilera Mira Fortuna A-Morridahn.*

She blinked in surprise. Both because she had expected *Daughter* as opposed to an exhaustive list of every name she possessed, and because the voice was not what she remembered. The soul shard she'd absorbed on Kyvren had been manic, its voice an over-enthusiastic chatter in her brain, incapable of slowing down. This was… cold. Clinical. A voice harsher than the steel in her hands.

The soul shard had been eager to talk to her, to have her talk back, to know her. They had liked her. She had assumed that the entirety of Lethe-Alihana's soul would be as that piece had been. But this half was seemingly unmoved by her presence. Before now, when she had attempted to talk to the house here—and therefore to them—they had never answered her requests, had never once reached out to her. Perhaps they could only talk to whomever held the sword, but given their silence now, they had clearly never asked Jevryn if they could speak with her. And as she realized now that this sword *was* the one she'd held in her Station—Jevryn hadn't gotten a different sword in order to spar with her, he had simply shifted the form of the one he already possessed—she realized they would have spoken to her then had they wanted to.

She pushed the unexpected sting of that rejection aside and focused on what she held. No wonder this dwelling reacted like a

Station when Jevryn wanted it too, yet failed to feel like one. The soul of Lethe-Alihana wasn't a part of the home, wasn't the structure itself, as Kaliaris was in her Station. That the power of creation that came with being the soul of a planet had built this place and could reforge it at will, she did not doubt. But Lethe-Alihana did not live within this dwelling. They lived within this sword.

And judging by how unconcerned Jevryn was at her being in possession of the weapon, he didn't expect her to know that. He didn't expect Lethe-Alihana to acknowledge her. But after enough time had passed he did hold out his hand, palm up in silent request.

An idea—a possibility—came to her so swiftly she didn't have time to consider it. She only had time to act. And yet she wavered, looking at Jevryn's—at her father's—empty hand, as if hoping he might somehow catch on and stop her.

"I'm sorry," she said softly.

He mistook her meaning, and his expression softened, as it had softened toward Griff the night before. It seemed that what Jevryn A-Morridahn needed in order to lower his walls was for someone else to lower theirs first. She wished she'd known that sooner.

"Think nothing of it, *na'tria*. And you should know that I do not call you that because I feel you have ruined my life. The truth is closer to the opposite."

Guilt was a hard, hot spike through her chest. "I know. That's why I'm sorry." She steeled her resolve, Constance flowing from sword-form back into a bracer on her arm. "I'll bring it back."

Understanding dawned on his face but if he spoke words, she was portaling before she had time to hear them. She landed in her room, Hiding both herself and Lethe-Alihana as she went, grabbed the bottle illusions from the drawer she'd stashed them in, and portaled out just as Jevryn arrived in the room behind her.

Death magic rippled from him in waves. The little pulses were not meant to harm but to seek any life in the room, though they would, by nature of his magic, cause slight injury to anyone without her affinity for death. Her Hidden magic fired in response, fending off the seeking pulses.

At the same time Jevryn's death magic sought to locate her, he reached with his portaling ability, attempting to ground her to this place through his greater dominance over portal magic. But his ability couldn't find her beneath the cloak of her Hiding, and she wasn't there long enough for his suspicion that she *was* there to break that cloak.

She landed next to her anchor on Earth, just outside the Station. As soon as her feet hit the ground she line-of-sight portaled as far away as she could manage. A glance back showed Jevryn had followed. He couldn't see the trail of her portal magic, Hidden as she was, but he could guess easily enough that if she needed an exit in a hurry, this was the only place in the universe, outside of his home, that she had an anchor to.

When he didn't see her, he vanished. She exhaled, flooded by a wave of relief—until he reappeared a moment later, Kaden in tow. The latter knelt, a wave of magic pulsing out from him, searching. For her. His magic slammed into her, battering against the cloak of her Hiding, drawing Hidden magic out of her in a torrent in a desperate bid to keep her from notice.

Kaden's head snapped up, his gaze scanning the area. He said something to Jevryn, and Nyx didn't have to be a mind reader to guess what it was. His magic had pinged just enough to tell him she was here, but the Hiding made it impossible for him to pinpoint her location. Another wave of magic swept from him, another assault on her Hiding.

Shit. She couldn't stay here. If Kaden kept hammering magic at her, the cloak of her Hiding would unravel. Jevryn would find her. Without the benefit of surprise, she wouldn't get away from him another time. He would drag her inside the Station grounds and she would never be free again. But where was she going to go?

She dumped magic into her Hiding on autopilot, the rest of her focused on summoning the planetary map. She knew very little of the universe, so her safe options were limited: Lehine, Kyvren, or Tenebris Umbra.

Jevryn would no doubt check Lehine, and she would be all too easy to find there. If she were capable of it, returning to Kyvren would be the smart choice. The Meerkin would give her a place to stay, she had no doubt, would hide her. But the very thought made nausea roil in her gut, tears pricking at the backs of her eyes. She couldn't do it. She couldn't be *there* again, not yet.

That left Tenebris Umbra. That option was painful too, but there were few places in the universe she knew the way to that didn't bear Seth's mark. And there were few better places to lose oneself than in the Shadow Market.

She closed her eyes and portaled. When she reopened her eyes, the red dirt of Tenebris Umbra was beneath her feet. She had portaled, on instinct, to the place she'd landed when she had first come here looking for Seth. It felt like a lifetime ago that she'd been chasing him, unable to remember who he was to her, following the instinctual feeling that if she only caught him, he could answer every question she had.

The wind blew, streaking the tears slipping silently down her cheeks. She wiped her face with the back of her free hand. The other still held Jevryn's sword close to her chest. She flipped her grip on the hilt and lowered it, staring at the length of steel. A pulse of magic went through the sword.

You ought not to have done this, child of Jevryn A-Morridahn. The tone of their voice in her mind was at odds with their words, as if they didn't mind at all that she had done what they claimed she shouldn't.

"Why not?" she asked.

But Lethe-Alihana did not deign to answer her. Instead, they continued on as if she hadn't asked. *And if you* were *to do this, you ought at least to have brought the warrior with you.*

She blinked. *You think I should have brought* Kaden?

He is useful, they said.

She didn't dignify that with a response. Yeah, sure, Kaden was useful. To her *father.* Which probably explained why Lethe-Alihana wanted him. They were used to being attached at the hip to Jevryn, and all the influence *he* wielded. They were sadly mistaken if they expected her to have the same level of reach.

She put their "advice" out of her mind and considered her options for carrying the sword. The thing was large—not heavy, but the length of the blade was longer than was practical for her to use in a fight, though Jevryn, with his greater height, had had little difficulty with it. And while she knew it could shift into something more manageable, she didn't think Lethe-Alihana would do so for her, given their attitude towards her thus far.

Constance, on the other hand, had no such reservations. The bracer flowed off her arm and slithered around Lethe-Alihana, forming a scabbard complete with a harness made out of wide, fine chainmail straps which connected with small clips. It was a back sheath—if she tried a hip sheath the damn thing would drag the ground—and she strapped it on. She'd carried a short sword like this the last time she was here, but the shorter length had made that weapon feasible to draw. The only way she could draw this sword without unclipping the harness first would be if Constance obligingly melted for her. Which they would probably do.

She gave Constance's new form a grateful pat, sucked in a breath, and walked down to the city.

4

Navigation wasn't Nyx Fortuna's greatest strength. She'd learned Evra was one of those people who could be dropped into the middle of a foreign metropolis and within twenty-four hours be able to find her way to everywhere of importance. If she was returned there ten years later, she would remember all the streets and businesses and bitch about how her favorite noodle shop on the corner of such-and-such avenue had been replaced with a bakery.

Nyx wasn't blessed with that kind of memory. She'd still been pretty wide-eyed about the universe when she'd first come to Tenebris Umbra, and since she'd been surrounded by people who had known where they were going, she'd left the navigating to them and focused on things like personal safety. Wrapped in a Hiding, she didn't have to worry about personal safety now, but she was disadvantaged at finding her way. She speed-walked through the bustling city, dodging passersby. She might not remember the exact route they'd traveled before, but she could and did move unerringly toward the center of the city, where the Keeper's spire rose like a sentinel above the rest of the buildings.

She took whatever roads led her in that direction, having to double back a few times whenever a street she took ended up not connecting to any other in the direction she needed. As she walked, she couldn't help but feel that there was something different about the Market, but it took her nearly the entire trek to the spire to put her finger on what that something was: it wasn't that the Market felt safe, precisely, but it did feel saf*er*. It was in the way people moved as they walked through the streets—still alert, certainly, but that alertness lacked the razor sharp edge she'd felt the last time she'd been here. She also spotted no few number of soldiers in the Keeper's uniforms, and while they moved through the streets with purpose, that purpose was less people-to-kill and more streets-to-patrol. Maybe, now that Bryn had more control, she was finally making those changes she'd said she wanted.

Nyx reached the Keeper's spire, pausing to stare up at the black edifice, to take in the white death moat that surrounded it. She didn't feel like the same person who had been here before, who had stood in this exact spot and wondered at the wideness of the universe. She remembered Evra pinning a necklace to the spire's interior wall with a dagger, and a smile curved her lips. Then she remembered everything that had come after, and the smile died. She turned her back to the spire. She wasn't here for it, she was here to use it as an orientation point. Remembering the twists and turns of every street might not be her strength, but she could remember general directions.

So she oriented herself and started walking again. It took longer than it should have to find the right spot. First, because so much had changed in so relatively short an amount of time. The slave pens were gone, new buildings in their place. The rearrangement of a city she'd seen only once, and seen very little of at that, made it difficult to ensure she had found the correct place.

The second delay was caused by the sirens that abruptly split the air, warning of the impending flaying winds. Nyx had cursed her biological father many times, for many reasons, some of them long before she'd known the nature of his relationship to her. Now, she added another curse, this one for his refusal to teach her how to craft the insulating atmospheric spells the first galactic travelers had used to avoid dying when confronted with less than ideal planetary conditions. Like, say, winds that picked up debris—regolith, as Maruca would have said—that would flay the skin from the body.

But no. Jevryn, in his infinite wisdom, had decided that, since she was not going to be portaling anywhere unknown any time soon—he had said this with a pointed look, clearly meant to convey a strong paternal warning—she didn't need to understand how the protective spell worked.

In other words, he thought if he kept the risk level high, she would be a good girl and stay home. When she'd tried to point out the possibility of her being taken somewhere against her will, which had happened twice in the last year, he'd informed her that no one would be abducting her from his private residence, nor would he be doing so himself, therefore the argument was moot.

All of which meant that instead of wrapping herself in sorcery and carrying on her merry way, Nyx found herself joining the crowd of fast-moving persons into the buildings built atop the old slave grounds. She remained Hidden—when she'd been here before, simply being in need of shelter during the flaying winds was not reason enough for the owner of a building to let a stranger seek shelter within it, and so she thought to sneak in—though curiously, it didn't appear she actually needed to. Everyone in the nearby radius was flocking to the two buildings, and none were being denied entrance. No one even guarded the doors.

Nyx slipped across the threshold, accidentally jostling someone and suffering a quick drain on her magic for her trouble. She didn't know why she stayed Hidden, save that she didn't want to talk to anyone, even strangers. She didn't want to be perceived, and it was easier—simpler—to remain unknown. It didn't escape her notice that she was, in this moment, as she had been all those years in Dead Earth: unseen, unknown, and forgotten. The difference was, this time around, that was precisely how she wanted it.

The building doors clanged shut. Sconces along the walls glowed with soft red light. She guessed they served the same function as the lights in Calista had—a visual indicator that the outside world was not yet safe. The thought brought a bitter smile to Nyx's lips. As if anything in the outside world was ever *safe*.

She drifted through the surprisingly calm crowd. "Calm" was not a word she typically thought of when she thought of the inhabitants of the Shadow Market. The last time she'd come here, Morgen had told her that few people lived here permanently, because "If you're even a third of a decent person, you can't stomach it for long".

But as she watched the people around her, she wondered if that was still true. Evra had once told her that Bryn Morrigan wanted to change the Market. She had come from a destitute planet, one where emigration by legal means was almost impossible. The chance for a better future had never been in Bryn's cards, and she'd sought a way around it, not just for herself, but for others like her, in similar situations. It was to that end that she'd become the Keeper of Shadows, the one person with a stranglehold on the illegal portaling market.

While she'd attained the position, her ability to do anything with it had been hampered by the fact that Seth had stolen the key to the Keeper's library, where the collection of stones from every ley-line-connected planet in the verse waited to be spelled. Without that collection, she couldn't truly *be* the Keeper, and she'd worked diligently to cover up the fact. Since Nyx had made Seth turn that key over, Bryn was the Keeper in truth as well as in name. The things she'd claimed she wanted to do, she now could.

Nyx had known Bryn had shut the slave market down, and her walk through the city had indicated she had made at least some progress in turning the Shadow Market into a less lawless place, but the people in this building were more a testament to change than anything else she'd seen so far. They had not only been calm and orderly as they entered the building, but they remained so inside, despite how packed the space was. Despite the fact that flaying winds could last anywhere from an hour to several days, and people in even the best conditions tended to become unruly at the knowledge they might be confined for an unspecified amount of time.

The faces around her seemed…ordinary. And as she looked, she realized there were children interspersed among the adults. While she was fully aware that bad people could and did have children, those children tended to show the signs of having been born to such people. These were just…children. Some happy, some bored, some throwing screaming tantrums, as children often did when they were forced into doing something they didn't want to do—like wait around in a crowded building.

These, Nyx suspected, were the people Bryn Morrigan had sought to move throughout the universe, from desperate circumstances into better ones. Were these people making a home in the Shadow Market, were they trying to reshape the culture of the Market itself, or were they only here as a waypoint to somewhere else in the universe?

She could ask them—find an inconspicuous corner to drop her Hiding and then strike up a conversation with someone. The Nyx who only remembered Dead Earth would have done it in a heartbeat, thrilled at any new connection and happy to learn anything about anyone who was willing to tell it. The Nyx who had regained her memories would have still wanted to do it, but the eagerness would have been tempered from a lifetime of feeling rejected and awkward, knowing her childhood was abnormal and she didn't truly belong. The Nyx she was now felt the curiosity at a fraction of the intensity she would have before. The inclination was there, the desire to know and find out, but it was like a passing breeze. Enough to stir her interest, but not enough to make her do something about it.

She turned away, wrapping the cloak of her Hiding more firmly about her, and walked to where plaques were set into the nearest wall. She was naturally drawn to any written words in a room, to find out what information others thought was worth displaying. And she was curious about these buildings—where they had come from, what their purpose was.

The plaques were metal, dozens of them spanning the entirety of the wall, each taller than she was and a foot wide. Above them, a smaller plaque read: *For those who have been lost, and those who have been found. If you belong, write your name. If you are missing someone, write theirs.*

Names were etched into the plaques. Name after name after name, and beside each one was a designation: *Lost* or *Found.*

Nyx's heart gave a painful thud in her chest as she realized what this must be, and she searched the plaques for a specific name. Was the list alphabetized? By first or last name? And in what language? She reached out, fingertips brushing the plaque before her, and as she did she felt some magic in the plaques respond to her inquiry, her need to know. The names rearranged, until the one she was looking for came to rest beneath her fingertips.

Kalvar Zurin: Found. A pang went through her. Had he seen this? He'd stayed behind in the Market with Kaden and Maruca when the rest of them had gone home. She didn't know where the Moors had made their base of operations before Kalvar had come back to the Station and Kaden had gone to work for Jevryn. She didn't know when the plaques had gone up.

For all she knew, they'd been Kalvar's idea. It hit her then—really hit her—that she hadn't been aware enough to see him off. He'd been so worried, but hopeful, about his exam and gaining entrance to the Governance Academy. About his future. She wanted good things—the best things—for him. She also wanted him to know that no matter what happened, he would always be welcome in the Station. He hadn't thought he had a home of his own. But no matter how much he grew up or how financially stable his life became, he would always have a home in the Station. She'd wanted him to know that and she hadn't even been there to tell him.

But if she could go back, she wouldn't be able to change the way she'd felt in the aftermath of Seth's death. Because she could still feel all of it, trapped beneath her breastbone, waiting for a weak moment to claw its way to the surface. To remind her that everything was now as it had been then, and the only thing that had changed was distance from the event.

She distracted herself from that thought—from those feelings—by reading the list. Name after name after name. She would never remember them all. Would hardly remember any of them. But they deserved to have someone read them. To have them known, if only for the briefest of moments.

When she couldn't read anymore she unclipped Lethe-Alihana's harness and slid down against the wall, settling the scabbard across her legs. Her back pressed to the cold plaster, she waited, staring into nothing. Her mind went...not blank precisely. It was never truly empty, never truly quiet, and never had been. It was more that it went in circles, traveling well-worn paths that were easy to slip into and relive while her face, had anyone been capable of seeing it, went as blank as she *wished* her mind was.

Nyx blinked out of her fog when the crowd around her began to move. The sconces on the wall had shifted from red to white. The flaying winds had passed, for now. She let the crowd disperse ahead of her, having no interest in fighting through the tightly packed individuals, no matter if they could see her or not. Only once they'd cleared did she stand, re-strap Lethe-Alihana to her back, and make her way out of the building.

Once outside, she walked around the buildings, until she could recognize the lay of land behind them, overlapping what she currently saw with what had existed the previous time she'd been here. Until she found the place where she'd seen him, leaning against a building, his arms crossed, his expression unusually neutral.

She struck out, walking around the side of the building to the ladder, bolted to the wall, that she'd once chased him up. She climbed it, much slower than she'd done when she was chasing Seth, and emerged onto the flat roof above. She felt the phantom memory of his breath against her ear, his quiet, purred, "Looking for someone, Nyxi?"

You, she thought. *I was looking for* you. *I always was. And now I always will be.* She walked to the edge of the roof. The last time, she'd jumped across it to the next, though there was no need, now. But she stared out across it for a long moment, remembering the chase, the moment she'd caught him and something in her had known that everything was going to be fixed now. That every question she had, he could answer if she only made him.

She turned away and walked to the side of the roof opposite the one that held the ladder, finding the long rail bolted to the wall. She slid down, landing on the hard stone of the alley beneath and following it to where it dead-ended. She didn't even try to remember the pattern Seth had traced on the stones beneath her feet. She would never be able to recall it. She'd been too busy wondering if she was about to be shredded apart by airborne regolith at the time to bother memorizing what amounted to the code for an alien keypad.

Instead, she dropped to her knees, pressed her hands to the ground, removed her Hiding, and waited. The answer was instantaneous. A two-by-two-slab of the ground lifted up and slid aside, revealing a pit below, lighted this time, instead of dark as it had been the first. Nyx swung her legs over the lip and dropped, landing lightly on the hard-packed dirt below.

Seth wasn't here to pull the stone doorway back into place this time, and before Nyx could do it, Calista did.

"Thanks," she whispered, unsure if she meant for closing the doorway or for letting her inside in the first place. She hadn't been sure Calista would want to see her. Nyx had taken Seth away from them, and he'd been their only company other than Laiveran. Considering Laiveran had been asleep for a few centuries until Nyx came along, and before that had been the cause of Calista's death as a planet, Nyx figured he hadn't really counted as company.

She walked out of the entry space, into the tunnels behind them. She wanted to go to the room Seth had occupied, but found that path was closed to her. Instead, she found herself walking the direction that eventually led to Calista's portal room, to the hexagonal cosmic floor between the six silver posts. That floor was open and inviting, leading to Calista's Heart.

Nyx set foot on the white spiral staircase, descending into the pervasive white mist that transitioned her from breathing the air above to breathing the not-quite-air that permeated all the Stations' Hearts. Or at least, Nyx assumed it permeated them all, since that feature was the same between Kaliaris and Calista, even if Kaliaris made that transition much more unpleasant. Or had. Now that Kaliaris had taken a shine to Nyx, they no longer tormented her with an unpleasant trip into their Heart, for which she was grateful.

She hit the ground, where the white mist was joined by a cotton candy confection of other mists in every color in the rainbow. Where the true Heart of Kaliaris was a vine-wrapped pedestal, Calista's was a fountain spilling into a small basin.

<Hello, Nyx Fortuna.> Calista's voice, soft and cool like fresh-powdered snow, filled the space. <You are making a habit of bringing me the most interesting surprises.>

Nyx frowned. She hadn't brought Calista anything.

<May I?> The Heart's rainbow mist swirled around the space above Nyx's shoulder, indicating—but not quite touching—the sword hilt there.

Nyx froze. She hadn't precisely forgotten what she was carrying on her back, but given that Lethe-Alihana had been impersonating the inanimate weapon they inhabited, it was easy enough for Nyx to forget they were with her. She hesitated. "That decision isn't up to me."

<A good answer. Ask if they will speak with me?>

"You can't ask yourself?" Then, figuring how that must sound, Nyx hastened to add: "They don't like me very much. You might have better luck on your own."

The water moving through the fountain changed pace for a

moment before resuming its normal flow. <You bear the vessel that contains them.>

"That doesn't mean they *like* me. They're actually a little upset about my current possession of them. I...might have stolen them."

Calista pondered this for a moment. <Perhaps it is not my place to argue with you, but I will do so all the same. The flexibility afforded to Lethe-Alihana, given they were never turned into a Station, is akin to my own now. I was bound here, and to Laiveran's control, but in his absence I do as I wish. Lethe-Alihana, sundered, was bound to Jevryn and Kiev A-Morridahn. The piece of Lethe-Alihana in that sword is not bound to obey *you*. Had they wished not to be stolen, they would not have been. Did they wish to get away from you now, they could. So you see, they must like you at least a little.>

Or, Nyx thought as she grasped the hilt, *they want something they think I can give them.*

Did it truly take you until now to consider that possibility? Lethe-Alihana asked.

They could read her thoughts. Great. Kaliaris couldn't read her thoughts.

You are not Kaliaris's child.

She snorted. *And I'm yours? The shard of your soul was happy enough to claim me, but you don't seem to want to.*

The blood in your veins originated on the planet I once gave life to, Lethe-Alihana said. *You would not exist without me. So yes, you are mine, whether I wish it or not.*

Ouch. *Can you read my mind all the time or only when I'm touching you?*

Physical contact is required for us to speak mind-to-mind.

Great news. If she didn't want the soul of her dead planet reading her mind, all she had to do was not touch the sword. *Do you want to talk to Calista or not?*

I am amenable to it.

The scabbard that was Constance split in half, letting Nyx draw the sword easily. She held it out to Calista. Mist swirled, lifting Lethe-Alihana from her grasp. In the initial moment when the sword left her, she had a mild sense of panic that she shouldn't have let it go. But it wasn't as if she could have stopped Calista had they wanted to take Lethe-Alihana by force, so she tried to relax and just wait.

Several minutes passed. The mist that had almost entirely hidden the sword from view now danced and shifted colors as the soul of one planet spoke to another. When the mist went still, Nyx felt Calista's sadness when they finally gave Lethe-Alihana back to her.

<Seth is gone.>

Nyx's fingers curled around Lethe-Alihana's hilt. Why had they told Calista that? "Yes."

<I missed him, after he left. I had hoped to see him again.>

That sense of crushing guilt constricted her chest again. "I'm sorry."

Calista's bafflement was apparent in the flux of colors in the mist. "What do you have to be sorry for?"

It was my fault. She didn't say the words out loud. She couldn't. But that didn't make them any less true. She was the one who always knew where Seth was, no matter what. She was the one who'd given that fact away to Kiev when they'd been in the prisons of Eravendrin. She was the one who'd been stupid enough to look for Seth, so certain Kiev was gone and needing to reassure herself that Seth was fine, that he was alive.

You are a fool, Lethe-Alihana said coldly. As if she didn't already know that. *If you intend to persist in this maudlin line of thought, kindly return me to storage so I need not drown in your self-recriminations.*

Fuck you, she thought, but even in her head, the words lacked any true bite.

Your father is correct. You lack eloquence.

Heat flushed her cheeks and ears, but she ignored Lethe-Alihana and flipped the sword over her shoulder, blade flat against her back, letting Constance reform into a scabbard around them.

She didn't answer Calista's question. Instead, she said, "If you don't want me here, I understand. If you want me to leave, I will."

Another pulse of colors in the mist. <Why would I wish you to leave? You have only just arrived.>

Nyx shrugged.

<Though your company is welcome, I must ask—why have you come?>

Nyx hesitated. "Did Lethe-Alihana tell you what happened?

When Seth—" She couldn't finish the sentence. Couldn't say the words.

<They did.> The admission was gently spoken.

"I need to find Kiev A-Morridahn. I can't go home until I do. And now that I took this"—she tapped the sword—"from Jevryn, I need a place to stay. Somewhere no one can find me."

<You once hoped, with some desperation, that I might know the identity of your parents. You have found your father, but now you refer to him by his name?>

Lethe-Alihana, it seemed, had loose lips.

<Why?>

"Sometimes family isn't all it's cracked up to be."

The mist pulsed, producing a skeptical sound. But Calista moved on. <So you have come to me to hide from the world, then?>

"If you'll let me."

Calista was quiet, the seconds stretching out, then: <In the centuries I have been here, I have been a haven to many who wished to hide themselves away. It appears to be a calling of mine that I am weak to resist. The reasons people wished to hide took many forms, but only one form matched your own, and that belonged to the first of my inhabitants.>

It took Nyx longer than it should have to parse what Calista was saying. *Laiveran* had built Calista. Laiveran had hidden away here as he attempted to find a way to use the planets he'd harvested to bring back his wife, Nyaera, before the Council had wrested the Harvester and its contents from him.

As she thought this last thing, it occurred to her that she didn't have any idea how the Harvester had passed from Laiveran to the Council. How he had lost this one critically important item, and yet been left to his own devices to all but hibernate within Calista's walls for centuries, until Nyx had unwittingly brought the Harvester back to him, rousing him from his slumber.

"I'm not Laiveran."

<And yet I know you to possess what he once did, and you stand here with the same pain pouring from you that he once felt. It is a pain that reshaped the universe. You can, perhaps, understand my concern.>

Nyx thought her response through carefully. She didn't think a flippant *You don't need to worry about it* was going to do the trick. "If someone came to me with irrefutable proof that they could give Seth back to me, and I believed it, and the only thing I had to do was kill someone else in his stead, I wouldn't do it. I *hurt*, Calista. I hurt so much I can't stand it, and I don't know how to deal with it." *I don't know if I can* keep *dealing with it.* "But I wouldn't kill a single person to undo it, much less billions."

<And yet there is one person you intend to kill.>

So Lethe-Alihana had gleaned that from her thoughts, and felt the need to share it with Calista. Why? "Kiev A-Morridahn," Nyx said, the name sticking to her tongue like poison, "needs to die. All he does is hurt people." *Griff, Lana, Fari, Temerex, Seth.* "Jevryn should have done it a long time ago. Kiev's his brother, he's Jevryn's responsibility. But since it's clear he's never going to, that makes it *my* responsibility."

Kiev was her uncle. And while her chances of success weren't great—though slightly improved, now that she had Lethe-Alihana— they were still better than anyone else's save Jevryn's or another councilor's. Somehow, she doubted she was going to luck out and one of the remaining ten other councilors was going to decide to take Kiev out of the picture after centuries of careful coexistence.

<Have you not considered that perhaps there is a reason your father has not done so?>

"I don't care." Jevryn had said he had a reason. If he did, Nyx couldn't see it. And if he couldn't bother to tell her, how important could it be?

<If you continue down this path, you may come to regret that opinion.>

Nyx didn't answer. She'd already said she didn't care. Calista could no doubt feel that lack of concern.

Calista's mist rippled like a sigh. <You may stay, while you embark on this fool's errand.>

Relief spread through Nyx. She honestly had no idea where else she could have remained hidden from Jevryn.

<But Nyx? Take care with Lethe-Alihana. They and I were always very different planets. A being that births death as a facet of its inhabitants' lives is fundamentally different than most. And that was *before* they were sundered. You travel with half of a soul most considered mad long before its breaking. Do not forget that.>

"I'll do my best." What else was she supposed to say to that? They were hardly comforting words.

<That is, I think, enough for today. You are exhausted.>

Nyx started to protest that she wasn't—the day, for her, hadn't begun that many hours ago—but then she realized Calista was right. She might have been sleeping too much these last few months, but it hadn't been restful sleep. It had almost been as if, the more she slept, the more tired she became.

<Would you like his room?> Calista asked. <Or a different one?>

Nyx swallowed past the lump in her throat. "I don't want a different one." She hadn't been able to bring herself to go in Seth's room at the Station. It had been too filled with him. His things, his scent, the phantom memory of his smile.

But it was different here. She exited Calista's Heart and made her way through the tunnels, to the room that had once been Seth's. She refused to look around, to take it in, to remember being in this room with him. She only dimmed the lights and went to the small bed. Standing before it, she bent over and took off her boots. She slid them to the side of the bed, her hands lingering on the buckles.

They were not her mercury boots. She'd left those on Kyvren, in her room in the den, traded out for footwear designed to survive the fire rains. Jevryn had retrieved them, along with the other clothing she'd left there, and returned them to her. He'd done so wordlessly, thanklessly. He'd carried them into her room, placed them by the door, and left.

He could have kept the boots. They'd been a gift to him from Griff. He'd wanted them back, he'd had them in his grasp, and he'd brought them to her instead. Had left them for her, even though she had never put them back on. She'd thrown them in a corner of the room and let them collect dust.

She should have said thank you. She should have told Jevryn to keep them. She should have put the damn things back on.

Her hands slipped from the buckles of her very ordinary boots and reached instead for the buckles of the sword harness so she could shrug out of it. After a moment's consideration, she laid down with the sword hilt gripped in her hand, the scabbard running down the length of her, as if it were a body pillow she snuggled. She didn't quite trust leaving the sword to its own devices, even if the contact meant Lethe-Alihana could read every turbulent thought she had. In this moment, they were welcome to her thoughts. Stars knew she was sick of them.

I suspect I will soon be sick of them as well, Lethe-Alihana suggested.

"Has anyone ever told you you're an asshole?" she muttered.

Your father did, once, express something of a similar nature.

"Only the once?"

I made life quite unpleasant for him after the insult.

"I thought you were bound to obey him."

All bindings have limits. Still, the presence of them is important. Between you and I, there are none. You would be wise to let Jevryn find you and reclaim me.

Nyx really wished her soul sword would shut up. "If Calista's right and you voluntarily let me steal you, why are you advising me to let Jevryn take you back?"

Because I know you will not do it. I do take pleasure in advising people of the poor nature of their choices when I know it will do no good, as then I am allowed to watch the consequences unfold knowing that I had warned them it could have all been different.

"Like I said, you're kind of an asshole. Now shut up and go to sleep."

I do not require sleep, Nyx Fortuna.

"Then meditate or something. I don't really give a fuck so long as you aren't talking."

Nyx immediately felt a sharp bite of guilt for her snappishness. At least until Lethe-Alihana sighed and said, *Yes, a complete lack of eloquence.*

She ignored them and closed her eyes. In the dark, she could almost imagine that Seth was there beside her. That she would wake up, as she had once before in this bed, to find him wrapped around her.

5

Coffee, as Nyx discovered over the next few days, was impossible to find in the Shadow Market. Calista's attempts to reproduce some version of it, based on Nyx's explanations, had resulted in a concoction not even the most desperate of individuals would be able to stomach. When Nyx had asked why Kaliaris could manage it and Calista couldn't, she'd inadvertently offended them and received an icy explanation that amounted to Kaliaris being bound to a planet—Earth—where coffee beans originated naturally, while no one had ever brought coffee into Calista in any form.

As a result, Calista was miffed at her, and Nyx was buying the closest thing to coffee she could find at a shop near one of the Station's exits. On her fourth morning in the Market, she paid for her coffee substitute with some money Seth had left behind in the room, and wrapped herself back under a Hiding as soon as the transaction was finished. She told herself the need to be Hidden when she was out and about was a need born from caution. There was no reason to go advertising her presence, in case Jevryn had people out looking for her.

But if she was being honest with herself, that wasn't why she did it. She simply didn't want to be perceived. The weight of eyes on her, even those of strangers who had no intention of speaking to her, felt like too much. It was easier to not be there, to flit like a ghost through the crowds. It didn't escape her notice that she was now actively choosing to live in a way that had caused her no end of pain when she'd been in Dead Earth, wanting *anyone* to see her and knowing no one could.

But that was the way of anything in life, she supposed—have no choice in a matter and it became a constraint, choose it and it felt like an empowerment. The difference between how she'd lived in Dead Earth and how she was living now was that she could dispense with this Hiding whenever she chose. If she wanted people to see her now, it was within her control to make them.

She sipped her beverage, lamenting the fact that it wasn't actually coffee. It was an infusion made from a local plant root, kind of like chicory on Earth. Nyx had never liked the taste of chicory, but this had a deeper, less nutty flavor that Nyx found more palatable, albeit altogether less satisfying than coffee. Knowing her luck, it was probably *good* for her, or something. Still, it was hot, and the ritual of having a drink in hand was its own kind of comfort. By the time she finished it, she'd arrived at the day's destination.

The glossy black stone of the Keeper's spire cut through the sameness of the sea of red stone buildings around it. A matching narrow black bridge stretched from the spire, over a lake of white sand, to the Market street. Nyx stepped over the torch-and-circle emblem of the Keeper of Shadows that was etched into the foot of the bridge, barely sparing a glance for the white sand that was a potent reminder that if she happened to tumble off that bridge, the only thing left of her would be dust. She'd christened it a death moat before and the name still felt fitting, the low hum of energy beneath the bridge disturbing her as much now as it had then. But unlike then, she didn't dwell on it. She pushed it aside, burying it down deep in the same place she buried all of her unwanted feelings these days.

On the other side of the bridge, she stepped through the wide doors into the spire, the same empty round room greeting her. Unlike before, the doors didn't close after her. Then, she'd suspected that either someone was watching the room, or the door had a trip ward on it that triggered the doors to close whenever someone crossed the threshold. Whichever it was, she was Hidden now, and the building didn't react to her presence.

The first morning she'd woken up in Calista, she'd realized that there was no point in finding Kiev before she found a source of portal magic. So, after careful consideration of her options, she'd decided to risk a trip to Lehine. She'd had the magic to get there and back, even if something went wrong and she had to leave before accessing the portal magic well. She hadn't doubted that Jevryn was just stubborn enough to drop Kaden there with orders to Track the area for her every fifteen minutes in the event she showed up.

She'd arrived on Lehine, grateful that Jevryn had at least taught her how to follow a portal magic trail—in this case her own—not just to a planet, but to the exact location on that planet where the portaler had departed from or arrived to. Given that Lehine was uninhabitable outside of its prison, following the trail she'd left upon departure meant she could safely arrive within the prison's confines. It also meant she'd arrived back in the portal well room, rather than having to face the cells outside of it.

But she hadn't found what she'd expected to. For a long moment after her arrival, she'd simply stared in incredulity. Once she'd accepted what she was seeing, she'd been forced to admit that her father crafted plans that were far out of her league. He hadn't left Kaden on Lehine to watch for her. He hadn't left anyone there. He'd simply taken the one thing she would have come to Lehine for.

The portal well was empty, like a swimming pool drained for the winter, not a spec of magic left. It boggled her mind to think of a single person moving that much magic. What had he even stored it in? She would have been impressed by the feat, if it hadn't pissed her off so badly. Especially because Jevryn had left her, in the center of the empty well, at its deepest point, a single portal stone. A brush of her fingers against it and she'd felt the now-familiar tug towards Jevryn's house. The message couldn't have been more clear: *Come home.*

No doubt he'd hoped she would have enough magic to get to Lehine but not enough to leave, and thus have no choice *but* to return. But while he'd made her plan decidedly more difficult to complete, she had no intention of giving up. So she couldn't get magic from Lehine. She knew where another portal well was. She just had to find a way to access it.

Which was why she was now sitting cross-legged in the Keeper's spire, her back against the wall, Lethe-Alihana in her lap, waiting. She'd spent the last few days getting a grip on the layout of the Market around her entrance to Calista, and following any of the Keeper's minions that she could find. She had hoped, given Bryn's new control over the Market, that the Keeper would have relaxed her security protocols a bit. It had to be tedious and resource-consuming to portal her employees in and out of the Keep constantly, and Nyx had imagined that, just maybe, there might be a physical doorway into the Keep somewhere that she could find.

Unfortunately for her, it looked like Bryn was just as paranoid as ever, because not a single person Nyx had tailed had led her to a physical entrance to Bryn's stronghold. None of them even portaled there. They had barracks in the Market that they returned to each night, so possibly Bryn *was* concerned with conserving resources and was doing it by not shifting her people in and out of the Keep with any regularity. So Nyx had come here, to the spire, where Bryn's portal witches had taken them through before. Odds were, this would be the point of arrival or departure, and Nyx intended to be here when the next portal opened.

She was careful, as she sat and waited, to keep her hands off Lethe-Alihana's hilt. Conversation wasn't what she was in the mood for. She wasn't in the mood for the thoughts tumbling around in her brain, either, but she couldn't get rid of them, and nothing seemed to calm her mind these days. Back when she hadn't known who she was, she'd been prone to panic attacks. Breathing exercises had helped her then, with that specific problem. But somewhere between then and now, the focus on her own breath had gone from calming her to making her *more* anxious. It didn't matter what kind she did—whether box breathing or simply the meditative kind where she was supposed to envision her breath entering and exiting her lungs and count the instances—it spiked her anxiety. It was like the more she focused on breathing, the more she felt like she *couldn't* breathe. The deeper she inhaled, the less oxygen it felt like she actually consumed.

And she'd never been able to meditate, had never been able to accept that anyone's brain could ever truly be quiet, because hers was utterly incapable of it. Her mind was a kaleidoscope of thoughts, and she could force it to focus on a particular one, but she couldn't make it simply be still. She'd read once that meditating wasn't actually about having a blank mind, but about focusing on one specific thing and noticing when your mind wandered from it.

That explanation hadn't helped her much either. Especially since, right now, none of the thoughts she could focus on were positive.

So she sat with her mind running in circles while an hour ticked by, then another. She got up and walked the circumference of the room, over and over until that lost appeal and she sat back down. She'd had no sign of any of the Keeper's portal witches. She'd had no sign of anyone at all. Only when her mind was veering into darker territory, when she'd withdrawn the quarter from her pocket —the one Seth had carried from Dead Earth and then throughout the universe during all that time he couldn't even remember her— and turned it over and over between her fingers for a full hour, did she take desperate measures.

After tucking the quarter back into her pocket, she grasped Lethe-Alihana's hilt. They sighed. How a being that did not have, and had never had, functioning lungs had picked up the ability to mentally sigh, she didn't know. Maybe it was nine centuries with Jevryn that had done it.

Your mind is so very like your father's.

"Don't say that," she whispered.

You both dwell incessantly on things that cannot be changed, things that bring you nothing but sorrow. You have the same notion of fairness, the same foolish idea that there should be justice in the universe, and that if that justice does not occur organically, you will have to create it for yourself.

Nyx did not want to agree with her father on anything, but… "What's so wrong with that?" The creating justice part, not the dwelling incessantly part. Wasn't justice entirely a created concept? She'd seen too much to believe in any karmic force, and "justice systems" as they existed only did so because someone, at some point in time, had created them.

You tend to exclude all else—people and things—in service to the notion. Jevryn has practically been a hermit for nine centuries. It makes my life dreadfully dull. I once experienced the lives of millions and now I am reduced to one.

"Is that why you came with me?" she asked, a little incredulous. "So you could see more people?"

No. Though I admit the change of pace is refreshing, even if you allow me to see so very little of the world.

The desire to ask why they *had* come with her warred with a grudging curiosity. "You can't see anything unless I'm touching you?"

I am inhabiting a sword, they said, enunciating each word with careful slowness, as if she were particularly dim. *With what eyes am I to see, if not yours?*

She hadn't thought about it. Probably because: "You don't seem all that confused about what's going on whenever I *do* talk to you." If they were in the dark unless she was touching them, shouldn't they be more confused whenever she checked in?

I am not senseless, Lethe-Alihana said irritably. *I hear what goes on around me.*

With what ears? she asked, layering the question with false innocence.

Sound is merely vibration, they snapped.

Merely, she thought back.

And my ability to sense the magic of those around me is, I dare say, far superior to yours. My situational awareness is not nonexistent.

Clearly. A moment later, her own irritation with them relented, as she reminded herself that, while Lethe-Alihana was rude and snobbish, they were also the sundered soul of a planet trapped in a sword and bound to her father. It was a long way to fall from being a planet that had created and sustained life.

And she couldn't help but remember that, for all her father was not a terribly giving person, she had often seen his hand going to his sword hilt. Before, she'd always taken it as a sign of his impatience, or of a hidden propensity towards violence. Now she suspected it had been a kindness towards Lethe-Alihana.

Allowing me some experience is the least he can do, they said, an uncomfortable reminder that they were privy to her thoughts when she was touching them.

"How did you end up like this?" she asked. After their soul had been removed from the Harvester, how had it become sundered, this half bound to Jevryn? For all his faults, she did not want to think her father would have willingly done this to the soul of any planet, much less the one he'd been born to.

Ask what you truly want to ask, Lethe-Alihana said. *The two answers are related.*

Fine. "Why did you come with me?"

Because I wish to be whole once more.

Of course. She was going after Kiev. Kiev possessed the other half of Lethe-Alihana's soul. The answer was so obvious she couldn't believe it hadn't occurred to her before.

You are young, Lethe-Alihana said patronizingly. *Some allowances must be made.*

Gee, thanks. "You said the two answers were related." Their wanting to come with her, and the sundering of their soul. "How did this happen to you?"

Kiev was in the process of binding my soul when his brother found him. Jevryn attempted to stop him. They fought. Unfortunately, the binding process was too far gone, by that point. Jevryn's interruption of it—and his fight with Kiev—caused a fracture in me, and when it was done I was bound to Jevryn, the lost part of me to Kiev.

Nyx waited, trying not to think anything at all. Lethe-Alihana's pause was pregnant, and she had the sense that if she could just be quiet, they would continue. And they did.

Your father cannot kill Kiev. It is not that he is unwilling to do it, though I do sometimes wonder—his mind is more difficult to read than yours—but that he physically cannot. There is a symbiosis in a binding such as the one Kiev placed on me. Kiev cannot harm me—either part of me —and since I am bound to Jevryn and would die if Jevryn did, he cannot kill him. The same restriction applies to Jevryn where Kiev is concerned.

Nyx frowned. "They fought on Kyvren."

They fight whenever the opportunity arises. But neither of them will ever deliver a killing blow. They cannot. And through Jevryn I cannot. But through you, who I am not bound to? That is an entirely different matter.

"But Kiev *did* almost kill Jevryn," she protested.

Lethe-Alihana parsed what she meant from her mind. *The death Kiev issued in Eravendrin was, if you will recall, intended for* you. *If you place a sword in the middle of a room and someone happens to walk in, pick it up, and impale themselves on it, you can hardly be said to have murdered them.*

Lethe-Alihana's voice practically dripped with irritation. *I told him to leave it, that you would be fine, but no, he had to go and nearly kill both of us because he couldn't bear the thought of anything happening to his precious daughter.*

A jolt went through her, as if a cold rain had drenched her without warning. "What did you say?"

Is your self-esteem truly so low that you never guessed? Congratula-

tions, in the entirety of his very long life, Jevryn A-Morridahn has managed to love precisely two people: Arradin, and you. I assure you, it was quite a shock to him to discover he was capable of non-romantic love. He required some time to come to terms with it.

"No." She spoke the word so softly it wouldn't be audible to a being who couldn't also hear inside her mind. She had been coming around to the idea that Jevryn might not hate her. That he might even feel something like...well, affection seemed like a stretch, but grudging acceptance for her, perhaps. Having initially been rejected by him so thoroughly, she wasn't ready to hear anything more.

Oh yes. Why do you think I resent you? Jevryn is an absolute fool when he loves. Having experienced the emotion so rarely, he cannot be rational about it. He becomes reckless, occasionally desperate, and since my own existence is now tied to his, I find this fact highly inconvenient.

Nyx wasn't given the luxury of time to come to terms with this revelation. The moment she'd been waiting for arrived, a portal yawning open in the room. It spat out two people and Nyx shot to her feet, fumbling for the anchor she'd made before coming here, a simple pebble she'd picked up and Hidden. She chunked it at the portal as it snapped closed. Not all of it made it through, the portal's closing shearing the pebble in half. Her Hiding held, splitting to cover the half now in the Keep along with the half on the spire's floor.

She exhaled heavily in relief, waiting for the two new arrivals to exit the room.

I had forgotten how disheartening it is to be required to rely on the plans of the young and inexperienced, Lethe-Alihana grumbled.

Nyx took that as her cue to put Lethe-Alihana back in their scabbard. Once the spire was empty, she retrieved the Hidden half of the pebble and moved it to the side of the room, out of the way, to use as a return anchor. Then she followed the line of her magic to the pebble piece now inside the Keep. She felt it, glowing strong, deep underground and several miles away. Smart of the original Keeper not to build the Keep directly beneath the spire. At some point, someone had to have attempted digging beneath the earth in the immediate vicinity of the spire, in the hopes the Keep lay beneath it.

She wondered, idly, as she pulled a stream of portal magic from one of her bracelets, who that first Keeper had been. She remembered Seth telling her that only the first Keeper of Shadows had retired from the position—the rest had all been killed by their successors. Given that the Keep was a labyrinth built belowground on an epic scale, and given that it held a portal well, and the Keeper controlled the portal witches and the secret to making the portal stones, she knew that first Keeper had to have been one of the original portal witches. She just didn't know which one.

Laiveran would make a lot of sense—he'd been on this planet, had built Calista—but she didn't think it had been him for two reasons. For one, Jevryn had told her the councilors had seeded portal stone magic, as it was used today, to obscure the fact the magic could be used in other ways. For another, if Laiveran had built the Keeper empire, why then give it all up and sleep for a few centuries inside Calista?

It made her wonder which of the councilors' hands were in the making of the Keep. Made her wonder which ones might still, on occasion, influence them. When she'd first learned about the Shadow Market, she'd been angry that the All Council, and the Enforcers by proxy, allowed it to continue existing. Now she wondered if one or more of them didn't check back in regularly on their little pet portal witch project to make sure all was going according to plan.

She bit the inside of her cheek. There was a lot she didn't know —about the All Council, about her father's place in it. She didn't know if he would tell her about it. But she thought, if she made it out of all of this alive, that it would finally be time to ask.

As the portal into the Keep formed before her, Nyx's Hidden magic, already wrapped around the portal magic, stretched to cover the portal itself. Seth had once told her that magic was blunted inside the Keep for anyone who wasn't the Keeper of Shadows, but she hadn't tried to use magic the last time she was in the Keep. This time, Nyx didn't feel any difficulty in relation to the portal—and it made sense that portal magic wouldn't be restricted when, to the Keeper's knowledge, everyone who could wield it was under their control—but as she stepped through into the Keep itself, she felt the sudden drag on her Hidden ability.

It was the difference between walking on dry land versus trudging through two feet of mud. It wasn't that it took more magic to keep herself Hidden, it was that accessing her magic and forcing it to do her bidding was twice as difficult. She felt like she was trying to do work that required the dexterous use of her fingers while wearing oversized gloves.

There was a moment where her Hiding flickered, threatening to dissolve. She forced it into place. Once it was solid, the pressure dissipated. Likely because whatever kept magic blunted in the Keep could no longer find hers.

The room was as Nyx remembered, a large, warehouse-sized space with arched openings set at intervals along each of the walls. There weren't as many portal witches as Nyx remembered filling the space, so either Bryn wasn't allowing as many people in and out as before, or Nyx had come on a slow day.

She retrieved the anchor pebble, tucked it into her pocket, and turned to the problem of finding her way to Bryn's throne room, which contained the portal well. The problem was that all of the archways in the rectangular room were identical, and they all led to stairs that descended down. When she'd last been here, Bryn's general, Essteria, had led them through an archway along one of the longer walls. It had been the wall to Nyx's right last time, but she had no way of knowing if she was facing the same direction now as she had been then.

In the absence of a better option, she hoped that she was, and went through the archway she thought they'd gone through. It didn't take long for Nyx to feel hopelessly lost. The building was an intentionally designed maze, all the stairs and doorways identical, and it had been a long time since she'd been here. She wandered down, dodging others on the stairwell and trying to remember how many flights they'd descended before, how many connecting door-ways they'd gone through.

Just when she was certain she was hopelessly lost, she felt it—the gentle pull of nearby portal magic tugging her into the correct room. She'd had a plan—get in, place her anchor somewhere unobtrusive, refill her bracelets, get out. But Bryn's empty throne caught her eye and that fist of grief squeezed Nyx's heart again as she remembered Seth lounging there, taunting Bryn.

Why had Nyx thought coming here would be easier than going to Kyvren? The Shadow Market made more strategic sense—it had the portal well—but it wasn't any less painful. But then, none of the places she knew her way to in the universe were safe. Everywhere she had been that Seth could go with her, he had. His memory was pervasive, a constant aching reminder. Earth, Tenebris Umbra, Amentia Furor, Nethrayne, Kyvren—he'd left his mark on all of them.

As she stared at Bryn's throne, that fist around her heart squeezing tighter, she wondered if she hadn't chosen the Shadow Market *because* it was where he'd been all those years they'd spent apart from each other. If she hadn't come here specifically to remember him. To feel like she could reclaim some part of that time she'd lost. But how could she? He wasn't here, to show her how he'd lived, to tell her what she'd missed.

But he'd been missing her while he was here, and it felt fitting in some way that in missing him, she should be here too. The only difference between them was that he hadn't known what it was he was missing, and once he'd remembered, he'd found her again. She knew exactly what she was missing, and she knew she would never find it again. She would never find *him* again.

She tore her gaze from the throne and walked to the portal well. The trip to Lehine and back had fully drained two of her bracelets, half of the third, and all of her rings—it was *far* out into the universe —and she refilled them now. The magic in this well wasn't as potent as that in Jevryn's home reservoir, but it was stronger than what she remembered from Lehine. A mid-grade strength. She shuffled the arrangement of her bracelets, placing those containing the lower strength magic on her right, and the one containing the remnants of Jevryn's more potent magic on her left.

Then, with the magic of the entire well at her disposal, she summoned the portal map and searched, as her father had once taught her to, for Kiev A-Morridahn.

Nyx found her uncle's signature on a planet at the very edge of her map. Somehow, it didn't surprise her that she should find him at the limits of her reach. She wondered if he was hiding from her. He must have known Jevryn would never voluntarily let her come after him, and that without access to a well, her limited experience meant her efficiency was nowhere near good enough to reach a planet so far away.

She hoped he *was* hiding. She hoped whatever she'd done to

him, when she'd screamed with the darkness inside her and the shard of Lethe-Alihana's soul, had injured him. She hoped he *hurt.*

She contemplated the planet, twinkling on the map so far off in the universe. She wanted to reach for it without caution, without thought. But for once in her life, Nyx showed restraint. She couldn't afford a mistake because she couldn't fail. She *wouldn't* fail. Not at this.

Reaching over her shoulder, she grasped the hilt of Lethe-Alihana. "If I go there, do I have enough magic to get back using my anchors here?"

No answer.

"Lethe."

A shiver went through the sword. *I do hope you are not attempting to give me a nickname.*

"Lethe-Alihana is a mouthful. Suggest something else and I'll be happy to use it. Otherwise, you're Lethe."

You cannot simply remove half of a being's name and expect that it retains the same meaning.

"Aren't you half a soul right now? I'd think that matters more than half a name."

I am beginning to regret my decision to come with you.

"I'm regretting my decision to bring you," Nyx snapped. "'Steal a talking sword,' I said to myself. 'What could go wrong?' I said to myself. 'It's not like it'll have the ego and superiority complex of a millennia-old planet.'"

A beat of silence, then: *Oh, was I expected to find that little tirade amusing and laugh? I do apologize. Ha ha.*

"You know, the jury just came back, and you're still an asshole. Do you want to tell me if I can make it back here, or should I just go and potentially strand us? If I die, you can be lost on another planet and never have any hope of putting the pieces of yourself back together again."

What makes you think me capable of such evaluation?

"You did give me a spiel about how the blood in my veins comes from the planet you gave life to, or something like that. If you made people with death magic then you also made people with the ability to channel portal magic. Shouldn't you just know what I can do?"

Lethe-Alihana's pause this time was lengthier than the previous one. *I am not a god, as you conceive of them on Earth,* they said eventually. *None of my kindred are. I do not possess the ability to look into your soul and weigh the measure of your talent. It is important to me that you understand this.*

"Why?"

Because people who believe they have a god at their disposal make terrible decisions. One has only to look to your uncle to see proof of that.

"So you don't know if we can get back?" He could have just said that. Also: "Can't you just, I don't know, *make* portal magic?" She should have asked this sooner.

That is not within my ability.

"But A-Lethe could portal infinitely. And the Stations had that ability transformed into the ley lines."

I am half *a soul, Nyx Fortuna, and I did not fracture along clean lines. I am certain it is my deepest regret to inform you that, at the time of my sundering, I did not manage to retain that part of myself. Had I known I would some day meet an angry descendant in need of an endless supply of portal magic to compensate for her lack of skill, it would no doubt have motivated me to greater effort at that time.*

Stars, Lethe-Alihana was a piece of work. No wonder her father was perpetually irritated. He'd been listening to *this* for nearly a millennium.

On the contrary, your father and I do not feel the need for endless chatter. We once went an entire century with less than ten words spoken between us. I do treasure the memory now, given the situation I currently find myself in.

Piece. Of. Work. "Out of the two of us, you're the one who's talking more."

It only appears that way because you cannot recognize the intrusiveness of your own thoughts.

Fuck this. She'd just go outside, find a pebble in the Shadow Market, and sink enough magic into it to make it into a portal stone. That would work, right? She let go of Lethe-Alihana's hilt.

A line of heat seared across her back. She yelped, jumped, and Constance fell off her, removing the source of the brand. Gingerly, Nyx slipped her fingers beneath her shirt, touching the skin beneath the areas where the scabbard had rested. It was warm but it wasn't, thankfully, burned, since Constance had reacted so quickly.

She glared down at the sword. Lethe-Alihana had heated up in less than a second, hot enough to heat Constance and make Nyx feel it, even through her shirt. The sword vibrated, rattling against the ground.

"I'm not picking you up," she snapped. "I don't need third degree burns in my life right now."

The sword ceased rattling, and began to smoke the way dry ice did.

"I don't need frostbite either."

The smoke vanished, condensation dripping off Constance.

"Do that again," she warned, "and I'll just leave you with Calista until I need you. She's not letting anyone else into her Heart to come retrieve you." After careful consideration of which digit she found least critical, she cautiously touched the tip of her right pinky to Lethe-Alihana's hilt.

I required your attention.

"Be less of an asshole and I won't take it away in the first place. And next time, if you feel the need to talk with me in a hurry, go the ice route. Or, better yet, shift your form into something more manageable. Like a nice dagger."

That would be so much easier. She could strap it to her thigh and not look completely weird if she needed to talk to Lethe-Alihana while in public and not Hidden.

I must be within a certain proximity of Jevryn to change form, and he must allow it.

"Exactly what kind of binding did Kiev place on you? How does it work?" It stood to reason that it would be the same kind that had been used to bind the other souls into the framework that made them the Stations. If she understood how that worked, she could—

I do not know.

Nyx blinked. "How can you not know? You were there."

My mind is not a human one. I do not function the same way that you do. That answer lies with the other half of me. So if you want it, return me to your back and do not do anything so foolish as collecting rocks.

Inside Nyx's mind, it felt like Lethe-Alihana shook their head. She decidedly disliked the feeling. They continued on, voice dripping with disapproval. *I told your father that failing to train you further was a mistake, but no, he was terrified to allow you around so much as a drop of portal magic, afraid you would go and do precisely what you are doing now. Fortunately, I can correct the oversight.*

Their voice shifted into a more lecturing tone. *Stones, being such a poor replacement for proper portaling, require time to make. The stone must be saturated with magic, allowed to cure, so to speak, and then saturated again, and then a third time. It is a sloppy waste of magic and, if I recall, Jevryn did have the sense to tell you that a portal stone is far less useful than an actual anchor, the latter of which you have here.*

"If I recall," Nyx said, mimicking Lethe-Alihana's tone, "having an anchor isn't a guarantee I can reach a place. And though I do know that portal stones are less effective than anchors, *you* might recall that I once *effectively* used them to get to an anchor that would otherwise have been out of my reach."

Lethe-Alihana's sigh rippled through Nyx's mind. *Yes, I will admit that was clever. Regardless, the portal stones are time-consuming to make and, furthermore, unnecessary. You have the magic you require to return to your anchor here.*

Nyx gritted her teeth. *Just stop arguing with them, just stop arguing with them, just stop—* "What happened to 'I'm not an all-knowing being to tell you what you're capable of'?"

That remains true. However, I have spent several centuries with your father. It has made me quite adept at gauging things such as this. Especially considering I was privy to all of his own thoughts in regards to evaluating your capabilities.

"You couldn't have just led with that? We had to have this whole fucking argument that ended with you nearly branding a sword-line into my back?"

I would not have sustained the temperature long enough to cause you permanent damage. May we go now?

You know what? Fuck it. Anything was better than continuing to argue with a damn sword.

You do understand that I am not actually a sword, yes? That is merely the current form I have been forced to take.

Nyx didn't answer. She flipped the sword over her shoulder, Constance refastening the harness across her chest, and checked that the cloak of her Hiding was still securely fastened. Portal magic flowed over her hands as she reached for the distant planet, and the portal blossomed into existence.

6

Nyx stared in stunned wonder as the portal closed behind her. She had expected Kiev A-Morridahn to hide somewhere dark. A gritty, overbuilt city, perhaps, where the buildings were so tall they blotted out the sun, and it felt like death was always a single misstep away. What she hadn't expected was to follow his trail to a fairy tale princess palace.

Or, more accurately, a fairy tale princess palace rising from the heart of a fairy tale princess city. The space where she stood was on the outskirts of it all, and she had the odd experience of both looking down on the city and across at the palace. The city itself was built in a deep valley she stood on the lip of, while in the center the ground had been built up, so the base of the palace rested on level with the ground Nyx currently stood on. Almost as if the city were a living moat for the structure.

Everything, from the residential buildings, to the walls that zig-zagged through the city, to the palace itself, was built of gleaming, pearlescent white stone. And everywhere, dripping from the walls, bursting from planters, pervasive throughout the city, were plants and trees flowering in colors so vivid they didn't look real. Blues and reds and pinks and yellows in every shade from pastel to deep, intensely saturated hues. It was as if someone had taken the idea of the hanging gardens of Babylon and created its fantasy equivalent on a city scale.

Mist hung in the air, coating it all in another surreal layer, as if she'd stepped into a dreamworld. The grass beneath her boots looked too delicate to be real, and she crouched, running her palm over blades as soft as spun sugar. She had the absurd notion that if she laid down on it she would fall into a magical sleep, one she wouldn't manage to wake from for a hundred or a thousand years.

You just want to cosplay Sleeping Beauty so I have to kiss you awake. They were Seth's words, what she knew, without question, he would have said to her. But she couldn't hear his voice, couldn't recreate it in her mind and she *wanted* to. She wanted the richness and familiarity of it, the teasing undercurrent that was present beneath almost everything he said. If he was here, he would tug her against him, his lips quirked in that familiar half-smile.

She squeezed her eyes shut, trying to block out the want, the insistent aching need for something she could not have. She could not think about what he would do if he were here, about how he would find this place as captivating as she did. It hurt too much, because he *should* be here—he should be with *her*—and if she thought about that too long the blackness lurking in the back of her mind would lash out and swallow her whole.

Kiev. Think about Kiev. Because thinking about Kiev brought a flush of red-hot anger, and anger was the only thing that kept the darkness at bay. She let the weight of it overtake her. It was familiar, and soothing in that familiarity.

She rose from her crouch and began the descent into the city, heading to the open space where the perimeter wall broke, allowing entrance to a street. She thought the wonder of the place might wear off upon closer inspection, but she was wrong. Butterfly-like insects danced in the air around her, their wings iridescent gold. Every now and then the grass would rustle near her and a furry red face would pop up, revealing a stoat-like creature that would then vanish as quickly as it had appeared.

The sound of running water hit her ears as she approached the outer wall of the city, but it took her a moment to find the source. Putting her hand to one wall, she found the stone cold to the touch. The wall's height was just a foot above her own and she jumped, grabbing the lip, her hands finding purchase between two vining plants that were flowering a brilliant indigo. She strained, pulling herself up so she could peer down the center of the wall.

Its interior was hollow, and water rushed through it, the current stirring plant roots that curled and undulated. She didn't think the movement was entirely caused by the water, and she got the distinct impression that sticking her hand into the water would be a terrible idea.

Nyx dropped to the ground, frowning as she surveyed the structure. Where did the water come from? Was it the city's drinking water source, the plants some kind of filtration system, or was it merely irrigation for the abundance of greenery? And where did it all go? She stood at the entrance to one of the city's streets, the perimeter wall to either side of her dead-ending. But the water wasn't spilling over the sides. Presumably it had an outlet underground—maybe a piping system, or discharge to a lake somewhere? She didn't know, and she supposed it didn't matter. It was just one of those things that made her curious.

Setting aside her curiosity, she started down the street. The sun was low in the sky, but rather than the city winding down, it appeared to be ramping up. The streets were flooded with people. They wore garb as brightly colored as the flora of their city, loose, flowing garments that looked both comfortable and practical. There was something about their features that looked familiar to her, but she couldn't place it.

She had to ignore the desire to simply wander through the city and observe them. Everything about this place felt peaceful. Beautiful. It felt like the kind of place where nothing bad could ever happen, and it was such a nice fantasy that she wanted to escape into it.

But bad things did happen, no matter how idyllic a place might look on the surface. The very fact that Kiev had come here was a guarantee that somewhere, hidden beneath the glittering jewel of the city, terrible things were indeed occurring. But it did beg the question: why *had* he come here? And was he even still on the planet?

The signature she'd followed felt old, and while it was the last signature she could find for Kiev—which in theory meant he was still here—it had occurred to her that if he'd wanted to obscure his location from Jevryn and her, he could travel by portal stone. Or by ley line. Either of those options wouldn't leave a trail that led back to him, because neither involved his personal use of portal magic. If she didn't have the ability to Hide both herself and her portaling signature, she would be traveling that way to cover her own tracks.

But she had no better option to try, which meant ruling out this possibility took priority. She hesitated, then touched two fingers to Lethe-Alihana's hilt. "Can you sense if Kiev's here?"

Were he—and my other half—within a hundred feet of me, yes. Outside of that range, no.

"If you sense him, give me an ice indicator." She let go of the hilt without waiting for a response. She'd wasted enough time arguing with Lethe-Alihana in the Keep. She didn't need to stand in the middle of a crowded street arguing with them, getting bumped by passersby who couldn't see her but whose accidental physical interaction with her caused a drain on her Hidden magic.

She walked quickly through the streets, aiming for the palace. While Kiev could be anywhere in the city—indeed, anywhere on the planet—she was betting his pride wouldn't allow him to hide out in some hole-in-the-wall building. If he was still here, he would be at the city's seat of power, so that was where she went.

Two hours later, Nyx had decided that, really, there was something to automobile travel after all. The city was the very definition of sprawling. It had looked far more manageable from her initial vantage point, but now that she was down in the thick of the buildings, it became readily apparent just how much city lay between her and the palace. Even if she'd been willing to risk her return trip to the Shadow Market—which she wasn't—by line-of-sight portaling to speed her journey, actually doing it was impossible. The streets were so crowded, there was nowhere safe to portal *to*. A space that was empty one moment was filled the next, people navigating the streets and each other with the ease of long practice.

The buildings were packed tightly together, turning the streets into a maze. Despite that she could see the palace at all times, given its height over the rest of the city, reaching it was not a simple matter of walking in a straight line. Nyx couldn't identify any organization to the streets, frequently wandering into dead ends, or following roads that headed toward the palace for a long stretch before breaking abruptly in a different direction.

She had never longed so much for the ability to fly. There had to be a faster way to move through the city, but if there was, she couldn't find it. Everyone walked, no sign of riding animals anywhere in sight, nor any other means of magical conveyance. She'd been avoiding communicating with Lethe-Alihana specifically because they were rude and she didn't want to need their help. But after her third hour of walking, where she'd still moved farther laterally than she had forward, she found a small nook between buildings, out of the way of the milling pedestrians, to tuck herself into, and grasped Lethe-Alihana's hilt.

Have you been here before? she thought at them.

Most likely.

You don't remember?

A ripple went through her mind like a shrug. *All planets appear drab and unremarkable compared to the magnificence I once created.*

Yeah, okay. *Could you try remembering the name of the planet?*

Another unconcerned ripple through her mind. *Jevryn travels as infrequently as he can, and I can tell you that this planet—whichever one it might be—was not under his purview. So no, I am afraid I do not recall it.*

You're lying to me. She was certain of it. They were being entirely too cavalier.

Perhaps.

Should I be concerned? She wasn't getting any sense of fear or danger from them, but would she? Their being able to sense *her* emotions didn't mean she could also sense *theirs.*

If I wanted you dead, Nyx Fortuna, I could simply kill you. Jevryn is not here to restrain me.

Well, that was comforting. *Why don't you want me to know where we are?*

Because, they said irritably, *I desire to see how you navigate without me. Allowing you to take me from Jevryn's home poses no small amount of risk to me. If you cannot manage a single unknown planet without my help, it may be that I should rethink my choice.*

And they had decided to wait until *now* to come to that conclusion? *Seriously?* she asked.

They did not answer. Nyx shook her head and let go of the hilt, merged back into the street's foot traffic, and kept walking. Half an hour later, the sun fully set. The city plunged into darkness. The instant night fell, everyone on the streets around her paused.

For a moment the darkness was absolute—no streetlamps, no magical means of shedding light, no glowing nighttime flowers—and the stillness was alarming, as if the city held its breath. Then the palace began to glow. Faintly at first, emitting a pale white light that gradually intensified, until the streets were bathed in its soft luminescence.

The city exhaled. The people began to move about their business once more and Nyx was the only one left standing still, unseen, staring up at the palace. It was so beautiful. So ethereal and surreal and perfect. Her doubt that Kiev was here somewhere vanished. She would like to believe that beauty such as this could exist without consequence. But she'd grown up knowing that pretty exteriors often held rotting cores.

Her mother had been—*was*, Nyx supposed—beautiful. And look what had lurked beneath *her* skin. At least Nyx never had to see Elena Fortuna again. She'd gotten what she'd needed from her mother. And she'd gotten closure, if one could call coming to the realization that your mother would never become a decent human being, and was in fact worse than you could have possibly imagined, "closure".

She dragged her gaze from the glowing palace back to the streets and resumed her trek. Soon her stomach rumbled, reminding her that she was alive and needed to eat. She'd been existing, these last few months, in a state of constant irritation with her body's need for basic necessities like food and water and sleep. It wasn't that she wanted to *not* eat, precisely, it was more that when she was hungry, she resented the effort necessary to fix the problem. On a logical level, she understood what it meant that she found such a basic task a herculean effort. She could tick off her symptoms like she was watching one of those commercials for depression medication that had once been so ubiquitous on television. Are you constantly fatigued? Check. Do you no longer have energy for the things that once brought you joy? Check.

Intellectually, she *wanted* to care about things, she just…couldn't make herself. She ignored the hunger pains for a while—she had water, as she'd started traveling everywhere with a canteen and some water purification tablets after the string of bad luck that had proved she was more likely to need the precaution than to not—but eventually she had to admit that she'd been walking for hours and she was getting lightheaded. She hadn't exactly been eating well prior to today, and it was having a compounding effect.

She was annoyed with herself over it—she'd tried to find the energy to fix the problem before now by reminding herself that eating affected the physical condition of her body, and the physical condition of her body affected her ability to carry out her plans where Kiev was concerned, but it hadn't made a difference. Because Kiev had felt so far out of her reach. Now he was potentially *in* reach, and she wasn't in the ideal condition for it.

Grudgingly, she came to terms with the fact that she was going to have to do better. Starting now. Given the native species on this planet was base Human, it was likely safe to eat the food here. But she wasn't carrying universal currency, and it was better not to chance it, anyway. Knowing her luck, she would end up eating the one thing a slight biological difference didn't allow for, and spend the next week sick.

Besides, even if she stayed, she wasn't reaching the palace any time soon. There was no dearth of distance between her and it. She could leave an anchor at this point, return to the Shadow Market to eat—and do some research that would hopefully tell her where *here* was, since Lethe-Alihana wouldn't—and come back tomorrow. There was no rush. The trail Kiev had left when he came here was at least a couple months old. Either he'd left the planet by portal stone, in which case he wasn't here anymore, or he hadn't left yet, in which case the odds of him deciding to do so in the next day or so were slim. A little more time was nothing.

She explored buildings in the area until she found one that appeared abandoned—peeling paint, empty interior—and then reached for the pouch of throwing stars on her belt. She pulled one free, covering it in a Hiding independent of the one that Hid her and everything she wore. She stared at the star for a moment, feeling the weight of it in her palm and remembering its maker.

"You never got to see this place," she whispered, "but I can leave a piece of you here." She pressed a kiss to the cold metal, then flicked her wrist, watching the trajectory of the star as it embedded itself high in the side of the abandoned building.

Then she felt for the tug of her other anchors, zeroing in on the one in Bryn's throne room. Briefly, she wondered how other portal witches—ones who had to have their anchors made for them—

differentiated between those anchors. For her, it was easy. Every Hiding had its own signature, its own unique mark. She didn't think she *could* rely on someone else to make her anchors, but then, maybe that was only a reaction born from having had the privilege of never needing anyone to. Her heritage, as painful as it might be, had nonetheless combined in such a way as to afford her a good number of magical privileges. She supposed she could comfort herself with that thought at night, if the weight of being a scion of two dying breeds of magic grew too heavy.

The thought made her snort, and she was still laughing as she portaled back into Bryn's throne room. She heard voices and abruptly ceased laughing. It wasn't that her Hiding wouldn't cover the sound—it would—but the voices were familiar.

"What exactly are you suggesting I do?" Bryn Morrigan demanded. Her voice was cool, authoritative, and clipped, just as Nyx remembered.

Another familiar voice answered the Keeper of Shadows. "I am suggesting you use her," NuReyva Duraven said. When Reyva had left the Station, Nyx had guessed that the next time she saw her, the woman would be at Bryn's side. Looked like she'd guessed right.

The pair strode directly to the portal well. Nyx pulled at the edges of her Hidden cloak, tugging it tight as she backed away, to the wall. Bryn didn't answer Reyva's comment. Her face was a mask, her eyes hard, and she wore the same armor she had when Nyx had first met her, although this time it wasn't covered in blood and gore. She stopped at the edge of the well and swiped her hand through it. She froze briefly, hand still plunged into the well, her brows drawing together in a frown. The frown never left her face, but her hand eventually continued its movement, coming away from the well covered in cotton-candy strands of portal magic.

Nyx blinked. So Bryn was a portal witch, then. Did Evra know? Nyx was willing to bet not. The two had broken up before Bryn had attained the Keeper position, and it seemed like their relationship had been rocky even before then. Bryn didn't strike Nyx as the type to overshare, even with her lovers. And as tight-lipped as Evra could be, if she'd known the woman was a portal witch, Nyx was pretty sure the Amazon would have told her. Given what Nyx was, the information was too relevant to her for her best friend not to pass it on.

"I don't use children," Bryn replied icily, pulling a small stone from her pocket and winding the portal magic around it.

How could she not feel the tug toward something *more*, Nyx wondered. Yes, she knew the portal witches left scattered throughout the universe had all been of minimal ability, and yes, she knew the idea had been seeded in them that spelling stones—in essence making anchors—was the only way to use portal magic, but Bryn was standing right next to a well. She had all the magic she could want at her disposal, and she couldn't feel that itch to do *more?*

"She isn't a child anymore," Reyva countered. "By her people's standards, she's allowed to make her own decisions. And you and I were making harder ones at younger ages."

Bryn's fingers paused in their magic winding. She turned her head, the entirety of her attention on Reyva. "I don't deny that your life has been difficult. You have suffered terrible loss. But she was forced to make choices I would not wish on anyone. And you may quibble with me over whether her age makes her an adult or a child and by whose standards, but she irrefutably was a child when she had to make those choices."

Reyva, from what Nyx had gleaned in her brief time around the woman, had a tendency to simply fire off whatever was on her mind. Her mouth opened, and then Nyx watched her take hold of herself, restraining that initial impulse. She thought for a moment, then said, "You treat her too cautiously because of her sister."

"Reyva," Bryn warned.

Reyva held up a hand, palm out. "I'm not jealous." Her head tilted slightly. "Well, maybe I am, a little. But what I meant is that you aren't treating her as her own person. You are treating her as your ex-girlfriend's little sister. All she has to do is talk to him. She *wants* something to do."

"She has been given things to do."

"She wants something *meaningful* to do. This is something meaningful."

Bryn returned to wrapping the stone in portal magic, her expression one of deep concentration, though Nyx thought the concentration was for what Reyva had said, not for the task she was performing with methodical precision, as if she'd done it a thousand times. When Bryn was finished and the portal magic had saturated the stone, she stared at it a moment before closing her fist around it. "Send her to me, then."

Reyva left. Nyx didn't. While it was certainly possible that Bryn Morrigan had more than one ex-girlfriend who had a traumatized younger sister, Nyx wouldn't bet money on that being the current scenario.

Bryn settled onto her throne, waiting, tossing the newly made portal stone up then catching it, over and over again. The door opposite the throne creaked open. Bryn caught the portal stone, snapping her fingers closed, and held it as Tamrin al'Daemon walked into the room. The younger woman's expression was bored but laced with the kind of low-level anger that could simmer in perpetuity without ever needing a new fuel source.

What had happened to her? Admittedly, Nyx had only known her for a short time, but while Tamrin had been at the Station, she hadn't been like this. Unwilling to speak about her time on Arkadia, even to her sister? Yes. Upset that Evra was making her return home? Yes again. But none of that held a candle to the fury boiling off the girl now.

Neither she nor Bryn spoke. Most seventeen-year-olds, if called to a room and then summarily ignored, would ask to know why they were there. Tamrin just waited.

Nyx waited too. She didn't know if Bryn was making a point, or if she and Tamrin were in a silent battle of wills to see which of them would crack and speak first, but in the end it was Bryn who straightened.

"I have a task for you."

"What is it today? Does the library need dusting?"

"Manual labor is—"

"Mind clearing. Yeah. I got that from the last ten lectures. Just hand me the dust cloth already so I can get it over with."

"Aren't you tired of wasting your time?"

Tamrin shrugged. "You know why I'm here. I'm not leaving until I get what I want. Making me clean things isn't going to scare me off."

Bryn leaned forward, resting her forearms on her thighs. "I am not trying to scare you off. I am giving you time to change your mind."

"Why does everyone act like I'm the only one who doesn't know my own mind when I'm the only one who *can* know it?" Tamrin bit out.

"Because you are young, and you may know what you want right now, but you don't yet understand how your mind will change as you grow older. How the things you do now are going to haunt you later."

"I'm already haunted!" Tamrin shouted. Bryn's eyes narrowed and Tamrin snapped her mouth shut.

"Is that why you want to kill people for me? To bury one bad memory under a litany of others? Because it won't work. All it's going to do is bury *you*."

"I have to *do* something, Bryn. My mother treats me like I'm glass, Evra treats me like I'm glass, everyone wants to just look straight through me *like I'm glass*."

"I'm not going to apprentice you."

"Fine." Tamrin turned on her heel.

"But I will let you do something else."

Tamrin stopped, turned back, suspicion in her eyes. "Like what?"

Bryn chucked the recently made portal stone at her and Tamrin caught it. "I want you to go talk to Kalvar Zurin for me. I've tried, but he's refused to see me. Apparently he's making a nice normal life for himself and wants nothing more to do with the Shadow Market. I even tried sending Reyva."

Tamrin snorted. "Could have told you playing up the fellow Tiagren angle wouldn't work. Just like sending me won't work."

"I think it will. You're close in age and you went through something together that anyone who wasn't there will never be able to understand, even if they want to. That type of experience bonds people."

Tamrin laughed. "The only person Kalvar was interested in bonding with wasn't me. This is a waste of time."

"And here I thought you had nothing better to do. Or should I get you that dust cloth?"

Tamrin's eyes narrowed. "Fine, I'll go. *If* you take me with you next time. I won't get involved. I won't do anything but be your shadow. Just take me with you."

Bryn made a noise in her throat that was the closest human vocal cords could come to a growl. "Your sister is going to kill me."

"Who's going to tell her?"

Me, Nyx thought. *I am going to tell her.*

"She doesn't even know I'm here. She thinks I'm staying at home like a good girl. Do we have a deal or not?"

Bryn exhaled heavily. "Yes, we have a deal."

Tamrin bared her teeth in what might be considered a grin, if one was feeling charitable in their interpretation, crushed the stone, and stepped through the resultant portal. Once she was gone, Bryn's gaze shifted back to the portal well. Something about the look on her face, the way she scrutinized the well…she couldn't possibly know some of the magic was missing, could she?

Nyx didn't know, but she found herself shrinking deeper into her Hiding, until she was almost inside herself. There was something about Bryn Morrigan that was too intense, that made her feel like the woman could see straight through her. Nyx didn't actually think she could, but since Hidden magic was based in belief, that meant it required Nyx's own belief to work. If she started having fanciful notions of Bryn's powers of perception, she'd cause her own damn Hiding to fail.

Fortunately, after staring deeply into the flickering blue depths of the portal magic for several long moments, Bryn stood and left the room. Only then did Nyx refill her own cache of magic and portal back to the anchor in the spire. She swiped that anchor and placed it near Calista, where it could serve as a nearby arrival point without being inside the bounds of Calista's dominance.

Inside the Station, she labored over her letter to Evra, crumpling up a dozen different drafts before settling on one that relayed the bare facts.

Evra,

Tamrin's with Bryn. She hasn't killed anyone yet. Bryn's been making her clean things. I thought you should know.

She didn't sign her name. Evra would know it was from her anyway, but it felt easier not to. Just like, in the end, it had been easier to write four just-the-facts sentences than to say anything that was actually on her mind. Like acknowledging that she missed her best friend. Part of her wanted to reach out, but it was too much right now. The thought of talking, of interacting. Of trying to playact herself because she had no energy to *be* herself.

Strangers were easier, because strangers didn't expect anything out of her. They didn't have any preconceived notions of who she was or how she was supposed to act. Nyx couldn't be the person Evra and Morgen and Griff knew right now. She couldn't go back to taking Arrivals and Departures, to quietly reading books in the morning over coffee and sitting on the back porch, couldn't do game night and movie night or anything else they'd expect out of her so they could reassure themselves that she was okay.

Because she wasn't okay. And she wasn't ready to pretend that she was just to make everyone else feel better. So she walked out of Calista's area of dominance, pulled herself through to the anchor outside the Station, and slid the note across the boundary. Griff would find it.

Then she left, before anyone could notice she'd been there.

7

Nyx's attempts at research that night did not yield promising results as to what planet she'd been traipsing around. Calista didn't know—being severed from the ley lines meant they weren't physically connected to the other planets—and they didn't have a connection to the Archives. Asking around the market led her to one rare books dealer with an outdated, stripped edition of the Archives that hadn't seen a connection to update its information in a century or two, and which she was charged a sum that amounted to highway robbery for the privilege of accessing.

It was also money uselessly spent. Every descriptor she searched by—flora, fauna, architecture, and inhabitants—wasn't specific enough to narrow the possibilities down beyond a couple dozen planets. That might have been enough if the Archives had had pictures, but it was a *very* stripped edition.

She'd thought about just asking someone while she was on the planet, but if she had, she might as well have worn a sign painted with neon letters proclaiming that she was there illegally. It wasn't possible to travel the ley lines and not know what planet you'd ended up on. She didn't need to draw that kind of attention to herself, especially considering that whoever she asked might not even tell her.

Still, she could probably at least pick up a city name today, and if the outdated Archives she had access to weren't completely useless, she could use the city name to find out the planet's. So decided, the next morning she packed a lunch into a small pack, stepped outside Calista's area of influence, and portaled to the anchor she'd left in Bryn's throne room.

The second she arrived, all of her plans went out the proverbial window. The throne room was brimming with people. Bryn sat on her throne, surrounded by dozens of her guards. The Keeper was tense, the guards were tense, and the woman standing before the throne, wearing black combat gear, her blonde hair plaited down her back, was—well, Evra al'Daemon did not look *tense* so much as she looked *pissed*.

"Where is she?" Evra's cool, sure voice filled the room.

Bryn's lips twisted. "I can explain why I allowed—"

"You don't need to explain anything." Tamrin stepped out from behind the other rank-and-file members of the Keeper's guard, her chin jutting out defiantly. To Evra, she said, "You can't just come here and—"

Evra quelled her sister with a single sharp glance and even sharper words. "I am not here for you." A mixture of disbelief and quickly concealed hurt flashed in Tamrin's eyes. Evra continued. "You said you wished to be a stranger to me, so that is what you will be."

Tamrin had told Evra that? When?

Maybe if you'd been around, if you'd been home, you would know, she thought to herself harshly.

"And I do not travel across the universe to save strangers from their own folly. I only do that for my family." Evra's gaze swiveled back to Bryn. "So I will ask you again. Where is Nyx?"

Oh shit.

Bryn's brow furrowed. "I have not seen her since the last time she was here with you."

"And yet I have this." Evra pulled Nyx's letter from her pocket and handed it to Bryn.

Nyx briefly squeezed her eyes shut. She'd known better than to send that when she was doing it. But she hadn't thought Evra would come here. At least, not looking for *her.* She hadn't thought Evra would think *she,* like Tamrin, was living in the Keep, though in retrospect, it was an obvious conclusion to jump to.

"So do not lie to me. I know she is here and I *will* see her."

"She is *not* here. Not by any knowledge or allowance of mine."

Evra's hand went to her sword hilt. When she spoke, her words had that particular tone that said she was done discussing matters. "I am not in the mood to—"

Nyx let the cloak of her Hiding unravel. She couldn't let Evra get into a fight with Bryn over her, not when Bryn was telling the truth. "I'm right here." Every eye in the room came to rest on her.

Bryn shoved off her throne. "How did you—" She cut off abruptly, eyes smoldering with heat that might be a little more literal than figurative, considering what Nyx had seen of her magic, and spat a single name like a curse: "*Hawthorne.*"

The name was a fist in Nyx's gut, punching all the air from her lungs.

"I thought I told you to keep his sorry ass off my planet. Where is he?" Bryn demanded.

"Not here," Evra said quickly.

Bryn snorted. "Oh, I am sure." She glared at Nyx. "Where?"

Nyx spoke a single, soft word: "Dead." She had thought it to herself a thousand times, but she'd never said it out loud. She only barely managed it now, a scant whisper, and verbalizing it made her feel like a part of her was dying too.

Bryn halted mid-stride. Reyva's face went shocked, then blank. She looked at Evra. "Is that true?"

Evra's hands clenched. "Yes. And I will discuss it with both of you later to your heart's content, if that is what you wish, but at this moment I need a private conversation with Nyx." She strode over and grabbed Nyx's wrist. "Let's go." It was very obvious, by Evra's tone of voice, that she expected Nyx to portal them out, immediately.

The old Nyx would have been concerned with the consequences of that action. With Bryn knowing she was a portal witch, with the fact that she'd just revealed what she was to anyone smart enough to realize that no bottle illusion was good enough to mimic invisibility. The new Nyx just didn't care. She'd spent so much time being afraid. Worrying what would happen if people knew who she was, what she was. Worrying what she might lose.

Now it didn't matter. None of it had mattered. What was anyone going to do to her? She'd been so cautious and then she'd lost what mattered most anyway. And she'd lost it, not to some stranger who might seek to use her, but to her own flesh and blood.

Bryn strode angrily toward them. "You are not taking her anywhere until I understand how she—"

Nyx drew a fresh stream of magic from the well, opened a portal to her anchor outside Calista, and dragged Evra with her. As she closed the portal someone fought to keep it open—Bryn, most likely —but the attempt was fumbling and rudimentary, the ability weak. Nyx clamped her will on the magic and the portal snapped shut.

Turning to Evra, Nyx opened her mouth, but the fierce look on Evra's face didn't exactly invite immediate conversation. Nyx settled for leading her into Calista, and they walked in silence down the tunnels to Seth's old room. Once inside, Nyx waited.

"Four lines?" Evra finally said, voice harsh. "You've been gone for six months and when you finally decide to remember I exist I only merit four fucking lines?"

Nyx opened her mouth. No words came out. She was experiencing a complicated range of emotions and she didn't know what to do with them.

"Well?" Evra demanded.

"I thought you'd want to know about Tamrin," she said weakly. "I didn't know about...about what she'd said to you."

Evra's eyes blazed hotter. "Of course you didn't know. How could you? I haven't seen you since you cracked three of my ribs."

Nyx winced. "I'm sorry."

"Oh, good. Now that I've tracked you down across the universe, you're sorry. Well, that just makes it all better, then. Since that is cleared up, do I merit any further amount of your time, or should I see myself out?"

"Why are you being such a bitch?" The words just snapped out of her and she couldn't call them back. She wasn't sure she wanted to. Why the hell had she felt guilty for being gone and silent all this time if *this* was how Evra was going to treat her? She knew Evra wasn't exactly a hugs-and-sympathy person, but she couldn't even muster a cliche "Sorry for your loss"?

"Because it seems to be the only way to get your attention!" Evra let out a breath that was half frustration, half growl. "We have been worried about you, Nyx. But we were letting it be because you were with Jevryn. We were trying to give you time to come home on your own. And then we find out you've stolen Jevryn's sword and run away from him to no-one-knew-where, and *then* you send me a letter with *four fucking lines* only pertaining to my sister's whereabouts. I understand what you lost—"

"Do you?" Nyx interrupted. "It's easy enough to say, but do you actually understand?"

Evra spread her arms wide in invitation. "If you think I don't, then explain it. I am listening."

How did she condense the entirety of her relationship with Seth into words? "He was everything to me." The only good presence in her life for its first eighteen years, the only person she'd been able to rely on. The one she'd shared everything with, who'd shared everything with her. The beat of her heart, a tattoo inked over it that would never again have a match.

"Then what am I?" Evra asked, her voice dangerously low. "If he was everything, am I nothing? Morgen, Griff, Kaliaris—are we all *nothing* to you?"

The words hit Nyx like a blow, and she staggered back a step. "I didn't mean—"

"You said you wanted a family. You *built us* into a family. I'm supposed to be your best friend and what do I get for the trouble? A few broken ribs and being tossed aside to deal with my own problems."

"Evra—"

"Do you think you are the only one who is dealing with shit?" Evra demanded. "Yes, Seth meant more to you, but he was our friend too. Griff thought of him as a son. We *all* lost him. And then we all lost you. I lost my sister, who wants nothing to do with me and I don't even understand why. Morgen has basically been abandoned by *his* brother and sister because they're too caught up dealing with their own shit and they don't appear to have given him a second thought because everyone thinks, *Oh, Morgen's the happy one, so of course he couldn't need anyone.*"

Guilt had Nyx snapping back, "It's been six months, Evra, not six years."

"Oh, so a temporary abandonment is fine. I see. I am so glad you are explaining the rules to me." Her voice practically dripped caustic. "We both know I'm terrible with emotion, so I am sure I could never have figured that out on my own."

Okay, that was enough of that. "I didn't want to drag you down with me! Any of you. Do you think I would have been fun to be around? Do you think if I'd come home I would have just gone back to normal in a blink and been what *you* needed? For someone who's saying I'm making it all about me, you sure seem to be making it all about you. Tell me more about how I should have just gotten over it all and gone back to being happy, nice Nyx, so grateful to not be homeless and to have people who can remember she exists."

"No one would have expected you to *just get over it.*"

Nyx crossed her arms. "Really? Because I distinctly remember you trying to drag me out of bed."

"Because I didn't want you to lie there until you died! And say whatever you like but that what's you were hellbent on doing. If Griff hadn't asked Jevryn to take you, what do you think would have happened?"

"I guess we'll never know because Jevryn *did* take me. You just shipped me off to be someone else's problem to fix. That's what you all wanted, wasn't it? For me to fix myself out of sight and come back and *be normal?*" Tears pricked like needles at the backs of her eyes. Maybe it had been the right decision at the time, sending her to Jevryn—she didn't know—but it didn't change that in that moment she'd felt abandoned. Like they hadn't wanted to deal with her, so they'd sent her to someone else.

"If we had wanted you gone I would not be here yelling at you for *being* gone," Evra gritted out. "And for the last time, no one expects you to be *normal*, whatever in the stars that even means. As for 'shipping you off', forgive us for trying to save your life. In case you hadn't noticed, if you go off the rails, you're too powerful for any of us to deal with, between death magic and your control over the Station.

"You threw me out of your room. You wouldn't respond to Morgen. You hadn't yet started fighting Griff, but after the difficulty he had restraining you during your memory issues, he didn't want to risk that you might lock yourself in a part of the Station where he couldn't reach you. Jevryn was capable of countering your abilities, so we let him. *You* are the one who refused to let us visit—"

"Like you even tried," Nyx cut in.

"We *did* try. *You* didn't want to see us."

"I think I'd remember if you'd shown up in Jevryn's living room and I sent you away."

"We weren't allowed to come without prior permission. We asked Jevryn if we could visit. He said he asked you and you said, quote, 'I don't want to see anyone'."

A sinking feeling hit in Nyx's chest. "When was this?"

"About a month after you left. Why?"

"Because he didn't tell me that *you'd* asked to see *me*. He just asked if I was ready to see anyone else."

"And you said no," Evra bellowed. "You didn't want us, you refused to come home, you literally *ran away*."

Evra's tone made Nyx retort, unthinking, "When you're an adult, it's not called *running away*, it's called *leaving*."

"So that's it then?" Evra demanded. "You're leaving? You're done with us? We should pack up and leave the Station?"

"I never said that." Panic clawed at Nyx's throat. "I miss you, okay? I miss you and Morgen and Griff and I wanted to see you, I *want* to come home. But I can't. Not until I—" She snapped her mouth shut.

"Until you *what?*"

"Until I kill Kiev!" she shouted. Evra stared at her, and suddenly Nyx needed her to understand. She needed *someone* to understand. "It's my fault. *I* insisted on going to Kyvren. *I* showed Kiev in Eravendrin that I knew where Seth was even under illusion. *I* looked for Seth after the battle because I was stupid enough to think Kiev was gone. I'm the one Kiev fixated on because I'm his niece. If it weren't for me, none of this would have happened." If it weren't for her, Seth wouldn't have lost his father to Elena Fortuna's magic. He would have grown up somewhere normal, somewhere far away from the poison that was *Nyx*, and he would be alive and happy and safe.

For a moment, silence reigned. Then Evra did the most un-Evra-al'Daemon-like thing Nyx had ever seen her do. She pulled Nyx into a hug. A fierce hug that made Nyx's bones creak. "None of what happened was your fault. Do you hear me?" Evra squeezed tighter, and the upper portion of Nyx's spinal column threatened to collapse under the pressure. "You did nothing wrong. Kiev's actions are his responsibility alone. You bear no blame for them."

Nyx squeezed Evra back. She wanted to believe her. She *really* wanted to. But she didn't. "Then why do I feel so shitty?"

"Because it hurts. Because if you blame yourself, it at least feels like you had some control, and if you had some control *then*, maybe you still do now. It feels like you could still change it. But you can't. You couldn't change it then, and you can't change it now, and accepting that fucking *hurts*."

The dam on Nyx's emotions, the one that had been in place for months, preventing anything more than shallow, silent tears, broke. She cried, and let her best friend hold her.

Nyx had forgotten just how much she hated crying. The aftermath always left her curiously drained, feeling monotone and hollowed out rather than actually feeling better. Her eyes were puffy, her nose was stopped up, and that was the state she was in when the door opened and Morgen and Kaden walked in.

The accusing glare she settled on Evra could have scorched ice.

"It's not what you think," Evra said.

Nyx folded her arms across her chest and turned her glare on Kaden, because she had significant doubts about this *not* being what she thought, no matter what he'd obviously told Evra to convince her to let him come with her to the Shadow Market. He stared back, expressionless. Typical Kaden Moor.

Nyx snorted, which was apparently today's magical lever to pull to make him speak words.

"I'm not here to take you back."

She arched an eyebrow. "Why don't I believe that? Oh, wait, I know why—because there's no way Jevryn didn't tell you to find me and bring me back, and you always do what he says."

Kaden shrugged. "Things change."

Things, maybe, but people? She had her doubts. "Then why are you here?"

He didn't answer. Of *course* he didn't answer.

Morgen cleared his throat. "Because I asked him to be." There was an uncertainty in Morgen's eyes as he looked at her that she hated—hated knowing she'd put there. Especially with Evra's recent reminder that Morgen's good nature made it easy for people to think he didn't need anything. He was the peacekeeper and the scholar, the one always ready to smooth over an argument or answer a question on theoretical magic. He'd taken the shitty hand dealt to him—from the day of the Harvester's theft, to his dismissal from the Enforcers, to his resultant life living under the radar and all the dangerous adventures his association with Nyx had gotten him into—and he'd never once complained.

"I'm sorry," she said.

Evra huffed. "I get *Why are you being such a bitch* and he gets *I'm sorry* without qualification?"

"Yeah, well, you did the hard work of making me feel guilty." To Morgen, she asked, "Do you hate me?"

Morgen sighed. "No, little Guardian, I don't hate you. But I do wish everyone I care about would stop having crises. It's not that I particularly want to have one of my own, you understand, but I'd like to know there's space for it if I find myself in need of one."

"Sorry," she said again.

"It's okay." He opened his arms and she dove into them, letting the comforting, familiar steadiness that was Morgen envelop her. "Does this mean we can go home now?" he asked. "Temerex misses you, and that damn cat you brought home is a kleptomaniac."

Nyx blinked. Fangs? "What is she stealing?"

"Half of my lab supplies, before I had Griff lock her out."

"Huh. That's weird."

"Yes. Are you coming home to deal with the weird?" The question made her stiffen, and Morgen sighed again. "I'm guessing that's a *no*. What are we doing, then?"

Before Nyx could respond that there was no "we"—they'd helped her with enough illegal things, they didn't need to add assassinating a councilor and going against the wishes of another to the list—Evra answered for her. "Killing Kiev A-Morridahn."

I f Nyx had expected an outcry at this revelation, she didn't get it. Instead, she received two weighty, intense stares. Of the two of them, Morgen's was easier to bear. There was something in Kaden's eyes she couldn't read and didn't want to. So she looked away from him and back to Morgen, who said, "You ran away from your father to kill your uncle?"

He didn't have to put it like that, but: "Yes."

Morgen blinked. "And you stole your father's sword because…?"

Lethe-Alihana chilled against her back, cold seeping through Constance and her clothes to freeze her skin. She lifted one finger out in front of her. "Hold that thought."

As soon as she grasped Lethe-Alihana's hilt, they said, *Do you intend to reveal my true nature to them?*

Is that my decision to make?

They pondered the question. *There is, ultimately, nothing I could do to stop you, save ending your life. And as doing so would not get me what I want, and without your Hiding of me I should be reclaimed by Jevryn shortly, I suppose I shall do nothing.*

Nyx would have rolled her eyes, but Lethe-Alihana wouldn't have been able to see it. *Do you* want *me to keep it a secret?*

As I have said, there is little of a reversible nature that I could do to sway you from the decision, should I oppose it.

Do you want me to keep it to myself or not? she asked.

I see no reason I should be making decisions when I have no power.

Exasperated, she thought, *You have the power to tell* me *yes or* no.

Lethe-Alihana didn't answer, and she had the feeling they were doing the equivalent of staring off into space and pretending to be uninterested in what was going on around them. The reason hit her, and she snorted. *You* do *want me to tell them, you just want to pretend that it was all my idea in the event something bad comes out of the decision.*

Lethe-Alihana huffed. *You try going unseen and unheard by almost everyone for centuries, and decide if you don't want to end the silence too.*

Nyx did roll her eyes this time. *Did you seriously just tell* me *I don't understand what it's like to go unnoticed? To feel like you're hidden from the world, and no matter how hard you try, no one can notice you exist? Think about that real hard for two seconds, Lethe.*

The silence that followed was, undoubtedly, Lethe-Alihana's attempt to come to terms with the fact they had no good rebuttal to that and they knew it. *Perhaps I spoke too hastily. You may share the nature of my existence with your…comrades.*

Thank you, ever so much, Your Esteemed Planetariness.

Would this invented title rank higher or lower than His Immortal Awesomeness?

When had they pulled her title for Jevryn out of her head? *Consider you and Jevryn's meaningless titles to be equal.* Constance let the scabbard they formed split in half as Nyx flipped the sword over her shoulder. Everyone was giving her strange looks. Well, everyone except Kaden. Maybe he'd been around Jevryn long enough to guess she was talking to the sword.

"This isn't Jevryn's sword," she explained. "Or, well, it isn't *only* Jevryn's sword. This is the soul of the planet that was once Lethe-Alihana. Jevryn's homeworld. This is why he's never killed Kiev. Because of the way he's bound to the soul, he can't."

For a moment, there was only stunned silence. Then Evra said, "That sword contains the soul of a planet? Of *Jevryn A-Morridahn's* planet?"

Nyx nodded.

"And you stole it from him?"

She nodded again.

"We're all dead," Evra said flatly. "I survived my mother's raising of me, her rage at my loss of Tamrin and subsequent severing of my bloodline, and now I am to be murdered by my best friend's father."

Morgen patted her on the back while looking at Kaden. "You told me you didn't know why she would take the sword." There was a warning in his voice. It made Nyx suspect that, prior to their arrival here, Morgen and Kaden had had a heart-to-heart wherein Morgen had laid down some ground rules. Good for him.

"I didn't," Kaden said.

"And yet you don't seem surprised that there is a Station inside the sword."

I am not a Station.

"Lethe-Alihana would like to object that they aren't a Station," Nyx dutifully relayed.

"My apologies," Morgen told Lethe-Alihana smoothly, his attention still on Kaden.

"I did say I suspected it was more than a sword," Kaden gritted out. "Which anyone could guess because she bothered to steal it. Had I known it contained the soul of a planet, I would have said,

'Morgen, I think the sword contains the soul of a planet'. I assumed she took it because he's attached to it."

Nyx looked at Kaden, parsing what he didn't say in those words. "I didn't take it to hurt him."

Kaden studied her for a beat, then: "Didn't you?"

"No. I took it because it's the advantage I need to kill Kiev." As soon as she realized what she'd said—and why—she glared at him. "Don't manipulate me into saying things. If you want to know something, just ask."

"I wasn't—" He cut off. His jaw clenched, and he spoke through it. "Never mind."

Evra steered the conversation back to the problem at hand. "You said the sword—Lethe-Alihana—was the reason Jevryn has not killed Kiev. Yet you stole it to help *you* kill him?"

"Jevryn's the one who can't act against Kiev. According to Lethe-Alihana, they *can*, so long as Jevryn isn't the one wielding them."

Morgen frowned. "Why does Jevryn's bond to the soul prevent him from killing Kiev?"

"Because the bond prevents Jevryn from intentionally harming the soul, and this is only half of it. Kiev is bound to the other half. Jevryn interrupted him when he was in the process of binding it and the interruption split Lethe-Alihana's soul, half bound to Jevryn, half bound to Kiev. Except for…"

"Except for?" Evra prompted.

"You remember A-Lethe?" She forced herself to focus only on the explanation surrounding the spectral dog, and not remember the events that had surrounded that time in her life. "Kiev chipped off a shard of Lethe-Alihana's soul to make the construct. That's why A-Lethe could portal. Unfortunately, he got the half of Lethe-Alihana that makes portal magic. I need to skim off Bryn's well. Which is going to be a lot harder now that she knows I've been doing it."

Evra must have agreed with this assessment because she asked, "Can you not reach the well you found on Lehine?"

"It was only a reservoir. And I can reach the spot where it *used* to be," Nyx said glumly. "Jevryn drained it."

Morgen blinked. "And…how did he do that?"

Nyx shrugged. "He's Jevryn A-Morridahn?" she offered.

"He compressed the magic into a sphere, locked it in a thalacite chest, and portaled it out," Kaden said.

Nyx wasn't sure what she was more shocked by—that Kaden had volunteered information, or: "He compressed *all* the magic in the reservoir? Like, all of it at once?"

"No, it took him a little over an hour."

"Oh, well, that's fine, then." His Immortal Awesomeness had needed an entire hour to compress into a ball more magic than Nyx could ever fathom using. "I'm no longer impressed, since it took him a whole sixty minutes to move it. So glad he took the time out of his busy schedule to block me from the one easy portal magic source no one would have missed."

Kaden raised an eyebrow. "You did block *his* access to his own reservoir."

"I didn't—oh, shit." She looked down at the sword still in her hands.

Lethe-Alihana's laughter echoed through her mind. *Yes, child, the reservoir was sealed when we left. And he requires me to access it.*

"Oh, shit?" Evra echoed, prompting Nyx to explain. For a moment after she did, they all stared at each other. Then Evra, Morgen, and Nyx all burst out laughing at the same time.

Nyx managed, through gasps for air, to say, "He's going to kill me." For some reason, it made her laugh harder. If Seth was here, he'd make some crack about how her methods of endearing herself to people were in serious question.

Her laughter cut off as abruptly as the thought had flashed through her mind. A hard knot coiled in her stomach and she felt suddenly sick.

"Excuse me for a minute." She shot to her feet and fled to the bathroom, locking it behind her. Her back to the door, she slid down until her butt hit the ground, then dropped her head onto her knees, taking shallow breaths.

Her body wanted to cry, to release the pressure building up inside her, but *she* didn't want to. Bad enough that she'd fled so quickly that everyone would know something was wrong. She didn't need to return with a blotchy face and swollen eyes. So she shoved it down. All the pain, the confusion of having felt *normal* for a moment, when normal didn't exist anymore. Not knowing if she hated herself for having had that moment, or if she only thought she should.

Turned out there wasn't a handbook for grief. Well, *someone* had probably written one, but even so, she wouldn't read it. She didn't want to be guided through the steps of loss, to be told how to feel or not feel, or that anything she did or didn't feel was fine. The truth was, most days, she didn't want to feel anything at all.

Someone approached the door. She couldn't say how she knew. There were no audible footsteps, and the doors in Calista did not have gaps beneath which a shadow could be seen. But she felt someone there. She braced herself, waiting for the questions, for the gentle but concerned, "Nyx? Are you all right?"

The question never came. No words did, and that alone told her who was on the other side. She sat there, trying to keep her breaths from making any noise, hugging her knees to her chest as if squeezing them tightly enough could make her fold in on herself. Her Hidden magic awoke in answer to her distress, a silken cocoon that enveloped her.

Eventually, she felt that waiting presence on the other side leave. For several breaths longer she stayed where she was, curled in on herself, not wanting to move. But she had to. Because she'd started something, and she was going to finish it.

She stood, went to the sink and splashed icy water onto her face. Then she shrugged off the comforting wrap of Hidden magic and went out to face her friends.

"So," she said, voice full of forced brightness, "who wants to play Name that Planet?"

By the time Nyx filled everyone in on what little she knew about Kiev's location—the description wasn't enough to make any of them think they could give a positive identification of the planet, although there was a betraying tightening of Kaden's eyes that made Nyx think he had suspicions—her friends were making poor attempts to disguise their exhaustion. It was barely noon on Tenebris Umbra, but a quick glance at Nyx's watch, still syncing with Earth's twenty-four-hour cycle, showed that for her friends it was nearly three in the morning.

When Evra fought a yawn so hard her jaw cracked, Nyx finally suggested, "Maybe you guys should get some sleep?"

Evra shook herself, her face saying she was ready to deny she was anything but alert and full of energy, before seeming to remember that she was among friends and didn't have to put on a show. "Perhaps a short respite is in order," she said cautiously.

"Uh-huh. Go to bed," Nyx said, "Calista can wake you up in the morning."

"A short respite," Evra repeated. "If we are leaving for a semi-unknown planet tomorrow then there is gear to purchase and preparations to be made."

"I can get whatever you need."

Evra's face took on a carefully neutral expression that meant she was trying to figure out how to say no one was purchasing her gear but her without being rude. "I am very exacting in what I require in supplies," she said carefully. "It truly is too onerous of a chore to place upon someone else."

Nyx rolled her eyes. "Fine, go take a beauty nap, I'll wake you up in a few hours and we can all go shopping together."

Evra's shoulders relaxed. "I do not see what beauty has to do with sleep, or why appearances should be of any importance at present, but yes, do wake us in a few hours. No more than three, if you would."

The response was so Evra, from her over-serious response to Earth sayings and phrases that didn't quite translate, to her insistence on giving excess consideration to the appropriate length of a nap, that Nyx smiled. The smile punched her in the gut the same way laughing with them earlier had. These moments of ordinary life in which she forgot, however briefly, to feel miserable. This time, though, she was ready for it, and she shoved her feelings down deep.

As Morgen and Evra turned to leave, Calista having helpfully illuminated a path to a prepared room across the hall for them, something else occurred to Nyx and she caught Evra's arm. "You know we don't have to leave first thing in the morning, right? I doubt Kiev's still on that planet, and even if he is, he isn't likely to move on in the next twenty-four hours."

Evra frowned. "I do not understand. What cause would we have to delay?"

"Tamrin," Nyx explained, dropping her hold on Evra. "I could go with you to the Keep tomorrow. Maybe I could—"

Evra shook her head. "I appreciate the offer, but in retrospect, this turn of events is probably the best scenario I could have asked for."

Nyx blinked. "Now I'm the one who doesn't understand." She'd assumed Evra would want to at least talk to Tamrin. Or if not Tamrin, Bryn. She was relatively certain that, regardless, Bryn would want to talk to Evra.

"I have been trying to talk to Tamrin for months. I cannot get her attention. Judging by how she has responded to every attempt I have made, I was convinced she did not want *my* attention. It was not until I was in the Keep, and legitimately there for you and not her, that I realized perhaps she *does* want it after all. At the very least, her pride was pricked that I was not there for her. I think perhaps my being present and ignoring her might actually do some good."

It made a certain kind of sense. "And Bryn?"

"What about her?"

"She's, ah, probably upset about me being in her supposed-to-be-impenetrable Keep?"

"Oh, that," Evra said, voice perfectly even. "She can—how is it phrased on Earth?" She asked this last bit to Morgen.

Apparently, they had picked up couples' telepathy, because with no further hint at what she'd intended to say, he offered, "Get over it?"

Evra nodded. "Yes. That."

"Right," Nyx said around the sudden lump in her throat. Watching them together, it was impossible not to remember that she'd been that in-tune with someone before, and she never would be again. The loss crashed in on her anew, the sudden reprieve and lightness at being surrounded by her friends buried once more beneath the black cloud of reality. Beneath the guilt at having felt, for even a brief time, normal. "Great," she said, striving for upbeat and coming out hollow. "I'll see you guys in a few hours."

Evra frowned and opened her mouth, but Morgen wrapped his arm around her waist and steered her toward the door. "See you in a few."

Only once they were gone, and had been for almost a full minute, did she realize that Kaden hadn't left. He hadn't spoken much at all during their conversation, fading into the background like he was so adept at doing.

Right now that background was near the door, his hands shoved into his pockets. As if he was trying to intrude on her space as little as possible. He hadn't come very far into the room the entire evening, and he'd said next to nothing that Morgen hadn't prompted him to say first.

What was he *doing* here? She didn't realize she'd asked the question aloud until he shrugged. She could have meant two things by the question—what was he doing here on Tenebris Umbra, or what was he still doing in her room—but she suspected the answer was the same in either case.

"You always did lurk whenever Jevryn left the house. What, are you oathbound not to let me out of your sight when I'm away from him?"

Some flicker of emotion rippled in the depths of his eyes, rising toward the placid surface of his face but failing to break it before sinking back down. He shook his head and turned to walk out.

"Why are you still working for him? Why were you *ever* working for him?" She didn't know why she needed to know. Not knowing had irritated her, on Kyvren—especially once she'd understood that that work had entailed him also working for Kiev—but now the curiosity had festered, had turned into a sore she could pick at as a pain to distract herself from other, deeper pains. So she picked.

He kept walking.

"Why?"

Another step.

"Or should I just ask Calista what time you leave tonight to tell my father where I am?" It hadn't escaped her notice that Kaden had only promised he wasn't here to take her back. He hadn't promised not to report on her.

He paused on the threshold, hands grasping the doorframe to either side of him, his head bowed. Finally, he said, "Have Calista track whatever you want. I'm not leaving until this is over. As for your original question, the answer would be shockingly obvious if you bothered to think about it."

He walked out and Calista closed the door behind him. Nyx sank onto the small bed, knees drawn up to her chest. If the answer was shockingly obvious, then she was shockingly oblivious, because she couldn't find it.

8

The next morning, shopping expeditions having been completed to Evra's satisfaction the prior afternoon, they had breakfast, geared up, and set off for the boundary of Calista's grounds, so they could portal off-planet. This plan was interrupted by the presence of Bryn's soldiers outside Calista. Lots and lots of soldiers, in a line Nyx suspected was actually a ring surrounding the entirety of the Station. The multiple projectile weapons aimed directly at them would have discouraged Nyx from opening a portal, even if she wasn't still standing on Calista's ground, where competing dominance made that impossible.

The line of soldiers snapped to more rigid attention as Bryn's black-clad figure stalked into view. Reyva followed in her wake, and the sight of the Tiagren woman made Nyx's stomach twist again. First with the memory of finally being made to speak that one word she'd avoided all this time, and then with anger because, when Reyva got close enough, Nyx saw her eyes were tinged with red, as if she'd been crying.

What the fuck right did she have to cry over Seth? The small voice of rationality in the back of Nyx's mind, the remaining sliver that grief hadn't smothered entirely, said that more people than herself were allowed to feel pain at his loss. But it was a fractional piece of rationality, and the chasm of darkness inside her was endless.

Death magic spiraled through her, suffusing her with that heady power she'd first felt on Arkadia what felt like a lifetime ago.

"Little Guardian," Morgen said, a soft warning. Or maybe it was a question—she couldn't tell.

She could feel all the points of her body where death bolstered her, where the lines of her veins ran black beneath the skin. Down arms and fingers, up the column of her throat, teasing at her jaw. Part of her wanted to let it crawl up her face, until she looked like something out of a nightmare, just to see what everyone would do. The soldiers nearest Nyx were already shifting uneasily at what they could see.

Bryn's hard eyes narrowed further. "Are you sick?"

Nyx laughed. Was she sick? "Absolutely."

Sick of waking up every morning in a world that didn't have Seth in it. Sick of carrying around the weight of obligation that was her accursed uncle. Sick of the weight of the Harvester hanging around her neck, an object created by a man who had suffered her same loss and felt he had the right to extinguish billions to not feel that way anymore.

"She's not sick," Evra growled, casting Nyx an irritated look. Probably because all of the soldiers' hands were suddenly twitching towards weaponry.

"I'm sick of being threatened," Nyx said. But she focused on the death magic that had spiraled out from her core, pulling it back in until the black left her veins. "See?" She waggled her fingers at Bryn. "All better. Now could you and your goons get off my lawn?"

Bryn frowned, shooting Evra a look. "Goons?" she asked, carefully pronouncing the word, a dead giveaway that it hadn't translated.

Nyx answered before Evra could. "Henchmen. Underlings. People you pay to do whatever you tell them to. They're in my territory and I don't like it." Technically, they were surrounding her territory—they were ringing the ground that encompassed Calista rather than stepping onto it, as if they knew exactly where the line that separated Station grounds from ordinary grounds lay. Which they probably did. Bryn and her other portal witches could likely feel it.

"The Shadow Market is *my* territory."

Nyx arched an eyebrow. "That's presumptuous of you. Do you

personally own all of this land? If you take three steps forward, can you open the door to the building below?"

A muscle in Bryn's jaw feathered, and Nyx felt a line of magic encompass her, Reyva, Evra, Morgen, and Kaden. She could feel the boundaries of the magic, though not what it did. Since Morgen could no doubt feel it too, being highly sensitive to magic, and he wasn't shifting warily, Nyx decided not to worry about it.

"This is where Hawthorne used to disappear," Bryn said.

Nyx flinched. She couldn't help it. Mention of his name was like pouring salt in an open wound. She pulled the hurt into herself and kept going. "I'm assuming you never managed to enter it." Her gaze flicked to Reyva. "Or you."

The look in Reyva's eyes confirmed it, and though it shouldn't have mattered, something in Nyx eased a fraction. She hadn't begrudged Seth his relationship with Reyva, or with anyone else he'd spent time with. She was, truly, glad he hadn't been alone all the time they'd been apart. But she was also glad that he'd never brought Reyva here. That the space Calista had made for him, the space that Nyx now inhabited, had only ever been his.

"It's a Station," Reyva accused, steel in her voice, and Nyx was annoyed that she'd ever taught the wardbreaker to recognize the nature of the doors she couldn't get through.

"There is no Station on Tenebris Umbra," Bryn objected, and it was obvious they'd had this argument before. Just as it was obvious they were looking for Nyx to solve the dispute. Nyx shrugged.

"How did you manage to infiltrate the Keep?"

Nyx nodded at the guards behind Bryn. "You sure you want to ask that question in front of all of them?"

"They can't hear us."

So that was what the bubble of Bryn's magic surrounding them was for, then: privacy.

"Well?" Bryn asked.

Nyx shrugged again.

"You're a portal witch," Bryn accused.

"So are you."

"I can't use the magic like *that*." The irritation in her voice said she'd tried, after seeing Nyx do it. The dark circles under her eyes said she'd probably tried all night. "How can you?" When Nyx's silence went on long enough, Bryn said, "Tell me, and I'll let the issue of how you managed entry into the Keep go without answer."

That was a big give, where Bryn was concerned. The woman was militant about her Keep. She *really* wanted to know how to portal without using rocks. But that was a secret Nyx wouldn't be giving away. The stakes on it were too high. If a portal witch ended up on Amentia Furor, they would likely be killed. And whether they were or weren't, it might relaunch an intergalactic war. Nyx had enough guilt to carry around. She didn't need to add universal war to it.

And it wasn't as if she was denying portal witches some innate part of their natures. They could still use the portal magic. She was just making sure they took surface roads with it instead of jumping on the highway. So instead of answering that, she pulled one of the bottle illusions from her pocket and held it up. "Infiltrating your Keep isn't that difficult with the right equipment."

Reyva shook her head. "Not even Seth's bottle illusions were that good. I used enough of them to know."

Nyx's fingers closed in a fist around the bottle. "And you honestly think he gave you the best he had to offer?" Reyva's head jerked back. "Trust me, you never saw half of what he was capable of."

"He's still dead, isn't he?" Reyva spat back, harshly. "I wonder how that happened."

Nyx didn't need the implication spelled out. Seth had survived seven years of the Shadow Market's dangers. He'd barely survived a year with Nyx. But if Reyva thought to cut her, she missed only because the wound was already deeper than her slice. Because what she said was nothing Nyx hadn't already thought. "Pleasant as it's been seeing you both again, I'm afraid we have to be going," she bit out.

Bryn shook her head. "You cannot portal on the ground you're standing on. I am well aware of that fact. And you are not leaving until I have answers."

A zing of cold against her back was Lethe-Alihana asking for attention. "'Let' implies you have the upper hand." She grasped the sword hilt, bringing the blade to a guard position in front of her. The dangerous thing about drawing a magical sword you had no bond with, and therefore no ability to control? It did what it felt was in its best interests without waiting for your permission.

A burst of wind emanated from Lethe-Alihana. It wasn't ordinary wind, but the ice winds that whipped at Nyx every time she made the internal descent into A-Queltr. These were the winds that surrounded death, that leached the warmth from a body in seconds, that gave ordinary people a sense of doom rather than of peace. They swept forward in an arc, blasting Bryn, Reva, and the nearest guards back.

Well, shit. "We should go," Nyx said to a group that was already moving, herself included.

The second she hit Station-free ground she opened a portal, waving the others forward. Morgen and Kaden ran through, and then she and Evra leapt across together. As she snapped the portal shut, Nyx caught sight of Bryn's furious face on the other side as the Keeper gained her feet. Nyx was extremely grateful, in that moment, that her current anchor was inside an abandoned building, and therefore didn't offer many clues to where she'd gone.

"Not to criticize, little Guardian, but are you certain that was the wisest course of action?" Morgen brushed imaginary dirt off the sleeves of his shirt and was clearly doing his best to look as non-critical as he claimed to be.

"It wasn't exactly my decision." Nyx frowned at Lethe-Alihana. "Did you have to do that?"

The conversation was growing tedious. And should the Keeper have decided it was in her best interests for her pathetic army to take you into her custody, I would find the situation entirely too *tedious. I have waited centuries for Kiev A-Morridahn's death. I do not intend to wait even a few days more than I must.*

"You know, Kaliaris's long life has granted *them* a certain *lack* of urgency, where time is concerned."

I am not Kaliaris. If Lethe-Alihana had been a person, Nyx had the distinct impression this would have been said with a sniff and their nose stuck in the air.

"Clearly." Deciding that was about enough of that, she shifted her grip on the hilt, but Lethe-Alihana protested before she could return them to Constance's scabbard.

Must you? I grow so bored, locked in darkness. I should like to see something of this planet.

A tiny prick of guilt stabbed at Nyx. The only way they could see something of this planet was if she had contact with them. But walking around holding a naked blade was just asking for trouble. She could Hide it from everyone, as opposed to just having it Hidden from Jevryn, but holding it aloft as they walked would grow tiresome, even light as it was. As would grasping the hilt over her shoulder. But she also couldn't carry the sword at her hip. She was significantly shorter than her father, and the blade was long enough that it would drag the ground.

Lethe-Alihana, catching her internal objections, said, *I understand. But I do wish to see the planet. As such, in this one instance, I would allow your knight to carry me.*

Nyx choked on empty air. "I'm sorry, my *what?*" Had she missed someone in clanking armor following her around?

Lethe-Alihana must have pulled the image of a medieval knight from her head, because distaste dripped from their voice as they asked, *Why in all the stars would anyone dress in such a manner? No, perhaps the word did not translate correctly.*

Which meant…her translator spells were translating Lethe-Alihana's thoughts directly into her mind?

My *translator spell,* Lethe-Alihana corrected. *Jevryn and Kiev wiped Salyrian from the common models.* This correction issued, Lethe-Alihana continued with their prior thought. *Let us try chevalier, then? Paladin? Champion?*

"I don't have a—" She cut off before she said "champion" out loud, suddenly reminded, by Morgen's delicate cough, that other people were present and she was engaged in an argument of which only her own half could be heard. She held up a finger to the three faces staring at her quizzically and forced herself to give her responses mentally rather than verbally.

Who are you talking about? I don't have a knight or a champion or whatever the hell else you mentioned.

There was a long pause, followed by muttering she couldn't make out, and yes, it disturbed her that Lethe-Alihana could mutter *in her own mind* and she could be unable to parse out what the words were. Eventually, they said, *Kaden. I would allow Kaden to carry me for a time. He is of the correct height for it to be no issue.*

Nyx stiffened, but she managed to keep her thoughts to herself this time. At least where "to herself" more or less meant very carefully not *having* thoughts. Or rather, very carefully directing her thoughts to the more neutral, practical ones.

I don't think giving you to Kaden is a great idea. Do you want *to end up back with Jevryn?*

In time, yes, they answered. *Your father is…a friend, inasmuch as a being such as myself can be said to have one. I simply require distance from him at this moment. And at this moment, your knight will be no issue in that regard.*

Nyx's thoughts were cold but calm, so her words couldn't be mistaken for a fit of temper. *Do not ever call him that again. Whatever he is, he is nothing of mine.*

A flicker of heat went through the sword's hilt, as if Lethe-Alihana were dismissing her. *A-Morridahns. Undoubtedly the most stubborn bloodline to ever tread my ground. But as you wish. Suffice it to say I have no fear that Kaden Moor will attempt to return me to Jevryn before I am ready.*

Won't touching you hurt him?

Why ever would it?

Because Griff panicked when I picked you up in the Station, because apparently touching a death sword if you don't have death magic is painful?

She felt Lethe-Alihana's sigh in her mind. *It is true that this vessel I reside in began as an imbued weapon, thus your Griff's concern, but that was long before I inhabited it. And while I can imbue the metal with death, I need not. Now may we get on with this?*

No. You don't even have a scabbard.

I am certain Constance can continue to accommodate.

"You want me to give him Constance, too?" And she was back to shouting her objections aloud. Wonderful.

Constance, picking up either the thread of what Lethe-Alihana wanted, or Nyx's distress, melted and flowed in a circle of cool liquid metal over her shoulders, around her neck, then up to her cheek. It felt a little like a cat walking all over her in an attempt to be comforting.

"Great. Now you've upset my"—what did she call Constance? It wasn't wholly a weapon, being of such a malleable nature. Eventually she just settled on—"Constance."

Lethe-Alihana's irritation was obvious. *Oh, very well, let me speak with her.*

Interesting that Lethe-Alihana called Constance "her". Nyx had been getting the same impression, but hadn't wanted to presume.

She coaxed Constance into her hand. At first the liquid metal settled in her palm but then, catching her intent, coated her skin like a flexible glove. Nyx grasped Lethe-Alihana's hilt with her metal-covered hand.

She didn't know exactly how Lethe-Alihana could talk to Constance, but after a few moments they must have convinced her of what they wanted, because the metal flowed off Nyx, reforming a scabbard around the sword, this time with a belt designed to buckle around the hips.

She has agreed to a temporary arrangement, if you give your permission. With the caveat that, should she feel you need her, I will be abandoned.

Nyx blew out a breath. "Fine." She stalked over to Kaden and thrust the sword into his hands. "Here. You're tall, and Lethe-Alihana wants human contact so they can see the planet. Don't make me regret this and don't put any moves on Constance."

Kaden raised an eyebrow, but he took the sword and buckled it on. "Moves?"

"Yeah. She's mine."

His hand settled on the hilt of the sword, and Lethe-Alihana must have said something Kaden didn't like, because his mouth twisted into a grimace. Nyx didn't ask. The soul of her father's planet was Kaden's problem for the next few hours. If she felt naked and vulnerable, divested of both the sword and Constance, she tried not to let it show. Or to wonder if Lethe-Alihana had really been interested in seeing the city, or if they'd manipulated her because they wanted to talk to Kaden. After all, Morgen and Evra were both close in height to Kaden. Surely anyone other than Nyx would have done.

She took a single step toward the door, then turned back to the others.

"Problem?" Evra asked.

In a manner of speaking. When she'd been here before, she'd simply Hidden herself. But if the streets were as busy as they'd been previously, four Hidden people would get bumped into. A lot. Every time someone ran into one of them it would be an added drain on her magic, and if it caused enough of a commotion—like, say, they accidentally tripped someone—that several people took notice, she might not be able to hold it. And four people seeming to pop into existence out of nowhere would generate a lot of attention.

Besides which, they were going to need to talk to people. Yes, she thought if Kiev was here, it would be in the palace, but gathering more information regarding that suspicion before they got to said palace seemed like the smart idea. And if they were going to ask locals prying questions meant to lead them to Kiev A-Morridahn, questions likely to get them remembered, it would probably be best if they didn't look like themselves.

She slipped her hand into her pocket, fingers brushing over one of the small vials. Everything in her rebelled at using it. At letting others use it.

She pulled the vial out, tipping a quarter of the contents into Morgen's hand, another quarter into Kaden's, another into Evra's. Bottle illusions typically lasted anywhere from one to twelve hours, depending on the quality you paid for. Anything above that cost a fortune. Seth could bottle twenty-four hours' worth in his sleep, and he'd done so a lot at the Station, both to bleed off excess magic and to set aside a cache for Griff. Since Nyx had an unfortunate habit of disappearing from the Station without warning, there was always a good chance Griff would need to impersonate her to run the Arrivals and Departures.

Bottle illusions, Seth had once told her, were both easier and harder to make than spinning an illusion oneself. Easier, in the sense that they weren't adaptive. When Seth spun an illusion, it changed in answer to his whims. It responded to the environment around him, to the minds it touched. In short, it was active and thus required varying amounts of magic to sustain. Bottle illusions were designed to make a single change—obscure or alter the user's features, or make an object appear as something else. Once a user put it on, they couldn't decide six hours into use that it would be better if they were a brunette instead of a blonde. The illusion was set, and couldn't be terminated early or adapted to new use.

Even within this set of restrictions, not every Illusionist could bottle the magic. Distilling one's magic into a vessel for others to use was a tricky business, because the magic was designed to answer to the person from whom it came. Many couldn't help but influence it, which was why most Illusionists with a basic aptitude for the practice only made predesigned illusions. Those that, once applied, would make the user appear as a specific race and gender, with predetermined features and clothing.

Distilling illusion magic into a bottle, with all the potential of its use and only the directive to follow the first request of the person who withdrew that magic, was more difficult. Nyx poured the remaining quarter of the bottle's contents into her hand and turned away from the others. Seth's magic spun in her palm, warm and layered and achingly familiar. She didn't want to use it. She wanted to keep it, to curl into it and pretend that Seth was here. She didn't want to use up this small piece of him that was still with her.

"Nyx?" Evra asked softly.

The magic spun and spun in her palm, waiting. She tried to think. To focus enough to give the magic form. With another bottle illusion, the magic might have already dissipated, having not been put to immediate use. But Seth's magic had always liked her, and so it stayed, awaiting her direction. But to direct illusion magic to change you, you had to *want* something. A different face, a different height, a different body. She couldn't muster the energy—the will— to want. The only thing she wanted was Seth.

The magic curled in her palm struck out, snapping around her. Horror blossomed behind her breastbone as she realized what it was doing.

No. Hell no, fuck *no.*

But it was too late. In a moment of stupid inattention, she had wanted, and the magic had done its job and given her an imitation of that want. She looked down at her hands—at *his* hands. Long, tapered fingers. Warm brown, bronzed skin. Hands that had brushed hers a thousand times, had held her and touched her and loved her.

She closed her eyes against the sick panic beating in her chest and exhaled a single word: "Fuck." There wasn't much else to say when you'd accidentally donned your dead boyfriend's likeness.

"Nyx?" Morgen asked hesitantly.

She made herself open her eyes. Made herself speak. "I didn't mean to do this," she said, Seth's rich voice pouring out in place of her own. "But it can't be undone." Bottle illusions were restrictive in that way. They did what you asked them to, and they did it for as long as the magic lasted. If you tried to place another bottle illusion over the first, the layers clashed, and it was obvious you were looking at two different, competing illusions.

The only way to shorten the effect was to put more draw on the magic by questioning the presented illusion. If she was lucky, her own disbelief at the situation would make hers wear off faster than the six hours a quarter vial's worth should have given her. "So if it's all the same to everyone else, I'd really like it if we could all pretend it wasn't happening."

She turned around. They'd known what was coming. They'd heard Seth's voice come out of her. They'd seen her clothes and her hair change to his. But Morgen still flinched when he saw her—Seth's—face, and Evra's cheeks lost most of their color. The only one who remained outwardly unaffected was Kaden.

"Are you sure—" Evra started, but Nyx cut her off.

"Pretend it's not happening," she repeated. "Please." Because if they didn't, she was going to throw up.

9

"Are you sure this is where Kiev is?" Kaden asked the question the moment they stepped outside of the building. He hadn't used illusion to change his voice, so she recognized him easily enough, though she would have anyway. Unlike her spectacular mishap, the others had gone for the expedient option of slightly altering their base features.

Kaden had dropped a couple inches of height and about half his muscle mass. His hair had lengthened and shifted from blonde to brown, and his facial features had all sharpened. Morgen had gained the couple inches Kaden had lost, his face taking on a more angular shape, his skin darkening to an even deeper black. Evra still looked like an Amazon. Her build was almost identical to her natural one, but her braid was gone, her hair completely shaved on one side of her head, the remaining locks dark black and barely skimming her shoulders.

"I'm sure this is the last place Kiev portaled to using his own magic," Nyx said. "If he used a portal stone or left here with another councilor, I can't know that. Why?"

Kaden hesitated for only a moment before he said, "Because this is Endalna."

"Okay. And that's important because…?" She could guess it wasn't going to be anything good, because Evra's and Morgen's gazes were fixed on the palace in the distance, and they both looked like they'd bitten into something sour.

None of them answered. In fact, all of them looked like they would rather dive into a merciless enemy horde alone with no armor than answer her.

"What?" she demanded.

Morgen rubbed at the back of his neck. "It is the seat of power of the Kormadin royal family."

Nyx knew the blood in her veins couldn't actually freeze, but it certainly felt as if it did in that moment. The Kormadin royal family. As in Dianara Kormadin, runaway royal currently hiding out in Earth Between. Kormadin royal family, as in the one Evra had told Nyx was so powerful it would take an army to make them bow to the law.

But most importantly? Kormadin royal family, as in Emerik Kormadin, husband of Elena Fortuna, and Nyx's stepfather.

She reached across to Kaden and grabbed Lethe-Alihana's hilt. *You knew,* she said accusingly. *This is why you wouldn't tell me where we were.* They didn't answer, which was answer enough in itself. Since they were intent on ignoring her, she released their hilt and she refocused her ire on someone else.

"You don't seem surprised, so clearly you recognized the city from my description," she said to Kaden, her voice carrying more than a hint of accusation. And it was so weird to have *her* inflections coming out in Seth's voice. Stars, she wished this day could just be over. She wished she didn't need to talk again until this illusion wore off. "Is there a reason you didn't mention we were going to my fucking mother's planet?"

He shrugged. Actually fucking shrugged. "There was a chance, from the description, that it could have been Gildan or Hileen."

She stared at him. He did not magically sprout a conscience and apologize. It was almost impossible to deal with someone who never apologized and probably never thought he did anything wrong. "The next time there is a thirty-three-point-three-repeating percent chance that we are going to *my fucking mother's* planet, warn me in advance."

He didn't respond. Nyx closed her eyes. She needed a minute. Or two. Surely one-hundred-and-twenty seconds would be long enough to dissipate the urge she had to jump out of her skin and scream *Are you fucking kidding me?* at the sky. Inhaling deeply and exhaling slowly did not help.

She gave up and asked Kaden, "Does Kiev have a working relationship with my mother?"

He didn't answer. Before she could explain to him exactly why not answering her right now was a very bad idea, Morgen asked, "Why would he know that?"

Nyx looked between them, confused. "I thought you two caught up."

"We did," Kaden gritted out.

"Clearly not enough." Morgen's tone was as tense as Kaden's.

"I said there were things I couldn't tell you."

"Things you can't tell me but you can obviously tell her? I'm your brother for fuck's sake."

"Yes, well, her father didn't choose to bind my tongue where she's concerned the same way as he did with everyone else."

"When you say 'bind'," Nyx interrupted, "do you mean that literally? Like Griff is bound?"

Kaden's non-answer was answer enough. Nyx's anger was a sharp burst of death magic pulsing through her body, there and then gone. When this was all over, she was going to have a long, long talk with Jevryn about what kind of behavior was and was not acceptable. As soon as she thought it, she realized two things. One, that she had every intention of returning to Jevryn once this was over. Not forever—she wasn't moving back in—but she did want to see him again. For all her resentment of his constantly being there—pushing her, never letting her wallow, never letting her rest—he *had* been there. She just hadn't realized that had mattered to her until she'd left.

And two, that she thought Jevryn would actually listen to her. Oh, she had no delusions that he would immediately jump to his feet in haste to do as she suggested, but she did think if she pointed out that he'd bound Kaden's will in a manner similar to Griff's own binding, she could make him see the similarity. He would no doubt icily explain to her that she was young and didn't understand the hard choices people sometimes had to make, but she thought there was a fifty-fifty chance that if she argued with him long enough, she could get him to reverse the decision.

But for now… She looked at Morgen. "I'm sorry, but I need to talk to him." She jerked her head at Kaden, who followed her back inside the building. She repeated her question. "Does Kiev have a working relationship with my mother?"

"Yes."

Nyx closed her eyes briefly. "How much of a working relationship?"

"I don't know the extent of it. Like I told you before, he didn't exactly trust me when I was…in his employment." Kaden's expression flattened more than usual, and for a moment he looked as dead-eyed as he had during the time he'd spent in Earth's Station as her "hostage".

She couldn't help but remember Kiev's words to her in Eravendrin, when he'd told her he'd made Kaden do things that had broken worse men. She almost asked. But she was still mad at Kaden, and it wasn't her business, and she doubted he would thank her for asking him to dredge it back up. And maybe it made her a coward, but she also wasn't certain she wanted to know. Wasn't certain she could handle knowing.

Not with everything that had happened. Not with how much bad was in the world, how it felt like there was nothing *but* the bad, now that Seth was gone.

"He visited this planet three times that I know of," Kaden said. "I think…"

"What?"

"I think your mother may have contacted him. After she returned from Earth. It's only a guess. She tried to hide her fear when I brought her to Jevryn, but she's terrified of your father."

"She fucking should be," Nyx spat. Kaden's eyes widened, and she remembered that while he might guess she didn't have a great relationship with her mother, he hadn't been privy to the fucked-up circumstances regarding Nyx's conception.

"What happened between them?" he asked.

She shook her head. "That's personal, but let me put it this way —if Jevryn decides to kill her at some point, it won't surprise me and I won't blame him." It was a harsh thing to say about her own mother. But any childish hope she'd clung to that her mother could either be reformed, or choose to reform herself, had died when Elena Fortuna had dispassionately recited those past events as if she'd done nothing wrong, and furthermore was the wronged party herself. She'd been a terrible mother. She'd driven Seth's father insane and then gotten him killed when it suited her purposes. She'd been intentionally cruel in giving Seth the choice to either stay with a Nyx who couldn't remember him, or abandon her, all because it had irked her that he actually liked Nyx. The woman was a walking plague of selfishness.

Nyx crossed her arms, tapping her fingers against her biceps. "So you think she reached out to Kiev to…what? Gain some sort of foothold with him so she could put him between her and Jevryn?"

"It's no secret, among those who have connections to the All Council, that the A-Morridahn brothers do not get along."

Do not get along was putting it mildly. But what he said made sense. And it was exactly the kind of step her mother would take. But to get Kiev's attention… "Do you think she told him what she is?"

"Possibly. She isn't high enough in the Kormadin family to command a meeting with him based on her status alone." His pause was meaningful before he said, "Based on my observation of her, I don't believe she would have revealed that she was Hidden. But she would have had to offer him *something* to pique his interest."

Sick heat blossomed in Nyx's stomach like a poison flower. "When did he meet with her the first time?"

Kaden's brow furrowed, and she could see him trying to remember when it had happened, and roughly how long ago that was in Earth's timekeeping system. "Around nine months ago?"

Nine months ago. Not terribly long after Nyx's mother had fixed her memories. And almost exactly around the time A-Lethe had begun stalking her whenever she stepped out into Earth Between. "She gave him me."

Oh, Elena wouldn't have told Kiev that Nyx was *her* daughter—she wouldn't have wanted the stain of that connection or the dangers that came with it. And she likely wouldn't have wanted to give up the truth of what she was. But offering up to Kiev the knowledge that Jevryn had a daughter? One he very much wanted to keep secret? One Elena could tell him the identity of?

She would have given Nyx up in a heartbeat. It would have solved all of Elena's problems neatly if Kiev took Nyx out of the picture. No more concerns over Emerik finding out who Nyx was and ruining Elena's meticulously cultivated new life. And if he killed Nyx, well, Elena had another child to fulfill her need for a magical feedback loop now. She didn't *need* her first daughter for that anymore.

Nyx's anger detonated. Death poured out of that endless void inside of her, suffusing her body, until she couldn't contain it anymore and it spilled out. The floor beneath her feet rotted, then crumbled into dust that blackened as if burned. The dark stain spread, eating up the floorboards around her in ever-widening concentric circles.

Kaden retreated from the sea of death emanating from her. "Nyx?"

"Get out."

"Can you—"

"Get out!" she yelled. She couldn't stop this. She didn't *want* to stop it. Everything Jevryn had wanted to teach her had been about control. Spin death out, reel it back in. Focus. Balance on the knife-thin precipice between this world and the void that lay beyond. Stay calm. Stay centered.

She'd never told him that it didn't help. That it kept the anger in her at bay but it didn't dissipate it. That she could perform the control he wanted her to have but it was *only* performative. Because she wasn't calm. She wasn't fucking centered. She was spiraling out of herself and she needed to.

Kaden had the good sense to recognize it because he left, closing the door to the building behind him. And once he was gone? All that anger and pain—months of it smoldering inside her, now stoked into burning fire by her mother's latest betrayal—tore out of her throat on a scream, and death was in her voice.

On Kyvren, when she'd loosed the soul shard of A-Lethe, Nyx thought she had screamed because she'd swallowed the shard and that was the natural way to free it. But Jevryn had explained that there was a very specific use of death magic, a way of honing it into a targeted force, in an attack that roughly translated to a banshee's wail.

He'd said it was a use that could never be learned or practiced, because it was fueled by primal rage, and those who dealt in death came to it only in the depths of their emotions. And then he had told her never to sink into those emotions again, because a banshee's wail, once loosed, could not be controlled, and once it started, sometimes it couldn't be stopped.

But Nyx was not her father. She couldn't remain perpetually in the state of icy detachment he lived his life in. In this moment, she did not care about control. So she screamed, the sound vibrating out of her throat, so loud it hurt her ears, and she didn't stop.

Death poured out of her, coating the support beams in front of her. The wood cracked, drying, rotting. She screamed again, and again, and again, until the pressure from it made her feel as if her eyes would pop out of her head. Until the support beams reduced to dust and the ceiling collapsed five feet in front of her, the resultant gust of air coating her in dust and ash.

She stared at the destruction, hands clasped in fists at her sides, her breath coming in hard, jagged pulls. She didn't feel better, exactly, but she felt...emptied. Like she'd lanced a wound, but knew the infection would return and she'd soon have to purge it all over again.

The door to the building creaked open an inch. After a lengthy pause, no doubt meant to ascertain if Nyx was going to scream again, the door opened wider and Evra strode inside, shutting the door behind her. A laugh bubbled out of Nyx. For some reason, it was unbearably funny that Evra had taken the time to shut the door when half the damn building was in ruins.

Evra stopped beside Nyx, making her own survey of the collapsed building. "Impressive," she offered.

"Thanks." The word rasped out of Nyx, the back of her throat raw.

"Kaden indicated your mother did something? He couldn't get all of the particulars out, given his...restrictions."

Nyx only nodded. She stared at the rubble some more and tried not to wince. Evra noticed.

"If it helps, when my mother severed my bloodline, I went to a tavern the most violent gang in my city is known to frequent, and picked a fight with one of their members. She had ten people with her and the resultant brawl destroyed all of the furniture, half of the liquor, and put holes in three of the exterior walls. I was black and blue for two weeks after, I spent a fortune in reparations to the establishment's owner, and I regret nothing."

Nyx contemplated this as the door to the building swung open again, Morgen and Kaden entering. "That sounds more impressive than screaming until half of a building falls down."

"Speaking of a building falling down," Morgen said, "we need to go. Like right now. I think half the city guard is a block away."

Nyx pulled her anchor from the wall and they exited onto the street on the opposite side of the building from the one they'd emerged onto earlier. Once they were far enough away to be certain they wouldn't be tied to the infrastructure damage she'd just done, they found an out-of-the-way spot to regroup.

"Not to be indelicate, little Guardian, but do we have a plan?"

"Yes. I'm going to have words with my mother."

"I understand this is a delicate matter," Morgen said diplomatically, "and familial disagreements have a way of heightening emotions, but I feel obligated to point out that she is married to Emerik Kormadin. While I'm sure Kaden's prior knowledge of the palace security, combined with your unique skill set, will allow us to reach her, leaving again may not be so simple."

"You don't have to come." She didn't mean it harshly. Marching into the Kormadin palace with her was probably a really dumb idea. A selfish part of her wished none of them were here, because if they weren't here, then she didn't have to think or care or worry about them. She didn't have to wonder if she was just going to get them killed.

There was a blissful simplicity to the isolation she'd begun this quest in. A soothing calm in the knowledge that her actions only affected *her,* that if someone was hurt or killed it was only *her.* And she was torn between wanting to keep this reconnection to her friends, and wanting them gone so she could sink back into cold detachment. So she didn't have to dredge up enough energy to convince them that she cared whether she made it out of this alive or not.

Her fingers brushed over the portal magic bracelets lining her forearm. "I can send you home."

"No," they all said in unison.

"But—"

"We're with you on this," Morgen said. "I'm merely suggesting we should think about an exit strategy."

Nyx waved a hand down her arm, the down-swipe unwinding

the Hiding over her portal magic long enough for them to see the bracelets, the up-sweep putting the Hiding back in place. "I'm the exit strategy."

Morgen muttered something under his breath that she couldn't quite catch, but which had the tone and cadence of *Stars help us.* "Little Guardian, I implore you to think waaaay back to when we first met. You were—" He cut off.

Nyx arched an eyebrow. "No, no, go on. I'm all curious now. I was…?"

He cleared his throat. "I was going to say you were a more cautious creature, but then I remembered you insisted on going to a prison planet approximately five minutes after finding out the universe was a bigger place than you remembered knowing."

She shrugged. "Impulsivity is in my nature, but fine, I'll fact-check first." She turned to Kaden. "When you abducted my mother, did you portal out of the palace?"

"Yes."

Nyx had never been more grateful for Kaden's tendency to deliver monosyllabic replies in a neutral tone that made it impossible to determine how he felt about a situation. "Great, then we have a plan. We walk to the palace, I Hide us and we go inside, I restrain myself from committing matricide while finding out where Kiev is. We portal out."

"Good plan," Evra said. Nyx couldn't tell if she was being serious or just trying to be supportive. Probably the latter. It was, after all, a shit plan that was thin on specifics.

"Have you considered that your mother may have put failsafes in place to detect your magic?" Morgen asked.

Nyx shook her head. "She wouldn't. One, her magic is probably a secret known only to her and Emerik, and she wouldn't want anyone else to be able to detect her or Serenity. Two, she doesn't know I can leave the Station." Elena had been locked in one of the Station's rooms for Nyx's Nethrayne absence and subsequent memory-skipping-induced Station meltdown. "Three, even if she did suspect I could leave, I don't actually believe her opinion of me is low enough to think I would come here. She hates me, but I'm not sure she thinks I'm stupid."

Morgen held up a finger. "You do understand what you just implied there, yes?"

That coming here and going into the Kormadin palace on her current plan was stupid? Yeah, she understood that. She just didn't care. "My offer to send you home still stands."

Three people crossed their arms and glowered at her.

Okay, then.

10

The city streets were once again too crowded to risk portaling by line-of-sight, but navigating them was significantly easier with Kaden in the lead. The route he chose made no sense to Nyx, veering off some streets and onto others when Nyx was certain doing so would only lead them in a circle, but she couldn't deny they were getting closer to their destination much faster than she had been managing on her own.

Especially since, now that she knew her mother was involved, there was no longer any need to ask locals prying questions. Which also meant there wasn't much need for the illusions they'd taken on. Kaden and Morgen, technically still being wanted fugitives, even if that was probably old news by intergalactic standards at this point, were still probably best off not showing as their real selves, but Nyx and Evra weren't likewise constrained. The ultimate lack of necessity made Nyx feel even more bitter about the guise she was currently wearing.

Her mood wasn't improved by the realization, the longer they walked, that she had forgotten how to exist around others. Oh, she had been able to have the hard conversations that had needed to be had, and to make plans that needed to be made, but just...normal conversation? She didn't remember how to *do* that.

She and Jevryn had not had normal conversation. He had attempted it once or twice, during the first month she'd spent with him, and each time she had pointedly stared at him until he'd quit trying. She and Kaden had hardly spoken at all, two silent shadows passing each other in rooms and hallways. She hadn't *felt* her social skills atrophying, but as she walked behind Evra and Morgen, listening to them talk about anything and everything, the ease of their communication felt foreign. It was like she was fourteen again, back in that mall, trying to talk to other girls for the first time and realizing she didn't know how.

Evra and Morgen kept trying to draw her into the conversation, and the best she could manage in return were one-word responses and vague grunts of assent or dissent. Even Kaden, for all his taciturn nature, was managing better than she was. His responses were frequently in hand gestures that meant nothing to Nyx, but Morgen read as if they were entire essays, laughing or agreeing or rolling his eyes. She had the feeling that she no longer fit. Not inside herself, not inside the group.

Before, she'd had an almost crushing need to belong. To rely on others because she *could*. Now...every plan she'd made in the last six months had been made in her head, with only internal answers to be found. She was no longer used to looking outside herself for solutions. Her mind felt like a container she had trapped herself in, and now she didn't know how to get out. Or if she even wanted to get out, and if anyone could really want her around if she did. Because whose fault was it that she didn't fit anymore? She was the one who'd left. She was the one who'd stayed gone. She was the one who—

"Hawthorne?" called a voice behind her.

Nyx's shoulders went bow-strung tight. She kept walking, desperately hoping she was experiencing an auditory hallucination.

"Hawthorne!"

This time, Morgen and Evra tensed, then sped up their walk. So much for auditory hallucinations. She increased her pace, hoping it wasn't obvious they were all speeding up. How was Seth being recognized *here*, of all places? She was relatively certain if he'd ever come to Endalna—or at least spent any significant time here—he would have realized her mother was here and they wouldn't have needed Jevryn to track Elena down for them.

Please do not make me have to pretend to be my dead boyfriend, please do not make me have to pretend to be my dead—

Footsteps sounded close and a hand landed on her shoulder, pulling her around. Wide-set blue eyes stared into hers from the pale face of a brown-haired man roughly Seth's own height. She felt her illusion drawing more heavily on the magic that powered it, working to convince the person touching her that she was Seth's height, and not her own significantly shorter build. She didn't recognize the man, but then, she didn't exactly expect to. It wasn't that Seth hadn't ever talked about events that had occurred during the years he'd spent away from her, it was that when he'd mentioned people he'd worked with, there hadn't been any reason for him to give her a physical description of them.

"Shit, it is you," the guy said, like he hadn't really believed it. "What are you doing here? Are you insane? You need to fix your face before one of Taizen's people recognizes you." He waited, expectantly, for Nyx to cover herself in a different illusion. Which she could not do.

She shrugged, trying to mimic Seth's usual cavalier manner. "All tapped out at the moment, I'm afraid."

The guy's eyes widened, but before he could say anything Morgen was at her side. "Sorry to cut your reunion short, Hawthorne, but we're on a tight schedule. We need to move."

"No," the guy said, "you need to get *him*"—he jerked a finger at Nyx—"off the street before you all end up dead." He shook his head. "Why am I even talking about this? Let's go."

He gave Nyx a shove towards a side alley and then moved in front of her, leading the way. She didn't follow, shooting a look at Evra and Morgen, who were looking between each other and Kaden, on that wavelength of silent communication she was out of sync with.

The stranger paused in the alley and looked back, realizing they weren't following. "You want to stay out here? Fine. It's your fucking funeral. You want to stay alive? Come on." He started back down the alley.

She took a hesitant step after him.

"Nyx." All Evra said was her name, and maybe Nyx hadn't lost *all* of that unspoken language that passed between friends, because she understood what Evra meant. They didn't know this person. They were here to do one thing, and it was not follow strangers down back alleys. Nyx might not be able to Hide their entire group on the busy streets without draining her magic, but if wearing Seth's face around was actually a danger, she could Hide herself until the illusion wore off.

There was no reason to go with this person. And yet...he'd known Seth. He'd known Seth and Nyx hadn't known him, and it felt like she couldn't just walk away. And it must have been written on her face because Evra just blew out a breath and said, "Okay."

Nyx trotted down the alley, following the stranger. A few twists and turns later they darted through a nondescript wooden door, up three flights of a narrow staircase, and into a dark, cramped apartment. The guy clicked three mechanical locks, activated the kind of ward Nyx suspected was reserved for emergencies, like when you thought the mafia was coming after you, and then pulled the curtains on the apartment's one window closed, plunging the room into absolute darkness for the space of a breath before wall sconces sputtered awake with soft light.

The guy—she wondered what his name was, but she couldn't exactly ask, since Seth would already know it—turned away from the window, giving her a hard appraisal that pulled heavily on the magic fueling her illusion. She should probably be worried about that—about the illusion failing while she was in the room with this unknown person—but she couldn't bring herself to be concerned about that when she *wanted* the illusion to fail. Wanted out of this false skin.

The stranger kept staring, as if he knew something about her wasn't quite right, but he couldn't put his finger on it. She almost just told him that she wasn't Seth. But she didn't know this person. He'd *seemed* genuinely concerned for Seth when he'd found them on the street, but plenty of people were better liars than Nyx, and Seth had been involved in a lot of business that wasn't exactly legal. So she thought of Seth's bored insouciance as he'd sat on Bryn's throne in the Shadow Keep and did her best to recreate it, the illusion magic coating her giving a boost to the attempt. She cocked an eyebrow at him and waited, unconcerned and expectant.

The stranger's shoulders relaxed and he huffed out a short laugh. "You always were an asshole," he said, a level of fondness in his voice that made Nyx want to snap that Seth was *hers*. Except he wasn't. He wasn't anyone's. Not anymore.

The stranger's gaze shifted to the others, and he jerked his head toward a narrow hallway to his left. "Can you give us a minute?" When no one moved, he looked at Nyx like he expected her—Seth—to fix it.

"It's fine," she said. "They're practically family."

Something like hurt flashed in his eyes, quickly followed by disbelief. "Since when do you have anyone who's 'practically fami-ly'?" He took a step toward her. "What is going on with you? I know we didn't part on the best terms, and I know I shouldn't have —" His gaze flicked to the others and he shook his head. "Whatever. But you just disappeared. You didn't even cancel your jobs, you just dropped 'em. Hell, I picked up Cato's so he wouldn't ask for your head on a pike, but I wasn't good enough to cover your shipment for Taizen, hence the reason you should *really* know better than to show your face here."

He paused, and just when Nyx was afraid it was going to be a long enough pause that she would be expected to give something resembling an explanation, he wound himself up again. "I mean, what the fuck? I ran into Reyva in the Market a couple months back and she said you were on Earth of all places, and if I really wanted to know why you left, I should go find you there. And I must be some kind of stupid because I actually did. Found a couple people in Earth Between who admitted to knowing you, but no one would tell me if you were around. Hell, by the looks they gave me when I asked, I thought you were dead."

Nyx flinched. It was an automatic response, and it was one Seth never would have made in a million years. Seth would have laughed and given a flippant response if someone had erroneously thought him dead. But she couldn't summon the energy to cover the flinch, to dredge up a *Clearly, reports of my death have been greatly exaggerated*, which he totally would have said because he would have found it twice as funny that no one save her would get the reference.

She couldn't bring herself to keep lying to this person, because the longer he'd talked, the more certain she'd become that he was just a man. Just someone Seth had known. Someone who cared if Seth was alive or dead. And it felt wrong to keep sitting here and pretending to be that person.

When she said nothing in response, the magic fueling her illu-sion took another hit as a fresh wave of the stranger's disbelief crashed against it. She felt it fraying, about to pull apart at the seams, from three hours of regular use followed by a series of disbelief-fueled barrages. She looked at her hands—at Seth's hands—and added her own disbelief to the stranger's. Not Seth's hands. Not Seth.

Magic curled back from her fingertips, revealing her own hands as the magic dissipated like mist evaporating with the rising sun. The illusion peeled from her body and soon she was only Nyx, and the relief was both weightlessness and crushing loss.

The stranger stared at her, eyes narrowed, clearly trying to determine what had happened. If she was Seth, his magic regenerated, playing a trick, or if she was the reality, the illusion stripped.

Nyx solved the mystery for him. "He is," she said simply, answering the last thing he'd said. "Dead. And I guess I just wanted to talk to someone who knew him during the time I didn't." Someone who wasn't Reyva, because as much as Nyx *wanted* to like Reyva, there was friction there in the best of times. They certainly weren't going to bond over Nyx's dead lover.

Dead. Funny how she kept thinking it—saying it—now that she was around other people again. It wasn't that she'd been ignoring the reality of it in her time alone, it was more that there had been no reason to dwell on the word, on the specific thought. She'd thought of *him* often enough—constant memories, a constant sense of loss— but she hadn't sat around repeating the "D" word in her head.

And if the look on the stranger's face was any indication, he might have been worried by the reactions he'd gotten in Earth Between, but he hadn't *actually* thought Seth was gone. Nyx watched his face go through a multitude of expressions. Denial. Consideration. Then, his gaze landing on the raven's feather earring dangling from her left earlobe, belief. She watched the reaction and she wondered if that was what her own face had looked like. Wondered, for a moment, if she hadn't been trying to be cruel in telling him, rather than kind.

He met her gaze. "How?"

The stranger's name was Mauri, and sitting around his kitchen table, Nyx told him what he'd asked to know. Or a version of it, at least. A version that left out councilors and planets they weren't supposed to have been on, and a civil war no one had known was being waged.

Mauri didn't ask any questions. He didn't show anything in response. Not like he had when she'd first told him. She'd gathered, from what he'd said about covering Seth's jobs, that he was an Illusionist too, and she suspected he'd recovered from the surprise enough to hide any of his true feelings behind a facade of calm.

The only thing he asked, finally, was: "And they are?" he indicated Morgen and Evra and Kaden again, who had been patiently impersonating ornamental statuary this whole time.

"Family," Nyx answered, leaving off the "practically" this time. "Mine, and later his." Maybe Kaden didn't quite fit that bill, but she didn't think she had to explain that.

A flicker of something showed through Mauri's expression before it vanished. "I think he always wanted one."

I want to have a family with you, Nyxi.

Her throat closed, and the burning at the backs of her eyes wasn't from sadness, it was from anger. Anger at everything that had been taken. Everything Seth would never get to have. "Yeah. He did."

They sat in silence, and it was heavy and awkward, until Mauri said, "Don't take this the wrong way. He was my friend, and I get that you were his, but I don't know you, and…"

"You'd like us to leave?" Nyx finished for him.

"Yeah."

"That's fair." Truthfully, she didn't want to be here any longer either. She knew the impulse that had driven her to follow Mauri, to find out who he was, but she didn't know what she'd hoped to gain from talking to him, and so she didn't know if she'd found it or not.

She and the others headed for the door, but there was something —in Mauri's eyes, in the weight that filled the room—that made her hand dip into her pocket, coming to rest against the remaining vials of Seth's illusion magic. She didn't want to part with a single one. But she did know how she would feel if she'd had nothing of him left.

She clenched a single vial in her fist, walked back to Mauri and placed it on the table before him. He picked it up, and she knew he recognized the magic. She walked away, but she didn't make it out before he called after her.

"It looked like you were heading to the palace. Are you?"

She shrugged. "Maybe."

He looked at the vial still clenched in his fist. "I don't know how recent your information is, but they changed their security protocols a little while ago. Apparently someone abducted the head of the Sixth House's wife right outside of the dining hall. Anyway, all the secured entrances now require dual magic keys activated simultaneously."

Nyx nodded her thanks for the offered information, and they left. Since she intended on line-of-sight portaling beyond all magical defenses while Hidden, the heightened security measures shouldn't be an issue.

The heightened security measures were an issue. Mauri had failed to relay that those magically sealed entrances he'd mentioned were also opaque. Another new development, according to Kaden. Most magic wards were invisible. They stretched across the opening they were meant to guard, but nothing prevented a person from *seeing* through them—only from walking through them without the proper key.

It was early evening on this planet, perhaps an hour or two away from nightfall, which meant even the outermost entrance to the palace grounds was unmanned. According to Kaden, the further-most entrance was always sealed, but manned during what Nyx would consider "normal business hours" to allow people in and out. Palaces apparently did not sustain themselves, and required such things as deliveries and laborers. These were not normal business hours.

Nyx stared at the closed, white metal gate, the open spaces between the bars obscured by an impenetrable gray fog, and found herself unhappily reminded that her mother was actually intelligent. Because Elena Fortuna was both selfish and vain, she gave off the impression that she was either incapable of, or unwilling to engage in, complex higher thought. For Nyx's entire childhood,

Elena had hidden the parts of herself that were cunning and calculating, but she had proved, when she'd finally made her escape from Earth, that she excelled at manipulation and longterm planning. And one did not excel at those things without an ability to plan for multiple contingencies.

Elena had spent time in Jevryn A-Morridahn's orbit when she was younger. She had seen him portal. She had *been* portaled by him. Nyx, considering the opaque barrier currently blocking her view, could only conclude that her mother had seen Jevryn line-of-sight portal at some point, and deduced he had to be able to see where he was going to do it. Having been recently abducted by someone working for Jevryn, Elena had clearly taken extra precautions to protect against a repeat occurrence.

What was perhaps most annoying about the situation was that it proved how very much Elena *didn't* know about Jevryn. *He* wouldn't be inhibited by these measures. He was perfectly capable of deciding to portal five feet from where he was standing without needing to know what existed at the destination. But Nyx was not so experienced, and so her mother's precautions, while useless against Jevryn, were quite effective against her.

"Thoughts?" Morgen asked quietly. Nyx's Hiding of them all, placed before they'd come within view of any palace staff or guards, flexed a little, cloaking the sound of his voice.

Nyx scanned their options. Ideally, they would find higher ground, from which she could see over the wall surrounding the palace and line-of-sight portal them onto the grounds from there. But there was no higher ground. The city surrounding the structure was lower on all sides. Even the land on the outskirts of the city, where Nyx had come in, had only been on level with the ground the palace sat on.

She looked up. The exterior wall was over twenty-feet high. She couldn't see the top, but she didn't have to. She could see the air above it. "I can get us on top of the wall and—"

But Kaden was already shaking his head. "Every brick used to build this wall was imbued by an energy mage. Touching it won't kill us, but it will paralyze us long enough for the guards to arrive."

Or, since her best plan involved them getting paralyzed on top of the wall, they could fall twenty feet to their probable deaths. "I'm guessing you'll tell me there's a reason we can't just shove a couple guards into the wall and steal their keys?"

"One, an energy mage alters the wall defenses not to harm on-duty guards at the start of every shift rotation. Two, magical keys are not like an apartment key. They're embedded in the skin and they only work in conjunction with the person they are assigned to."

Great. She didn't bother asking if he knew of any alternate routes in from his time as a guard. If he knew one that was possible for them to use, he would have mentioned it already. Kaden Moor might be laconic, but he hated wasting time.

The Kormadin royal palace was, according to her friends, one of the most heavily guarded places in the universe. Kaden, she'd learned, had only managed to abduct her mother because Jevryn had pulled enough strings to have him installed as a member of the Kormadin guard assigned to Elena's family. Obviously, that route was not open to them now. They'd all more or less been counting on Nyx to get them through, because her magic—both Hidden and portaling—was the only kind no one knew to guard against. Or so she'd hoped.

There had to be a way around this. Something niggled at the back of her mind, a solution on the tip of her tongue. She was distracted when an irritated expression crossed Kaden's face and his hand fell to the hilt of Lethe-Alihana. A moment later, he unbuckled the sword belt and handed both Constance and Lethe-Alihana to Nyx. "They want you." For Kaden, he sounded downright chipper as he relayed this information. What exactly had the soul of her planet been saying to him if he was this excited to get rid of them?

She accepted the sword and Lethe-Alihana's voice immediately poured into her mind. *Your lack of tutelage in the various uses of portal magic is truly appalling.*

Nyx sighed. *Good talking to you again too. How was your jaunt through the city? You and Kaden have any fun conversations?*

Lethe-Alihana was silent for approximately fifteen seconds. *I believe that was meant to be a joke. Since it was not terribly amusing, you must forgive me if I do not laugh.*

It was hilarious, she countered. *You just have no sense of humor. What's so appalling about my "lack of tutelage"?*

Your inability to portal a known distance to an unseen location.

She shook her head. *I'm not so sure that's the terrible disadvantage you're making it out to be. Griff's book was pretty explicit on the many gruesome ways I could die by portaling to places I can't see.*

Lethe-Alihana sniffed disdainfully. *Arradin Thesrani is overly cautious. Progress is achieved by taking risks.*

Spoken like someone who got to remain nice and safe inside their planet while they watched other people take risks and die in the name of progress.

Nyx felt a *whoosh* through her mind, like the sweep of a hand in a dismissive gesture. *Barring the possibility that someone walks by at precisely the moment you portal across, there is nothing on the other side of this gate but a packed road and empty air.*

Uh-huh. And if someone does *walk by at the precise moment I portal across, my body will end up spliced with theirs and the two-to-five minutes it takes us to die will be filled with pain and horror.* The illustrations in Griff's book of that particular calamity had given Nyx nightmares.

It only happened five times.

That you know of, she pointed out.

The danger is minimal.

Does my father ever do this type of portaling outside of a known environment? He did it all the time in his house, sure, but he knew the exact depth of the walls there, and what to expect on the other side of them.

When Lethe-Alihana gave no answer, Nyx said, *Yeah, that's what I thought.*

He did, *before Arradin filled his head with excess warnings about the various gruesome ways in which they could die.*

And I'm sure these "excess warnings" never came to any fruition, she thought sarcastically.

A beat passed. Two. *From what I've glimpsed in Jevryn's memories, there was a particularly close call in which Arradin was impaled on a stalagmite. Jevryn still has nightmares about it, occasionally.*

I think since he was *impaled, you don't get to call Griff "overly cautious".* It was also odd to think of Jevryn as being human enough to have nightmares.

Fine, he is a perfectly acceptable level of cautious. None of which changes the fact that the current risk level is so low as to be practically nonexistent. But if you do not want my help, do not take it. Your only remaining option is to gain employment with the Kormadin family. Their background searches are notoriously thorough, however, and they rarely take on unsolicited employees unless an individual possesses unusual skills. Kaden's position and false identity was obtained only through Jevryn's connections.

Nyx grimaced. She had the feeling Lethe-Alihana was manipulating her because they were impatient, but she was impatient too. She looked at Kaden. "If we come back tomorrow when the gate is manned, will the opaque factor dissipate when they allow people through?"

Kaden shrugged. "It would depend on how it was designed." He turned to Morgen. "Can you tell?"

"Not without alerting whoever's monitoring the defensive magic that I'm prying."

"Do it anyway?" Nyx asked. "They aren't going to find us if they come check, and I'd rather not try Lethe's suggestion if we could just come back tomorrow and do this the easy way."

Morgen nodded, a low, soft hum starting in the back of his throat. Nyx always wished she could see what he saw when he looked at the structure of magic. She was usually sensitive enough to feel magical use in her vicinity most of the time, but she couldn't see what it looked like the way Morgen could. He sustained his initial note for a few seconds, then adjusted to a new one, holding that for a bit longer before letting it fade.

"The obscuring spell is independent of the locking one."

So coming back tomorrow wouldn't change anything. "Guess we're going with Plan B, then."

"And Plan B is...?" Evra asked.

"I try to learn new magic on the fly from a cranky old planetary soul and hope we don't end up spliced into another human being or impaled on a stalagmite."

I am not cranky, Lethe-Alihana objected, *I am surrounded by inferior beings.*

Evra frowned. "I do not believe we are anywhere in the vicinity of a cave system, therefore stalagmite impalement would be unlikely."

Nyx waved her hand. "It's the principle of the matter. Everyone just...hang tight, I guess." To Lethe-Alihana she said, *All right. How does this work? Every time I tried it before, the portal just wouldn't take shape. I figured you must have to be able to portal the way Jevryn does, without making a physical doorway.*

You do.

Okay, but why?

To open a doorway, you must be able to picture a destination. When you think of traveling twenty feet away to a place you cannot see, what are you picturing?

Being twenty feet away.

Yes, but what are you seeing *in your mind?*

Nothing.

Exactly. Therefore the magic does nothing *in response.*

So…what? I need to imagine what I think is over there?

Do not, under any circumstances, do that. You will almost certainly imagine a different place you have actually seen, whether you realize it or not. In the best case scenario, nothing will happen. In the worst case scenario, your magic will lock onto the true place you are thinking of and take you there.

She blew out a frustrated breath. *This doesn't make any sense. I can open a doorway to a planet I've never seen before, but I can't open one to a space twenty feet away? I can't* see *what's on an unknown planet before I go there.*

Lethe-Alihana sighed. *It is—what is that term humans use?—a mental block, of sorts, that arises from the specificity of what you are attempting. The magic you wield is, in essence, possibility. The universe is filled with possibility. When you immerse yourself in the magic and the planetary map forms around you, it is reflecting those possibilities back to you. The reason you have no difficulty opening a doorway to another planet is because you know there is a planet to travel* to.

I know there's a space on the other side of the gate to travel to, Nyx said irritably.

Furthermore, Lethe-Alihana continued, as if she hadn't spoken, *you are not attempting to impose your own beliefs of what* might *be on the planet onto the magic. You are filled only with the curiosity of let-me-see-what-is-there, or the necessity of I-must-be-away-from-here. And in essence, it* is *a line-of-sight portal, because though the map you project is a creation of your own imagination, it is sight enough for the magic's purpose. What you are doing when you line-of-sight portal is not actually latching the magic on to the place you see, but providing a mental pathway down which the magic can travel to take you to your destination.*

Nyx thought about it. Then she thought about it again. *I don't know that that makes sense to me.*

Lethe-Alihana admitted, with an air of great reluctance, *It does not make sense to many—Arradin was one of the few who could grasp the finer workings—and rarely do portal witches themselves grasp it. A person must have a certain amount of reckless impulsivity to take the risk of portaling in the first place. Therefore, those capable of wrapping their minds around the more complex workings of the ability are certain not to have it. Though the ability is inherited, inevitably if anyone too sensible is born into a portal witch family, the ability skips them.*

Wow, okay. So I'm reckless, impulsive, and not very bright, which lets me open doorways to planets I haven't been to, but I'm not reckless and impulsive enough to imagine myself opening a portal to a specific space I can't see?

Precisely. If Lethe-Alihana had possessed a face, Nyx was certain it would have been beaming. *Now you see the difficulty we are working with.*

Nyx bit her tongue on the retort she wanted to give, because she suspected that, for once, Lethe-Alihana wasn't actually *trying* to be insulting.

It is your awareness *that you do not know precisely what is on the other side, while being close enough in proximity to feel as if you should, that is inhibiting you. The space is near enough to feel real, and the realness and proximity of it prevents you from opening a doorway when you lack specifics.*

Nyx rubbed at her temples. This was only making a loose sort of sense to her, and only if she didn't think about it too hard. *So how does portaling like Jevryn does, instead of opening a doorway, get around the issue?*

Because you are going to wrap yourself in portal magic, and think about jumping to the other side of this gate.

Nyx's brain immediately conjured an image of her leaping over the gate. If she had her damn mercury boots, that would be an actual possibility.

Not jumping in that sense, Lethe-Alihana reprimanded her. *Not over, but through.*

Right, she thought to herself. *Through. Such an easier way to think about it.*

Do cease whining and try.

Nyx sighed. Aloud, she said, "Okay, I'm going to try something. Nobody panic if I vanish."

She shifted Lethe-Alihana to her right hand and drew a stream of portal magic into her left, dragging the magic over her arm, like she was smearing on sunscreen. This was going to take forever. And way too much magic. And the reason she'd never tried to do this before, to try and portal like Jevryn did? She was terrified she was going to miss a half-inch of skin somewhere, portal, and find herself missing a fingertip or something.

What, in the name of the stars you seem to hold holy, are you doing? Lethe-Alihana demanded.

Coating myself in portal magic, as requested? Nyx offered.

You are thinking far too literally, child. Magic is not an inert object, like a pair of pants to be physically put on in the morning. What you are doing is clumsy and wasteful.

Irritation burst out of her. She was tired of Lethe-Alihana treating her like she was an uneducated four-year-old. Did they think she *wanted* to use an excess amount of magic? All she wanted was to coat herself in magic and get to the other side of the damn gate without having to listen to them *tut* their disapprov—

The magic she'd wiped onto her arm thinned and flowed, stretching along every inch of her skin. It closed last over her toes and fingertips and *snapped*. The world flickered, the shortest of disappearances, like the blink of an eye, and then she was no longer staring at the gate with her friends. She was on the other side of it, staring at the palace.

She was also completely naked and sans one talking sword, her fist now closed around empty air. Nyx had never been more grateful to be Hidden in her life. It gave her a minute to stand there and think *What in the actual fuck?* without having to worry about anyone seeing that she was naked in public.

It also gave her a moment to simply stare. Now that she was on this side of the gate, it was obvious that from the other side, some magic was at work obscuring the true size and structure of the palace. It hadn't changed entirely—it was still a massive, gleaming princess palace—but looking at it now, she realized that before she wouldn't have been able to tell you *how* tall it was, or anything specific about the layout of it.

The answer to the first question was *too* tall. Skyscraper tall, the building's peak obscured by thick white clouds. The walls from the bottom half of the building down were smooth with no outcroppings, while the upper half, which she guessed played host to the residential sections, boasted balconies dripping with greenery. She could have stared at it for hours, had a strong wind not blown up and reminded her that she was naked.

She folded her arms over her chest and turned to look back at the gate, mentally running through how she'd gotten here. She had wanted to be covered in magic and on the other side of the gate. Portal magic was will based. Her will to have these things happen had been very strong. Apparently, she had forgotten to include the will to have her clothes come with her.

She was phenomenally annoyed. Not because she was naked, though that wasn't great, but because all the time she'd spent on her own, trying to figure out how to do exactly what she'd just done, her failure had been caused by something so minor that it was beyond infuriating. It had been inhibited by her own *beliefs* about how portal magic worked. Specifically, how it worked for her.

She had thought she manipulated doorways. It was how she had always portaled, so it was how she thought the magic worked for her. She willed it to open doorways, and that was what it did. She couldn't open a doorway to an unknown nearby space for all the reasons Lethe-Alihana had just explained to her. And she had also not realized that the magic would respond to her will for it to move *around* her. She'd never understood how Jevryn wrapped them in magic when he portaled. She had half-suspected it was some *other* ability he was using to direct the magic around them. Not that its movement was a response to his desire for it to move.

She sat with it for a moment, accepted it, and turned around to face the gate again. Plucking a few strands in the Hiding that covered her, she removed the exceptions that allowed her friends to see her. She loved them, she did not want them to see her naked. A fresh strand of magic spilled into her palm. She hesitated over it. Open a doorway like she was used to, or try the new method?

She decided to test the new method again for her return trip, but fixed the surrounding area firmly in her mind, so she could open a doorway to bring her and everyone else back through. Somehow, she didn't think anyone but Morgen would find it funny if she accidentally portaled all of *them* without their clothes. Plus, it would be self-defeating if they kept having to portal back for said clothes.

Nyx gave the strand of portal magic a mental prod, willing it to wrap around her. It responded sluggishly, as if it were a piece of dough without much elasticity and, if stretched too quickly, would break. Magic could be such a frustrating thing. Will something unintentionally, because you were driven by intense emotion, and it would leap to do your bidding. Try to do the same thing purposefully and it was like pushing a boulder up a hill.

She tapped her foot, counting the seconds on her watch—because yes, her subconscious mind had not directed her magic to portal her clothes, but apparently her fear of being without a time-telling device was strong enough for it to include that particular item—and after fifty-seven of them had passed, the magic finally clicked into place around her.

While it might have been slow to cover her, the moment she thought of being across the gate, the world blinked and she was back to where she'd started.

"They're sure this is normal?" Morgen was asking Kaden, presumably because Kaden was once again in possession of Lethe-Alihana. "I know she said not to panic about the disappearing, but she didn't say anything about disappearing and leaving her clothes behind." He frowned. "I think there's a religious Earth myth about this, if I'm not mistaken."

"They claim she's fine." Kaden sounded irritated.

"What I want to know is, why will they talk to you and not me?" Morgen asked.

"Or me," Evra added.

It appeared that in the two or so minutes she'd been gone, her friends had played pass-the-talking-soul-sword around. She drew the exception to her Hiding off her clothes, laughing under her breath when Morgen jumped as they disappeared to his sight.

"Little Guardian?" he asked, cautiously.

She dressed quickly, then reworked her Hiding again to pop back into visible sight for the three of them. "Don't ask," she said.

"About the clothing?" Evra clarified.

"Yes. Don't ask about the clothing." She held her hand out to Kaden and he gave her back the soul sword.

An utterly appalling lack of—

Oh shove it, she interrupted. *You're a terrible teacher, I'm a terrible student, let's just move on. Anything important you would like to relay before I put you back in storage?*

No, they replied. It was a *no* full of seething sullenness.

Good. She laced her mental voice with enough false sugar to bake a dozen cakes. Then she strapped Constance and Lethe-Alihana back into place, opened a doorway to the other side of the gate, and waved everyone through. Once across, she let Kaden take the lead, since he was the only one of them who had been here before.

They encountered three more opaque, locked areas that required Nyx to put her newly learned portaling ability to the test. It was still a sluggish ability, when not fueled by her irritation, and she still only used it on herself. She could *feel* the magic slipping around her, and so knew when it had fully enveloped her—and, fortunately, a firm nudge meant she didn't lose her clothes again. But she wouldn't have that knowledge if she tried to wrap it around her friends, and she wasn't willing to take the risk of accidentally maiming one of them. Far better to portal herself, then open a doorway back to the space she'd just vacated to bring everyone else through.

As they moved through the palace grounds, then the palace itself, Nyx tried not to notice the beauty of the place. But that beauty was inescapable. It was in the architecture of the building, the master craftsmanship evident in everything from the gorgeous tile floors and tastefully placed ornate fountains, to the decorative moulding around entrances, to the statuary and artwork that graced niches and adorned walls. Out of the context of the situation, she would have loved it. The child in her that had grown up reading about faraway places that didn't exist would have thought it a fairy tale castle, would have kept herself Hidden for days just so she could wander and explore at will.

But *in* the context of the situation? The adult her walked these halls, slipped past carefully laid defenses and strategically placed guards, and felt her anger rising. All that time she'd been living in Tempe, memory-less and unseen and alone, her mother had been living *here.* Ensconced in decadent luxury in a place so beautiful it hurt to look at.

Nyx's feelings were a writhing, simmering mass she couldn't find an adequate word for. She had the uncomfortable suspicion they were waiting for the right moment to explode out of her, and the situation wasn't helped by the godawful number of stairs she'd been forced to climb since walking into the building.

The palace had a type of elevator that operated off magic rather than electricity, but according to Kaden, they couldn't use them because each movement of each elevator was tied to an alert and logged, in addition to being guarded. The alert wasn't something Nyx could Hide, because she didn't know whether what triggered the alert was magical or mechanical, and therefore wouldn't know what component to Hide. And she couldn't simply Hide the entire elevator, because the people guarding them would notice the sudden absence of an elevator, when she had nothing to replace it with. Seth's bottle illusions were strictly for people—not things—so she wouldn't be making a false elevator out of her remaining bottles.

Add in that the elevators were designed for one person—though two smaller individuals could probably squeeze in at once—and there was no way they were making four unnoticed trips. Especially since that would necessitate splitting up, and if there was one thing Nyx had learned from horror films, it was that you and your party should never, ever split up in hostile territory.

Hence the stairs. In a skyscraper-height building where the residential section didn't start until halfway up. Her legs burned. Her knees protested. Her lungs declared that surely no amount of cardio could prepare an individual for this scenario. Kaden and Morgen continued climbing with the stoic determination of those who know that a thing must be done, and so they are going to get it done. Ahead of them, Evra bounded—yes, *bounded*—up the steps, half a flight ahead of Kaden and Morgen, and a full flight above Nyx. While Nyx could not see Evra's face, the enthusiasm of the Amazon's gait made Nyx suspect she was wearing an expression of sheer joy. Or, rather, what passed for joy on the face of Evra al'Daemon.

Nyx climbed with the resignation of someone who knew that she was not in possession of enough portal magic to simply line-of-sight her way up the stairs, but really wished she was. It was the damn switchback nature of stairwell construction within a building. She could only see to the top of one flight. She'd have to initiate a new portal at every landing. One of the few pieces of portal magic lore Jevryn had imparted to her in the last six months was that the bulk of magic expenditure in portaling was involved in opening the portal.

The primary four factors in how much magic was used were the initial opening, the distance being traveled, the grade purity of the portal magic itself, and the efficiency of the wielder. So line-of-sight portaling could be extremely efficient across flat distances, where the wielder could see a long way. Not so efficient if she had to open over a hundred portals because she didn't want to climb some stairs, and she wasn't going to get stranded on a foreign planet without enough magic to get back to the Shadow Market simply because she was lazy. Besides which, magic use involved mental muscles in the same way climbing stairs involved physical muscles, and she hadn't had any opportunity to exercise the first ones in the last six months.

When Evra reached the next landing and Kaden called softly for her to stop there, Nyx was ridiculously grateful for the break. They lined up along the wall, because the stairwells were busy in a place this size, and being able to flatten themselves against the wall at a moment's notice was a necessity. Morgen and Evra took the wall to the far side of the door that broke the landing, and Kaden and Nyx took the other side.

Morgen, Kaden, and Evra's illusions had fully faded several flights ago, so the Amazon's expression one was one-hundred-percent Evra al'Daemon as she eyed Nyx critically. "Your cardio—"

"—capacity is atrocious and embarrassing," Nyx finished for her. "I'm aware." She'd actually done a *lot* of cardio in the last six months, she just tended to glide along at an easy pace for long stretches of time, rather than mix up the intensity, like Evra would. Nyx wasn't incapable of completing the task at hand, and she wouldn't find herself curled up in bed tomorrow unable to move, she just wasn't quite as unaffected by the task as everyone else, and her dislike of it made the climb feel worse than it was.

Evra shook her head. "I was making such progress with you, too. When we return home, I'll have to start all over."

Nyx groaned. "I hate you."

An actual smile crossed Evra's face. "I know."

"Don't worry," Morgen told Nyx, "after she runs you ragged, I'll make comforting *there there* statements and bring you coffee."

"Thank you," Nyx said. "I always knew I liked you better."

"Everyone always likes him better," Evra grumbled.

Nyx started to fire back that if Evra ever expressed her care for people via comforting statements and coffee, rather than by relentlessly driving them to be the best that they could be, she might occasionally come out on top in the popularity contest. Then reality punched Nyx in the gut. *Home. Cardio. Bitching about cardio. Evra bitching about how Morgen was always the popular one.*

It was all so fucking normal. *Too* fucking normal. Talking about going home like she'd never left, like they were just on any other trip and returning to the Station—going back to life-as-usual—afterward was a foregone conclusion, rather than one Nyx wasn't sure she could handle.

Elena Fortuna had once said that Nyx's sadness infected a room. That her negativity could spread through a space like smoke, bringing everyone down with her in seconds. And maybe there had been some truth in it, because the look on her friends' faces made it obvious they'd noticed her mood go from "joking" to "I had a normal interaction and now I would like to go curl into a ball and hurt for the next year".

Either that, or *they* had realized they'd been talking about Nyx going home like it was normal. Maybe they'd remembered, just as she had, that nothing was normal, that they could pretend they clicked together like they had before, but there was friction now. Maybe it was that, or maybe it was just Nyx's own guilt at having been gone for so long that that friction had had a chance to develop.

Whatever the cause, awkward uncertainty formed in the space between them. Nyx wrapped her arms around her stomach. It was something she hadn't done in a really long time, something she did when it felt like she needed to physically press all her emotions back into herself. As if she could squeeze herself tightly enough that she would fit back into the mould she'd obviously escaped from.

Kaden's gaze cut briefly to the movement. Morgen opened his mouth, hesitated, and in the hesitation, Kaden stepped in. "We didn't stop for idle chatter."

Nyx was so bloody relieved to be rescued from the awkwardness that she responded before anyone else could. "Then what did we stop for?"

He indicated the door. She stepped around him and reached for the square indent she'd seen other stairwell-goers use to open the doors, but Kaden put his hand to it first, blocking her. She looked up at him, brow quizzically raised.

"Your new portaling," he said. "How accurate are you?"

"How accurate are you hoping for?"

"If you needed to land in a square foot of space ten feet on the other side of a wall, could you do it?"

Nyx didn't even have to think about that one. "No." She'd used her newfound portaling method four times on the way up, and while she was more confident in the general use of it, saying she lacked precision was as obvious as saying a hammer was a blunt instrument. "Please tell me we didn't climb all of these stairs on the basis of your hope that I could do this. Because you could have just asked before we climbed the stairs."

He shook his head. "It was the more direct route, but there is another."

"On this floor?" Nyx asked hopefully.

The corners of his lips curved the minimum amount necessary to be considered a smile by Kaden Moor standards. He pointed up. Of *course* Option Number Two involved more stairs. She sighed and started climbing. Six flights later, she asked, "Could Jevryn have done it?"

He looked over his shoulder, held her gaze for two seconds in answer, and returned his attention to where he was walking. Right. Of *course* Jevryn could have done it.

11

By the time Kaden led them onto an actual floor, Nyx didn't want to see another stair for at least a year. Maybe two. She got a whole two minutes to catch her breath before Evra began impatiently tapping her foot, so Nyx sucked it up and followed as Kaden took them down several hallways and into an empty room so large that it seemed to stretch on forever to either side of her. Her footsteps echoed in the space each time her boots hit the glossy wood floor. They were halfway across the room before she realized what it was—a ballroom. A *massive* ballroom.

Nyx honestly had no idea how many people an average Earth ballroom of old was designed to hold—one hundred? Two hundred?—but whatever the number, she thought you could fit at least a dozen Victorian-era ballrooms into this space, possibly more, and it really put into perspective for her the amount of political and social intermingling that must be involved in a universe in which over a hundred planets all coexisted alongside one another. How many diplomats had occasion to visit other planets? And how would the universe fare if Nyx *did* eventually succeed in freeing the Stations, destroying the ley lines in the process? Of course, since there was a good chance she would die in this attempt to kill Kiev, maybe it would never matter.

They reached the side of the room opposite the one they'd

entered, a fifty-foot stretch of which was nothing but glass doors. Kaden slid one open and they poured onto the balcony outside. The temperature, which had been mild on the ground, was significantly chillier this high up, and it made her question why there was even a balcony here. Who would want to come out into the frigid air in a ballgown?

She hadn't realized she'd asked it out loud until Kaden said, "There are warming spells out here when the room is in use."

She rubbed her arms and frowned, looking back inside. "And how did you know it wouldn't be in use?"

"It's closed for renovations. For about five years now. Everyone agrees it needs repairs, but the budgeting committee cannot cease arguing about where the funds for them should come from."

It didn't appear to be in need of renovations, but what did she know? Still, good to see that bureaucracy was bureaucracy no matter where you went in the universe. "And we are out here because…?"

"Because that"—he pointed up, up, *up*, to a balcony she could just barely make out, so high that she suspected if she stood on it, she could reach up and brush a cloud—"is your mother's."

Nyx walked to the railing. She knew it was a bad idea and she did it anyway, ignoring all common advice that said "don't look down". *Down* was far enough away that her stomach flipped itself inside out. She gripped the railing, an irrational part of her afraid that thinking about falling would turn it into a reality. Before this moment, she would have said she didn't have a fear of heights. But she truly believed people were not meant to be this far off the ground.

"We couldn't have gone through a nice indoor path?" Nyx asked when Kaden came to stand beside her. She didn't expect an answer to that question and she didn't get one, because the obvious answer was that the only available indoor path was the one she wasn't a good enough portal witch to handle.

"And the balconies aren't spelled against people breaking in?"

Morgen clapped her on the shoulder, which made her jolt, which made her stupid heart think she was somehow going to fall through the solid stone floor beneath her feet. "Little Guardian, the ground is down there." He pointed to the way *way* down there. "The side of the building is sufficiently protected against being scaled, and the only flying race in the connected universe is the griffins. While they *can* survive on this planet, the gaseous makeup of the air on Endalna isn't ideal for them. If they physically exert themselves to the level needed to fly on this planet, they pass out about thirty feet into the air."

"These are the private sanctuaries of Endalna's elites," Kaden said. "There *are* guards at the higher levels, but they are tastefully hidden."

Something about guards being referred to as "tastefully hidden" made her snort. She eyed the next balcony. It was maybe fifty-feet further along the wall, and fifteen feet higher than the balcony they currently stood on. Her depth perception wasn't the best, so after she spun a tendril of portal magic from her bracelet and opened a doorway, she stuck her head through the portal rather than blithely leap through. She didn't particularly *enjoy* doing this, as she was all too aware that any lapse in attention that resulted in an unexpected closing of the portal would effectively decapitate her, but it was better than jumping through only to find out that it *looked* like she'd opened the portal above the balcony from over here, but in actuality it was a couple feet shy. Fortunately, her aim had been true, and she stepped through, followed by the others.

She repeated the process from balcony to balcony, and they moved steadily further up and along the building. The higher they went, the larger and more lavishly furnished and decorated the outdoor spaces became. By the time Nyx was staring up at her mother's balcony, she didn't think it could even rightly be called by that word. The ones they'd passed so far? Ones of stonework and railing, furnished with tables and chairs and hanging plants? Yes. But this one? Well, it might be humbly masquerading as a balcony, but it clearly had grander aspirations.

Nyx didn't know what marvel of engineering and magic had combined to create the space she saw, but it must have taken no small amount of both, because the area jutting into the sky was far too large to be possible without any visible signs of support. It sprawled along this side of the building and appeared to wrap around the corner of it to the other side as well, and if it was built from the same cold stone as the other balconies, she couldn't see it beneath all the greenery.

It was as if someone had taken a lush, manicured garden, carved it from the earth, and glued it to the palace wall. Grasses, flowers, bushes—even trees—held dominion, vines dripping from the sides, their leaves and tendrils rippling in the gentle breeze. Sections of the garden were terraced, grass steps leading up to smaller, more heavily manicured areas and—in one instance—a plateaued space furnished with an intricately carved stone table and chairs.

At that table, seated before a tea set that was far too delicate—and no doubt expensive—for a child, was a five-year-old girl. Her hair fell in white-blonde waves, her actions too poised for someone so young as she poured liquid into cups for the imaginary attendees to her tea party. At the bottom of the stairs that led up to the little picnic area stood what could only be the girl's bodyguard.

"Wait here," Nyx said.

"Nyx." Kaden grabbed her wrist, the rough calluses on his hand rasping against her skin.

She looked pointedly at his hand on her wrist, then lifted her gaze to his eyes. He didn't let go.

"What are you planning to do?" he asked.

"I haven't decided yet." She jerked her arm free, ripped open a narrow portal and stepped through, closing it before anyone could follow. She arrived on the grassy steps, already behind the body-guard's line of sight, so his vigilance for potential threats wouldn't cause any further drain on her Hidden magic. For a moment, Nyx merely stood there and watched as her sister talked animatedly to the non-existent occupants of the empty seats before her.

Well, Nyx supposed they weren't entirely empty. Two of the three seats held large stuffed animals—one a bizarre bird-like crea-ture with brilliant plumage, the other some relative of a feline—both clumsily Hidden. The net she'd drawn over them—and Nyx's mouth turned down in a frown at seeing that Serenity was making nets like their mother—was rudimentary, the threads of it sticking out into reality. Serenity must have intended it to hide the stuffed animals from only a few specific people—the bodyguard, for one, as Nyx could follow the rough threads of the Hiding to him—because she had no difficulty seeing the animals herself. And, because she wasn't included in the Hiding, she also had no difficulty seeing the structure of it.

Interesting. Nyx approached the one empty chair directly across from Serenity, resting her hands on the back of it. Her own Hiding, as it was meant to conceal her from everyone except her friends, was in no danger of being spotted by Serenity, even if the girl's aptitude were advanced enough to spot such a working without being led to it first, which Nyx doubted. Given the rough shape of the nets over the stuffed animals, it didn't appear Elena was being as demanding with Serenity's magical education as she'd been with Nyx's at the same age.

"Now," Serenity was saying to the brilliantly plumaged stuffed animal, "as I told you before, this meeting is of a most secret nature." She spoke as if she was mimicking the kind of language and mannerisms she'd heard adults use, rather than anything kids her own age would say. "Mommy mustn't know. She no longer approves of our association." She turned to the feline stuffed animal. "Or ours."

So, Elena had decided her daughter was too old for stuffed animals and pretend friends. Nyx was hardly shocked. As she listened to the child chatter, she got the impression of a girl having a pretend tea party not because she thought it was fun, but because she was lonely.

Nyx frowned. Where were Serenity's friends? Shouldn't a royal child be surrounded by them?

Nyx couldn't help what she did next. She'd always wanted a sibling, and she would likely never have another chance to meet this one without Elena's interference. And, yes, maybe there was a part of her that wanted to know what was so right with Elena Fortuna's second daughter that had been so wrong with the first.

Was it merely the appearance? That Serenity looked so much like Elena, whereas Nyx looked so much like Jevryn? Was it the way that, despite her obvious loneliness, the little girl still smiled and laughed and seemed to do both easily and often, whereas Nyx had been a quiet, subdued child?

Was it only the circumstances of her birth? That Nyx had landed Elena Fortuna in a secluded part of Earth, and Serenity had cemented Elena's status as the wife of a powerful scion of the Kormadin royal family? It was time to find out.

Nyx opened a single, careful exception to her Hiding. She expected Serenity to startle when Nyx suddenly popped into existence across from her, but the girl only went very still, cocking her head slightly and considering. After that moment of consideration, she drew herself up and said, in a perfect imitation of someone much older and stuffier than her, "I don't believe you are supposed to be here. You may go."

At these words the bodyguard whipped around, proving he listened to his young charge's idle chatter when his gaze focused on the space where Nyx stood and the drain on her magic intensified. But he must have been accustomed to Serenity talking to people who weren't there—or didn't appear to be there—because after a moment he relaxed and returned to facing the other direction.

Nyx rested her forearms on the chair back, hands clasped, and leaned forward. "Maybe I'm not *supposed* to be here, but I don't think you want me to go."

"Why not?"

"Because if I leave, I'll probably never see you again. And sisters should know each other, don't you think?"

Serenity blinked and, with a wary eye to the bodyguard, said quietly, "You're not my sister. You don't look like me."

"I look like my father. You look like our mother."

Serenity narrowed her eyes. Nyx hadn't exactly spent a lot of time around kids, but she was pretty sure a five-year-old wasn't supposed to look that shrewd. Tobi had certainly never put Nyx this off-kilter, even when the Congregation was speaking out of him. "*If you are my sister, prove it.*"

Nyx reached out and plucked a strand of the Hiding that covered the stuffed feline. "This is sloppy. If I tug on this strand, the entire thing will come undone."

Serenity lunged over the table, knocking Nyx's hand away. "Don't!" Her gaze shot to her bodyguard and then she whispered, "Mommy wants to get rid of them." Her hand clenched around the feline's big stuffed paw.

"Why?" Maybe Nyx had misjudged their relationship. When she'd seen them at the Station, she'd thought the three of them—Emerik, Elena, Serenity—had looked like a picture-perfect family. She'd thought Elena truly loved Serenity.

"She says I'm too old to be talking to them." Her shoulders hunched. "I know they're not real. And I know she wants what's best for me. But I don't have any other friends." She looked at Nyx, hope shining in her big blue eyes. "Are you here to be my friend?"

If there was a hell, Nyx was going to it. She should never have talked to the girl. Elena would never allow the two of them to have a relationship. But how was Nyx supposed to have known the Kormadin princess was lonely and she'd be getting her hopes up? "I think sisters can be friends," Nyx said carefully. And because she now felt like she owed her something, she said, "And friends help each other." She reached for the strands of the Hiding on the stuffed feline. "As it is, this will unravel on its own—see here, the ends aren't secured properly—but you can weave a better one."

She held out her hand for Serenity's, and her sister tentatively obliged. Nyx guided her control of the strands. Her mother had done this with her, when Nyx was very young, but Elena had always been impatient and harsh about it, so Nyx endeavored to be kinder. And Elena had always been attempting to make Nyx's workings look more like her own, whereas Nyx was now showing Serenity how to undo her current working and reweave it into something other than a net. It was a struggle to remember the simpler patterns she'd been able to manage at that age, but she finally found something basic enough that Serenity could follow it.

When they were finished, Serenity's eyes lit up. "It's a blanket!"

"I suppose it is." Though Nyx had started the working in her own cloak pattern, it was Serenity's magic and, since Nyx had allowed her freedom of expression, the girl had altered it as they progressed, and there was no denying it looked more like a blanket now. That was the way of Hidden workings—they were meant to be particular to their makers. It was why Serenity's original one had been so bad—she'd been attempting to copy Elena, and copying wouldn't work if it was in a style that wasn't intuitive to her.

This joint working convinced Serenity of Nyx's status as her sister in a way words hadn't, and Nyx couldn't bring herself to dim the resultant excited glow by refusing the cup of tea offered to her. When ordinary children had imaginary tea parties, was there typically real tea involved? Nyx wasn't one to know, so she took the cup —still surprisingly warm—sipped the fruity tea, and let Serenity talk.

The girl had barely said more than a sentence when suddenly she froze. Nyx stood and turned, following Serenity's gaze. Their mother had emerged onto the balcony, her husband at her back.

Elena's voice held a warning when she asked, "Serenity, who are you talking to?"

"No one," she said in a small voice.

Elena's eyes narrowed. She dismissed the bodyguard with a flick of her hand, waiting until he disappeared inside to speak again. "I'd like to give you one more opportunity to be truthful. Who were you talking to?"

Serenity said nothing. Nyx stepped sideways of the chair she'd vacated, guessing correctly that Elena's attention would focus on it. No doubt Elena expected one of the stuffed animals was Hidden there, and she wanted to break that Hiding. When she found nothing, her gaze shifted to the chair that held the stuffed bird.

The panicked look on Serenity's face was all the warning Nyx needed before the girl blurted out, "I was talking to my sister!"

Elena's face went ashen. She stopped focusing on the chair, gaze instead sweeping over the entire area. Nyx was ready for the tug on her magic as Elena sought her. For now, she fed her Hiding enough to keep it from breaking, biding her time.

Emerik cleared his throat. "You don't have a sister, sweetheart. And you remember your mother and I agreed you're getting too old to be playing make-believe like this." Given the gentle, indulgent tone of his voice, it sounded more like Elena had decided, and Emerik had reluctantly agreed.

But no amount of softness in his voice could prevent the outrage that crept across Serenity's face. Nyx couldn't help but smile. She knew that reaction. It was the deep-seated indignation born when someone called you a liar when you were telling the truth. Nyx had been accustomed to the feeling in her youth. It appeared she and her sister were more alike than a first glance would lead a person to believe.

Her little sister drew herself up. "I didn't make her up. She's right here! You just can't see her because she can do magic like Mommy and me."

"Sweetheart," Emerik began.

Elena cut him off, holding out her hand to her second daughter as Nyx's magic took another deep hit to keep her Hidden. "Come to me right now." Elena's voice brooked no disobedience. It was a tone Nyx was intimately familiar with but Serenity was clearly not.

Because if Serenity had had any notion of what typically followed that tone, she would have scurried to her mother's side, not indignantly said, "But I'm playing with my sister and I only just met her! I don't want to go."

"Serenity Arianna Kormadin, you come here right now or I swear to you I will—"

Nyx chose that moment to drop her Hiding. "That's really no way to speak to your daughter, is it?" The look on Elena's face was well worth the shitstorm this was going to unleash.

Serenity ran around the table to take Nyx's hand, grinning up at her before transferring the dazzling smile to Emerik. "See, Daddy? I have a sister!"

Emerik froze. The reaction—and the way he kept looking uncertainly between Nyx and Serenity—told her he didn't know what to do. He was stuck between the bizarre-to-him assertion that Nyx was Serenity's sister, the realization it might be true, since Nyx had appeared out of thin air, and the fear that Nyx would harm his daughter.

Half-a-dozen guards poured out of the balcony door at some unseen signal.

"Nyx!" Evra shouted from the other balcony. Another flux of Hidden magic poured out of Nyx to cover the sound of the shout, to keep the Hiding over her friends intact. Nyx subtly turned her hand palm out, telling Evra to wait. Just wait. Nyx drew Serenity in front of her, hands resting on the girl's shoulders. Emerik's face went bloodless. He motioned to the guards and they halted. Nyx felt a little guilty for using her sister as a human shield, but the Kormadin guards would never hurt her, and though Emerik didn't know it, Nyx would never hurt her either.

Elena went into full damage control mode. She glared at Nyx. "I don't know who you are, but—"

"I remember you," Emerik said. His voice was calm and reasonable. Clearly, since he couldn't throw guards at her, he'd chosen the talking-Nyx-down approach. "You're the Guardian. From Earth's Station, yes?" He frowned. "But how are you here?"

By the tightening of Elena's lips, Nyx could tell she hadn't counted on her husband remembering what the Guardian from Earth's Station looked like. Nyx was a little surprised too, if she was honest, but then, given the family he'd been born into, memorizing people and the positions they held had probably been a part of his training since his youth.

Emerik's gaze went to Nyx's hands on Serenity's shoulders, his concern for his daughter poorly disguised. "I don't know what you want, but—"

"I want a word with my mother." She flashed her teeth in a smile that would have made Evra proud, turning her attention to Elena. "I think you owe me that, after everything. Don't you?"

12

Emerik looked from Nyx to Elena to Serenity, then back to Elena. His jaw clenched. He dismissed the guards with a single flick of his hand, and in less than ten seconds, it was only him and the three women on the balcony once more.

He turned to his wife. "Is what she claims true?"

Elena had only a brief moment to decide how to play this. Nyx saw the calculations flash through her eyes before her head suddenly dipped, eyes downcast, lashes fluttering in a tremble. "I didn't know how to tell you. She's *his* daughter. V-Viktor's. I had no choice in the matter, I—"

"Stop *lying*," Nyx said harshly. "For once in your life, take some responsibility for your actions." Nyx looked at Emerik. "I am not Viktor Hawthorne's daughter. And Viktor was never holding her captive. You didn't rescue her from an abusive man, you ended the life of a man she had ensorcelled beyond all reason. The only thing you rescued her from was the consequences of her own actions."

Silence descended. Nyx was willing to bet the story Elena had told her husband about Viktor was not common knowledge. She wouldn't have wanted the stigma of a prior, supposedly abusive, relationship following her into the Kormadin family. So Nyx knowing it—knowing to deny it—meant something.

Serenity tugged hard on Nyx's hand. "What's going on? Why are Mommy and Daddy upset?"

Nyx dropped into a crouch. She owed her sister the truth. "Mom and I don't exactly get along. She would rather I didn't exist. That's why she never told you about me."

Serenity's eyes filled up with tears. "Then you didn't really come here for me? You came here for Mommy?" She looked so betrayed, and Nyx couldn't really blame her. At the same time, it irritated her—that Serenity had so much that Nyx hadn't had, that her life had been so sheltered that it seemed as if this moment—realizing that Nyx hadn't come here to befriend *her*, specifically—was the worst of her life.

But it wasn't Serenity's fault that she'd had a pampered childhood and Nyx hadn't. Nyx's anger wasn't for the girl, so she put it aside.

"I came here for someone else entirely," Nyx said truthfully. "But I really did want to meet you. And I really do want to be your sister."

"That will not be happening," Elena said sharply.

Nyx flicked her gaze to her mother. "We'll discuss it later. Until then..." She looked back to Serenity. "I need to talk to Mom and your father alone. But I'll come say goodbye before I go." She reached up, tucking an errant lock of hair behind the girl's ear. As her fingers brushed her shoulder, she Hid a few threads of her clothing, creating an easy, safe anchor. "Okay?"

Serenity hesitated, then her jaw took on a stubborn set and she said, "You promise?"

Promises held weight with Hidden. And though this one wouldn't bind Nyx via her magic, if she was going to make it, it would mean something. Serenity knew that. "I promise."

"Okay." Serenity accepted this and walked back inside, much to the relief of both her parents, if the twin exhalations were any indication.

"You will not be seeing her before you go," Elena said. "You will not be seeing her ever again." She turned to Emerik. "Have her removed."

Emerik made no move to do so. He looked like a man who had felt someone rattle the foundation of his life, and he was now very much afraid it was going to crumble apart around him. "She's your daughter." It wasn't a question. "When we entered this marriage we said there would be no secrets between us. Yet you lied to me about the existence of an entire *person*. Do you have any idea what this will do to us if the family discovers it?"

Nyx crossed her arms. Good to know Emerik's primary concern was his family standing.

Elena retreated into ice and polish. "She should never have been a problem."

Emerik blinked. "How? How did you think another child wouldn't be a problem?"

Elena said nothing. Nyx raised her hand. "I can answer that."

Emerik turned back to her, his gaze cold in that way that spoke of a man who was accustomed to having his way and was now calculating how much damage control would need to be done, and how soon. Nyx's friends saw it too, if the fact that they were now unspooling a length of rope from the pack at Evra's feet, and was that—yes, yes that was a grappling hook they were pulling out. The walls might not be scalable, but apparently the balconies weren't grappling-hook proof. What had even made Evra think to bring that?

The Amazon threw twice before the hook caught on this railing —lucky for Evra that Hiding her had also meant Hiding everything she was carrying—then pulled the rope taut and tied it off on their balcony. Nyx sincerely hoped there was a magical component keeping the hook caught and the rope tied, because Evra swung fearlessly over the balcony and began walking her hands over each other along the rope.

Remembering she was supposed to be giving Emerik an explanation, not surreptitiously watching an event other people couldn't see, Nyx said, "She wiped my memories. Or rather, she *Hid* them. It's a long story, but I'm all better now."

Emerik opened his mouth, but Elena snapped, "What is it you want? If you think I will allow you to become a part of our lives here—"

Nyx laughed. She laughed so hard she almost doubled over and tears came out of her eyes. When she could finally talk again she said, "Stars, how self-centered do you have to be to think I would *ever* want to be a part of your life again? My sister's? Yes. It's not her fault she has you for a mother. But I'm not asking your permission for that."

She didn't *need* Elena's permission. All she needed was a portal anchor left, unseen, in the correct place.

"Then why are you here?" Elena ground out.

To Nyx's left, Evra reached the end of the rope, climbed over the balcony, and dropped onto the soft grass, followed by Morgen and then Kaden. It was everything Nyx could do not to stare at them and give away their presence.

"I am waiting," Elena reminded her.

Nyx was tempted to make her wait longer just for that comment, but she didn't. "Kiev A-Morridahn."

Elena and Emerik both went very still.

"Somehow, he found out about me. About what I am." She chose her words carefully. Let Emerik think she meant her Hidden abilities. "I'm curious, did you get anything in return for giving him my identity, or were you just hoping he'd clean up your dirty laundry for you?"

Elena crossed her arms, tapping her fingers against her bicep. It was such an un-Elena-like thing to do—Nyx thought her mother could remain glacially frozen even in the face of imminent torture—that Nyx narrowed her eyes. Before she could determine what it meant—if it meant anything at all—Kaden slipped up behind Elena and pressed a dagger to her throat.

What the hell was he doing? The draw his direct physical contact with Elena caused to Nyx's magic meant she had only a split-second to decide whether to drop the Hiding over her friends entirely, or to weave Elena and Emerik in as exceptions. She chose the former just as Evra and Morgen arrived at her side.

"Call them off," Kaden ordered, his voice low and full of violent promise. *"Now."*

Elena's fingers tapped against her arm again and this time, because Nyx was looking, she saw shadows retreat from windows high above the balcony.

"Archers," Evra said quietly, following Nyx's gaze.

So that's what her mother had been doing when she was tapping her fingers—summoning backup. Evra nodded to Kaden and he dropped his hold, coming to join Nyx and the others.

Elena's eyes flashed as she tracked his movement. *"You."*

Kaden inclined his head, as if he hadn't just had a blade pressed to her throat. As if he were greeting a person he didn't particularly like, but also didn't care enough to cause a scene over. "Lady Kormadin."

The calm, neutral recognition seemed to take Elena off guard. The tirade that had no doubt been coming never left her mouth, her gaze instead flicking several times between Kaden, Nyx, and the others before finally settling on her daughter, her lips curving into a smile. "I can't help but notice a rather prominent absence from your party. Did you get bored of the boy-next-door appeal? Or was it Seth who finally tired of you?"

Nyx wasn't consciously aware of moving, or of calling on that darker power inside her. She just knew that one moment she was standing there, and the next she had her mother pressed against the nearest hard surface, a hand veined in black wrapped around her throat, the two of them enveloped in a shifting wall of black shadow that blocked out all sight and sound around them. "Don't. Ever. Say his name. Again."

Elena's eyes were wide, and it was gratifying to see them filled with those same hints of terror Nyx had seen when Elena had been near Jevryn. She clawed ineffectually at Nyx's hand, and only then did Nyx realize her grip was tight enough that her mother couldn't breathe.

For a long, long moment, Nyx did nothing. There was a part of her—the part that had encased them both in an impenetrable sphere of death magic—that whispered she had already decided one person had to die, so what was one more? Her mother had caused so much suffering. She was selfish to her core, and Nyx didn't think she would ever change. Because Elena didn't ever believe anything she did was wrong. No matter the circumstances, she was always the victim.

Nyx's fingers tightened—and then released. Because no matter what had happened in her life recently, she wasn't going to kill her own mother.

Elena sucked in air, her eyes still wild. "What are you?"

It was such a funny question, coming from the woman who had given birth to her, and it had such an easy answer. "My father's daughter." Tendrils of black smoke streaked from the shifting wall, coiling around—but not quite touching—Elena's face. "That's what you told my uncle, isn't it?"

Elena said nothing. One of Nyx's tendrils lashed out and bit her cheek.

"Isn't it?"

Hatred burned in Elena's eyes. "Yes. Fine. I told him. Is that what you wanted to hear?"

It was, and it wasn't. Because it meant: "Seth's dead. Because of you." Another thing that was true…and wasn't. At least, not wholly true. Where did one lay the entirety of the blame for that death? With Nyx's mother, because she was the reason Kiev had taken an interest in Nyx? With Kiev, because he was the one who'd actually done it? Or with Nyx, because she was the reason Kiev had killed him?

Before Seth had died, if Nyx had been given this hypothetical scenario with other people, she would have said the blame rested only on the one who had taken the life. Now that she was the one in the middle of it, she wasn't so sure.

If she'd hoped this news would have any effect on her mother— that Elena would show some remorse—she'd hoped in vain. Her mother was what she was. Nyx might have forgotten that fact for a few years, when she'd forgotten herself, but now that her memories were in working order again, she could accept that she'd known it for a long time. She'd stopped hoping Elena would change not far into her adolescence.

"I think you'd deserve it," Nyx said softly, "if you died in recompense. But I'm not going to do it."

Elena let out a jagged breath.

"Serenity has to be taught how to use her magic, after all, and I don't feel much like becoming a surrogate parent at the moment." Not to mention, taking Serenity with *her* would be far too dangerous, and that was even if the girl *wanted* her life upended, which Nyx very much suspected she did not.

Serenity might not be allowed friends, at this moment, but while Elena might be strict with her in that regard, it was clear that in all other aspects, Elena doted on her daughter, as did Emerik. Serenity's childhood was not Nyx's. Serenity was a pampered, royal child, and Nyx didn't think she would appreciate having all of that stripped from her to go live in a Station with a depressed older sister who was also in possession of an item that all of the universe's most powerful people would kill her for, if they ever found out she had it.

No, what Serenity needed from Nyx was a tempering influence to keep her from absorbing all of the worst of Elena's beliefs and personality traits. At least until she was old enough to survive without Elena's guidance. After that…

Nyx bared her teeth at her mother. "But what was it you said Jevryn told you? That once I was grown and didn't need you anymore, you should run as far from him as possible? Perhaps I'll make you the same promise regarding Serenity. Enjoy your life as a Kormadin, Mother. Because once Serenity's grown, I might decide to take it from you.

"That is, if your husband doesn't do it first. He didn't look too thrilled by this turn of events. So if you don't want me to drop this wall and tell him exactly who my father is—somehow I can't imagine he'll appreciate knowing that a councilor has every reason to hate you—then you're going to tell me where to find Kiev."

Silence.

Nyx shrugged. "Have it your way, then." The darkness around them thinned, turning more gray than black.

"Wait," Elena gritted out.

Nyx did, the wall around them not growing any more translucent, though it didn't fully darken again. Nyx wasn't entirely sure how she was controlling it, other than by raw emotional intent. This —the wall and the tendrils—were facets of death magic Jevryn hadn't delved into with her yet, and it disturbed her a little that the tendrils moved in similar fashion to the phantom snakes Jevryn had made when he'd impersonated his twin.

"I don't know where he is."

Nyx waited, but her mother didn't elaborate. "You're not being very helpful."

"He isn't here."

"Still not terribly helpful. Why don't we start at the beginning. When *was* he here and what happened?"

"A little over four months ago."

Nyx blinked. She'd expected the time to line up with her own departure from Kyvren, but this would have been a few weeks after that.

"He was…" Elena's nose wrinkled in distaste. "He looked like half of him was dead. You can never see much of those two, the way they dress, but the left side of him was…wrong."

A small smile spread across Nyx's face, and there must have been something deranged in it, because Elena's face took on a wary expression. Nyx didn't care how she looked. She'd actually hurt Kiev. She'd screamed at him in anger, but she hadn't imagined she'd done any damage. Not given Kiev's assertion about how easy it was for an A-Morridahn to swallow one of their own deaths. But she hadn't considered what the shard of Lethe-Alihana, carried in her voice, might have done. Perhaps she was having trouble finding him because he was already gone.

As nice of a fantasy as it was, she doubted it. "What did he want?"

"He had magic with him. He wanted me to Hide it from everyone but him."

"You told him what you are?" Nyx asked skeptically. Giving away something like that about herself was not a very Elena-liked move.

Her mother's mouth twisted like she'd bitten into something sour. "No. He deduced you were Hidden and thus that I must be, so I have your carelessness to thank for that."

Nyx didn't even bother rolling her eyes. She supposed some things never changed—any problems in Elena's life were still all Nyx's fault.

"What kind of magic did he want you to Hide?" Nyx asked, but she knew. Of course she knew. It explained why Kiev's trail ended here, but he was gone.

"The kind your father uses to bypass the ley lines."

"Have you seen him since that day?"

"He returned once, for the same purpose."

"How long ago?"

Elena's voice clearly conveyed her irritation at continuing to have to answer questions. "Roughly one month."

"And how was my dear uncle's health at the time?"

"Improving." Elena sounded as annoyed about this fact as Nyx was. It was unfortunate for Nyx that taking care of Kiev was also going to take care of one of her mother's problems.

"Add me as an exception to the Hiding."

Elena's eyes narrowed. "Why? It won't do you any good unless you are already in his presence. And even if you *were,* that magic doesn't respond to anyone but him or Jevryn. I've tried."

"That isn't your problem, is it?"

Elena laughed. "An inherited ability, then."

Inwardly, Nyx cursed herself. Letting her mother figure out she was a portal witch was a terrible mistake that would no doubt come back to bite her in the ass at some future time.

"You're just like him," Elena continued. "I knew it the moment you were born. That you were all of his and nothing of mine."

Nyx sighed. "Yes, yes, I'm a terrible disappointment. You've expressed the sentiment before, but truthfully, I can't think of a better compliment than being nothing like you. Now add me as an exception, and I'll be out of your life."

Her mother's expression turned calculating. "And out of my daughter's." The way she said it, as if she only had the one, left no doubt that she didn't truly consider Nyx hers. It shouldn't have stung. It was nothing new. Yet it did, and Nyx had a feeling it always would.

"She's my sister," Nyx said simply. "And she's lonely. You've isolated her."

"Because she is too young to understand that her magic cannot be shown to others. In a few years she will grow out of that, and her status will guarantee her all the company she desires. She doesn't need *yours.*"

Nyx shook her head. "You've never really cared about anyone, have you? You've always just seen people as a means to an end, so it wouldn't have hurt you to not have friends. It hurts her." *It hurt* me. But she didn't say that, because her own pain wouldn't matter to Elena. "You won't be able to undo the damage you've done to her if she continues to have no one."

Elena lifted her chin. "She is stronger than you are."

It wasn't a matter of strength. "Maybe she is, maybe she isn't. But I won't agree not to see her, and if I were you, I wouldn't push me on it. If you refuse to help me, there's one foolproof way to end all of your Hidings."

Elena sneered. "You don't have it in you to kill me. You've already proved that."

"I don't need to." She reached for Lethe-Alihana's hilt.

Constance freed the sword and Nyx pressed it to her mother's throat.

Hello, betrayer. Heat rose from the blade.

Elena made a strangled noise. "That's *his* sword."

"It is," Nyx agreed. "Slightly more than a sword, as you can see, and with a mind of their own. They're bound to obey Jevryn. Me? Not so much. And me and this sword? We both want the same thing. And while I might hesitate to end your life, they won't. So what's it going to be, Mother?"

Do not actually kill her, Nyx told Lethe-Alihana silently.

The heat coming from Lethe-Alihana intensified. The sword jerked in Nyx's hand and a thin line of red opened on Elena's neck.

Lethe, Nyx warned.

Oh, do calm yourself, she required encouragement. See?

Elena's lips twisted into a snarl and her magic rose. Elena plucked and weaved the threads, her eyes burning with hostility. When she finished, Nyx drew a strand of portal magic from one of her bracelets, summoning the map, searching, and *there.* A trail that hadn't been there before, traces left of trips between this planet and others, but to one more than the rest, and that one—that one the space where he currently waited.

She closed the map and flipped Lethe-Alihana across her back, Constance re-closing around them. She let her mother go, drawing the magic of death back into herself. The wall around them dissolved, revealing that, in their absence, the world had fallen into utter chaos.

Morgen, Evra, and Kaden faced off against Emerik and half-a-dozen Kormadin guards

"Call them off," Nyx ordered.

Elena didn't. Not immediately. She had a smile on her face as she watched the chaos. "Do you see that?" She pointed at where Emerik struck at Kaden with a thin whip of silver magic. "All of that, because I disappeared for a few minutes. He is *mine.* All of *this* is mine. And nothing you've done here today will undo that. He's too invested."

It hit Nyx, in a moment of startling clarity, that everything she'd been so angry with her mother about as she'd walked through this palace was meaningless. She'd been furious over the different lives they'd led since they parted—Nyx alone and barely surviving while her mother rose to a position of power in the lap of luxury—but this life her mother led? *This* was nothing. It wasn't real. She'd seen Emerik's face when he'd learned who Nyx was. It hadn't been the face of a man who had been betrayed by the woman he loved. It had been the face of a man who had received an inconvenient twist in his orderly life, and now he would have to deal with it.

And Elena thought it was *worth* something. Nyx looked at her mother. "I don't give a shit about your marriage or your would-be kingdom. Call them off."

Elena did, the guards and Emerik halting at her command. Evra took the opportunity to clock the guard she'd been fighting in the temple with the hilt of her sword, a look of grim satisfaction on her face as they dropped like a brick. Evra's gaze found Nyx's, all-too-obvious relief on her face when she saw Nyx unharmed. It was so little, only a brief acknowledgment, and yet it was so much. Morgen gave Nyx a short nod, and Kaden's eyes found hers, held them for a moment before he looked away.

And there, in those three small gestures, was so much more than her mother had. So much more than her mother would *ever* have.

"You have Emerik Kormadin," Nyx agreed with her mother. "And you have your place here. You lied and tricked your way into both of them and maybe, since your husband's bought those lies hook, line, and sinker, he'll never give them up. But you don't have anything real, and he knows that now.

"Me? I have them." Nyx nodded at Evra, Morgen, and Kaden. "And I have never had to pretend to be anything other than what I am to earn their loyalty. They're my friends because of who I am, not because I play a role well." She hadn't appreciated that until this moment. That her friends—her *family*—were here for *her*. She had been gone, with no communication for almost half a year, and the second Evra and Morgen had realized she was somewhere they could reach her, they'd come. And Kaden, for all her complicated history with him, for all she'd worked to pretend he didn't exist these last months, was here too. Maybe she didn't fully understand *why*—maybe she didn't want to—but he was backing her up, the same as Evra and Morgen.

She looked back at Elena. "That's what you can't stand, isn't it? That's what you hated about Seth. That he loved me for who I was, when you hated me for it." Her mother didn't answer. Nyx hadn't expected her to, and in truth, she didn't want her to. But she did have one final thing to say. "His blood is on your hands, as much as it's on Kiev's." *As much as it's on mine.* "I won't forget that."

Nyx walked away from Elena, back to her friends. As she passed Emerik, she paused long enough to say, "Good luck with your wife, Lord Kormadin. I wouldn't wish her on anyone."

She reached Evra, Morgen, and Kaden, portaling them to the next balcony, and the next and the next, until they were far enough away from knowing eyes that she could slip them all beneath the comfortable cloak of her magic again, Hiding them from sight.

"Did you get what you needed?" Evra asked.

Nyx nodded. "Before we go, I have something I need to do." She hesitated, but in the end, she asked. Because she thought Serenity might like it. Thought it might do her some good to meet more people who existed beyond the sphere of the Kormadin family's influence. "If she wants to…would you all want to meet my sister?"

S erenity sat primly on her bed, waiting, when Nyx portaled into the room. When she saw what Nyx had brought with her, she lost the primness. "You saved them!"

Nyx handed her the two stuffed animals she had retrieved from the tea party table and waited while Serenity cooed over the treasures and settled them onto her bed. Once Serenity had done this to her satisfaction, she looked at Nyx, excitement warring with suspicion in her eyes.

"You came back."

"I promised I'd come say goodbye."

"So you're leaving?" Serenity asked sullenly. "And I probably won't see you again because Mommy doesn't like you."

Ouch, kid, way to say it bluntly. "I do need to leave soon, and while it's true that Mom would rather we didn't see each other, what she doesn't know won't hurt her." Lying to one's parents was probably not the best thing to be teaching a child, but then Serenity had Elena Fortuna for a mother, and Emerik Kormadin for a father. Surely anything Nyx had to teach her would be an improvement.

"So…you'll come back?" Serenity asked.

"If you'd like."

"I suppose," Serenity said, clearly striving for aloof disinterest. The mannerisms she chose to imitate made it abundantly clear that everyone she had to base imitations off of was an adult. "If you want to."

"I do."

"Are you leaving, then?"

"Soon. But if it's all right, I'd like you to meet my friends first. They think it's pretty cool that I have a sister."

Serenity perked up. "You have friends?"

Nyx nodded. "Can I bring them in?" Serenity gave her assent. Nyx opened a portal to the balcony she'd come from and her friends stepped through.

"Serenity, these are my friends, Evra, Morgen, and Kaden. Everyone, this is my sister, Serenity."

Serenity gave Nyx a horrified look, as if she had made an irreparable blunder, and drew herself up. "Greetings, friends of my sister. I am Serenity Arianna Kormadin, daughter of Elena Thererre Lyra Fortuna ne'Kormadin, and Emerik Fiall Kormadin, of the sixth house of Kormadin."

Nyx blinked. Did this kid have a speech tutor?

Serenity looked at Nyx's friends expectantly. Morgen was the first to respond. "Morgen Severell Drahl, son of Amelia Agate Drahl, and a father who isn't worth mentioning."

Serenity looked as if she didn't know whether to be charmed or horrified by the way he'd chosen to refer to his father. He winked at her. She quickly slid into "charmed" and asked, "Amelia Agate Drahl of Raveras?"

Morgen's face took on an expression that said he hadn't expected a kid to make any connections to his family name. "Uh, yes." Nyx arched her eyebrows at him in question, and he pretended not to notice.

"I look forward to associating with your family."

Morgen looked like he was about to protest, but Serenity had moved on to looking expectantly at Evra.

"Evra Helene al'Daemon." The Amazon hesitated, then said, "Sister to Tamrin Gale al'Daemon and Horus Octavius al'Daemon."

"You have a sister as well?" Serenity asked it like having a sister offered one membership to an exclusive club, and now she and Evra were in that club together.

"I do," Evra answered. "Though she and I are not getting along so well, right now."

"Why not?"

"I don't think—" Nyx began, but Evra waved her off.

The Amazon looked contemplative, as if she'd been trying to find that answer for some time, and finally had. "Something bad happened to her. It changed how she viewed the world. After, I tried to help her, by doing what I thought was best for her, because that is what older sisters are supposed to do. She disagreed. I think she needed someone to lash out at, and she chose me because she knows I will never abandon her." She smiled wryly. "That is what older sisters do—put up with the abuse of younger sisters."

"Thank you," Serenity said. "That is helpful." She looked at the final member of their party.

"Kaden," Kaden said. He did not offer his last name or any familial connections. Only Evra and Morgen having just stated their full names and connections made Nyx realize that she didn't know Kaden's either. Last name, yes. But if he had a middle name, she didn't know it, nor did she know his parents' names. She had never thought it odd that he hadn't talked about anything like that when they were together, because she had been trying so hard to avoid being asked similar things she couldn't answer.

Serenity waited. When Kaden didn't elaborate, she was either intuitive enough to realize he was never going to, or otherwise didn't know how to respond. Instead, she addressed the group as a whole. "It was nice to meet you all. Will you visit again when Nyx does?"

"If we can," Morgen promised.

Footsteps sounded in the hallway, and Elena called, "Serenity? Your father and I need to speak to you."

Serenity's eyes widened. "Go!" she whisper-yelled.

Nyx hastily Hid the very back corner of Serenity's bedside table to serve as a portal anchor for future visits, then opened a doorway to Tenebris Umbra.

13

When Nyx dropped them back into the throne room of the Shadow Keep, she wasn't surprised to find Bryn waiting. The Keeper was slumped on her throne, one elbow on the chair's arm, her chin resting on her palm. She stared out at the room, seemingly focused on nothing, but the increased magic needed to fuel Nyx's Hiding told her well enough that Bryn had been waiting for them.

It was a sound plan. Where else would a portal witch go, but back to the source of portal magic? The real question was, how long had she been waiting?

Nyx hesitated, looking between the portal well and Bryn. She had no doubt she could get what she'd come for without getting caught. But there was the small problem of her current base of operations being the Shadow Market which, to all intents and purposes, might as well belong to Bryn, who also knew precisely where to find Nyx to make her life uncomfortable. And there was Tamrin to consider, not to mention Nyx's desire to know why Bryn had wanted the girl to talk to Kalvar.

"Should we talk to her?" Nyx asked Evra.

"It might be best if we did so now. The longer she thinks, the angrier she tends to become. And considering how we left things outside Calista, the opportunity to sort this out alone, when she does not need to be concerned about her image as the Keeper in front of her people, is one we shouldn't pass up."

In other words, time to pay the piper. "Okay, then. Here we go." Nyx dropped the Hiding and waved at Bryn. "Long time no see."

Bryn didn't so much as blink. The only outward concession she made to four people popping into existence before her was a slight hardening of her expression. Well, that, and the fact the temperature in the room rose to a stifling degree, heat emanating from the Keeper. Nyx remembered Seth sitting on Bryn's throne as she heated it beneath him, and wondered if Bryn's magic extended only to temperature increases, or if it was more along the elemental lines of fire magic.

It was Evra who finally broke the silence. "Is it necessary for us to sweat through *every* layer of clothing?"

Bryn finally lifted her chin from her hand. "For all the difficulty you've caused me, I ought to turn you into human torches. Surely, once you are reduced to ash, your mere presence will no longer be enough to throw my operations into chaos."

Fire magic then, Nyx supposed. Despite the bite in Bryn's words, the temperature in the room mercifully cooled.

"Reyva is waiting outside that...place, with Essteria and two dozen soldiers. They're all convinced you were too intelligent to come back here."

Nyx raised an eyebrow. "Was that supposed to be an insult? I'm hurt."

"That." Bryn pointed at her. "That's why I knew you'd come here, right to this room. You have no sense of self-preservation. No wonder you and Hawthorne got on so well."

Nyx flinched. Was hearing his name ever going to stop feeling like a punch to the gut?

"Bryn," Evra warned.

But Bryn ignored her. "Yet he's barely cold in the ground and here you are, back with that one." She nodded at Kaden. "I'd have thought you'd wait a little longer, out of respect for the dead."

Nyx knew she was being baited—she hadn't even told Bryn *when* Seth had died—but it didn't matter. The pain was still too raw, her nerves still shot, and she couldn't stop herself. She portaled across the room in a blink, Lethe-Alihana pressed to Bryn's neck.

Still making excellent decisions, I see, they said acidly. Nyx ignored them.

The Keeper's eyes sparked. "How are you *doing* that?" She ignored the steel at her throat and reached her hand in the direction of the portal well. Magic streamed to her, a small tuft that settled into her palm. She held it out to Nyx. "Show me."

Nyx's entire body hummed with anger. "You used his name," she said, her voice low. "You implied I don't mourn him enough, all to bait me into portaling, and you think I'm going to show *you* how to do the same?" She shook her head and threw Bryn's own playbook back at her. "I'm beginning to understand why Evra left you."

Bryn bared her teeth. "You don't want to play with me, Earthling. You'll find it hazardous to your health."

"I wouldn't be worried about *my* health, if I were you." Nyx's gaze flicked significantly to Lethe-Alihana before she slowly drew the blade away, returning it to Constance's care. "As for playing"— she plucked the tuft of portal magic from Bryn's hand—"I think you'll find I don't lose easily."

Nyx felt a slight resistance as Bryn tried to hold on to the magic, but it was like an ant pushing against a boulder—the Keeper's ability for portaling was weak. No wonder the Council hadn't worried over the stray portal witches left in the universe finding their way anywhere they shouldn't. If this was representative of their capabilities, none of them would ever make it off a planet without an anchor. Or they'd make it to the closest uninhabitable planet and die in the attempt.

Nyx began funneling the ball of magic into various bracelets, her focus still on Bryn. "Now, I haven't had the best day. I had to talk to my mother, and that always puts me in a bad mood. So let's get the ground rules set now, hmm? I'm going to be in and out of this city for a while. And I'm going to use your portal magic well. There's not much you can do about either, considering..." She Hid herself. The magic drain needed to do it right in front of Bryn's eyes was like sucking a pool dry in one gulp, but she needed a flashy display. She held it for five agonizing seconds, let it go and picked up her sentence where she'd left off. "You won't even know if I'm here."

Bryn's eyes lit with fire, a slow smile stretching across her face. "Can you survive portaling into this room if it's hot enough to melt steel?" The temperature around Bryn began to rise. "Because I can raise it that high and keep it there. Maybe you'll get lucky and arrive when I've cooled it to allow the other witches in." She shrugged. "Or maybe I'll never cool it, and I'll take all the magic they need to them."

Nyx once again contemplated the ways in which her life would be vastly easier—and safer—if Jevryn would just teach her the damn insulating atmospheric spell. But no, he seemed to think she would get into trouble with it. She couldn't imagine why.

Nyx crossed her arms. "You want to expend your magic keeping this room that hot all the time? Just to keep me away from a resource you'll never be able to deplete with your limited abilities?"

Bryn's jaw clenched.

"Evra?" Nyx called, without taking her eyes off the Keeper. "How long can she keep this place that hot?"

"The entire room? Approximately a week before her magic begins to cannibalize her body for resources."

Nyx nodded and held out her hand. Portal magic surged to her, far more than the amount that had come to Bryn. "I can take enough magic with me to last a week." She looked at Bryn. "And if you decide to take a break on the heat, I don't have to physically come in here to find out if the room's livable. I can check in regularly and stop by whenever you're resting."

Bryn's hands curled around the ends of the throne arms. "I will reduce that place you're living to rubble."

"Don't tempt me to do the same here."

Morgen coughed, loudly and pointedly, drawing their attention. "If I might be so bold as to offer an alternative solution to theft and infrastructure destruction?" He smiled at Nyx. "You've already wrecked one building today."

Bryn gave Nyx a reassessing look, which had undoubtedly been Morgen's intention. "Alternatives?" she asked, her voice dropping back into a bored, disinterested tone.

Morgen waved his hand, indicating the portal well. "You have an abundance of resources."

"I'm under no obligation to share them."

He turned to Nyx. "And you have a skill she finds useful. Trade."

Nyx stared at him. What the hell was he doing? He'd been to Amentia Furor. He knew precisely why she shouldn't be teaching anyone the lesser-known facets of portal magic. "Can I talk to you in private for a moment?"

Without waiting for an answer, she locked her hand around his arm and pulled him to the far side of the room. "What are you doing?" she whispered. "I can't teach her to portal."

Morgen, his voice equally soft, lips barely moving, answered, "She doesn't have the aptitude to portal like you do. Teach her line-of-sight. She'll never make it off planet without an anchor stone."

Nyx's frustration ebbed a little. Morgen had a highly attuned ability to sense magic and tease out its limitations. He'd seen both her and Jevryn portal enough times now that if he said Bryn couldn't do it, Nyx believed him. And yet…

"I can portal a lot farther than I could when I started out. The more I practice, the easier it gets. And I'm sure everything"—she started to say Jevryn, then erred on the side of safety and said—"*he* can do is way more than he could when he started. This is a lot bigger than me ignoring his advice on what *I* should or shouldn't do."

"He's had an unnaturally long amount of time to practice. And your starting line is leagues beyond hers. Magic is a muscle, yes, but you're still limited by the body you're born with, so to speak."

"And what if she teaches someone else what I've taught her, and eventually it makes its way to someone who *does* have the ability to get off-planet? Griff said it's not impossible for an otherwise obscure portaling line to produce a once-in-a-generation talent. You saw Amentia Furor." She wanted to tell him she didn't have a burning desire to rekindle an intergalactic war, but Morgen—and Evra—didn't *know* about the Minethrans. It was one of the few secrets Nyx had kept from her friends, because knowing it would only put them in danger. But Morgen *did* know that the Council considered it a death sentence for anyone to set foot on Amentia Furor. "If Bryn accidentally ended up there, the absolute *best* case scenario is her dying quickly."

"I wouldn't ordinarily suggest this—"

"I can already tell I'm going to love where this is heading."

"—but you could come to a binding agreement."

Nyx blinked. "You mean like what Jevryn did to Kaden?"

"Exactly like that."

"I have no idea how that works. And she'll never agree to it."

"I can walk you through it, and you might be surprised what people will agree to when they want something badly enough," he said, a trace of bitterness in his voice.

Nyx wasn't touching the latter half of that statement. She had a feeling he was talking about Kaden, and she didn't want to know. "I don't know that I *want* to come to an agreement with her."

Evra might be on good terms with the Keeper these days, but Evra's history with Bryn meant that she was always going to be treated with more generosity than ordinary people. Nyx wasn't so fortunate. While her last deal with Bryn hadn't gone badly, there had been plenty of room for it to.

And though she didn't exactly *dis*like Bryn, she didn't exactly like her either. The woman hadn't clawed her way into the Keeper position by being warm and friendly. She was cutthroat when it came to gaining advantages for herself and her newly gained empire, and while Nyx respected her dogged determination from afar, she didn't appreciate being on the receiving end of Bryn's machinations in the up-close and personal.

"Do you want to refuse to deal with her more than you want to find Kiev?" Morgen asked.

He just had to come back with the logic and reasoning, didn't he? Of course she would deal with Bryn if it meant finding Kiev, but she didn't want to be tied up with the Keeper any longer than necessary. Maybe, if she worked this right, she could get out of the bargain without actually having to offer too much.

She'd likely need direct access to the well to find Kiev, if she didn't want to expend all her stored portal magic, but it wasn't like she was going to need to come back. Once she found him—well, one way or another, it would be finished, after that. If she survived, it would be time to return to the Station, and once she did that... She glanced at the tattoo on her hand, the stylized *one* standing out starkly against her skin.

She had one more time Kaliaris would allow her to leave them. Realistically, how much more portal magic could she need?

Making up her mind, she stalked back across the room to Bryn. "Here's the deal: I'll give you half-an-hour's worth of instruction each time I need to use the well *if* you make a binding agreement not to intentionally pass on what you know to any other portal witch *and* do everything within your power to ensure no other witch learns it some other way."

The last thing she needed was Bryn explaining it to a non-portal witch, like, say, Reyva, who could then turn around and pass it on to the rest of Bryn's witches.

Bryn shook her head. "I have no idea how much time is involved in learning what I want to know. *And* you owe me for however many times you snuck in here and stole magic behind my back. I want to learn the foundation of the ability as back-payment for what you've already taken. Once I've seen how that goes, we can determine reasonable payment for each use of the well."

Nyx crossed her arms. "I'm not giving you back-pay. You wouldn't give it to me if I were inept enough to let *you* steal something from *me*."

Bryn's jaw clenched.

"And as for the time needed, *I* learned line-of-sight portaling in a few minutes. I'm being generous with half an hour per use."

Having pricked Bryn's pride twice in rapid succession, Nyx got the response she wanted. Mostly.

"Fine. You have a deal. But if I'm not satisfied with the results, I will end it, and you will find me quite creative in the ways I can keep you from that well should I choose to."

"Fair enough." Nyx didn't bother making any threats in return. Bryn was certainly the type who might try to take the baseline knowledge Nyx provided her with and extrapolate from there, thus obviating the need for any further instruction and allowing her to bar Nyx from future well access. But from Nyx's own experience, she knew that even if Bryn *wanted* to do that, her need to know more would ensure that the next time Nyx wanted to make a trade, Bryn would take it.

"All right. Let's get this over with."

After thirty minutes, Nyx had learned three things: one, she hated teaching, two, Bryn wasn't a gracious student, and three, Morgen had been spot-on in his assessment of Bryn's natural aptitude. Nyx didn't consider herself to be very efficient with her magic use—even though her efficiency had improved since her first fumbling attempts—likely because Jevryn so thoroughly outstripped her in that regard and frequently reminded her of the fact.

But compared to Bryn? Nyx might as well be a savant. After forty-three minutes of instruction—Nyx could be generous when the student was struggling—Bryn had managed to open a window the size of a grapefruit to the other side of the room. So, you know, if Bryn needed to send a butterfly through a portal to a space twenty feet away, that was now an option for her. At least, provided she had access to the well's limitless supply of portal magic. The Keeper's efficiency was *terrible.* Nyx tried not to cringe at how much Bryn was using, but it was a little like watching someone continuing to dump gas into a vehicle that got half a mile to the gallon and topped out at five miles-per-hour.

Even Bryn could admit it. "How is this practical?" she demanded. Sweat glistened on her brow, and she stubbornly held the small portal open another second before letting it close.

"It gets easier," Nyx offered. Which had the benefit of being true without her having to explain why Bryn was having so much more difficulty with it than Nyx had. Namely, genetics. "Keep practicing. Work on getting the full-size portal and your magic requirements should go down with time. But for stars' sake, don't go *through* the portal unless you're sure you can hold it open. If you accidentally bisect yourself, I don't want to be accused of murdering the Keeper of Shadows. And I really don't want your job."

Bryn glared at her.

Nyx lifted her hands, palms out. "I'm just saying, portaling is an inherently dangerous activity and I am not responsible for any loss of limb or life arising from your unsupervised actions. Now, if you don't mind, I have places to be and people to kill."

Bryn stared at her, as if unsure whether to take her seriously or not, while Nyx's half of the room went uncomfortably silent. What? She couldn't joke about it? If she didn't have morbid humor in this moment, what exactly was she supposed to cling to?

Shaking her head, she sank her hands into the portal well and pulled up the planetary map. She went to look for Kiev, but she was more attuned to Jevryn, and so found him first. Guilt nipped at her as she followed his criss-crossing paths. He'd been *everywhere* looking for her. Lehine. Earth. Kyvren. A dozen other planets she couldn't name. Here.

Shit. He'd been *here*. "Bryn? You haven't had any…distinguished visitors recently, have you?"

"I couldn't say. Your definition of 'distinguished' and mine might not align."

That sounded like a *no*. "If you do get one, don't tell them I'm on the planet, and *definitely* don't tell them I showed you how to line-of-sight portal."

"Perhaps you could be more specific on who *they* might be?"

Nyx shook her head. "Trust me, you'll know them if you see them." Currently, Jevryn was at his home. His signature glowed more brightly from that location, and she was surprised to feel a pang of longing for the quiet library in the heart of his home. It was nothing akin to the longing she felt for Earth's dot, but still, it was something. His home was a refuge away from the wider universe, an isolated place of calm where time seemed to stand still. Maybe that was why he liked it. Maybe that was why she wanted, for a moment, to return there.

The weight of the portal stone he'd left her in Lehine's empty reservoir weighed heavily in her pocket. She realized, with the sudden stark clarity of one who has been utterly focused on a single goal for months and never paused to draw breath long enough to think about it, that she didn't have to do this. Her path wasn't written in the stars and planets she gazed out upon. No cosmic force compelled her to continue down it.

She could quit. Use the portal stone and give Lethe-Alihana back to Jevryn. He would forgive her. She hadn't realized that fact until the moment before she'd left, when she'd apologized to him and she'd seen, finally, a hint of the sentiments he kept buried so well. He would forgive her, as her friends had forgiven her for her absence, as Griff and Kaliaris no doubt would.

She could go *home*. All she had to do was give up. To tell herself that there was nothing she could do. That Kiev was a problem too big for her, one she had little hope of solving, and that Seth wouldn't want her to risk it.

The aching chasm inside her yawned a little wider at the thought of him. He would never have wanted her to do this. If he'd known in advance what would happen, how it would happen, he would tell her to let it all go. To let *him* go and move on with her life. He would want her to *have* a life.

But what she was doing now…it wasn't about what he would have wanted. It wouldn't ever be about what he would have wanted again, because he was gone. That was the whole point. The living made their choices based on the fact that they had to keep living. It didn't matter that Seth would never have wanted this for her, because she could never have him back. *She* had to go on living, and she could not live with herself in a world where Kiev moved through the universe with no one to curtail him.

Kiev did what he wanted because Jevryn *couldn't* stop him, and if any of the other councilors were powerful enough to do so, they had chosen not to. Nyx was not a councilor. Nyx was not her father. Nyx was only *Nyx*, but she was going to remove the filth that was her uncle from the face of the universe or she was going to die trying.

She looked past all the traces of Jevryn, until she found Kiev. The planet his trail led to was one she didn't recognize, though that was hardly surprising. Her own lessons on portal magic had ground to a halt, with Jevryn favoring death magic training in its stead, and being rightfully concerned about letting her near portal magic in any quantity.

A shadow fell over her.

"Where?" Kaden asked.

Nyx pointed.

"Can you widen the scope of the map?"

Nyx did so, bringing more of the surrounding planets into view. Kaden's lips thinned.

"You know what planet it is?" she demanded.

"It's…not a planet, exactly. It's"—his gaze flicked to Bryn and he both eschewed names and lowered his voice—"*his* private refuge."

A hot ball of anger rose in Nyx's chest. "You didn't think to mention that he has a private refuge? That would have been really useful information before I had to go endure *my mother.* I know you have difficulty with words, but surely even you could have mustered a 'Hey, Nyx, by the way, that guy you're looking for? Yeah, he has a private refuge he might have retreated to, and I know where it is'."

He looked at her. Silently. Pointedly. She disliked how very much the silentness and pointedness made her feel brash and emotional when, really, she thought her irritation perfectly justifiable.

"*If* I had known where it was, I might have mentioned it."

She pointed at the map. "You clearly know where it is."

"I know how to recognize it based on the surrounding markers." He pointed out the nearby planets. "I recognize the formation because when he portals places, he doesn't bother to hide the map from anyone. He went there *once* in the entire time I worked for him. I memorized the map so I could recognize it again in case it ever proved useful. I couldn't tell you how to find it, because I don't know what inhabited planets it might be near.

"If you hadn't had a lead on him already, I might have mentioned it, but you could have searched this map for years and never found it, even if you had the magic at your disposal to waste, which at the time, you didn't."

Under normal circumstances, she would have let it go. But there was something...not *nice*, exactly, about arguing with him, but stress relieving. A temporary outlet for all the useless fury she felt. "You still should have said something."

They were close, by virtue of the necessity of having this argument in harsh whispers, given Bryn's proximity. Close enough that she saw the brief spark of anger in his eyes.

"I'm sorry," he said in a slow, measured, caustic voice. "I didn't realize we now had a collaborative working relationship, and you would have taken my suggestions seriously, as opposed to accusing me of setting an elaborate trap to take you back to your father."

Nyx bit the inside of her cheek to stop herself from snapping back a retort. He was right. She *would* have thought that. She also didn't care, and wanted to keep arguing with him just to feel anything other than the raw aching wound inside her. But she wanted to find Kiev more. So she turned back to the map, studying the place her magic had drawn her to.

"So this is his hideout. How guarded is it?"

Out of the corner of her eye, she saw a muscle in his jaw tick, and for a few long seconds, he didn't answer. Maybe she'd pissed him off too much to get a response. Finally, he said, "I don't know. I've never been there. He doesn't take *anyone* there."

Nyx considered this. It was Kiev's private stronghold. Jevryn had one too—the place Nyx had lived for the last six months. Her father, before she and Kaden had come to stay with him, had lived alone. He had no staff, no guards, no companions. Jevryn and Kiev, however different they might be, *were* siblings. Twins. They had been raised the same and had—despite clearly different natures and choices—ended up in very similar positions in life.

Was it too much to hope for that Kiev was every bit as paranoid as his brother, and he too lived alone in an isolated dwelling with no one to assist him?

Probably. But there was only one way to find out—by going there. Part of her wanted to do it right then. Just open a portal and walk through. Common sense, inconvenient as it was, prevailed. Having trekked all over a different planet *and* interacted with her mother today, she was tired. If she portaled to Kiev's location now, she would be doing him the favor of delivering herself on a silver platter.

And there was the fact that if she went now, leaving Kaden and Evra and Morgen behind would not be an option. They would insist on coming with her. When she'd hatched this plan, it had been with every intention of carrying it out alone. Then Evra had shown up and started using "we" language, and Nyx had felt guilty for being gone so long. She'd missed her best friend and wanted to keep her and Morgen around for as long as she could. Taking them to her mother's planet hadn't felt all that dangerous, because it was just a normal planet, and one she hadn't actually expected to find Kiev on.

But taking them to a location she knew was Kiev's personal lair, for lack of a better word, and which she knew nothing about, felt a lot like signing their death warrants. She couldn't live through that again—losing someone else. Losing her family, when she'd only just gotten them back. What she had was rare, and maybe she didn't deserve it, but she had it and she could not—would not—risk it. Would not risk *them*.

If she told them her fears, they would insist on coming with her anyway. If she pushed the argument, impressing that they might not come back from this, they would use that as an opportunity to logically counter that if it was that dangerous, she shouldn't go either. Answering with "I don't care if I come back or not" wasn't likely to get her anywhere. Well, it would get her *somewhere*—namely, right back to the Station where everyone could keep an eye on her.

No, the only way she was getting to Kiev alone was if she made damn sure her friends didn't know she was leaving. So, for now, she would just pretend that they were all going together, and make the choices she would make if they were.

She spun a fresh strand of portal magic and opened a doorway to her anchor outside Calista. Unsurprisingly, she saw Reyva on the other side. Nyx drew from the well—thankfully, it hadn't occurred to Bryn to put a limit on how *much* Nyx could use each visit—and widened the portal from the typical door-size she usually created to one easily ten times that in length and double it in height.

She did this, not so she could see Essteria and the soldiers with Reyva, but so *they* could see through to the room she stood in—and Bryn behind her.

"Hi," Nyx said to a thoroughly stunned Reyva. "I'll ask nicely once. Get off my property."

"And if we don't?" Reyva shifted from stunned to angry in a fraction of a second.

Reyva's tone spiked Nyx's irritation. She wanted to grab Reyva and drag her through whether the woman wanted to come or not. The desire traveled down the portal magic sifting through Nyx's hands. It lashed out, wrapped around Reyva, and yanked her from Calista's grounds to the inside of Bryn's throne room.

Well, shit. Now that she had expanded the horizons of her portal magic abilities, she was really going to have to be careful what she wished for. Thankfully, Reyva was unharmed, all limbs and clothing portaled with her. Save for looking completely stunned, the ward-breaker was no worse for wear for her unexpected portal trip.

Nyx tried to look like she'd meant to do what she had. "Anyone else want an involuntary trip?" she asked the remaining people outside Calista. "Or would you rather walk through the portal nice and easy of your own volition?"

Essteria's hard, reptilian gaze looked over Nyx's shoulder to Bryn. Nyx also looked at Bryn, arching her eyebrows. The Keeper made a "come here" motion with her fingers, and Essteria and the rest of her people came through the portal, eyeing it warily with each step.

"Wonderful doing business with you," Nyx told Bryn, ushering her own people through to Calista's grounds. "I'll be in touch."

She stepped across the portal and snapped it shut.

14

Nyx spent the evening in Seth's room in Calista, trying to look interested in hammering out possible courses of action she had no intention of implementing. She sat cross-legged on her bed and let Evra, Morgen, and Kaden carry the bulk of the discussion, interjecting enough questions and occasional comments to not draw suspicion. When it grew late enough, she made all the right noises about being exhausted and continuing this discussion in the morning.

Kaden and Morgen left, but Evra lingered. "I am sorry," she offered.

Nyx frowned. "For what?"

"Your mother."

Nyx had not forgotten Elena Fortuna so much as she had pointedly buried the woman in a deep corner of her mind to not think about again until it couldn't be helped.

"As difficult as my relationship with my own mother can be, she would never..." Evra trailed off.

"Sell you out to someone hoping they would remove you as a problem in her life?" Nyx gave a dry, humorless laugh. "Yeah, I'm fortunate that way."

"Do you want to talk about it?"

Maybe she *should* want to, but she shook her head. She'd

stopped wanting to understand her mother after talking to her in the Station's cafe. With her memories restored, a lifetime's history of Elena Fortuna once more in her mind, she'd realized that she *already* understood her mother. And she wished she didn't.

Because no amount of understanding who a person was made up for how they treated you. And no amount of *talking* now would change what had been or what was. It could only bring the pain of it to the forefront, and Nyx had no interest in harming herself in that manner, in continuing to dwell on unpleasantness, as if giving her mental energy to it would somehow force meaning from it.

Which was hilarious considering she had no problem causing just such harm to herself by dwelling on another person. Oh, she *tried* to think of Seth as little as possible, because each thought was another small cut added to the thousands of others that refused to close. Sometimes she even succeeded. Sometimes, she could go entire days blocking out the memory of him. Other times, all she did was remember.

Evra stood. She was studying Nyx with an inscrutable expression. "I could stay," she offered, "if you do not want to be alone." The subtext clear in the words was that Evra didn't think Nyx *should* be alone. Or, perhaps, that Evra didn't trust what Nyx would do if left alone.

But then, Evra had always been sharp.

"I'm fine," Nyx lied. "Are you fine? Because I seem to remember you giving Serenity a speech about older sisters taking abuse."

"A few sentences is not a speech."

"Uh-huh. Look, all I'm saying is yesterday it was all 'my sister has said we're strangers' and 'I'll try ignoring her while being in her immediate vicinity' and today you're imparting the wisdom of sisterly sufferance to a five-year-old."

Nyx expected Evra to blow her off, but instead her face grew serious. "Serenity...reminded me of Tamrin, when she was that age. Tam very much wanted to be older than she was. I was her closest sibling and I was so much older than her—Mother always liked to say Tam was the result of a spectacular argument with our father followed by too much enthusiasm working it out—and Tam always wanted my approval.

"She wanted to go everywhere I went, do everything I did. In her eyes, I was infallible. And then I did fail. I failed *her.* She's never blamed me for what happened, but I think, on top of whatever she experienced on Arkadia, it shook her foundations to discover that I was not perfect. And after all of that, despite everything, she still wanted to be wherever I was, and I sent her away."

This was the first time Nyx had ever heard the Amazon sound uncertain about anything. "Evra...you did what was best for her."

Evra drummed her fingers on her thigh. "Did I? At the time, I thought so. I thought it was her only chance at a normal future. Seeing her now, I do not believe that normal future was ever a possibility for her, after Arkadia. And someone has recently explained to me that I should not expect people to simply 'be normal' after they have experienced certain things."

"I didn't mean—"

Evra waved her off. "I know. But...the advice is still sound. When Tam returned from Arkadia, I treated her like a stubborn child who couldn't be trusted to make her own decisions. I thought I was doing what she needed when perhaps all she needed was for me to be there. And I was not. Now I have to find out if I can rectify that."

"She's still mad," Nyx pointed out.

"Why do you say that as if it is a positive thing?"

"She wouldn't be mad if she didn't still want you around. She didn't hide out at your ex-girlfriend's and really expect that you wouldn't eventually learn she was there. Trust me—she wants to work it out with you."

"I hope that you are right."

Nyx started to say "See you in the morning," but was afraid the lie would show itself on her face. Instead, she said, "You should get some rest."

"As should you." Evra gave her an appraising once-over, and then said, "Hug?"

Nyx stared. She stared long enough that Evra demanded, "What?"

"Hug?" Nyx repeated.

"You say it all the time."

"Yes, exactly. It's my line. You borrowing it is odd *and* you hugged me yesterday." Nyx pressed the backs of her fingertips to Evra's forehead. "You don't *feel* like you're coming down with something. Don't tell me you've been in therapy while I've been gone and now you're in touch with your emotions."

Evra batted Nyx's hand away, scowling. "Do you want the damn hug or not?"

"Of course I do." Because this conversation with Evra had erased any lingering doubts Nyx had had about going to Kiev's alone. She could not put her friends at risk for her personal vendetta. She couldn't lose them. She couldn't be the reason Tamrin lost Evra.

She was glad that Evra was in a hugging mood, because she didn't know when she would get one from her again. Even if Nyx survived her trip to Kiev's, this would probably be the last time in a very long while that Evra would be feeling emotionally generous. Because if you didn't see your best friend for six months and they tracked you down across multiple planets, pissed off at you for ignoring them, and then you chose to go off without them again? Well, what were the chances said best friend was forgiving you for that?

So, yeah, she took the damn hug. Though she kind of regretted it when an acute stab of pain went through her right shoulder blade. "I don't mean to be critical, but your technique needs work," she grumbled. Unless she was mistaken, that was Evra's thumb digging into her. "You do know you're not trying to stab the other person with your fingers, right? Also, do you work out specifically for finger strength or something?"

Evra's thumb quit digging into her. "If you are going to complain, the next time you want a hug I am going to say *no*." Evra released Nyx and stepped back. "I'll see you in the morning."

After she left, Nyx stared at the closed door. She didn't feel conflicted, exactly—for once, she was relatively certain she was making the right choice—but she felt…sad. She hadn't realized how much she'd missed Evra and Morgen until they'd shown up. She was suddenly, intensely glad she'd seen them again. Spoken to them. And she was just as suddenly aware that if this went poorly, she wouldn't have that same chance with Griff and Jevryn.

Briefly, she considered writing her fathers a letter. But what would she say? And would it help them, even if she knew *what* to say? Seth's words, left in his birthday maze for her, hadn't helped her, they'd broken her. Because she'd been reminded so viscerally of exactly what she didn't have anymore. Of exactly what she never would have again.

Maybe death, when it came, was best if it was sudden and left no remnant of a person behind. Or maybe she just didn't know what to say.

You're not going to die, she reminded herself. *Probably.* She should feel more fear at the possibility of it, but fear required an energy she didn't currently possess. *Do what you came here for. Worry about everything else after.*

She stalked to the bed, where Lethe-Alihana, secure in the molded scabbard of Constance, rested on the mattress. She'd avoided communication with them since she'd threatened Bryn earlier, and she wasn't looking forward to hearing their thoughts on everything that had happened in the times she hadn't been connected to them.

Nyx took a fortifying breath and grasped the hilt.

Ah, so you finally deign to—

Do you know how Kiev's residence is laid out? Nyx asked, interrupting them.

Let us see if you have actually *found him*, they said, and she didn't know if she could feel them moving through her thoughts, or if she was imagining the sensation. She wasn't sure how much of her mental activity they were able to access. They didn't, thank the stars, seem to be capable of riffling through her memories at will, but rather seemed to pick up on whatever thoughts, no matter how stray or insignificant, crossed her mind.

She tested the theory and, rather than telling them everything that had happened, she focused on the moment she'd traced Kiev through the portal map.

They made a contemplative noise in her mind. *This is... interesting.*

Interesting like we're fucked, or interesting like we can work with this?

The latter. Mostly.

What the hell does mostly *mean?*

It means Jevryn has been there, but not in three centuries or so, as I believe that was the last time Kiev sufficiently irritated him into invading his domain.

So your information on it is three-hundred years out of date? She'd more or less counted on Lethe-Alihana being able to tell her everything she needed to know. If they couldn't…

Three centuries is like three years when you have lived as long as the A-Morridahn brothers. Do you completely rearrange your home every three years? Most people do not. They establish things the way they like them and, if terribly inspired at some point, might change the color scheme.

Nyx supposed that Lethe-Alihana, having hosted several centuries of humanity on their planet before being reduced to their current state, would know this better than she would.

Kiev is rarely inspired. He likes things functional and, so long as they are, doesn't overly concern himself with them. Allow me to show you how it was the last time I was there.

Images appeared in her mind's eye, as if she was remembering something she'd seen before, except she'd never seen *this*. Because it wasn't her memory, but Lethe-Alihana's. Or, rather, it would be Jevryn's memory, shared with Lethe-Alihana.

It started in that split-second between portal departure and arrival, the moment when she appeared in a small square room, the walls a sharp white. Distaste rippled through her. White was such an abhorrent color, all harshness, stark and unyielding. But then, Kiev had always preferred the sterility of it to the warmth of anything with true color. Even as a child, he'd gravitated to emptiness.

Nyx jolted and the scene froze. She wasn't simply seeing her father's memories, looking back in time through his eyes, she was feeling what he'd *felt* at the time, reliving his thoughts.

You do not approve, Lethe-Alihana said.

Can you turn the thought replay off? I shouldn't be feeling what he's feeling, he wouldn't want that. She doubted anyone would, but he would like it less than most. If there was one thing she'd come to know about Jevryn A-Morridahn, it was that he was a deeply private person.

I cannot. By virtue of my nature, I am capable of perfect recall, but I cannot filter the sight from the feelings.

Nyx's fingers flexed on the sword's hilt. *Can't you just tell me what to expect?*

I could try. But you will not fully understand. If you wish to have some chance of success in this endeavor, you should take what I can show you. Your father's thoughts are not so personal in this sequence that it should cause either of you undue discomfort for your knowing them. There is nothing of you in them, after all. You were not even born yet, nor was your mother, nor any of your line back multiple generations. The Jevryn A-Morridahn whose memories you now walk might as well be a stranger to you.

She almost snapped back that the Jevryn A-Morridahn who existed *now* might as well be a stranger to her, but then it occurred to her that that wasn't true anymore. She didn't know him well, but he wasn't a stranger. And that was exactly why she didn't want to be prying into his personal thoughts. Did she want to know her father better? Yes. Did she want it to be because she'd stolen into his memories rather than because he'd offered the information? No.

But...Lethe-Alihana was right. Nothing she saw or felt in this memory would be related to her, specifically. It made it feel less intrusive.

Fine. Show me.

The still shot in her mind lurched back into motion and Jevryn stepped out of the small white room that was the only place one could portal into Kiev A-Morridahn's residence. Once, even this would not have been accessible to him. As the half of Lethe-Alihana's soul that Kiev possessed was the half which had retained the planet's ability for creating portal magic, Kiev's home retained the same dominance as any of the Stations.

But Kiev had erred, when he had carved a splinter free to create A-Lethe. He had already lost most of Lethe-Alihana's regard the day he had bound their soul to him. He had lost the rest on the day of A-Lethe's creation, and slicing the shard from the soul had damaged the soul's bond to him in the process. That damage had created this pocket of space where the soul's dominance held no sway.

Once Kiev had become aware of the weak point—after Jevryn had exploited it—he had chosen to make it an official entrance, so he could decorate what lay beyond it in a way that his only regular visitor would find most distasteful. Because of this, Jevryn was grateful that he did not have occasion to visit often.

Even Kiev himself rarely did so. Unlike Jevryn, Kiev enjoyed playing at godhood, and so he spent his time flitting between planets, propping up one government or another while quietly ensuring the failures of others. He did not typically come to this private residence.

No, Kiev only ever came here for one of two reasons—either he wished to add something to the macabre collection of trophies that lined either side of the hallway that stretched before Jevryn, or he had met with a mishap that had injured him greatly, and he had retreated here to recover.

In these latter instances, Jevryn made it a point to visit. To pass through the labyrinth of traps and wards Kiev had layered this place in to make himself feel safe, so that Jevryn could remind him that only a bond kept him alive. Remind him that no matter how many layers of magic he shrouded his home in, Jevryn had always been more adept than him in these matters. If Jevryn could not kill Kiev then he would remind him, as often as possible, that Kiev had always been—and would always be—the lesser of the two of them.

Jevryn passed through the entrance hall in all its macabre grandeur, his gaze fixed firmly ahead. He already knew what lay encased in the walls to either side and had no desire to fixate on them. As for the crowning centerpiece displayed in the octagonal foyer at the end of the hall, well, there was no avoiding *that.*

Would that the figure on the pedestal there were a statue. That would be far less disturbing than the reality, and yet he could not stop himself from looking at the face that stared down at him, eyes locked forever in the brilliant amethyst of surprise, lips parted. Forever dead, and never gone.

As always, he considered breaking the spell that held the figure in place, considered allowing his magic to slip free and turn that figure to dust. But, as always, he did not. As disturbing as he found this display, he thought it was perhaps one of the only things Kiev had ever done that he might regret. The only thing that might make him doubt. So Jevryn left it, moving around the display to the door directly beyond it. Magic spilled down his arms, crackling between his fingertips, and he stepped into the first of Kiev's tests.

Nyx swayed as her vision cleared. She no longer stood in Kiev's home, but in Seth's old bedroom at Calista. Her body felt odd, torso and limbs too short. Even her hair was too short and not heavy enough, until she blinked away the feeling of having inhabited Jevryn's body, Jevryn's thoughts, Jevryn's mood.

Then she wished she could claw it back. Or at least latch on once more to the inurement Jevryn had felt, because the things she'd just seen made her stomach revolt. She'd known Kiev was twisted, but what kind of man had *that* as the welcoming display in his home? Who would want to pass it every time they returned there?

In her mind, Lethe-Alihana sighed. *Will your revulsion be an issue, Nyx Ilera?*

She vehemently wished they had a physical body capable of feeling pain that she could slap, because calling her *Nyx Ilera* after what she'd just seen was both cruel and intentional.

She swallowed the revulsion they had mentioned. *No.*

Excellent. Let us gather your friends and go, then. I prefer not to linger. I have waited far too long for this.

Nyx's hands clenched around the sword hilt. *I'm not taking them.*

That is beyond foolish. You have seen what you must navigate.

Jevryn did it by himself.

You are not your father.

Nyx shrugged. *I understood what he did. I can do it too. I'm not going to get my friends killed.*

A brief pause ensued, during which she could practically feel the wheels in Lethe-Alihana's mind turning. Finally, they said. *Very well. I understand your sentimental attachment to your friends' well-being.*

Thanks ever so much, she answered, the sarcastic bite in her words sharp enough to cut glass.

But will you not at least take Kaden? Unless I am much mistaken, you do not consider him a friend.

What is your obsession with Kaden? First they'd bemoaned her leaving him behind when she left Jevryn's, then they'd wanted her to let him carry them on Endalna. *Do you have a hard-on for him or something?*

I am the soul of a planet, they said acidly. *I do not have, nor have I ever had, sexual urges.*

That's nice for you, I guess. Why are you obsessed with him?

I am not obsessed. I find him useful. He is extremely competent. Have you any idea how rare competent individuals are? I've lived far more millennia than you would be comfortable counting, and I can assure you, my experience across that time is that few people are deserving of the label.

Nyx blinked. *So, what, you like having him around because he scratches your itch for competence porn?*

I believe I explicitly stated that I do not have—

—sexual urges, Nyx finished for them. *I got it. Hate to disappoint you, but no, I'm not taking him.* She'd already gotten her boyfriend killed. No sense in adding her ex-boyfriend to the list. Whether or not she counted him among her friends. And that…that was an entirely different can of worms she would not be opening for inspection.

In her mind, Lethe-Alihana sighed. *You are so very like your father. You both insist on taking responsibility for things outside of your control. It is the height of hubris to assume that everything happens or does not happen because of you.*

Anger flared in Nyx. *Kiev took Seth because I was a shiny toy he wanted to play with and I refused to let him. He warned me he would take something from me. If you want the height of hubris, it was me thinking I could get away from that encounter without him making good on the threat.*

You wished to help your friends, the Meerkin.

And look where that got me. I put everyone I loved in danger except Griff, and only because Griff physically couldn't be there.

You do not make the choices of others for them. Do you think you are the only one allowed to choose to risk themself? That it is fine for you to risk your life in service to others but they are not allowed to make the same choice for themselves? Your Seth was not one to divest himself of responsibility.

Nyx squeezed her eyes shut. *You don't understand. He would have done anything for me.* He'd never been able to deny her anything. If he knew she wanted something, if he knew she cared about it, she didn't even have to ask—he just did whatever it took to make sure she had it.

So no, she hadn't forced him to help with the Meerkin. She hadn't had to. He'd known she cared, and that was all it had taken for him to commit himself fully.

Just as you would have done anything for him. Lethe-Alihana's reply was oddly gentle. *That type of love, that level of trust, is rare. Do not think for a moment that I do not understand that. That I do not understand what you have lost. But had your positions been reversed, you would not have wanted Seth to blame himself for your death. You would tell him he was being foolish not to rely on his friends.*

Nyx let out a soft laugh. *Thanks for attempting to be my therapist, but I know what you're doing. You want me to take them because it ups my chance of success, and killing Kiev is all you care about. You don't care if they die. You don't care if I die. You just want* him *gone. Well, I want him gone too. But I care about them more than I care about revenge.*

And it was a relief—a vast tidal wave of it—to realize that was true. It gave her hope that if she survived this, there would still be something of herself worth dredging up and living with.

15

Nyx needed supplies, which Calista grudgingly provided once it was clear they wouldn't be talking Nyx out of her chosen course of action.

<Have you considered the consequences if you fail?> Calista asked.

Nyx stood next to the hexagonal floor that had once been Calista's connection to the ley lines, before that connection had been sundered. The path to Calista's Heart yawned open, allowing their voice to reach more easily into Nyx's mind.

<Your Hidings will not survive your death. If I cannot urge you to reconsider for your own sake, consider what will happen should you fail and the Harvester fall into Kiev's hands.>

"I could leave it with you." Except she knew she could not, even before Calista responded.

<Should your Hiding fail, even I cannot keep it safe forever. From ordinary people? Certainly. But it will become a beacon to those who know what to look for, and without Laiveran here, the combined might of the councilors can overcome my ability to keep them out.>

There was only one option, really. "I'll handle it."

A sigh rippled through her mind. <Do try not to die, Nyx Fortuna. I long for the deliverance you promised us all. Beyond that, I find I have grown fond of you.>

Nyx swallowed. "I'll do my best." It was true, even if her best would be given not because she didn't want to die, but because she didn't want to fail.

She returned to her room, where she scratched out a quick note and added an exception to the Harvester's Hiding. After a moment's deliberation, she then added two more. Just in case.

She slipped the Harvester off the chain around her neck, refastening it with Jevryn's ring still on it. She tucked it back beneath her shirt, sliding her hand up to brush briefly against the rock, held in the hollow of her throat by a length of soft cord, that was all that was left of the man she loved. Any doubts she had about what she was doing evaporated. She took the Harvester, the note, and the portal stone Jevryn had left her in Lehine's empty well, and went to one of the doors across the hall from her room.

Calista unlocked it for her, and Nyx slipped in as soundlessly as she could manage. She stopped just inside the doorway, taking time for her eyes to adjust to the dim light. Her breathing was shallow and yet it sounded too loud. But when she could finally make out more than dim outlines, the form lying in the room's bed was still asleep.

Nyx crept across the floor, stopping next to the bedside table. She hesitated, watching the steady rise and fall of Kaden's chest. She hadn't watched anyone sleep since Seth had... Just, since Seth. There was something hypnotic about how even a person's breath became when they slept, and something in that regularity always calmed Nyx.

Her fingers clenched around the Harvester. Maybe it wasn't fair, to dump this burden on Kaden. But then, it hadn't exactly been fair when he'd dumped it on her in the first place. Considering he'd brought it into her life—and what he'd done to ensure she would keep it—maybe it actually *was* fair. Karmically so.

Besides, it wasn't as if he would have to carry it for long. She stretched her hand forward, placing the note, the Harvester, and the portal stone on the nightstand. She was careful not to make a sound, setting down the items and then holding them a moment to make sure neither the Harvester nor the portal stone would roll off the table.

A line of ice seared against her back, Lethe-Alihana shocking her with sudden cold. Nyx jerked in surprise, the Harvester and the portal stone scraping slightly against the table.

Are you fucking serious, Lethe?

Kaden woke. His hand shot out, grabbing her wrist and jerking it back, sending everything she'd placed on the table clattering across the room. He moved before she could, sweeping her legs from beneath her.

Nyx's back hit the floor, Lethe-Alihana trapped awkwardly beneath her, digging into her flesh. She let out a sharp yelp as the impact knocked the breath from her lungs. Kaden was on her in a flash, pinning her down. His left hand clamped her right wrist. His right hand drove a dagger at her chest.

Panic was a pulse of death magic in Nyx's veins, pushing unnatural strength into her arms. Her free hand lashed up, and she was quick, but not quick enough. The tip of the dagger cut through her shirt, nicking her skin before she caught Kaden's wrist.

Calista flooded the room with light. In the sudden brilliance, Nyx saw all too clearly that Kaden's eyes held no recognition. He wasn't seeing *her*. It was worse than the time in the Station, when he'd thought she was a hallucination conjured by a Mindwitch. Then, he'd known who she was, even if he'd thought she wasn't real.

Now, it was as if he didn't see her at all, as if he wasn't even awake, his body reacting to a perceived threat on autopilot. She pushed his arm up, creating some breathing room between his dagger and her flesh. He tried to wrench his wrist from her grasp and almost succeeded, even with her death-strengthened grip.

"It's me," she gritted out. "Could you snap out of it?"

He gave no indication he'd heard her. The door burst open. She couldn't see who came in, from her position flat on her back, but there were only two people it *could* be.

"What the hell?" Evra demanded.

Kaden's head snapped up.

"Kaden?" Morgen asked softly.

By the way Kaden simply remained where he was, motionless, assessing, she could tell he was still trapped in whatever altered state he was in.

"It's all right," Morgen said, and this time his voice wasn't only his voice. It held a Siren's lilt, honeyed magic in the words. "No one here is a threat. You're fine, and you need to wake up."

Kaden blinked. It wasn't until he did so that she realized he hadn't been blinking prior to that moment. He looked down and the glassy emptiness was gone, replaced by recognition, and he stopped trying to force the dagger into her chest.

Relief flooded her, and she relaxed her grip on his wrist. Kaden didn't say anything. The only shift in him had been that initial moment of recognition. Beyond that, his expression was as blank and impenetrable as ever. He let her go and stood. His dagger disappeared to wherever he'd pulled it from, the movement so quick she missed it. The dagger was simply there one moment and gone the next. Then he stood there, waiting.

Something was deeply wrong with him. It was that same something she'd noticed when she'd forced him to stay at the Station all those months ago, only she'd missed that over the last few months it had been left to sink its claws in and hook them deeper.

He'd never been like this before. Difficult to read and taciturn? Yes. Awakened by the slightest of noises? Also yes. But he'd never been unclear on what was happening when he woke. He'd never attacked her. Even in the Station, after Arkadia, he hadn't been unaware, as if his actions were disconnected from his body. And if he had, back then he would have at least acknowledged the slip. He wouldn't have just stood off to the side like nothing had happened.

What had Kiev done to him? What had Kiev *made* him do, for this to be who he was now?

It's not your problem. Nyx sat up, looking away from him, to the door where Evra and Morgen stood, and her stomach tied up in knots. Evra held her sword in a defensive position, her hair free of its normal plait. The only thing she wore was Morgen's shirt and her underwear. Morgen's sword was also in his hand, though he'd let the point drop upon seeing that there wasn't an intruder in the Station. He was even less dressed than Evra, considering his shirt was on her body.

In addition to Nyx's stomach tying up, her heart chose that moment to constrict. If you took away the swords and the concerned expressions morphing into suspicion, they painted such a domestic picture. Such an intimate one. Go back six months and that could have been Nyx and Seth awakened in the middle of the night, rushing into a room to make sure their friends were all right, working as a unit, silent communication rippling between them.

Evra finally lowered the tip of her sword, her voice low thunder. "Someone explain what is going on, or I swear by the stars I will—" She cut off when the Harvester rolled across the floor, coming to a stop against her bare foot.

Nyx gritted her teeth—the Harvester hadn't suddenly decided to roll across a perfectly level floor all of its own accord. Calista had clearly decided that if Nyx was already caught out, they were going to make certain she was *thoroughly* caught.

Evra swiped the Harvester, her eyes flashing angrily even before a sudden breeze kicked up in the windowless room, blowing Nyx's note right to the Amazon. Evra snatched it from the air. She read, then wordlessly passed the paper to Morgen.

Nyx had written the briefest note that could convey what she needed to: *If I don't make it back, take the Harvester to Jevryn.*

When Morgen handed the note back to Evra, she crumpled it in her fist, then got straight to the point. "What. The. Fuck?"

Nyx didn't answer. She couldn't quite get herself to meet Evra's gaze. There was a reason she'd been sneaking out in the middle of the night. Namely that she knew Evra wouldn't take well to being left behind. Nyx was prepared for some yelling, some anger. She could handle that.

But Evra didn't get angry. When Nyx didn't answer her first question, the Amazon asked a simpler one: "Why?"

Nyx briefly pressed the heels of her palms into her eyes before saying, "Why do you think? I already got one person I loved killed."

Evra stalked across the room, crouched, and took Nyx's jaw in her hand so she couldn't look away. "I have already told you that you did no such thing. I cannot make you believe it. So let me make you believe something else instead. I am not going to be left behind. *We* are not going to be left behind. Where you go, we go, no matter the consequences. That's what family *does.* Have I made myself clear?"

Tears pricked at the backs of Nyx's eyes. She blinked them away and nodded. Or tried to. Evra still had Nyx's jaw in an iron grip.

"If I did not believe this was something worth doing, I would not go along with it, Nyx. Believe me when I say I would have knocked you out and dragged you back to the Station for Griff and

Jevryn to deal with, not dug a latent tracking spell into your back so I could follow you when you inevitably did *this.*"

Nyx blinked. No wonder that hug had been so painful. She'd been getting the magical equivalent of a microchip. She should probably be upset about that, but she couldn't bring herself to be mad. Not when she knew she'd have done the same thing if their positions were reversed.

She closed her eyes. "I don't want you to get hurt. Any of you."

Evra's grip gentled. "*We* don't want *you* to get hurt. So you will have to come to terms with the fact that we are all going in order to ensure our own ends. Now, since I do not trust you to remain on this planet without supervision, Morgen and I are going to get dressed, and then we will all plan our next moves. Together.

"While we are gone, the two of you"—she pointed between Kaden and Nyx—"will remain here." Her tone brooked no room for argument. "If either of you is upset over what just happened, or are otherwise holding onto any issues that will make it difficult for you to work together tomorrow, sort them out." She looked at Nyx. "You want us all to make it out alive? Ensure we can function as a team." She looked at Kaden. "As for you, I would advise speaking more than five words."

Evra ushered Morgen out of the room, shutting the door firmly behind them. Nyx and Kaden looked at each other. Neither said a word.

<h1 style="text-align:center">16</h1>

Six months ago, Nyx would not have been capable of holding a staring contest with Kaden Moor. That Nyx took awkward silences and felt the need to fill them. She *felt* things—usually anger or betrayal, but occasionally guilt, where Kaden was concerned—and she couldn't help but express them. Present Nyx's feelings were blunted and subdued, buried beneath a haze of numb despondence that was only ever traded out for anger. That buried part of her wondered what the hell had happened to him, and if he was likely to snap in the middle of this venture, given what she'd just experienced. But her ordinarily insatiable curiosity didn't have the will to express itself.

She didn't really think he would lose it. Not while he was awake. Neither did Morgen, or he would have said something instead of leaving Nyx and Kaden alone together. So to Nyx's mind, there was nothing to work out. She understood why Evra thought there was— given what they were going to walk into together, the four of them needed to be able to trust each other without reservation. At least when it came to keeping each other alive.

She could see why Evra thought Nyx and Kaden would be the weak point. They both spent most of their time pretending the other didn't exist, and when they did interact, it was usually Nyx being pissed and Kaden impersonating a statue. But that had never really mattered when things needed to be done. She had worked with him fine on Kyvren, despite it all. She could work with him now. Clearly, he felt the same way, since he also didn't feel the need to fill the silence.

Or so she thought, until he opened his mouth and said, "What the fuck were you thinking?"

Her numbness receded somewhat in the wake of anger. Why exactly did he think he got to judge her choices? "Congratulations," she told him. "You've spoken one more word than the five Evra said were required." She made for the door. "I'm glad we had this little chat."

He moved. He didn't *look* like he was hurrying, yet he managed to put himself between her and the door, forcing her to either stop or run into him. She stopped. "What?"

"You aren't stupid."

"Really? Wow, thanks." She stepped left to go around him, but he moved with her. She stopped again.

"You aren't stupid," he repeated. "But going there alone is one of the most asinine things you could do. I understand not wanting to bring Morgen and Evra to Kiev's attention, but I am already in it. You should have taken *me*."

Ice cold along her back was Lethe-Alihana wanting attention. She ignored them, not wanting to hear some version of *I told you so.* "Take *you*?" She laughed. "You almost drove a dagger through my chest a couple minutes ago."

His jaw tightened and his gaze dipped briefly to the slice in her shirt. There was an art to reading Kaden's facial features. They were always so minuscule that it would be impossible for a layperson to tell the difference between them. Between his jaw tightening in anger versus in shame. It was the latter cause, this time, the Kaden Moor equivalent of a flinch, and she knew she should feel terrible. Knew it more when he drew that dagger and placed the hilt into her left palm, then closed both her hands over the leather wrapping, the blade tip pointed at his chest.

"Go ahead," he said. "Make us even."

For a moment, she just held there, her hands on the dagger, his hands on both. She didn't want to hurt him. But she couldn't deny she had an urge to hurt *something*. His hands gentled around hers and she flicked her gaze up to his. She had the uncomfortable feeling he understood everything she felt in this moment, and she hated that. She tore her hands out of his and flung the dagger away. It hit the floor with a clatter, skidding out of reach.

Anger welled up in her, more potent than ever. "If you have a death wish, Kaden, that's your problem. But don't you dare fucking try to use *me* to deliver it."

His gaze measured her. "Most people would say you're the one with a death wish, going after Kiev."

"Then why the fuck do you want to come?"

He leaned toward her, his eyes flashing. "Because *I* want him dead."

Kiev's words replayed in her memory. *The things I've had him do have made worse men snap.* Cocooned in the exclusionary embrace of her own pain, she'd conveniently forgotten that he had suffered at Kiev's hands too. The look in Kaden's eyes said he would never forget.

The door opened and Evra stalked in, Morgen on her heels. "You two good?" the latter asked.

Nyx didn't know if *good* was the right word. But she had a reason, now, for Kaden's presence. One that made sense to her, that she could understand and even sympathize with. Her anger died. "Yeah. We're good."

Evra's gaze went to the dagger Nyx had flung across the room. The Amazon snorted. "Clearly."

"We're good," Nyx repeated, but this time, it wasn't Morgen or Evra she was saying it for. Kaden dipped his head in acknowledgment, the movement so minuscule she'd have missed it if she hadn't been looking for it.

"Very well," Evra conceded. "We can get to work, then. Since I do not know what we will be facing, I will need to visit several of the Market's vendors, to prepare for various possibilities. We will need to discuss gear and—" She broke off, scanning Nyx. "Were you truly going to take *nothing* but the sword?"

Nyx rolled her eyes. "I have a med bag packed."

"Emergency rations? Water? Extra weapons?"

"We're going to Kiev's house, not back to the wilds of Amentia Furor," Nyx said defensively. "We won't be there long enough to need snacks."

"You say that as if you *do* know how long to expect we'll be there."

Nyx sighed. "Jevryn's been there multiple times. Lethe-Alihana shared the most recent experience with me. Kiev has a testing ground between him and his visitors. It isn't fun, but it isn't going to take us three days to navigate."

"How long *will* it take?" Evra asked.

"Jevryn can get through it in about twelve minutes."

"How long do you expect it will take us?"

"Longer," Nyx admitted.

"Define—" Evra began, but Morgen gently cut her off.

"Perhaps, little Guardian, you could just tell us what we can expect? In enough detail to allay Evra's concerns?"

Evra huffed out a breath. Nyx let out another sigh and surrendered to her fate.

17

Nyx portaled them into the Shadow Keep's throne room early the next morning. She had talked Evra down from three duffel bags full of supplemental gear to one. Nyx still didn't see the point in bringing it—none of them could afford the loss of maneuverability to carry it through Kiev's testing ground, so it would have to be left outside the entrance—but it didn't really cost Nyx anything to bring it, so she did.

Only four people were in the Shadow Keep's throne room when they arrived, and as Nyx's Hidden magic cloaked her own party, the presence of Bryn's people made little difference. They were stationed around the well, obviously intended as guards, though why Bryn thought they would be effective, Nyx had no idea. Though the guards wouldn't prevent Nyx from accessing the well, the Keeper would still know Nyx had been here—Nyx's one lesson with her had revealed that the woman's ability to sense portal magic quantities was off the charts. She might not be very good at using it, but she could tell how *much* had been used down to a microgram. So, yeah, Bryn would know some of her magic was missing, but Nyx was putting herself on the buy-now-pay-later plan, so to speak.

To this end, she walked to the throne and dropped a rectangular piece of paper onto the seat. Calista had provided Nyx with scissors that cut with a fancy edge, which Nyx had used to cut a prettily bordered rectangle from heavy paper, and a fancy pen, which Nyx had used to write: *This ticket entitles Bryn Morrigan to one half-hour magic lesson with Nyx Fortuna, redeemable in person at Earth's Station.* She had a feeling when Bryn found it the ticket would burst into flames, and Nyx's only regret was that she wouldn't be around to see it happen.

Of course, she would be seeing a very pissed off Keeper of Shadows in person later, but that was Future Nyx's problem. If Future Nyx existed beyond the next few hours, anyway.

That is not the attitude to carry into battle, Lethe-Alihana grumbled. Nyx held their sword in her left hand, rather than leave them in their scabbard. They had been to Kiev's home as many times as Jevryn had, and she wanted any advantage they could give her. In light of this, Constance had shifted, forming a bracer on Nyx's arm, ready to offer protection or shift into a needed form at a moment's notice.

Nyx didn't bother answering Lethe-Alihana, even with a stray thought. The momentary levity she'd gained from her note to Bryn evaporated as she strode to the portal well, the weight of what she was about to do settling heavily onto her shoulders. She touched her fingertips to the stone nestled in the hollow of her throat.

I wish you were here. I wish you were with me. I wish none of this was necessary. But she'd learned, in her youth, that wishing was pointless. No amount of it ever achieved anything.

She returned to where Evra, Morgen, and Kaden waited by the portal well, sank into the abundance of magic, and pulled them from the Keep.

They arrived in the white square room she'd seen in Jevryn's memory. Calling it a room was charitable—it was smaller than an elevator, and with the four of them all together, the space was practically claustrophobic. Nyx was sandwiched between Evra and Morgen, with Kaden at her back, but they all just stood, waiting. For her.

She stepped out, sensing with the death side of her magic, even though Jevryn's memories told her she would find nothing here. There was a reason Kiev had chosen to turn this flawed space into an entranceway. If one of the councilors had the nerve to come here, or sent someone else, Kiev wanted his garishly displayed trophies to be the first thing they saw.

So Nyx walked forward. She tried not to look. She'd caught only glimpses, in the memory, because Jevryn had not looked. But one could not block out one's peripheral vision, and so she knew what to expect. The walls were clear and behind them, posed in their moments of death, were bodies.

She kept her head pointed resolutely forward. No one spoke as they followed her, but she felt their unease. The hall was wide enough that they fanned out beside her, as if trying to insulate her. They were almost out of the mouth of the hall when Kaden stopped. He shifted until he faced the body on the right, immortalized forever in their moment of passing.

Nyx did not look at them. She did not want to see the remnants of what had once been a person, and she knew that when Jevryn had last been here, that space had been empty. That was over three-hundred years ago, so this space could have been filled at any time since then. But she knew, by the way Kaden stared—by the way he'd gone rigid—that it had been filled much, much more recently.

She did not know if she still loved Kaden, in any sense. Given how little it turned out she'd known him in the beginning, she did not know if what she'd thought of as love then could truly be considered it now. But she did know she had cared, once, and that some part of her still did.

She never looked at the body behind the glass. Kaden's demons were his own, and she didn't want to know them. But she stepped in between the body and him, waiting until his eyes flicked dispassionately down to meet her own.

"What's done is done," she said. Wasn't that what everyone kept telling her? "But we can make sure it never happens again."

His lips parted, but she wasn't terribly surprised when no words followed. He gave her a curt nod, turned away, and they walked into the small foyer the hallway led into, where a final body waited. This one, Nyx did look at.

She could see the echoes of herself in the face, could trace her ancestry in the shape of the hands. Those hands were curved around the crossguard of the sword buried in the woman's stomach. Blood had seeped into the pure white of her robes, her face forever frozen, not in pain, but in surprise. There was something odd about her posture, as if, though her body had been displayed standing, she had been in repose at the time of her death.

The plaque beneath the pedestal read: *Ilera Hedaad A-Morridahn. Beloved mother.*

"Is that..." Morgen trailed off, as if he couldn't quite get himself to believe it.

"My grandmother."

"Did Kiev—"

"Yes." The fact that Ilera's body was here, the crowning achievement in Kiev's trophy room, was evidence enough, even if Nyx hadn't felt the truth of it in Jevryn's memories. Kiev had killed his own mother. She could tell, from bits and pieces Jevryn had mentioned in passing, that Ilera A-Morridahn had not been the gentlest of souls. But while his feelings for her were obviously complex, if they had ever tended toward the hatred that Nyx bore for her own mother, those feelings had tempered over time. And Nyx, despite what she'd threatened on Endalna, would never drive a sword through her own mother's gut.

"And he put her...here?" Morgen asked incredulously.

"She's family," Nyx said bitterly. "Family always gets a place of honor." She did not reach out and cut the threads of death magic that preserved her grandmother's body. But she did make Ilera A-Morridahn a silent promise: *If I survive this, I will give you the dignity that was denied you.* Her, and everyone else in this macabre museum. A statue was one thing. A literal corpse on display for centuries was another.

She stepped around the pedestal and immediately stopped again. "Fuck."

The door directly ahead, the one Jevryn had gone through in the memory she'd lived, no longer existed. Instead, a new door, one that hadn't been there before, was cut into the wall to Nyx's left.

In her hand, Lethe-Alihana vibrated with satisfaction. *He is afraid,* they whispered in her mind.

Of what?

You.

That's ridiculous.

Is it? Only the councilors—and you—can reach him in this place. Of them, only you and Jevryn, or those in your company, are likely to survive the trials within. And Jevryn cannot kill him. You can. You injured him on

Kyvren, and he ran to your mother to Hide his location from you, for fear of you doing precisely what you are doing now.

Morgen stepped up to her side. "Problem?"

"Give me a minute." *If it was so obvious, why didn't you expect that he would seal off the route we planned to take?*

Oh, I did. But I did not wish to risk you delaying our journey. And the memory was useful. You needed to understand how Kiev thinks.

The funny thing about rage was that sometimes it burned hot enough to have a tempering effect, and Nyx's did so now. It flared bright, hitting its zenith and bursting, the afterglow spreading through her veins like a cleansing fire. An eerie sort of calm settled over her.

Let me be clear with you. If any of my friends die here today because you misled me, I will bury you. I will take you to the outer reaches of space where nothing lives and I will Hide you there, and then I will convince Serenity to continue Hiding you after my death, and every generation of Hidden thereafter.

You will be the next Harvester, she continued, *forgotten and alone, drifting where no one will ever find you, in a vessel that cannot see the vast expanse of nothingness you exist in. Do I make myself clear?*

A soft wave of approval rippled through the sword. *Ah, there is that A-Morridahn spine. There is the scion of the most ruthless bloodline I ever gave life to.*

Nyx recoiled. If that was how Lethe-Alihana thought, it was a wonder they didn't consider Kiev their crowning achievement.

He had the potential, but he has no respect for life. If you wish to understand death, to truly master it, then you must also treasure life. Neither of the A-Morridahn brothers do, even though neither will kill indiscriminately. Kiev will not, because he views death as a resource, and he does not waste resources. Jevryn comes closer to an actual respect for life —he understands the value of it as a concept—and that is why he will not kill simply because it suits him. But he does not care, save for those rare individuals who find a way into his heart. And then, for them, he loves beyond all reason.

You are similar, but you are different. You do *care about life, as more than a resource or an abstract concept. You care about people. And yet, at the core of you, there is still* me. *My* legacy, *my* power, *my* drive to *vengeance. You may be the purest expression of me yet.*

The quiet of her rage boiled suddenly before returning to a

simmer. For someone who claimed they were not a god, Lethe-Alihana certainly sounded in that moment as if they thought themselves one. But perhaps they were only proving their connection to humanity on a deeper level than they intended, falling prey to the hubris all parents seemed to share, in one form or another—the belief that whatever they found to like in their children was a result of that child being *their* child, while any faults belonged wholly to the offspring.

Beam approval, if it makes you feel better, Nyx answered. *But I highly doubt you will enjoy my following through on the promise. Help me keep them alive, or you will regret it.*

A sigh rippled through her. *As you wish.*

Aloud, Nyx said, "Remember how we spent three hours yesterday going over, in excruciating detail, what I saw when Jevryn came through here?" Three heads nodded. "Well, none of that is accurate anymore. Stay behind me and don't touch anything."

She strode to the door on her left. There was no handle, nor were there any visible hinges, so presumably it opened inward. She pressed her fingertips to the lacquered wood. Death nipped at them. The magic wasn't the concentrated torrent that would be necessary to end a life, but if she weren't A-Morridahn-born, the sharp bite would have killed the skin that touched the wood, would have eaten through that skin to the tissues and vessels beneath.

Nyx drew her fingers in an ever-widening circle on the door, pulling the magic to her as if she were gathering up a cobweb. She rolled it into a golf-ball sized sphere, clenching it tight in her right fist, her left hand still gripping Lethe-Alihana's hilt, and nudged the door open with her foot. She expected an instant attack. When none came, it had the effect of ratcheting her tension higher, rather than relieving it.

The room beyond was lit, though dimly so, sickly yellow light filtering down from far above. She couldn't actually see the ceiling because a thick gray fog hung in the air, obscuring what lay above. Cautiously, Nyx stepped inside. After a moment, she motioned the others to follow, with a terse, "Don't touch the walls." They were painted with death magic, and while she could clear the areas she touched, she couldn't draw Kiev's magic to her without that touch. She was more than a little surprised the floor she stood upon wasn't coated in it as well.

Her friends crowded in behind and around her, just inside the door. The air was thick and wet and stifling, the humidity cloying. A single exit lurked on the wall directly opposite the door they'd entered through. The way to it was not straightforward. For one, the room was easily fifty feet in length, though narrow, spanning only twenty feet or so in width. But the length wasn't the problem. The problem was that, rather than having a floor, the room had a lake.

The stone surface they stood on, just inside the door, was like a very short dock that gave way almost immediately to crimson water. Other patches of stone broke the water's surface, dotted here and there, seemingly without rhyme or reason. Some were small and empty, little more than one-foot-square stepping stones, placed as if some giant had scooped a handful of them and hurled them into the lake like they were pebbles to be tossed. Others were as large as the dock Nyx stood on, four-by-six foot floating islands atop which perched…things.

Nyx supposed they were, in the general sense of the word, plants. No two were alike, but each shared basic plant anatomy— stems, branches, leaves, and the obvious roots. Obvious, because the islands the plants sat atop were shallow things, if the one nearest to her was any indication. It seemed no more than a floating mat an inch or two thick, into which the nearest plant had sunk its roots, the tendrils punching through the thin substrate to the water beneath. That water, though crimson-tinted and difficult to see through, was not entirely opaque, and while she couldn't make out much else, she could identify the trailing roots beneath. They moved, and whether it was by some unseen current or because the roots were capable of independent action, Nyx couldn't tell.

"Little Guardian?" Morgen asked.

"Hmm?"

"While I, too, am enjoying taking in the scenery, would now perhaps be a good time to…?" He mimed opening a portal to the opposite side of the room.

"Oh. Did I forget to mention? When Kiev's here, his half of Lethe-Alihana's soul grants the residence the dominance of a Station. I can only portal into the entrance because it created a fault in Lethe-Alihana's power when Kiev chipped a shard from the soul to make A-Lethe."

Everyone stared at her. "Yes," Evra said slowly, "you failed to mention that."

"I can walk everyone back to the entrance," Nyx offered. "My willingness to return you home unharmed still stands."

They stared at her again in answer. No one had a sense of humor these days.

"No portaling, then." Morgen said. "Moving on. Question: Is this room giving anyone else the creeps?"

"Yes," Evra answered.

Kaden grunted.

"Anyone recognize the plants?" Nyx asked.

Slowly, as if the admission pained him greatly, Morgen said, "No. But the variety of flora on any single planet is astounding. Most inhabitants of a region can't recognize all of the species in their own area, much less their whole planet, much less the entire universe."

Which Nyx figured was Morgen's way of saying that, whether it was unreasonable to expect someone to recognize the plants or not, he was irritated that he didn't.

"It is a garden," Evra said. "*His* garden."

The assertion seemed at once both obvious—what was a collection of plants in a large indoor room if *not* a garden?—and wrong. The word *garden* evoked feelings of serenity and calm. Of hours spent tending and providing care, of nurturing. This room evoked the opposite of calm, and Kiev A-Morridahn was not a man who nurtured. Yet…the plants were here, and if he did not tend them with at least some regularity, they would have died.

So, yes, she supposed this *was* a garden. But what kind of garden did someone like Kiev bother to keep alive? One with a purpose, obviously, or it would not be located *here*, would not be part of the tests intruders had to face if they wished to find him.

Kaden stepped to the edge of the platform, eyeing the only stepping stone within jumping distance. Nyx threw her arm across his chest, like they were driving in a car and he wasn't wearing a seatbelt, and she was trying to keep him from going into the windshield from a hard brake.

"We agreed I would go first. Every room, every time." There was no denying that Evra, Kaden, and Morgen were deadlier than Nyx in a one-on-one fight—at least if one ignored her recently awakened death magic—but there was also no denying that Nyx was better equipped to handle the traps and curve balls Kiev might have left for them.

Kaden turned his head to look at her. "We agreed to that because you knew where you were going. Now you don't."

She shook her head. "We agreed because, in this one particular environment, I'm less breakable than the rest of you." Without waiting for the argument that was sure to follow, she jumped to the nearest stepping stone three feet away. She half-expected it to sink beneath her sudden weight, but it remained stable. The sharp bite of death magic nipped at her where the soles of her boots touched.

Once again, the thin layer was nowhere near the amount needed to kill. This first stone, in fact, would do nothing more than wear at the soles of her boots. Lifting first one foot, then the other, Nyx placed a protective coating of her own death magic on the bottoms of the boots, the tread already worn down from Kiev's magic. Though she suspected she would wish she had her mercury boots by the end of this, for now she was glad they were back in Jevryn's home. Maybe the wider universe had cobblers who specialized in magical footwear, but if not, she didn't want the boots ruined.

Resting the flat of Lethe-Alihana against her shoulder, she crouched, placed her free hand on the stone, and made the same circles she had on the door, lifting each foot one at a time to gather the coating of death magic. She added it to the ball in her hand. It was Kiev's magic, so she couldn't do much with it, but one never knew when a ball of ready death magic might be useful for hurling at something.

She considered that magic—what she'd scraped off the stepping stone, what she'd scraped off the door—and then considered the complete lack of death magic on the landing area just inside the room. That lack, she was certain, had been intentional, designed to lull the entrant into a false sense of safety, into thinking that standing on the floor was safe, and that jumping to the first stepping stone would likewise be safe. And while those highly sensitive to magic, like Morgen, might recognize the minuscule coating of magic on this stone and decide to turn back before it was too late, most wouldn't. They'd lose a little of their footwear to decay without realizing it and jump on to the next stone, which she was certain would have another, slightly thicker coating of magic, and so on and so forth, until they were too deep into the room to avoid Kiev's trap snapping closed around them.

That it *was* a trap, Nyx had no doubt. This place might be where Kiev came to feel safe and lick his wounds in private, but while another person might lead with overwhelming force against an intruder in such a place, Kiev liked to play. She didn't even need Jevryn's memories of this place to tell her that. Kiev's careful stalking of her via A-Lethe for months, and his behavior on Kyvren, proved it well enough.

Kiev wouldn't *want* an intruder to turn back at this stage and go home, even if that end result would be the safest thing for him. No, he would want an intruder to feel threatened enough to believe they'd already recognized the danger they were in, but confident enough to believe they could overcome it.

It would be in his nature, Lethe-Alihana agreed. Nyx had almost forgotten about them, the sword feeling more like an extension of her hand than another being. But it wasn't an extension of her hand, and holding it while she jumped greater distances across the room meant throwing off her balance and having one less hand available should she need it.

Any sage words or insights before I give you back to Constance? Nyx asked.

I believe falling in the water would be inadvisable.

Really? And here I went to the trouble of jumping to this stepping stone because I thought swimming across the room was a perfectly viable, expedient option.

She flipped the sword over her shoulder and Constance spilled from her arm, reforming into a scabbard around the blade. Nyx let go of the hilt, cutting off Lethe-Alihana's acerbic response about how she was not nearly as amusing as she thought she was. She'd barely let go when ice chilled her back. Cursing, she grasped the hilt again.

Yes?

Check in with me at each new stone. I cannot advise you if I cannot see.

She grumbled her assent and released the hilt. Before rising, she peered into the murky water, leaning forward to glimpse beneath the stone she was on. She could just make out the slender stem of a support jutting down from the center of the stone, as if what she stood on was as sunken pillar that had been sheared off from whatever it was originally meant to support.

Her gaze traveled wider, farther, but while she could make out the shape of nearby moving things beneath the surface—like the roots of the plant on the nearest island—she could not see more than a foot or so deep. No ripples broke the stagnant calm. She wasn't optimistic enough to hope nothing lived in the water—just pessimistic enough to suspect anything swimming through it would stay deep enough to remain unseen until someone had the misfortune to fall into the lake.

"Nyx?" Evra asked. Her voice was unusually tense, and Nyx realized she'd been crouching there, staring into the crimson depths, for some time.

She rose. "He painted the step in death magic. I've cleared it." She explained her theory that Kiev *wanted* people to continue past this point, the better to trap them, which prompted various versions of *obviously* in response. Nyx studied the room, and the zig-zagging path she would have to take to reach the door on the other side.

"I don't suppose you guys would wait to follow until I make it all the way across?" Three identical hard stares answered that question. She sighed. "Keep to the steps I've been on, then."

She jumped to the next stepping stone, then the next and the next, peeling off coatings of death magic as she went, the available steps leading her to the right in a diagonal line from the room's entry door. Directly behind her was Evra, followed by Morgen, then Kaden. Evra's precious duffel bag of supplemental items remained on the entryway landing, for obvious reasons. Nyx really didn't know why Evra had bothered to bring it.

They pressed forward in silence. The cloying warmth and humidity of the room made Nyx sweat profusely, and her clothes were soon soaked through. She wondered how the wicking spells on Evra's clothing were holding up under these conditions, but after one glimpse at the Amazon, decided not to ask. Evra's face could have been in the dictionary next to the word *tense*, and the atmosphere in the room didn't leave much space for levity.

Nyx kept leaping across stones and clearing death magic, growing more tense herself the more nothing happened. Yes, the amount of magic on the stones kept increasing—if she or her boots had been normal, the latter would have been eaten through, and she doubted her feet would be in any condition to hold her body weight —but so far that was the only obviously dangerous thing in the room. She kept glancing behind her, reassuring herself that the others were still there, afraid that one time she would look back to find they'd all disappeared, silently taken while her back was turned.

She should have been more focused on herself. Though even if she had been, it wouldn't have mattered. Three-quarters of the way across the room she jumped onto the next stepping stone—and fell into the water as if the stone wasn't even there. Because it *wasn't* there. It was all illusion, no substance, and the force of her leap meant she dropped like a rock, the water closing over her head.

She scissor-kicked her legs, driving up, face breaking the water. The others were yelling at her. She barely had time to register the fact, to take a single large gulp of air, before the water around her erupted. Tentacle-like tendrils shot up, clamped her, and dragged her under.

18

Nyx hated opening her eyes underwater, but panic had them flying wide now, desperate to see through the murky red liquid. The light above the surface receded at a rapid pace as the tendrils dragged her farther and farther from it. She thrashed, but the tendrils—or were they roots?—had wrapped around her torso, pinning her arms to her sides. Kicking did nothing, because there was nothing to kick.

Terror blossomed in her chest, screaming at her to breathe, but if she breathed, she would drown. The wellspring of death within her geysered, flooding her with power and strength. She wrenched her left arm free and clamped her fist around a section of vines. Death poured from her fingertips. The roots convulsed. Not in pain, but in something that felt disgustingly like ecstasy. They drank her magic down as if they needed it to survive, and when she cut the flow of it, they writhed in protest.

What the fuck?

Constance morphed from the scabbard form, the metal strap that held Lethe-Alihana to her sprouting a thin, three-inch wide blade that severed the vines around Nyx's chest. Somewhere deep beneath her, a pained screech tore through the water like metal scraping across a chalkboard.

She grasped the hilt of Lethe-Alihana. Constance let the sword go, flowing down Nyx's other arm. She dropped the ball she'd gathered of Kiev's death magic and grabbed Constance as it reformed in her hand as a twelve-inch knife. Nyx pressed the dull side to her body and slid the blade between her and the remaining roots that clutched at her waist and hips.

Another enraged screech rent the water. Nyx kicked up. The weight of water in her boots dragged at her, but she doubted the deadly plant beneath would wait patiently for her to unbuckle her boots and slide them off. She drove herself mercilessly upward, broke the surface and sucked in a glorious lungful of air.

Lethe-Alihana's cross voice spilled into her mind. *I told you not to fall in—*

Roots grabbed her ankles and yanked her down. The speed and force of it nearly knocked the new breath from her lungs. Her arms took the path of least resistance, the current of the water driving them up above her head, and she nearly lost hold of Constance and Lethe-Alihana.

Death magic punched through her again, demanding release. It wanted to kill, because killing would make her safe. Except it *couldn't* kill this. Kiev A-Morridahn had a garden of plants that ate death. Because of course he fucking did.

The roots swarmed up her body, over her thighs and hips, as if they felt the swell of that magic inside her and were desperate to find it. They reached her stomach, the tips of two tendrils probing at her skin, searching. They stabbed into her, twin punctures in her flesh, taking root inside her body. They convulsed in a motion like a throat swallowing, and she felt the flow of death magic in her body being carried into them.

Agony lanced through her, the roots burrowing deeper, taking more, draining her. She wrestled against their pull, willing her magic to remain *hers*, to give her strength she desperately needed. She fought against the drag of the water, got her arms down and slashed with Constance, severing the tendrils that had taken root. Others swarmed up, trying to take their place, and she hacked those back too. All the while her body screamed for air, and if she didn't get it soon she was going to open her mouth and breathe the lake into her lungs.

She contorted herself in half, the two punctures in her stomach screaming, and swung her sword in an arc. Lethe-Alihana super-heated the blade, the water boiling and easing the resistance of the water. She didn't try to cut the roots *on* her body, but cut lower, through their base in the water beneath her feet, severing their connection to the main body of the thing that ensnared her.

As she did, her body tilted and she saw down, to just what that thing was. A gaping maw yawned open before her, its lips feathered like those of a Venus flytrap's. Spiraling out from the mouth were four throats, leading to four stomachs. One was empty. Two contained things in stages of digestion too advanced for Nyx to identify, for which she was grateful.

From the fourth, a horrified face stared up at her through the clear membrane of the stomach. The face had belonged to a Dresidian in life, their eyes wide, tentacles frozen around their face. Revulsion hit Nyx hard and swift, and she nearly opened her mouth and sucked the crimson water into her lungs. Air. She needed *air*.

But already more roots snaked toward her with lightning quickness. If she raced them for the surface, she would lose. Out of the corner of her eye, she saw the floating ball of Kiev's death magic. Constance molded into a bracer, freeing her to reach out and grab that ball. She fed more of her own magic into it, mixing the two, and just before the roots reached her she hurled the ball down, straight into the plant's mouth.

Like a Venus flytrap sensing a meal, the mouth snapped closed, lips meeting. The long hair-like teeth, protruding from the edges of the lips like eyelashes, twined together. The plant shuddered in ecstasy, the tendrils of its roots stilling.

Nyx kicked, driving herself upward against Lethe-Alihana's orders to stay and deal a killing blow. Killing the plant wouldn't matter if she drowned. She broke the surface once more, gulping down greedy lungfuls of air. Then she took a final one and dove back into the depths. The euphoria the hit of death magic had induced in the plant was wearing off by the time Nyx reached its mouth again, the monstrous maw opening, the waving tendrils around it shooting up to search for her.

She hurled another golf-ball sized bit of death magic into the mouth, and it closed and stilled again. She plunged the sword down —not at the mouth, but at the places where that mouth connected to the stomachs. Lethe-Alihana warmed again, boiling the water, cauterizing the wounds they made as Nyx dragged the sword in an arc around the mouth, severing it from the rest of its body.

The roots went inert. It wasn't that they died when the mouth was severed—she suspected that, just as a flower could live in a vase for several days without its roots, so too would the roots continue to live without a connection to the mouth—but while she didn't think the plant possessed a brain or even primitive consciousness, it obviously had a central control, and Nyx had just severed it. In the wake of that lost connection the roots, lacking direction, drifted aimlessly.

Nyx didn't stay to witness anything further. She refastened Lethe-Alihana to her back, freeing her arms to swim. Her abdomen protested with each kick of her legs and stroke of her arms, and she tried very hard not to think about *why*. She could think about *why* later. When she was back on dry land.

Her face broke the surface. She sucked in a deep lungful of air— and realized the room had come alive in her absence. The floating islands teemed with awakened life, the plants whipped into a frenzy by her fall into the water.

Evra stood on the stepping stone Nyx had leapt off before her fall, hacking furiously at the vines that reached for her from the neighboring island. But swords weren't designed for hacking, and a one-foot-square stone didn't give the Amazon a lot of space to maneuver. For every vine she cut off, another took its place.

Nyx swam for her. A bulbous protrusion on one of the vines burst. Evra had ducked the second before it exploded, and the spray of green liquid that shot out went over her head, hitting the water with a hiss and an effusion of smoke. The vines slithered away from Evra, dropped below the surface, grabbed the pillar supporting the stone Evra stood on, and pulled.

The floating island the plant rested on shot forward, its nearest bank slamming into the stone's edge. Evra struck with speed and precision, her sword a blur as she cut through the vines that had snared the pillar beneath her. The remaining ones recoiled, waving angrily. The plant drew back, the vines splaying out around its main body like a peacock's fan, safely out of reach of Evra's sword.

Dozens of bulbous protrusions grew on the vines, fattening like fruit. Evra shifted her grip on her sword and began to spin it in a circle, the flat of the blade parallel to her body. She started slowly, hands close together out in front of her, passing the hilt seamlessly from one hand to the next, as if she were spinning a bo staff, only this was more difficult because a bo staff was evenly weighted for spinning while a sword was not.

Evra spun faster and faster, until the metal was a blur in front of her. When she hit peak speed, her hands swapping places so rapidly on the hilt that it seemed impossible not to fumble it, magic abruptly surged out of her and snapped onto the blade. The lesions on the plant's vines burst. A barrage of acid shot out—and splashed harmlessly against Evra's spinning shield of magic and steel.

For a moment, Nyx only stared. She hadn't thought Evra possessed any innate magic, though she hadn't realized that until this moment. In truth, the Amazon's possession or lack of magic was something Nyx had never given much thought to. Evra was death with a sword, and magic wasn't something she'd ever seemed to *need.* But it was very obviously there as Evra shifted the momentum of the blade. She transferred the spin to the side and, on the backswing—when the tip of the blade was pointed directly behind her—reclaimed a two-handed grip and drove the blade's momentum forward. It was as if the sword pulled the Amazon forward, as if she flew at the heart of the plant's mass, her feet inches above the ground.

Nyx knew Evra wasn't *actually* flying. She'd launched herself off the pillar, toward the plant, driving with her legs, but there was no denying the flash of magic along the blade had something to do with the speed and fluidity with which Evra moved. The sword's tip pierced the center of the plant, drove deeper, deeper, until the crossguard was flush with the vegetative matter. Evra twisted, then jerked the blade straight up, splitting the main body of the plant in half. Viscous red fluid sprayed out, coating Evra from her face down to her toes. It quickly sloughed off her clothes, and the completely irrelevant thought Nyx's brain conjured at that moment was: *Well, I guess the wicking spells are holding up just fine.*

Nyx swam for the island as Evra continued to hack pieces off the plant, ensuring its demise.

"Can a girl get a hand?" Nyx asked.

Evra stopped hacking and spun, relief flashing across her face. "Thank the stars." She transferred her blade to her left hand and dashed to the bank of the island, gripping Nyx's hand and hauling her up. Nyx made a small, hurt noise as her stomach—and the two hacked-off roots still embedded in it—scraped the side of the bank.

Evra's gaze dropped, her eyes widening. Before Nyx could say anything, a sound to Evra's left drew both their attention. Morgen was caught in a cocoon of interwoven leaves, each one as big as Nyx's head. His mouth was covered by one of the waxy, four-lobed leaves, as if it had been pasted and glued to his face. The plant must have been trying to take away his voice, but as it hadn't covered his nose, he could still hum. A haunting melody built in his throat, and the cocoon stilled. Hesitantly, slowly, the leaves began to gently unwind from his body.

They did so too slowly for Evra's liking. The Amazon was already moving. She took a running start and leapt from the island she and Nyx stood on, across two stepping stones and to the island where Morgen had been ensnared. She cut through leaves and stems like a machine, spinning and hacking until Morgen jerked his arms free.

Where Nyx would have, in his position, taken the returned use of her hands to peel the leaves from her body, Morgen's hands went to the covering on his mouth, ripping away the one there. The leaf took skin with it, bright red blood blossoming in patches around his lips.

He didn't seem to notice. His eyes were alight with fire and fury, and yet when he opened his mouth, the song that poured forth was the most beautiful thing Nyx had ever heard. His strong voice saturated the room, and even though the song wasn't tuned to her, wasn't meant to affect her, she felt its power nonetheless, and for a moment she was struck immobile, in awe of the perfection of Morgen's voice as he poured a Siren's power into the wordless notes he sang.

It took less than five seconds for everything to stop. Every plant —every root and vine and stem in the room—stilled. Caught in the hypnotic lull of Morgen's song, the flora that had been intent on killing them all mere moments before was sung into sleep. When Morgen finished, the fury in his eyes wasn't gone, but it had dimmed. He looked at Evra and grinned.

The Amazon glowered at him in return. "I am relieved that one of us is having fun," she bit out.

He opened his mouth but Nyx, a new fear striking her as she realized something was missing from the room, spoke first. "Where's Kaden?"

The three of them scanned the room. The plants were still, lulled into passivity by Morgen's voice, but Kaden was nowhere to be seen. The water lay placid once more, the room quiet.

Nyx's heartbeat thudded in her chest, pounded harshly in her ears, a sick feeling in the pit of her stomach. This couldn't be happening. She couldn't lose someone. Not again.

She spun in a circle, eyes narrowed, straining to see a scrap of black fabric or a shock of golden hair, but it was all too obvious, in the silent stillness of the room, that Kaden wasn't there. She dropped to her knees, hands on the edge of the island, and peered into the water. As if she could see more than a few feet down. As if, even if she could, he would by some miracle be in this exact portion of the lake.

The darkness that lived deep within Nyx pulsed again, unwinding, spiraling out with nowhere to go but the cage of her body. Because what lived inside her couldn't *fix* anything. What was the point of being a bearer of death, when death couldn't save? She'd once thought Jevryn so powerful for that ability, so unbreakable, and maybe he was. For himself. Maybe that was the true meaning of the A-Morridahn motto, *never broken*—that they themselves were never broken, but everything around them was.

Her heart pulsed hard against her chest, the strength of her magic pulsing with it. The urge to scream rose up in her again, wanting to pour out a torrent of rage, but what fucking *good* would it do?

Above her, something shifted. She jerked her gaze up, drawing Lethe-Alihana on instinct, but she couldn't see through the thick gray clouds. At this point, she was ready for anything, and if snakes with glowing eyes decided to rain from the strange indoor sky, she wouldn't be terribly surprised. It would give her something to focus her fear and anger on.

But what fell through the fog was *not* a deluge of serpents. There was another series of sounds—rustling, slicing, thrashing—and Kaden Moor dropped from the clouds, a knife gripped in one hand, severed bits of dark purple vegetation clinging to his body. He hit the water with a massive splash, disappearing beneath the surface.

Every plant in the room twitched, trying to wake. Morgen's voice rang out, more commanding than before, and that bit of movement stilled. Kaden bobbed up from beneath the lake, swam to

Nyx's island, and pulled himself onto dry land. Red welts covered the exposed skin on his neck, face, and hands. While he did not collapse in joy at finding himself once more on solid ground—Nyx didn't think he was capable of expressing that much relief openly—he rested on all fours for a minute, taking long inhales and exhales.

Nyx did collapse—onto her back, which she immediately regretted for two reasons. One, there was still a plant corpse on the island, and her head landed on a mass of hacked apart vegetative matter. Two, she'd forgotten precisely how much use of the abdominal muscles the movement involved and barely managed not to scream.

She breathed shallowly and deflected her pain through the judicious application of sarcasm. "So," she asked Kaden, "you drop in here often?"

Slowly, Kaden turned his head to look at her. The glare in his eyes and the harsh set of his jaw, combined with the letdown of fear and adrenaline, were too much. She laughed.

That laughter lasted all of two seconds and cut off with a wince. Kaden's gaze shot to her stomach, where the severed roots still plunged into her skin. She should probably do something about those. Yes, any minute now she would do just that.

Kaden rocked his weight onto his heels and tugged her shirt up a few inches. His eyes widened.

"What?" she asked. "You didn't get magic-sucking leech-roots on your Infiltrating the Villain's Lair bingo card?"

His glare, which had never entirely dissipated, returned in greater force. He touched his fingertips to the skin around the root and pressed. It *hurt*. The skin was hot and swollen and tender, a fact she hadn't realized until he'd decided to *poke the injury to see what happened,* and she felt warm liquid spill onto her skin, as if a blister had burst. She did not look because she did not want to know, right at that moment. Instead, she slapped his hand away and rattled off a string of curses that ended with: "What the *fuck?*"

"These need to come out."

She knocked his hand away again, because he was clearly intent on beginning the removal process immediately. "No shit, Sherlock." She could feel the roots trying to burrow deeper into her, which meant any traditional medical advice on leaving the foreign object puncturing one's body in place was out the window as far as she was concerned. "Maybe we could wait for someone to retrieve the bag with the medical supplies first?" Evra was just going to have a field day over her precious bag being useful.

"I have it," Morgen said, landing on the island directly behind her. He shifted a few feet so Evra could jump over after him. The four of them and the bag barely all fit together on the small island.

"I told you it was not over-preparation," Evra said smugly.

Nyx rolled her eyes and valiantly did not point out that if she hadn't killed the mother plant, and Morgen hadn't sang the others into submission, there would have been no reaching the bag which was, again, highly impractical to carry through dangerous terrain.

Morgen knelt. Like Kaden, he too apparently felt the need to prod at her wounds for the sake of scientific inquiry. "Would everyone please stop doing that?" she ground out. He'd touched the *other* one, and hot liquid hit her skin again. This time, she looked down. She immediately wished she hadn't.

"Oh, that is gross. That is so very, very gross." Sickly yellow-and-green pus oozed from around the roots.

"They need to come out," Morgen said, echoing Kaden's earlier assessment.

Kaden reached for the roots, and Nyx knocked his hands away again. "Evra can do it."

A muscle feathered in his jaw. He rose to his feet and let Evra take his place. She was the only one of them who looked to have escaped physical injury, and she was also the cleanest, since the wicking spells on her clothing meant she'd shedded most of the plant gore that had landed on her. She looked at Morgen and nodded. Morgen placed one hand on Nyx's hip and the other on her shoulder. She barely had time to register *why* before Evra grasped the roots, at the base where they bit into Nyx's skin, and jerked them free.

Nyx screamed. Morgen held her down, because her body very much wanted to bolt upright and run far, far away from the pain. The resistance as Evra had ripped the roots out had been very much like trying to unplug a particularly stiff electrical cord from an outlet that did not want to let it go.

Evra took over holding her down—even though Nyx wasn't trying to move anymore, now that the roots were gone—while Morgen wiped at her skin with an analgesic antiseptic. The wounds weren't bleeding, and Nyx wasn't sure if that was a good thing or a bad thing. If she'd been stabbed with a knife, she'd be bleeding. Why should it be any different for aquatic plant roots? Since she had nothing better to do, she asked.

"It appears the organism"—and yes, Nyx *loved* that Morgen called it an organism rather than a plant, as it made it feel all that much more disgusting—"had coagulating properties in its secretions."

"Morgen? Do me a favor. Never, ever again use the word 'secretions' to reference something a freaky death-magic-eating plant has put inside my body."

Evra snorted.

"Little Guardian, should you find yourself in a similar situation again, I'll have to question your life choices." He finished with the antiseptic and paused, meeting her gaze. "Is there any chance of you agreeing to leave and come back once you've healed from this?"

"Are the wounds going to kill me in the next three hours?" When he didn't answer soon enough for her liking, she prompted, "Well?"

He sighed. "The wounds themselves? No. But I have never seen roots burrow into a person before. I can't use an emergency regen kit because if the secretions—"

She glowered at him for that word.

"—are toxic, the regen kits don't nullify toxins and furthermore will cause them to spread more quickly."

Nyx wouldn't have taken the regen kit anyway, because they only had one and her not-bleeding wounds didn't seem to warrant using it when someone else might need it later. "Do you think they were toxic?"

"It's difficult to say. The skin around the puncture wounds is red and swollen, which indicates the possibility. Other side-effects, like nausea or dizziness, likely won't show for an hour or two."

"If we don't make it out of here in an hour or two, we're probably screwed anyway. Hit me with a painkiller and let's go."

"The longer a toxin is allowed to spread in the body the more difficult it becomes to treat, especially since this one is of unknown origin."

"Potential," Nyx corrected.

"I beg your pardon?"

"The *potential* toxin is of unknown origin. And the fact you aren't trying to force me to go back means you have a temporary solution. So let's do whatever that is and move on."

Morgen muttered something under his breath, unstoppered a vial of what looked like gray ooze, and coated her puncture wounds in it. "If it *is* a toxin, this will bind to it and slow the spread, but it is a temporary stop-gap. Six hours at most. If at any point you develop symptoms of nausea, dizziness, blurred vision, or difficulty thinking clearly—though I recognize that last one may be difficult to differentiate from your ordinary state—tell one of us or I will not be held responsible for strangling you."

"If I think I'm going to throw up, make sure you're the first to know. Got it. Do I get painkillers with this?"

"Yes," he said grudgingly. "I don't know why I insist on bouncing around the universe with people who continually get themselves seriously injured and then refuse to respond rationally to the fact."

"Evra, are you really going to let him talk about you that way?" Nyx asked, trying to distract herself from the needle Morgen had pulled out for the painkiller. As it turned out, the invention of medical needles was not isolated to Earth's machine-dominated landscape. Not when the rest of the universe had metal-inclined magic workers.

"I am uninjured," Evra replied.

"Seriously? You don't even have a scratch? Strained wrist muscle from pulling off whatever the fuck that spinning sword move wa—*ow.*" The needle bit into Nyx's skin, a sharp pinch followed by the burn of medicine as Morgen depressed the plunger.

"Unlike you, little Guardian, Evra has a very low injury rate. I understand now why Seth called you a trouble magnet."

Nyx's sarcastic levity died. Morgen froze as he realized what he'd said, a second syringe's worth of painkiller an inch away from her stomach. "Shit. I'm sorry, Nyx."

She made herself shrug. "It's okay. He wasn't wrong."

Morgen finished working on her in silence. Once she was bandaged and sitting up, he and Kaden assessed their own comparatively minor injuries, since they had the peace to do so at the moment and had no idea what might be waiting for them in the next room. While they worked, Nyx took off her boots and dumped out the water.

Evra crouched next to her and asked, voice low, "Are you okay?"

"I would be better if I were dry," she said, ignoring what Evra was really asking. Her pants and shirt weren't terrible—Calista had provided her with a replica of the spelled Talorean garments she'd worn the first time she'd gone to the Shadow Market, and they had shed most of the water without absorbing it. Unfortunately, she hadn't considered the possibility of falling in a lake, which meant her bra, panties, and socks were ordinary cloth, and beneath the Talorean outerwear, all were soaking wet.

"Give me your socks." Evra held out her hand.

Nyx peeled off her socks and deposited them in Evra's hand. Evra had *asked* for them, but Nyx still cringed, on account of they were socks, which had been on her feet and then drowned in a lake and probably smelled horrific, though Nyx's nose was clearly experiencing olfactory fatigue because she couldn't smell them herself.

Evra flicked her fingers and steam rose from the socks. She handed them back to Nyx, who took them, rubbing the now-dry wool between her fingers. Evra grabbed Nyx's boots and repeated this drying trick.

"What?" Evra asked, when Nyx only stared at her dry footwear instead of putting it back on.

"You have magic," Nyx said, pointing out the obvious. "Since when do you have magic?"

"They are simple drying charms, Nyx. You can buy them by the dozen at any traveler's supply store."

"Would this be the same place one buys wicking spells?"

"Yes."

"That would have been good information to have earlier, and why have I never seen one of these traveler's supply stores in Earth Between?"

Evra sighed. "Because no one, and I mean absolutely no one, is stopping by Earth Between to buy survival charms and supplies before heading off to somewhere else. It's the dead end of the universe, Nyx, the magic would fade while it's on the shelf."

Dead end of the universe. "Hey, you live there too."

"I am aware."

"And wicking spells and drying charms are not a magical sword shield. Pretty sure you can't buy *that* off the shelf."

Evra grimaced.

"You can spin a sword really fast in a circle until you generate a magic shield. This is important information and I am your best friend, how did I not know about this?"

"Maybe it would have come up if my *best friend* had spoken a single word to me in the last six months."

Ouch. That was fair, but also: *ouch.* "I *am* sorry, Evra."

"Apologies are only words."

"How philosophical of you. Is there an action you would like me to place behind the words?"

"Yes." Evra met her gaze. "If this doesn't go the way you want it to, do not disappear for another six months. Because if you do, next time, I will not be at the Station when you come back."

The words might have been a deserved punch to the gut, but they were still a punch. Nyx swallowed. "Okay. I got it. No more disappearing act."

Evra nodded.

Nyx put her socks back on. Halfway through tying her boot laces she said, "So…magic sword shield?"

Evra sighed. "You aren't going to let it go, are you?"

"It's *a magic sword shield.*"

"You haven't seen it before because it is almost never practical. It requires a great deal of practice to learn, yet one's enemies rarely give one enough time to go through the necessary forms to activate the magic, and if you stop spinning, it all falls apart."

"Huh." Nyx finished tying her laces. "Then why learn it at all?"

"Because sometimes, as you've seen, it *is* useful." Evra stood and offered Nyx a hand up.

"Anyone ever cut off a toe learning that trick?"

"Yes."

Nyx couldn't tell if Evra was joking. And now that she was on her feet again, her stomach injury pleasantly numbed, and Morgen and Kaden clearly ready to go, her brain returned to the task of getting to the next room. The illusory stepping stone had been critical to crossing the lake without having to jump onto one of the plant-inhabited islands. And while Morgen had put all of those plants to sleep, she didn't want to jump onto one of them only to discover it was illusory too, and furthermore didn't want to risk that accidentally coming into contact with one of the plants might be deadly, since Kaden's welts were rapidly accelerating towards something that looked like a poison ivy reaction, and which he was coating in a thick gray paste.

Besides, now that she knew the floating islands were literally floating and therefore movable, and furthermore knew the water was only around fifteen feet deep, she had a better idea. She unsheathed Lethe-Alihana and held them out to Kaden. "Can you take Lethe for a minute?" The soul of her dead planet was giving her the silent treatment, apparently unimpressed with her performance thus far.

Kaden eyed the sword warily, as if he would prefer vines descending from the ceiling and taking him captive once more to his taking possession of Lethe-Alihana. She was about to ask Evra instead—she'd gone for Kaden because Lethe-Alihana liked him, and she was trying to appease them—when Kaden took the hilt from her.

Nyx stepped to the tip of the island. It was shaped a little like a canoe, the end pointed and narrow, which served her purposes. Constance turned liquid and flowed to her hand, sensing what she needed. Nyx only hoped the metal could extend as far as she needed. She wasn't sure what Constance's limits were.

The metal first formed her familiar bo staff, but when she held it off to the side of the island, parallel to her body, it kept lengthening, down down down, until she felt the end hit the lake floor below.

"Hope everyone has good sea legs." She pushed off with Constance and the island glided forward on the water. It didn't move as easily as she'd hoped—it wasn't exactly designed for travel —but there was only twenty feet or so of space left to traverse, and she was able to pole the island across the room like a raft. Which turned out to be a fortunate thing, because when they reached the exit door, there was no dock for them to step onto.

She retracted Constance and retrieved Lethe-Alihana from Kaden. She had no idea what was on the other side of the door, but given that if a person reached it Kiev clearly wanted them to have no safe place to retreat to, she suspected that once they went through, whatever was on the other side would hit hard and fast.

I concur, Lethe-Alihana said.

Oh, are you talking to me again?

Yes.

Sarcasm. Apparently it flew right over the metaphorical head of a sword-bound soul.

She wished for the shield Constance had formed against A-Lethe when she'd been on Kyvren, but Lethe-Alihana was a two-handed sword, and despite what some poorly researched films would have one believe, there was no way to effectively use a two-handed sword with only one hand. Instead, Constance molded back into a bracer on her left forearm, offering some extra protection and the ready ability to morph shape as needed.

"Everyone ready?" Nyx received three grim nods in return and opened the door.

<h1 style="text-align:center">19</h1>

A gust of hot, fetid air hit Nyx's face, and two glowing eyes opened in the darkness of the room beyond, directly before her. She didn't think or hesitate, but drove Lethe-Alihana forward, into the stomach of the man-shaped thing in front of her. She thought it might once have *been* a man, but something was different about it now—wrong, on a visceral level. Its hands rose, clamping on the sword's blade.

Striking the torso will do nothing, Lethe-Alihana snapped. *It is already dead. Enough limbs must be severed to render the body nonfunctional.*

In a flash, Nyx remembered Jevryn's fight with Kiev on Kyvren, remembered the corpses that had leapt up at Kiev's command.

Ensure you tell your precious friends that if you want them to live, Lethe-Alihana added. Power built, swelling within the sword, and detonated. It was a pulse of true death—all of Lethe-Alihana's design and nothing of Nyx's own—that swept through the body and extinguished the facsimile of life that had given it animation. Nyx pulled Lethe-Alihana free as the body crumpled. Beyond it, she could see only a few feet, the space illuminated by the dim light filtering in from the doorway to the garden room.

A narrow stone bridge, like the drawbridge of a castle, stretched into the cavernous space, maybe four feet across. There was no railing, no lip at the sides, only slick black stone giving way to a fall of unknown depths. She had a second, maybe two, to register all this before something large dove at her from above on nearly silent wings. She ducked and rolled, barely missing the swipe of talons, grateful now for all the hours Evra had spent insisting Nyx perfect the art of rolling with a bladed weapon in hand.

The massive bird-like creature—Nyx couldn't tell *what* it was from the glimpse she'd caught, the room was so damn dark—flew up, and in that brief reprieve she yelled, "Everything in here is dead. They don't feel pain. You'll have to disable them."

She moved deeper into the room, dodging and countering the airborne creature's strikes. She knew once every member of her party had crossed the threshold, because the door slammed closed behind them and every sixth-stone on the bridge lit up like a torch, bathing the room in orange light. As if, now that they were all trapped, Kiev wanted to make sure they saw precisely what they were trapped in here *with.*

The stone sides of the bridge dropped twenty-feet down. Climbing up from the pits below, already halfway up, were dozens upon dozens of corpses.

Nyx dodged another swipe of talons and counter-slashed, the sword driving through flesh. A severed talon dropped at her feet, for all the good it did, the creature swooping away and circling to return. Flesh wounds didn't slow something that couldn't feel, for all that they must retain some of the instincts they'd had in life, or the creature wouldn't bother dodging her attacks and returning. She supposed she should be grateful for that. If it didn't retain a sense of self preservation, it would realize it could just land on her and peck away until it ripped out something vital. Then again, if it did that, she could drive Lethe-Alihana into its body and let *them* neutralize it.

Out of the corner of her eye, she caught glimpses of the others in similar situations, but she couldn't spare the focus from her own fight to tell anything more than that they were all still alive. An ill-advised glance down showed the first wave of non-winged hordes a foot or two from reaching the top of the bridge.

Can't you fix this? Nyx demanded of Lethe-Alihana. She remembered Jevryn driving Lethe-Alihana into the ground on Kyvren, a pulse of magic emanating from the sword, taking out all the moving corpses around him in a single blow, the way Lethe-Alihana had taken out the one she'd driven her sword through earlier.

Jevryn is the one who did that, Lethe-Alihana said, catching her memory. *I can see the world through you, through your senses, but I cannot take control of your body or your magic. If you shove me into a corpse, then I can disable the magic that fuels it, because I am touching it. But I cannot send my own power beyond what I am touching. If you want to do what your father did—and I very much suggest that you do—then you* are going to have to do it.

Nyx let out a short growl of frustration, and when the bird creature dove at her again, she took off the other talon. *Great,* she snapped at Lethe-Alihana. *How exactly do I do that?*

Find the ledge within you. Stand upon the cusp of death, and you are connected to death, to every iteration of it around you. Find those iterations, and reclaim them.

The bird creature dove at her again just as one of the climbing corpses, faster than the others, hauled itself onto the bridge. Nyx turned and drove her sword into the climber. It took less than two seconds for her to connect, for Lethe-Alihana to turn it from walking corpse to corpse-corpse, but it was two seconds too long. The bird creature hit her from behind, knocking her down.

She landed on her stomach, arms, sword, head and shoulders hanging off the bridge. She blinked, the face of another climber—this one belonging to a Livkai, the reptilian people Essteria hailed from—an inch from her own. She swung Lethe-Alihana down, slicing into the corpse's hide. The bird-creature's beak bit into the back of her shoulder and Nyx let out a guttural sound of pain and fury.

Magic pulsed from Lethe-Alihana. The Livkai corpse lost ambulatory control, dropping like a stone. Nyx rolled onto her back, fire arcing through her shoulder as she ripped free of the bird's beak. She jerked her head left, dodging the next strike. Her arms were still behind her, hanging off the ledge, and as the beak jabbed at her again she swung the sword up, the sharp edge biting into the beast's neck.

Magic jolted from Lethe-Alihana and two-hundred pounds of lifeless corpse collapsed on top of her. She reached for death and it flooded her eagerly, giving a boost to her physical strength. She heaved the body off her, sending it tumbling into the pit. Right now, she would have killed for Jevryn's fine control over death magic, for the ability to enhance her strength only a little, but for a longer period of time. Her "control" was mostly still impulse, and if she tried to hold it, she burned out fast. If she tried in this room, she'd have nothing left when she really needed it.

She rolled to her feet as Evra reached her, Morgen and Kaden on the Amazon's heels.

"Plan?" Evra barked, smoothly severing the head of a climber as it rose above the side of the bridge. Headless, it pushed itself up until Evra severed its hands and kicked it in the chest, sending it tumbling.

"I can neutralize them but I need time. Can you guys cover me?"

"Where?" Evra disabled another climber. "There's nowhere to put you to cover you."

If Kiev had an ounce of compassion, he would have given them a nice, wider spherical section in the middle of the bridge from which to make a last stand, but no, the damn bridge was four feet all the way across. Nyx faced one edge of the bridge, drove Lethe-Alihana into the skull of a rising climber and watched the body drop.

"I can handle what's right in front of me if you guys can cover the rest." She hoped that was true. Jevryn might be able to do what Lethe-Alihana had described in seconds, but Nyx wasn't him. She needed time and focus to reach death's ledge within herself.

"Got you here," Evra said. She had already moved ahead of Nyx, which now put her covering the bridge to Nyx's right, closest to the exit.

"And here," Morgen said to her left, on the side of the bridge facing the way they'd come in. That left Kaden as the solid presence at her back. Of *course* the one of them who took up the most physical space had to be back-to-back with her. If either of them moved too much and bumped into the other, one of them was going off the side of the bridge, and it was going to be her, because Kaden was a fucking immovable rock.

Focus, Lethe-Alihana snapped. *Find the ledge.*

That was so much easier said than done. She typically closed her eyes to find that space. She stabbed her sword left, through the temple of one climber, reversed the blade and stabbed right, into the temple of another. Even with the fighting advantage Lethe-Alihana gave her—all she had to do was stab and hold the contact long enough for them do the rest—she could not afford to close her eyes. The climbers weren't fast, but they were steady, and the pit below teemed with masses ready to replace each one they took down.

Focus. She resettled her grip on Lethe-Alihana's hilt and tried to follow that path inward. It had been easy to do in Jevryn's home, sitting cross-legged on floor mats with her eyes closed while his steady voice guided her. His home and his voice had been peaceful, as had the place she found within her.

There was nothing peaceful about her current circumstances. She could not close her eyes, Jevryn wasn't here, and if she didn't get this right, not only was she going to die, but her friends were too. And no matter what they said about free will and making their own damn choices, it would be her fault. She'd wanted to come alone. They should have *let her* come alone, shouldn't have cared enough to follow her, shouldn't have cared at all.

Because she wasn't worth it. She had failed in the worst way possible. She had failed to protect the person she loved most in the world. She had failed, and there were no second chances with death, no do-overs. She had failed.

Focus. To find the staircase, she had to do what she had never managed in Jevryn's home—she had to be both in her body, and in A-Queltr, but the two were at odds. Being in her body was the trial of living. Being in A-Queltr was the peace of death.

You must accept, Lethe-Alihana said, not unkindly, *that the two coexist, that neither is preferable to the other. That the one balances the other. Find that balance.*

Nyx struggled to make the connection. To accept what Lethe-Alihana told her when, if she thought of Seth, life was better than death, and when she thought of herself, her mind often went to the opposite conclusion. Then she felt the weight of the three people around her, and she felt herself dragged to a place midway between. A place where living did not feel as terrible, because they were here with her. Where the peace of death lost some of its allure, because it was static and unchanging, with no room for joy or laughter.

She found a place in her mind where she could accept her continued survival with as much grace as she had accepted the possibility of her death up to this moment. The first step on the spiral staircase that led to A-Queltr appeared, the mental imagery she usually evoked overlaying itself across the room.

She descended. Four or five steps down her determination wavered, the staircase growing hazy. Maybe she hadn't wanted to admit it, even to herself, but part of her had wanted to fail again, here, on her own behalf. She'd pretended to her friends that this wasn't an intentional suicide mission for her, that she while she recognized the danger, she didn't *want* to die. But she realized, standing on this bridge, hacking at corpses, that part of her thought she deserved to. That death would be the ultimate penance for her failure.

Had she come here alone, there would have been no chance of reaching A-Queltr. Maybe she would have survived the garden on her own, maybe not. But it was unlikely she would have survived *this*. She would have died buried beneath a mountain of corpses and she would have accepted that as a fitting end. That she should die, trying to avenge another death.

The staircase grew thinner, her foot beginning to sink through the step. She was losing the path, and if she lost it, her friends would die. There was no fitting end that also ended with Evra's death, and Morgen's, and Kaden's. She willed the stairs to remain.

There is no fitting end that also ends in your *death, Nyxi darling.* Seth's voice in her mind wasn't real. How many times had she gone to death's ledge, hoping to hear it, but never had? Whatever lay beyond the veil of life, if indeed anything did, it was not something even the death-touched living could reach.

Seth's voice in her head now was not *Seth*. It was her want of him, her memory of him, her need of him. It was her recognition, as death teetered perilously close, that what he would have said to her in that moment—what she had always known logically but been unable to make herself believe, what everyone who cared about her had tried to drill into her skull—was true.

Her death here and now, in this moment, in this place, would not be fitting. Her death would not be penance. It would only be death. And if playing at being an A-Morridahn had taught Nyx anything, it was that death was neither moral nor immoral, neither good nor bad.

Focus. The stairs solidified, and she started back down them.

Death simply *was.* And Nyx understood, finally, that she wanted to live. She had loved Seth. Impossibly, immeasurably, unshakably. But she was more than the love she had felt for a person who no longer existed. He had been so much a part of her for so long it felt like he was imprinted on her DNA. Losing him had ripped out chunks of her soul and the edges were still bleeding, might *always* be bleeding.

Focus. She reached the base of the stairs and the staircase vanished, leaving her at the edge of a mountain, the face of it covered in snow. Beneath the facade of the mountain, in the darkness of Kiev's home, she drove Lethe-Alihana into another corpse.

Focus. Yet if her soul still bled from Seth's loss, it also still lived. *She* still lived. And she realized, in that moment, that the greatest dishonor she could do to his memory would be to throw away her life as if it meant nothing. Because *he* had loved *her*, and if she said her life was worthless now, what was that except saying that he had loved poorly? That he had put his faith and his hope and his care into something undeserving.

Focus. She stepped onto the razor sharp ledge of death and the mountain vanished. It was only her, balancing on the thinnest of precipices, the void beneath her and the howling winds around her. Howling, because today death was not peaceful. Today, death was the storm of wrath that had not quieted in Nyx's chest since it had awakened, so many months ago.

Today, death was Nyx.

Focus. She linked with death, linked the void beneath her with the magic in her body, with the magic in Lethe-Alihana—and with the magic beyond. So many threads of it all around her, dark ribbons of promise, of an eternal mystery that could not be known until one walked into death's embrace.

She would not walk today.

Focus. She reached for the nearest threads encircling her. Lethe-Alihana had not told her to sever them, he had told her to reclaim them. She tried to grab them but they refused to come, slipping through her fingers like water.

She remembered the pulse of magic Jevryn had sent through the corpses on Kyvren. A person could not grasp death. Only death itself could do that.

Magic flooded through her, into Lethe-Alihana. She placed the tip of the sword to the bridge, anchoring Lethe-Alihana to the world, and pushed her magic *out*, toward the nearest whispers of death. Her magic skated past the living, avoiding Evra and Morgen and Kaden, wrapping instead around the snippets of death inside each corpse. Snippets that had already been severed and now only needed to be reclaimed.

They came easily, merging with her power. And then she pulled that magic back into herself. Corpses fell, the sounds of her friends' movements pausing as she bought them a reprieve.

She searched again, found more threads and sent a flood of her magic out to gather and draw them back to herself. She did it again and again, the waves of her magic traveling a little farther each time. A final wave, sent out and drawn in again, and there were no more dark threads in the room, calling to her with their wrongness, their loneliness. They had been returned to the main body of death, where they belonged…and where she did not.

She had had difficulty, in Jevryn's home, stepping away from death's ledge. Each time she balanced on it, a part of her considered slipping. That consideration was still there. She thought it might always be, thought perhaps it was human—or at least A-Morridahn —to contemplate death, but it did not tempt her as it had before.

She spun from the ledge and found the mountain face waiting, found the staircase and climbed up, back into the land of the living. There was no pain, as there usually was when she left A-Queltr. Because that pain, she finally understood, was a result of wanting to be in one place over the other, of being unable to balance the two. She let go of A-Queltr, the overlay of the staircase against the room dissolving, and found her friends staring at her.

Somewhere in that time, Kaden had spun her around, so she no longer faced the drop off the bridge but him, his hands on her elbows, steadying her as if afraid she might tumble back at any moment. Her gaze dropped to his hands and he removed them, stepping back the scant six inches available to him to do so.

She took a sideways step and looked over the edge of the bridge. Below, the floor was covered in mounds of unmoving flesh. So much death. So much waste. She thought Lethe-Alihana was wrong. They had claimed that Kiev did not kill indiscriminately, but there were dozens, if not hundreds, of bodies below to contradict that assertion. Bodies that were already beginning to stink.

It was not indiscriminate, Lethe-Alihana argued. *Each death here*

was dealt for a purpose. For this *purpose. For you. You may call it wasteful, you may call it horrific, but indiscriminate it most certainly was not.*

Nyx rolled her shoulders back, wincing as the wound where the bird-creature's beak had bit into her flesh burned with the movement. *Do me a favor. Don't talk to me again unless it's necessary for our survival.*

"You good?" Evra asked.

Nyx considered the question. "Yeah." The winds of wrath still stirred in her chest, sighing back and forth, waiting for the right moment to rip free. "I'm good."

Together, they crossed the bridge to the doorway. Here, Nyx hesitated—from Jevryn's memories, she knew Kiev typically placed three obstacles between himself and anyone entering his home. And from those memories, she knew the third one always packed the hardest punch.

She took comfort in the storm waiting inside her, grasped the handle, and walked into the next room.

20

Nyx shut the door behind her, the warmth of the Station's library folding around her like a hug. It was a welcome contrast to the cold outside, where the snow fell in thick white flakes. She loved the cold, yes, but part of what she loved about it—about winter—was the coziness of blankets and fireplaces, of hunkering down inside and spending time with the people she loved.

Motion caught her eye and Morgen dashed through the library, pursued by Evra. "For stars' sake woman, show mercy," he shouted.

"Be deserving of mercy," Evra snarled. Her expression was murderous, but there was humor beneath it. Whatever they were fighting about, Nyx didn't think they'd be fighting about it for long. They disappeared in the direction of Morgen's laboratory and Nyx shook her head, smiling.

Griff, sitting on a low-backed couch with his legs crossed, his golden wings draped behind him, lifted his spectacled gaze from the book in his lap. Nyx was still getting used to seeing him in the winged-human body he'd been born into, even though it had been over a year since they'd managed to return him to it.

But even in pressed slacks and a sweater vest, he was still Griff. A smile curved his lips when he saw her, and he nodded in the direction Evra and Morgen had disappeared. "I thought they would settle down eventually, but with each passing year the belief fades further."

"I don't think 'settle down' is in their vocabulary," Nyx agreed. She'd known them fifteen years now—and wow did she feel old when she thought about that fact. It made her chest physically hurt, a heartburn she pressed the heel of her hand against—and they were much the same as they'd always been. Steadfast, loyal, and absolutely untamable.

Her nose caught the scent of gumbo drifting in from the kitchen, and she groaned. "When is dinner ready?"

"That would be a question for the chef," Griff answered.

Nyx grinned. "Then I better go ask him." She crossed from the library into the Station's kitchen, taking a seat at the bar and resting her chin on her hand. "So, what's a girl gotta do to get a little service around here?"

Seth, stirring an enormous pot of gumbo and wearing a Kiss the Chef apron Morgen had bought him on his last trip into Dead Earth, sent her a smoldering look. "From you, Nyxi darling, I take down payments in kisses."

"Hmm." She drummed her fingers against her chin. "I suppose that could be arranged." She stood and walked around the counter, stopping halfway there as something thrummed in her chest. A fierce energy, her death magic beating against the cage of her body, insisting something was wrong.

But what could be wrong? Seth was here, smiling at her.

"What is it?" he asked, expression morphing into concern.

"I don't know." There was something about those words, that thought—*Seth was here*—that scratched at her mind. It was important, and if she could just—

Shrieks issued from the hallway and two torpedoes of pure energy masquerading as six-year-olds burst into the room, shattering the feeling of wrongness.

"Mommy! Mommy! Fari took my dagger!" Lana jumped at Nyx, knocking the wind out of her—having small children who could already access the strength advantages of death magic had been a rude awakening—but Nyx caught her, brushing silk black hair out of eyes gone red with anger. Lana, however, never liked to be held long, and when she immediately squirmed, Nyx put her down.

"Did not!" Fari screamed, crashing to a halt at Nyx's other side, her own irises pulsing with a kaleidoscope array of colors that telegraphed her own indignation. "I have *mine*. It's not my fault you lost yours!"

The "daggers" were blunt yet properly weighted practice weapons their "uncle" had given them for their sixth birthdays, and Nyx was still slightly unhappy about that choice of gifts. She settled a stern look on Fari—she *did* have a habit of liberating things that weren't hers. "Did you take your sister's dagger?"

Fari shook her head vehemently.

"You swear? Think carefully before you answer." *Think carefully before you answer* was code for *Don't make me get Veritas.* Nyx, of course, did not actually prick her daughters' fingers with a truth-telling dagger to solve their squabbles. Instead, she and Seth had convinced the two of them the dagger magically knew whether they were telling the truth no matter what, no blood necessary, by having Seth illusion the color change while they told obvious falsehoods like "Earth's sky is red".

However, since the usefulness of the tool would be lost if Seth had to base the illusion on his best guess about whether they were telling the truth or not and he got it wrong—their daughters got their lying ability from him, no doubt about it—extra chores were instated if Veritas had to be paraded out.

Fari looked up at her, eyes still spitting indignation. "I didn't take it!"

Nyx believed her. For one, she had Nyx's ingrained belief that the world should be a just place, and she took exception when something stood in opposition to this belief. She was taking a great deal of exception at present. For another, Lana was always losing her things.

"Lana, did you *see* your sister take your dagger?"

Lana scuffed her foot on the floor. "No," Lana said, drawing the word out. "But I can't find it. And I put it in my closet, I know I did!" Her eyes welled up with tears.

Nyx bent and pressed a kiss to her forehead. "Why don't you go ask your uncle Kaden to track it for you? He's in the gym."

The tears spilled over. "But then he'll know I lost it," she wailed. "And he just gave it to me. He'll be mad."

Nyx felt a migraine building. "Has Kaden *ever* been mad at you?"

Lana's chin wobbled. "N-no."

Of course he hadn't. Kaden had the stoic patience of a saint. Well, maybe not a saint, this was Kaden Moor they were talking about, but…something. He'd grown a lot in the last few years. He and Seth both had. They'd come a long way from trading punches at the back of the Station to being something close to friends, with Morgen as the common buffer between them.

She and Seth had never known quite how to explain Kaden to Lana and Fari, and since the girls had decided he was their uncle, they'd decided that was fine.

"I doubt he's going to start being mad today," Nyx pointed out. "Go ask him."

Lana pouted, but she took off in the direction of the gym. Fari glared at Nyx. "She said I lied."

"I know. But while she jumped to conclusions, I think she *did* believe you took it."

"So?" Fari put her hands on her hips. "It's not fair." She spun to Seth. "Tell her it's not fair, Dad!"

Seth's eyes danced with laughter, but he kept a somber expression. "So, so unfair."

Fari spun back to Nyx. "See?"

Nyx gave Seth a *you're dead* look. He winked at her. That pain in Nyx's chest rose again, a sweet, aching agony at seeing him. She loved him *so much* and it *hurt*. Death whipped wild winds in her chest, insisting something was *not right, not right, not right.* If she could just figure out *what* wasn't right, she could—

"What is unfair?" Jevryn asked. He stood on the threshold between the library and the kitchen, and his calm, steady voice quieted the feeling in her chest. Fari latched onto him, launching into a retelling of her cruel mistreatment.

"Ah, I see," Jevryn said when she finished, and since Jevryn was saying it, Fari took this as agreement with her.

"Lana was mistaken," Nyx said, shooting Seth and Jevryn warning glances, "and she will do something nice for Fari in apology."

"Fine," Fari huffed out. She turned her attention back to Jevryn. "Will you show me the ledge again?"

Nyx sighed. Where Lana just took the strength death magic offered, Fari was *obsessed* with the theoretical aspects, but she wasn't allowed to access A-Queltr without Jevryn there to make sure her balance didn't falter.

"If you wish," he said, letting her grab his hand and drag him off. He had taken his role as "Grandfather" haltingly at first, and he would never be as natural at it as Griff, but he was trying. It helped that he was thrilled to finally have a student who listened to what he said and followed his directions without complaint, something Nyx had never managed.

Once he and Fari were gone, Nyx groaned and slumped back into a seat at the kitchen bar, glaring at Seth. "I still can't believe I let you knock me up and you had to overachieve with twins."

"Don't blame me," Seth said, "twins run in your gene pool, not mine."

"It's still your fault," she insisted. "But I'll forgive you if you kiss me."

He lifted her hand, pressed a kiss to the back of her knuckles, and let it go quickly. Too quickly.

"I had something more substantial in mind," she grumbled.

"And yet, dinner is finished," he said, flicking off a burner. "I'm afraid you'll have to wait."

She raised her eyebrows. "Really? Since when has Mr. Dinner Is Infinitely Reheatable decided eating is more important than sex?"

That feeling of wrongness resurfaced and driving it was anger, fury, *wrath*. This was wrong. This was beyond wrong, it was cruel.

But she couldn't put her finger on *why*.

A deep thrumming ran through the Station. An Arrival. She'd forgotten she had one scheduled. She needed to go, needed to—

No. She planted herself in the chair and refused to move. Every time this feeling surfaced, something happened. Her children distracted her, Jevryn distracted her, an Arrival she'd forgotten about called to her. Well, nothing was going to distract her now. Because something wasn't right. Something with Seth or about Seth wasn't right, but that didn't make any sense, because Seth was the thing in her life that was *always* right.

He was responding to the last thing she'd said, but she didn't hear it. She stared at him, as if doing so long enough would explain why the only thing she felt when she looked at him right now was an overwhelming sense of grief. She swallowed the lump in her throat and felt the movement of a rock strung on a cord, resting against the hollow of her throat.

A rock that…

Nyx closed her eyes. Opened them. Seth was still there. His warm brown eyes, the slight quirk of his lips. His hair was mussed, a tendril brushing against his raven's feather earring.

Nyx lifted her hand to her left ear, where that feather was soft against her fingertips. And she heard another man's voice, this one pulled from her memory, from a time when she hadn't remembered Seth existed. *I guess I can't be blamed for letting them dredge you out of my memory. For seeing your face. Your body. The way you walk, the way you talk. They're burned into me.*

Seth was burned into Nyx. A tear spilled down her cheek. Seth's face creased in concern and he walked around the counter, stopping next to her. But he didn't touch her. "Hey, what's wrong?"

She looked into his eyes, memorizing them. But she'd already memorized them, hadn't she? She was *looking* at the memory of them, at the memory of him. And she told that memory what she never had in life. What she *should have*, in life. "I love you." The tears were making tracks down her face now, but she didn't try to stop them. "I love you *so much*. I always have."

"Hey, it's okay. I know. I love you too, Nyxi."

And there it was. She finally got to hear him say it, even if it was only a hallucination of him talking, something a Mindwitch had pulled out of her memories to distract her. To trap her here, in this perfect make-believe world, with what she wanted more than anything else.

Touch a Mindwitch's Construct long enough and it deconstructs, Kaden's voice whispered in her memory.

She should—touch Seth. Hold that touch until the false representation of him fell apart. But she couldn't. This wasn't real, but it *felt* real. She only knew the difference because she was fighting it. If she quit fighting, if she *wanted* to believe it, would it feel real?

The world beyond this space inside her mind was harsh and cold and empty. This place was warmth and longing and possibility. This was safety and happiness. This was the life she'd wanted to build. Would it be so wrong to stay?

She felt her determination faltering, felt herself starting to lose the urgency to act. She could stay, and have everything she'd lost. It would hurt no one but herself. She had nothing in the world beyond except—

—except Evra and Morgen and Kaden. If she stayed, would they survive? Would they realize what was happening to them in time to break free? And would she really risk their lives because she wanted to stay with the memory of a man more than she wanted to live?

She closed her eyes. Opened them back into Seth's. It took all of her will to say, "Kiss me."

He shook his head. "Not when you're acting like this."

Someone pounded on the front door, urgently, and she felt it rattle through her connection to the Station. She ignored it. "Kiss me."

Morgen and Evra ran back into the room. "Nyx," Evra said sharply, "you need to come. Quickly. Something's happened with Temerex and—"

Nyx shut out her voice. She wasn't real. The real version of her was in a different room, trapped in her own dreamworld, and Nyx had to get her out.

"Kiss me," she told Seth again. Because if she was going to shatter her perfect make-believe world, she was going to shatter it with a kiss.

He shook his head. "No. Not until you tell me what's wrong."

"Everything," she whispered. "Everything is wrong without you." She pushed onto her feet, wrapped her arms around him, and kissed him. For a few seconds he was hers again, the warmth of him against her, the taste of him in her mouth.

Then the dream shattered and her arms were wrapped around empty air, Lethe-Alihana clutched awkwardly in one hand. The Mindwitch sat before Nyx on a carved chair, her arms resting on the sides. Ropes of power splayed out from her, an unraveled one stitching itself back together as Nyx watched.

"He said you'd be difficult," she spat. "Now come here." The restitched rope whipped out. Pain lashed Nyx's mind and the room and the Mindwitch vanished.

She sat on the couch on the Station's back porch, her bare feet tucked beneath a blanket, a book open in one hand. Seth sat on the ground, leaning back against the couch, his unruly dark hair a contrast to the light gray fabric. The autumn evening had a slight chill to it, just the way she liked. Seth tipped his head back and smiled up at her, a devious glint in his brown eyes. He was—

Not real. The torrent of death magic threatening to burst out of her chest screamed it at her. *Not real, not Seth.*

She broke free again and it hurt twice as much this time, slamming back into the real world. Out of the corner of Nyx's eye, Kaden ran toward the Mindwitch, sword in hand. Unsurprising that he'd broken free too—of all of them, he had the most practice with Mindwitches—but it didn't matter. Just like the Mindwitch's power snaking toward her again didn't matter.

Because Nyx was *done.* Her pain erupted in a lash of magic that gripped the Mindwitch in a fist and squeezed. The Mindwitch froze. Her skin turned gray. Cracks formed over her face as if it was land that had gone too long without water. Then her skin blackened. The fist of Nyx's magic squeezed again, and the Mindwitch collapsed into dust.

Twin gasps were Evra and Morgen jerked abruptly back to reality. Nyx took a moment to reassure herself that they were fine, and then her attention focused on the space behind the chair the Mindwitch had occupied. A narrow hallway stretched to a chamber where a raised platform waited. Lying on it, hands crossed over his chest like a sleeping vampire, was Kiev A-Morridahn. Another form —a woman—was slumped across his stomach, as if she'd been holding vigil at his deathbed and fallen asleep.

"Stay here," she ordered Kaden and a barely lucid Morgen and Evra. They'd agreed that when they reached Kiev, he was *hers.* Her uncle could kill them too easily and she wouldn't allow it.

She sprinted down the hall. She didn't care about talking to Kiev. She didn't want to hear him rationalize, did not care if he apologized or begged for mercy. A man who had lived over nine-hundred years and still behaved the way Kiev did had no room for mercy or change in him.

Nyx had come this far. She had survived his fucked-up garden and his undead horde. She had seen the life that should have been hers, the children she would never have, the man she would never hold or kiss or love again, and Kiev was going to pay for taking it from her and then shoving a facsimile of it down her throat like acid, hoping she would choke on it.

He was going to *pay.*

She hit the end of the hallway and slammed into an invisible barrier. The impact jarred her. A sound like a gong being struck reverberated outward, and Kiev bolted upright. The form that had been slumped over him fell sideways, behind the platform and out of sight. Kiev's head jerked toward the hallway and she saw that half of him looked…dead. The skin she could see on the right half of his body—face and neck and hand—was grayish, his right eye clouded over. The left half of his mouth twisted into a snarl of hate, but she could see, beneath the hate, fear.

Lethe-Alihana had been right: Kiev was afraid of her. She'd forced him to swallow a shard of his planet's soul, and the cost had been steep.

He took a step toward her, left hand drawing a short sword from off the platform.

Yes, she thought. *Come here. Come to me and I will show you what you've wrought.*

Use me, Lethe-Alihana snapped. Their need was as insatiable as her own and Nyx did as bid, driving them into the invisible barrier. The point of the blade stuck and she threw her will and magic and muscle behind it, driving forward. She felt cracks form in the invisible barrier. Knew Kiev felt them too, because he halted. His gaze locked on the sword and recognition lit his eyes.

That's right, she thought. *The half of your planet you haven't bound to you wants to say* hello.

Kiev took a step back. Nyx screamed. It was the same scream she'd unleashed on Kyvren. Though it did not carry a soul shard with it, Lethe-Alihana's power yet welled up, joining the torrent of her own that poured out.

All color drained from Kiev's face. He stepped back, withdrew a stone from his pocket and crumbled it into dust. Portal magic ripped into the room.

No. "Don't you dare," she snarled. "Don't you *dare* run away from me you fucking coward."

He didn't answer. She shoved herself to the left without letting go of Lethe-Alihana, straining to make out anything of the portal's destination, but it was no use. It had opened facing *him* and the portals the stones opened were like mirrors. He could see it because he was facing it, but she—she was on the back side, where there was no reflective surface.

The barrier separating them exploded outward in a rain of invisible shards and Nyx stumbled into the room—just as the portal vanished.

21

Nyx stood inside the room's threshold, Lethe-Alihana clenched in one fist, and stared. At the space where Kiev had been. At the nothing that was there now. At the evidence, once again, of her failure.

Dimly, she was aware of a presence at her back, slightly to her right.

"Nyx?" Kaden asked.

"He's gone."

Another presence at her back, this one a little to her left.

"Where?" Evra's voice was off, as if whatever she'd seen in the Mindwitch's clutches hadn't left her yet.

"I don't know. He used a portal stone." Of *course* his bond to the other half of Lethe-Alihana's soul would let him circumvent the dominance they could generate. "I can't track a portal created by a stone." It wasn't Kiev's magic, so the familial trace wouldn't be there. And Kaden couldn't track him across planets. He'd only been able to do it with Nyx on Amentia Furor because he'd been Linked to her.

Kiev had planned this, she realized. He'd known she would come, and if she survived everything else and made it this far, he'd had a portal stone so he could run if he didn't like his chances. Run using a method she couldn't trace.

Lethe-Alihana vibrated with anger. *Find him.*

How do you propose I do that? she snapped. They didn't answer. Her body hummed, filled to the brim with magic that demanded an outlet and had none.

Morgen stepped past her into the room, and she only realized there were bodies—seven that she could see—sprawled around the room when he knelt beside one, checking for a pulse. He shook his head and moved on to the next. Then the next.

They bore no obvious signs of injury, nor did the room smell of decomposing flesh. When Nyx looked, she found the threads of death magic, preserving them as the corpses in the opening hall had been preserved. But these bodies were not trophies. No, it was simply that having corpses rot in the room with a person would be not only inconvenient and disgusting, but also unsanitary.

Why had he left them here in the first place? "Who were they?" she wondered aloud.

"His personal Shamans," Kaden said quietly. "He must have drained them trying to heal whatever you did to him on Kyvren."

She glanced sharply at him. "Shamans? Plural?" That couldn't be right. Every body in this room couldn't have been a Shaman. "How many did he have?"

"Ten," Kaden answered. "None of them by choice."

"*Ten?*" Evra asked, disbelief in her voice.

Shamans were both rare and precious. It didn't surprise Nyx that Kiev would have access to one or two, maybe even three, but *ten?* And calling them his personal Shamans implied that not only did Kiev have access to them, but no one else did.

"This one's alive," Morgen called. He had disappeared behind the stone platform Kiev had been lying on, and when Nyx walked around it she saw two more bodies—and the woman who had been slumped over Kiev. Morgen had helped her to sit up, her back propped against the side of the platform.

She was barely conscious, her eyes roving behind closed lids. "Water," she croaked. "Please."

They hadn't brought any with them—sloshing canteens of water didn't really sit well on a person in a fight, and they'd come here to fight—but something on the nearest wall must have been familiar enough to Evra that she recognized it as a sink, because she walked over to it and, after fiddling with a couple of the stones set into the wall, got a tap to turn on. Pressing against random places on the wall eventually popped open a cupboard door designed with a pressure release. She took a glass from the cupboard, filled it with water, and brought it back to the woman.

She grasped it with both hands, and only once she'd drained it did she open her eyes. "Thank you. I—" She cut off when she saw Kaden. The glass dropped from her hands. She tried to scramble away but only crashed against Morgen, her terrified gaze never leaving Kaden.

"Please," she whispered. "Please, I tried, I swear I tried. Look at them"—she gestured at the bodies—"they died but I didn't. I was helping, I'll still help, I'll—" She saw Nyx and hope blossomed in her eyes. "She's the one he wants. She's the one who did this to him. You don't need to kill me, you have her."

The look in Kaden's eyes…haunted didn't begin to cover it. Neither did self-loathing, or regret, or pain, but all of those things were there. All of those were things *Kiev* had put there. Nyx didn't know what Kaden had done for her uncle, and she didn't want to, either. She already had too good of an idea.

She stepped in front of Kaden. "He isn't going to hurt you."

The woman trembled. "You don't understand. What he is. He's—"

"Not going to hurt you," Nyx reiterated. "I know you think—"

Kaden's hand landed on her arm. She looked up, met his eyes, and saw in them the silent request for her to stop. Stop defending him. Stop trying to help. Stop trying to fix it.

"I'll be in the next room," he said. "Find me when you're done." He walked out.

Morgen looked at Nyx. "Do you need me?"

She shook her head. "Go." He nodded and went after Kaden.

The woman watched it all, her fear and confusion evident. "I don't understand." Her voice was barely a whisper. She looked as if her entire world had been turned on its head and nothing made sense anymore.

"What's your name?"

"Tira."

Well, Tira, I have no idea how to help you. If Nyx was going back to Earth…but she wasn't. Not without finishing what she'd started. "Is there somewhere I can send you?"

"Send me?" Tira repeated blankly.

"Do you have a home? Friends? Family? Someone Kiev took you from?"

"I've been with him since I was five. This is my home." She glanced to her left, and Nyx realized there was another small hallway, likely leading to bedrooms and living areas.

Fuck. Nyx couldn't take Tira with them. The woman was terrified of Kaden, and Nyx would only lead her right back into Kiev's path anyway. "Pack anything you want to take with you. I have someone I can send you to. She'll give you a place to stay until you decide what you want to do."

Bryn Morrigan was going to just *love* Nyx dumping an injured Shaman on her doorstep, but Nyx didn't have any other options.

Tira looked at Nyx like she'd lost her mind. "This is my home," she repeated.

"If Kiev comes back here he's not going to be in a good mood. You don't want to be here when that happens."

Tira drew herself up. "*When* he returns, I will help him. That is my job. I have done it for two centuries. *I* kept him alive when the others died. *I* siphoned the poison you shoved into his body and *I* will cure him when he returns and be rewarded."

Nyx stared at her. "Are you forgetting that a few minutes ago you were on the ground begging for water, afraid Kiev's lackey was going to execute you for doing a poor job? Pack your shit."

Tira's eyes flashed. "I am not going anywhere with you. All of this is your fault!" She indicated the bodies around the room. "They're all dead because of *you*."

Nyx drew back. "Fine. Stay here and rot in his tender care if that's what you want."

Tira shoved to her feet. She collapsed almost immediately, but she got up again and stumbled down the hall. A few seconds later, they heard a door slam.

Evra looked at Nyx. "That was…unlike you."

Maybe it's more like me than you think. Maybe I'm so nice because I shove the rest of it down all the time. Because I want people to care, so I care about them even when they treat me like trash. But she was tired— so tired—of giving.

"She is only scared," Evra said, "and she doesn't know anything else."

Nyx closed her eyes briefly. "I know. But she's not going to come with us willingly. And even if she did, she would turn around and sell us back to Kiev the first chance she got. If we take her forcefully, and we don't succeed in killing him, she'll run back to him on her own. What's the point?"

"So you are just going to leave her here." Evra still sounded incredulous.

"For now, yes. If Kiev left them for months or years at a time, she must have food and all the other necessities. Once we've finished this, I'll send Jevryn back for her." Surely he would know what to do with Tira. The Shaman might not like him, but she would respect him where she didn't respect Nyx.

"That's it?"

"What do you want me to do, Evra?"

"I want—" Evra cut off.

Nyx lifted her eyebrows. "For me to go back to being nice, *normal* Nyx?" she finished for her.

Evra blew out a breath. "No. I want for you to not lose yourself so completely that you can't find your way back."

Nyx's resistance softened. "I won't. And even if I were feeling fluffier, I would make the same decision. There's no point in taking her out of here while Kiev lives. She doesn't want to go. You can't help someone who doesn't want to be helped."

"Yes, I am well aware of that fact," Evra said pointedly.

"Are we really going to fight?" Nyx asked. *"Now?"*

Evra sighed. "No." She glanced at the hallway Tira had disappeared down. "She stays until we finish it, then. Where is Kiev likely to have fled?"

Nyx really did not want to answer that question with *I don't know.* Where *would* Kiev go? Somewhere he felt safe...or after someone he blamed. If he suspected Nyx's mother had shown her how to find him...

Nyx wasn't worried about her mother. Elena Fortuna could lie in the bed she'd made. But what about Serenity? Nyx highly doubted Kiev was above harming a child. She didn't know if that was where he'd gone, but she had to make certain it wasn't.

"Come on, we need to go. We need to go right now." She and Evra took off toward the Mindwitch room. They crossed the threshold, Morgen and Kaden turning as they ran in.

Morgen's eyes widened at their haste. "What—"

Pain, hot and blinding, stabbed through Nyx's ribcage. She stumbled, clutching her chest, expecting to feel the hot spill of blood, but there was nothing. Pain stabbed her again and again, ripping through her, until she would have collapsed if Evra hadn't shoved her arm beneath Nyx's shoulder, holding her up.

People were talking to her but she couldn't hear them. She was —*they were*—being ripped apart, a level of pain they hadn't felt since the world they'd given life to was harvested, their essence locked inside a cage of—

Something hot flared in their…hand? No, *her* hand. *Nyx's* hand. The agony she was experiencing was not her own. It was another's, a being she had bonded herself to with a thorn that bore a part of her life.

Kiev A-Morridahn was in her Station.

22

Nyx did not bother with subtlety or efficiency. Now that Kiev was gone from his home, taking his half of Lethe-Alihana's soul with him, nothing remained here to exert dominance over her use of portal magic. So she tore every ounce of that magic she possessed from her bracelets, wrapped it in a sphere that encompassed them all, heedless of the portions of the room it also touched, grasped hold of her anchor outside the Station and pulled. They crashed onto the ground just outside the Station's boundary, a portion of Kiev's floor landing beneath them.

She ran, crossing the boundary that meant *home* and immersing herself in the Station's senses. Pain engulfed her. She fought through it—it wasn't hers—and folded space, stepping from the edge of the boundary to the Arrival Room in a blink.

The portal bay floor, leading to the Heart, was open. Three deep gashes had rent it, two short parallel cuts and a longer one connecting to the ends of the other two, as if someone had drawn only three sides of a rectangle. Something had been levered underneath the longest edge to pry the floor up, like a lid on a tin can.

Her pulse thudded as she raced for the opening. This shouldn't be possible—the councilors had *some* control over the Stations, but they couldn't access their Hearts. If it was possible, even through force like this, no one would have been more motivated to achieve it than Jevryn had been when she and Griff had been in the Heart with Laiveran. Yet he hadn't managed it even then.

Kiev had help, Lethe-Alihana said. *The Soulsinger's.*

Nyx's blood went cold. Laiveran. Kiev was in her Station's heart *with Laiveran.*

She fell to her knees by the opening. "Kaliaris?"

A second went by with no answer. Three seconds. Five. Ten. If she jumped without Kaliaris's help, how far would she fall? Would she survive the landing?

Twenty seconds. Fuck it. She swung her legs over the opening. She shifted Lethe-Alihana to one hand, preparing to jump. A long, green vine shot up from below, wrapped around her waist, and pulled her down.

The descent was faster and more turbulent than usual, and three feet from the bottom the vine holding her went limp. She dropped to the barren ground. Barren, because the vines that should have been there were withered, revealing the dirt beneath.

Kaliaris's voice echoed weakly through her mind. <Save…him.>

Him. Not *me.* She heard the beating of wings and saw Griff, trapped in the prison that should have held Laiveran. All of Kaliaris's living vines were concentrated on that prison, crawling up the clear walls, offering as much protection as they could. It wasn't a prison, in this moment, but a panic room, a last bastion of safety. Kaliaris had shoved their oldest companion into it in an attempt to shelter Griff from Kiev, who hacked and slashed at the vines with a sword that dripped death. Vines tried to curl around Kiev, to rip him away, but each one that touched him shriveled and died.

"Hey, Uncle!" Nyx shouted. "You ran out on our family reunion."

Kiev stopped and spun.

"Nyx, run!" Griff roared.

"Yes," Kiev told her. "Run, and I might not chase you."

Hunger poured from Lethe-Alihana into her. "Freshen my memory—have I been running away from you, lately, or have *you* been running from *me?* You were so scared of me you went to my mother, of all people, for help."

She pulled on death, black arcing through her veins, reinforcing the weak point in her shoulder where a skeletal beak had torn her flesh. "So here's my counteroffer: drop your sword, kneel, and I'll make it quick. It's a mercy you don't deserve."

A sound of pure hatred left Kiev's throat, and he attacked. He was shockingly fast. Given his body's appearance, she'd expected him to be suffering a lack of full mobility, but whatever Tira had done, all of his limbs worked even though they looked dead.

Nyx caught his first strike on her blade and the force of it reverberated through her bones. *Holy shit.* It was as if she'd forgotten to reinforce her own body with death magic, except the spiderweb of black veins over her hands and arms were proof she hadn't. She drew more of that strength up as she parried and struck, each of his blows threatening to numb her hands.

He cannot keep it up overlong, Lethe-Alihana said. *He's pouring too much power into it.*

It didn't matter if he couldn't keep it up *overlong* if he killed her before that time ran out. She'd always known she was unlikely to best him when it came to strength or skill alone. Just as with Jevryn, there was a breadth of experience there she couldn't hope to overcome. Just as with Jevryn, she had to find a weak point. She had to make him stumble.

"Does it bother you?" she asked. "That you went to all the trouble to rearrange your defenses just for me, and I breezed through them anyway?"

He didn't answer. She evaded another strike, and another, but the next one she parried made her arms ache all the way up. The wound in her shoulder screamed, the surrounding muscles threatening to give.

"I killed your Mindwitch. I hope you weren't terribly attached to her."

"Dehla was growing tiresome."

He'd responded to that one. Dehla might have grown tiresome, but she'd been something else at some point.

"Still, you could have given me something a little more challenging. She barely put up a fight. I can only imagine how disappointed my grandmother would have been, had she known that *that* was the best you had to offer me."

The next strike Nyx countered had more in common with a brute-force blow from a club than it did with a swordsman's strike.

It *did* numb her arms for a second, and only the last six months of daily practice with Jevryn kept her moving despite the fact. But she wasn't entirely quick enough, and his blade bit into her upper arm. It was a shallow slice, but it didn't do her any favors.

Yes, Lethe-Alihana said, *Ilera A-Morridahn. That is the wound to press salt into.* And so they gave her more salt—Jevryn's memories of Kiev, careful wisps gathered over the years in those rare moments when her father's mind had been unguarded.

"But then again, maybe she wouldn't be disappointed. Maybe she knew, all along, that you were always second best next to Jevryn. Second into the world, second in talent. Less polished, less controlled."

Kiev rained down a rapid succession of blows, fast and devastating, but his form was slipping.

"Every time Ilera A-Morridahn looked at you, that was what she saw: a paler, weaker imitation of my father. A less desirable backup to be deployed when the best option was engaged elsewhere. You couldn't even carry on the family name, the one thing you might have been good for."

That, Nyx realized as Lethe-Alihana fed her the relevant information, was the root of Kiev's hatred for Griff. Kiev didn't care that his brother was gay. He would not, in other circumstances, have held any more contempt for Griff than he did for anyone he viewed as too soft—and therefore unsuitable—to be an A-Morridahn spouse.

No, he cared that the one time Jevryn A-Morridahn had refused their mother's wishes, throwing over an arranged marriage for the golden-winged man he'd met on another planet, Kiev had been the one required to take that marriage contract instead. And in so doing, discovered he was infertile. Not all types of infertility could be cured by Salyria's healers, and his could not. He had hated the marriage, but when it was dissolved on the grounds of his inability to provide an heir, and the A-Morridahn family had lost the valuable political connections it had provided, he had become all but invisible to Ilera A-Morridahn.

Rather than be angry at a system that based his worth on something out of his control, something that had no bearing on an individual's *actual* worth, Kiev instead blamed Jevryn and Griff. To Kiev's mind, Griff's entrance into Jevryn's life was the catalyst that caused Kiev's fall in the hierarchy of his family. He was a man caught in the failures of his past, no matter how many centuries behind him they might be removed, and they had as much power to wound and enrage him today as they'd had when freshly made.

Nyx's muscles screamed as she blocked, over and over, Kiev's ferocity leaving no room for an attack of her own, the power in her veins the only thing keeping her from faltering.

Keep pushing, Lethe-Alihana ordered.

"I saw her body. Her eyes, her shock. She was so surprised, wasn't she? That *you* of all people were her end."

Nyx's vision blurred at the edges. Too much. She was pulling on death too much, and if she didn't stop soon, Kiev wouldn't need to kill her—she'd tumble off that ledge inside her, into the abyss of her own accord.

I don't want to die. The thought was still a surprise to her, but it was true. Living hurt. Living was, sometimes, unbearable. But Nyx wanted to continue doing it.

Keep pushing him, the sword snapped.

She couldn't even feel her arms anymore as they moved, but she pushed. "You could take some pride in besting her if you'd actually fought her, but you didn't, did you? You drove a sword through her gut in her sleep like the coward you are."

His eyes sparked orange and this time when he struck, she blocked and let them come into a bind. A fresh wave of death's strength surged through her. Keeping pressure on the bind with her right hand she dropped the hilt with her left, snaking it over her right arm and grasping the pommel of Kiev's sword. She jerked her left hand up and over in a counterclockwise motion, wrenching the hilt from Kiev's hands and flinging it aside. The second it was no longer in his grasp, no longer touching *him* and therefore no longer imbued with the magic of death, one of Kaliaris's vines snagged the hilt and ripped it away.

Nyx drove the sword forward. Kiev caught the blade in his bare hands, the tip only just piercing his clothing and nicking the skin beneath. His hands were fists around the blade, holding it back, but they barely bled. Through Lethe-Alihana, she felt the coat of magic, brushed over his body like a second skin, lending extra protection to his hands, extra resistance to her attempt to drive the blade home.

Kiev's eyes blazed. He pushed the sword back, pushed *her* back. "Not good enough, *Niece.*"

She screamed—no magic in her voice this time, only anger and frustration and pain—and pulled recklessly on the power inside her. Kiev did the same. Blackness closed in around the edges of Nyx's vision. A little longer. If she could hold on a little longer—but holding wasn't enough. *She* wasn't enough, wasn't going to *be* enough. Her shoes slid on the floor as Kiev drove both her and the sword back. Both the cut on her upper arm and the beak wound in her shoulder threatened to make her remaining strength fail entirely.

No. She wouldn't get another chance. This was it. She couldn't fail.

But she was.

And then there was a weight at her back, slowing her slide. Kaden's arms came around her, closing over her own on the sword. "I've got you."

Another weight, this one at Kaden's back, and their slide stopped entirely. "So do I," Morgen said.

A final weight, behind Morgen. "And so do I." From the end of their line, Evra dug in her heels and *shoved.* Nyx surged forward. Her arms and Kaden's strained. The blade pushed forward, past Kiev's resistant magic, and slid home.

Her uncle's eyes turned the same stunned amethyst his mother's had in death. He tried to backpedal but she loosed one hand from the hilt, trusting Kaden to keep the sword in place, and locked her hand behind Kiev's neck. She dug deep, dragging out another surge of death's power. Her vision narrowed to the field of Kiev's face and she yanked him closer, her eyes boring into his.

"This is for Seth. And Griff, and Jevryn, and Lana and Fari, and Temerex, and Kaden, and my grandmother, and *me.* I hope there is no peace where you're going. I hope there is *nothing* after this life because no hell would ever make you feel remorse. The only thing you care about is yourself, so I hope you cease to be in any form, because the greatest punishment you could ever imagine for yourself is a total end.

"So *end.*" She put all her weight against the sword, shoving the blade through to the crossguard. Kiev's irises turned from the amethyst of surprise to the red of hatred. He opened his mouth and she twisted the blade, cutting him off. He didn't get to speak final words. He didn't deserve them. She wanted him to die just like this —silent. Unheard.

Constance shifted, flowing down her arm. Nyx lifted her left hand from the sword, grasped the dagger Constance became, and drove it into Kiev's neck. She dragged the blade, severing the carotid, and ripped it free.

A minute went by, Kiev's lifeblood pouring out, and then he slumped on the blade. Her vision swam—she was still holding onto the death magic that bolstered her strength, and she'd been pulling too much for too long. She let it go. Let Kaden push Kiev's body off Lethe-Alihana's blade. Watched it fall. Watched as they all disentangled from each other—her, Kaden, Morgen, Evra—and thought about how in death, the personality wiped from his face, Kiev finally looked like Jevryn to her.

Nyx shivered. Then the floor beneath her feet began to writhe. At first, she thought it was only Kaliaris's vines regrowing in the absence of Kiev's onslaught—and it *was* that, but it was more, too. It was concern.

<They are dying,> Kaliaris said in her mind. Their vines carried Kiev's sword to her. Placed near his body, she felt something flickering between Kiev and the sword, something she recognized the structure of, because it was the same thing that connected Griff to Kaliaris and Kaliaris to Griff: a bond. A bond that meant neither of them would survive the death of the other.

Like Jevryn, Kiev had placed his half of Lethe-Alihana's soul into his sword, and that soul was dying now. Too late, she remembered *why* Jevryn couldn't kill Kiev himself—because his binding to Lethe-Alihana meant he could not harm either half of the soul, and killing Kiev would kill the piece of soul he was bound to. It had never occurred to her that when *she* killed Kiev, she would be killing part of Lethe-Alihana as well. It should have, but she hadn't even thought about it because she had assumed Lethe-Alihana would never help her, if that was the case.

Horrified, she turned to them for help. But what she felt from them was a deep, purring satisfaction. Emotions and thoughts rolled through her mind, and she realized that Lethe-Alihana no longer viewed the other half of their soul as being part of *them*. They viewed it as an imposter—as something whose nature had split when it diverged from them. They had wanted to kill Kiev, yes. But their true aim, their true hunger, this entire time, had been to destroy the other part of themself.

Not only did Nyx not want the other half of her planet's soul to die, but they held the knowledge of how Kiev had created the bond that held them to him—this bond, and all the others. They were the key to understanding how the bonds worked, to freeing Griff. Holding Jevryn's sword in her left hand, she grasped the hilt of Kiev's with her right.

Magic arced through her, the half of Lethe-Alihana from Jevryn's sword using her body as a conduit to attack the other. She dropped Kiev's sword before the attack could connect, cursing. She tried to drop Jevryn's sword too, but Lethe-Alihana refused to let her let go. Desperate, she reached out with the only other resource she had, and tried to Hide the other half of the soul. If she could Hide it from the bond, then maybe as the bond died, it wouldn't take the soul with it.

But the drain on her magic was too intense. The bond *knew* the soul was there; its entire purpose was to latch onto it. Her mind raced. She couldn't Hide the soul from the bond, but maybe she could Hide the *bond* from the *soul*.

Kaliaris, if they feel the bond vanish, tell them not to try and hold it. Tell them to let it go.

She Hid the bond. At first, it was nearly as painful a drain as trying to Hide the soul had been. But Kaliaris must have gotten through, because then that drain dwindled from a torrent to a trickle. The soul could not entirely forget that they were bound, but they could *want* to forget. Enough that her magic could hold the Hiding in place. And so long as she held it, the effects of that bond were nullified.

If Kiev had been alive, the bond fully intact, she could never had managed this. But with the damage done, with the soul's compliance, she had just enough to hold the Hiding until the last of the magic fueling the bond died, and it blinked out. The soul inside Kiev's sword shuddered. Through Kaliaris, she felt them flicker, and feared they would die anyway.

<Weakened,> Kaliaris assured her. <But they will live.>

Through Jevryn's sword, Lethe-Alihana raged in her mind. The ferocity of it drove her to knees. They invaded her body, her senses, trying to reach *through* her to Kaliaris, and through Kaliaris to the other half of their soul.

"Nyx? What do you need?" It was Griff, at her side. She had a moment to feel relief—that he was safe, that he was unharmed—and then Lethe-Alihana tried to batter their way through her again.

"Get me and Kaden out of the Station. Throw us across the border if you have to."

Kaliaris drove them out of the Heart with record speed. She tried to leave Kiev's sword behind, but Jevryn's had latched onto it somehow, as if an invisible force locked the two together. Once in the Arrival Room, where Kaliaris no longer had fine control, Griff took over. Space folded and they were at the boundary. The ground beneath her bucked, tumbling her, Kaden, and Kiev's body over the border.

Kiev's sword moved, drawn toward Jevryn's. Nyx grabbed it, forcing the two away from each other, but the attraction between them was strong. She didn't know how long she could hold them apart, and if they clashed, she suspected one of them was dying.

Kaden grabbed on to the hilt of Kiev's sword with her, driving it into the ground. Then he grabbed Jevryn's, driving it into the ground as well. It helped, but it wouldn't for long.

"Portal stone in my right pocket," she told him. "I need Jevryn. *Now*." Her father was the only one who could control the half of the soul bonded to him, and since the sword wouldn't let her go, she would have to bring Jevryn to the sword. She would go herself, but if she portaled and the two halves of Lethe-Alihana went with her, would she lose control of them in the moment of transit? She didn't know and couldn't risk it. Holding them apart *now* was all she could focus on.

Kaden dug into her pocket, pulling out the stone Jevryn had left for her at the bottom of Lehine's well what seemed like a lifetime ago. He didn't waste time on words. He crushed the stone. She caught a glimpse of Jevryn's library, then Kaden was through and the portal closed behind him.

She clung to the sword, hoping Kaden and Jevryn would reappear, but the seconds, then minutes, dragged by. Her only saving grace was that Lethe-Alihana was so intent upon their other half that at first that they did not seem to recognize what was interfering with their ability to reach it: namely, Nyx.

Then the hilt began to heat. Nyx reached for Constance, changed her mind and unwound Gleipnir from her wrist. She didn't know how much stress Constance could withstand but Gleipnir was, in theory, unbreakable. She looped one end around Lethe-Alihana just as the heat became unbearable against her skin, looped the other end around her right hand several times, and held on.

Then Gleipnir too began to warm, heat traveling from Lethe-Alihana through the metal. *Shit. Shit, shit, shit.* At first it was just warm. Then uncomfortable. Then her skin began to burn.

A portal tore open, depositing her father and Kaden. Jevryn, thunder in his eyes, strode forward and wrenched Lethe-Alihana from the ground. The connection between the two swords wavered, then broke, and Gleipnir went cool in an instant. Nyx rapidly unwound the chain from her hand, wincing. She hadn't held it long enough for it to burn terribly—no worse than accidentally bumping her arm against the open door of a hot oven—but it was yet another injury at the end of a very long injury-filled day. Exhausted, trembling, the painkiller on her abdominal wounds wearing off at a rapid rate, Nyx looked into her father's furious face and said, "Hi."

That muscle beneath his left eye twitched. He slid Lethe-Alihana into its scabbard and a shifting circle of black smoke erupted around her and Jevryn, cutting off all outside sight and sound.

"*Hi?*" he echoed. "I have been scouring every corner of the universe for you for days. I have barely slept, I have barely eaten. I feared you dead or worse, which you very well might have been had I not returned home when I did to find Kaden waiting, and you open with *Hi?*

"Of all the inane, foolish, reckless things you could possibly have—"

Nyx took two steps and threw her arms around him in a tight hug, careful to keep her burned hand from actually touching anything. She hadn't realized she'd missed Jevryn until that moment. Hadn't realized that, for all she'd spent the last six months verbally sparring with him and being as difficult as possible, she had taken comfort in the fact that he had never given up on her. She'd thought he had done it out of a sense of obligation, because Griff had asked him to, but his eyes, as he'd gone on his tirade just now, had been a particular shade of orange that she now knew was fear.

Was he angry with her? Yes. But it was an anger born, at least partially, out of fear for her.

"I'm sorry," she said.

He blew out a breath. Carefully, awkwardly, he folded his arms around her. "It is selfish of me to ask, but please never do anything like this again. Do not force me to suffer your loss, child."

"I…" She couldn't exactly promise that. "I'll try. I'm not very good at staying away from trouble."

"I am aware. Please try diligently, anyway."

A very important fact clawed its way up her throat, one she had to get out. "Laiveran's gone. I don't know how, but he helped Kiev enter Kaliaris's Heart, and now he's just gone."

Jevryn's arms tensed around her, but all he said, was: "We will handle it." He let her go and stepped back, looking down. She followed his gaze, and only then did she realize Kiev's body was inside the death circle with them. It hit her, truly hit her, that she'd killed Jevryn's brother. Not just his brother, but his *twin*. Kiev had been terrible, yes. But he had also been family. Would Jevryn hold his death against her, just a little?

His face was as impassive as ever, but his irises were changing colors so quickly it was like looking into a spinning kaleidoscope. He crouched, studying the form that had once started out identical to his own, and gained distinction only as time and events had left their marks on them both.

"So this is what you've come to, after all this time," he said softly. Nyx didn't think he meant her to hear him, but it seemed he'd forgotten her for the moment. "I thought I might feel sorrow, when this moment finally came to pass. You were not entirely without moments of…fraternity, in our youth. But it appears you hollowed out all remnant care from me sometime throughout these many centuries. And I find, now, that I only feel as if one of the many stains I have left upon this universe has finally been wiped clean." He reached out, placing two fingers to Kiev's forehead. "I will that death would keep you, Brother, and never see fit to return any part of you to this world. Some things ought only be born once."

The body beneath Jevryn's fingers disintegrated, turning to ash.

But where he had once solidified the ash of Seth's body into the rock that now rested in the hollow of Nyx's throat, Kiev remained only ash. The individual specks began to glow with faint blue as Jevryn wrapped them in portal magic. Nyx felt for the intent—the destination—and the scope left her reeling as, several seconds later, Kiev's remains were scattered to a thousand different places in the universe. As if Jevryn never wanted any part of Kiev to be reunited with another. And there, left behind in the emptiness, was the soul shard Nyx had forced Kiev to swallow, the one that had been intent on poisoning him from the inside out.

For a long moment, Jevryn only stared at that shard. Then he stood, the kaleidoscope colors of his eyes settling once more to a calm silver, and collected the scrap of soul. He grimaced and offered it to her in the palm of his hand. "Hold on to this."

Nyx took it. *Daughter,* the shard babbled happily in her mind. *Daughter daughter daughterdaughter. You freed us.*

Nyx sighed and carefully tucked the shard into her pocket. She wasn't sure what it said about her that the only piece of Lethe-Alihana's soul that seemed genuinely fond of her was the unhinged piece.

"I am still quite angry with you," Jevryn informed her. "I have a severe lecture in mind. However, as you are injured, and I can only offer wild conjecture as to what is matted into your hair and staining your clothes, I will defer that lecture until we have all had a chance to rest. Arradin will wish to know that you are well, and I think you owe him a much lengthier apology than the one you have given to me."

Nyx winced. "Maybe we could wait to—"

Jevryn gave her a withering look and the death circle encompassing them vanished. "Kaden, please take possession of *that.*" He pointed at Kiev's sword, still plunged into the ground. His distaste of the weapon was obvious, and she wondered if it was because it was Kiev's, or if it was some remnant of Lethe-Alihana's dislike for their other half, expressing itself through him.

She didn't have much time to ponder it, as Kaden did as he was bid and Jevryn immediately helped Nyx—none-too-gently—across the boundary and onto her Station's grounds. Griff was waiting for them, looking worried, and this was much, much harder to deal with than an angry Jevryn.

Still, her first approach had worked out okay last time, so she tried it again. "Hi."

Griff and Jevryn shared a look.

"I leave her in your hands, Arradin," Jevryn said. He stepped past her, squeezed Griff's shoulder, and walked away to collect Kaden and the sword.

23

G riff raised one wing, forestalling anything further Nyx might say. "You are exhausted, and Morgen has informed me you have wounds that require prompt medical attention. You should shower and have your injuries treated. Anything else that needs to be discussed can wait."

Nyx did not like the phrasing of *anything else that needs to be discussed*, but she was barely on her feet. The more the painkiller on her stomach wore off, the more she very much wanted another one, so she went inside to take the recommended shower. In her room, she put the shard of Lethe-Alihana into a clear glass jar and placed it on her nightstand, where it glowed a soft blue, like a fairy lamp.

In the bathroom, struggling out of her clothes *hurt*, and she only managed it because, now that adrenaline and painkillers were wearing off, common sense was reminding her that roots had burrowed into her stomach in the recent past, and she would like actual medical attention for that. She left the waterproof bandage around her waist while she soaped up, then shampooed and conditioned her hair. When she finally peeled the bandaging off, wincing as it stuck to the wounds, she decided it was a good thing she'd attended to hygiene before unwrapping it. Because if she'd seen what her stomach looked like first off, she wouldn't have cleaned anything.

No, she would have done exactly what she did now, which was, more or less, panic. She turned off the water, dried as quickly as possible, and barely remembered to thrown on a pair of sweatpants and a bra before running into her bedroom.

"Griff, I think I need—" She cut off, as there were two occupants in her bedroom.

"Anti-toxin for a fourth-molt resurrection plant?" Jevryn finished for her. He stood next to Griff, a truly impressive glower on his face. "You should have mentioned this immediately. Lie down."

"If I had any idea what a fourth molt resurrection plant was, I'm sure I would have." But she did as ordered, dropping gingerly onto her mattress. The two punctures in her stomach had turned into hot, knotted areas the size of golf balls, her skin was angry and red, her abdomen was on fire, and now that she could partially feel again, it felt very wrong.

"A simple 'a carnivorous plant dug roots into my body' would have sufficed." Jevryn had absolutely no bedside manner, which meant he didn't warn her before jabbing her with another two needles full of painkiller.

"Fine. If I find myself in that situation again, I'll mention it straightaway." The injections burned as they spread through her, but when they melted into blissful numbness, she discovered this painkiller was *much* stronger than what Morgen had carried with him. So much stronger that it felt like her body, from midway down her ribcage all the way to her knees, had ceased to exist.

"I'm missing part of my body," she said. The words came out as loopy sounding as she suddenly felt. What the hell was in those injections?

"It will come back, I assure you," Jevryn said. "Arradin, would you mind?"

Griff jumped onto the bed, having shrunk to the size of a St. Bernard, and placed one heavy talon on her chest, as if he was there to prevent her from getting up.

"I'm not going anywhere," she told him happily. "I can't even feel my—wait, what the fuck are those for?" Panic tried valiantly to surface through her drugged state. Jevryn was holding a scalpel and what looked like a pair of forceps on steroids.

"Your language truly is appalling."

"No, you're just *old*."

"I shall remind myself that you cannot be blamed for what you say under the influence of Bliss. I do not recommend watching this."

"What are you going to *do?*" And who named a medical drug Bliss?

Jevryn cut across the first golf-ball sized legion. Nyx didn't feel a thing as her skin split open and blood gushed out, mixed with green and yellow ooze. She would have been nauseous, but apparently Bliss counteracted nausea, too.

"The resurrection plant was native to our homeworld."

Well, that explained why it ate death magic.

"In order to reproduce, it requires a host that carries death magic, and thus can provide the seedlings with the nutrients they require as they grow. Going anywhere near the lagoons in the breeding season is an invitation to a slow, painful death."

Nyx really, really did not like where this was going. Jevryn traded the scalpel for a pair of surgical retractors and used them to hold the cut open. Then he took a pair of forceps and plunged them into the incision.

"Once implanted, the seeds grow at an alarming rate. Fortunately, Morgen mistook the side effects of the plant's implantation process for a toxin, as the binding agent he used to slow a toxin is also capable of successfully paralyzing the seed's growth process until it wears off."

Jevryn made a clamping motion and, slowly and carefully, pulled the forceps up. A pale, bean-sized seed was clamped between the two metal arms, and it was *wriggling.* Long, spindly roots descended from the seed, disappearing into her stomach.

"Jevryn," her voice was high and panicked. Griff pressed firmly down on her chest, but she wasn't trying to move. She was too terrified that if she moved, the roots would break, and tiny pieces of them would be forever lodged inside her body.

"It will be fine, *na'tria.*"

"Do not leave pieces of that thing inside me."

"Their roots are very strong, even at this stage. They will not break off in you. That strength would be an issue had they been allowed to grow for another few minutes, but at this stage they have not wrapped around anything vital, and will not cause irreparable harm in the removal process." The last of the roots pulled free, and Jevryn dropped the seed into an Erlenmeyer flask filled with red liquid. Griff reached over and placed a wooden stopper into the flask.

"You're keeping it?" Nyx asked incredulously.

"I will dispose of it safely." Jevryn moved to the other puncture wound.

"Are you sure you got it all?"

"Quite sure."

"Please be certain. I do not want to be mother to the next generation of creepy corpse-eating plants. Why is this happening to me?"

Jevryn sliced across the other puncture and pried the incision open. "It is happening because you chose to impulsively walk directly into a trap set by a man who had no scruples about killing you in the most unpleasant way possible."

"Fine. Okay, but—wait. You said this thing grew on your planet? So Lethe-Alihana knew what it was?"

"It would be quite impossible for them not to, they did create it."

"They failed to mention it."

Jevryn paused, forceps poised above the incision, and gave her a look. "Of course they failed to mention it. Had they mentioned it, I have to believe that even you would have had the good sense to abandon your chosen folly and seek medical treatment, at which point they would not have gotten what they wanted.

"I have some fondness for Lethe-Alihana, but you must remember that they do not think in the same way that you do. They are not mortal. Consider that, the next time you decide to take off on an ill-advised vengeance quest under the guidance of something far more powerful than yourself."

Nyx had no good response for that, so she decided that perhaps now was the time to shut up and close her eyes, so she didn't have to see the thing that had almost used her as a breeding host as it was pulled out of her body. Closing her eyes, however, invited the exhaustion of the day to take hold, and she'd almost fallen asleep when she heard Jevryn talking.

"—will require twice-daily cleaning and regular checks for infection. And of course it will scar, but there is no helping that. I advise—"

She drifted off for a minute, then woke again to the soothing feel of Griff's talons stroking through her hair. Jevryn was gone.

"I'm sorry," Griff said, "I did not meant to wake you."

"It's okay."

He stretched and resettled his wings. "Nyx…there is something I need to say to you. I did not mean to make you feel abandoned, when I sent you to Jevryn. I did not mean to make you feel as if you were not wanted."

"Griff—"

He raised a wing. "Allow me to say this. I never intended to hurt you, and I am sorry that I did. But I was frightened, and I did not know how to help you. I thought perhaps he could, and if I could go back, I would still make the same decision. Because he did help you, and I am not certain that I could have.

"I hope you can forgive me for it. I hope you can understand that I was trying to do what was best for you, in the only way I knew how." He rose. "I will leave you to rest, now."

She reached for him and missed. "Wait." She struggled to rise, then gave up because she still couldn't feel most of the lower half of her body. Her head felt muzzy from the drugs, and thinking was difficult. "It did hurt. I was angry. It felt like everyone just wanted me to go away for a while and come back normal, with all of my problems fixed."

Griff's eyes closed, and she had the sense that she was messing this up, but it was so damn hard to think through the fog in her brain. "But I wasn't punishing you. I didn't stay away to hurt *you.* Jevryn was right. I didn't come home because I didn't think Kaliaris would let me leave again. Not for as long as I might need to be gone."

"I—" He broke off, head canted at that angle Nyx equated with a human frown. "I did not say that I felt you were punishing me. Or share Jevryn's conjectures on why you remained away."

Shit. This was what she got for talking while high on pain meds.

Griff's head straightened. "The missing illusion vials. You were *here.* And neither I nor Kaliaris knew. How?"

Busted. "Hidden magic. It only worked because Kaliaris wasn't expecting me to be here." And now that she'd said that out loud, and Kaliaris had certainly heard it, it was never going to work again. Great.

"Nyx," Griff began, his voice clearly uncomfortable, "precisely how long were you eavesdropping for?"

Given that Jevryn had appeared in his home library only a few minutes after she'd returned that night, she guessed that whatever they'd talked about that Griff didn't want her to have heard had been spoken of *before* she'd arrived.

"I walked by when you were talking about me being angry with you, and then I left when you asked Jevryn to stay."

"I see." He relaxed.

"Are you two…?"

"My personal relationship with Jevryn remains my personal relationship with Jevryn."

"Right. Sorry." Maybe she could ask Jevryn. "I just meant that if you *are*, I'm okay with it."

He gave her a look.

"I hear some people are weird about their parents getting back together, and I just want you to know that I'm not. Weird about it."

"Am I to take it your relationship with your father has improved?" Griff asked, pointedly evading the subject of him and Jevryn.

She winced. "Umm…I kind of implied he might be willing to kill his own daughter so I could throw him off guard long enough to steal his soul sword, which led to me accidentally locking him out of his own portal well, and then I disappeared, which apparently caused him stress, and then I killed his twin brother." Wow, it sounded bad when she put it like that.

Griff sighed, heavily.

She continued babbling, because this lovely drug she was on apparently made her babble. "But considering we didn't *have* a relationship before, maybe that counts as an improvement? Or at least, there is a relationship that can now be improved upon? What do you think?"

"I think you need rest." He pulled the blanket up, over her shoulders, and she snuggled into it. Yes, sleep sounded nice, except—

"I'm sorry I hurt you. I didn't mean to. I just—*I* hurt and I didn't know what to do with it." She still hurt. She still didn't know what to do with it. "I didn't know how to be around anyone."

Gently, he said, "You are not the only person to have shut someone out because you were in pain. You would not even be the only person in this room to have done so. And I assure you, six months is far less a time to ignore a person than eight-hundred years.

"So sleep, and do not worry over it." Griff tucked the blanket around her. "The hurt we have done each other is not of a kind that cannot be repaired."

She started to do just that, but another thought jerked her back to wakefulness. "Wait. Ilera."

Griff's head canted. "Ilera A-Morridahn?"

Nyx nodded. "Her body. Kiev kept it. I promised I wouldn't leave her like that."

"I understand."

"And there's a Shaman. Kiev's Shaman. Tira. In his home. She's loyal to him but she can't be left there."

"I will tell Jevryn. He will handle it. Rest."

24

The next morning, Nyx did not want to rest. She didn't entirely know what she wanted to do, or if *want* was even the right word, but she knew that lying in bed was not it. She had had enough of her own thoughts, and if people were right that vengeance didn't fix anything, it *had* quieted the voice in her head that said she hadn't done enough.

She wasn't sorry Kiev was dead. She didn't regret her actions. His presence in the universe was no longer a weight upon her shoulders. He would never again harm anyone else. He would never again take away someone's lover or daughter or brother or friend. He would never again taunt Griff and Jevryn with the servitude he had locked Griff into.

He would never again do *anything*. And that? That was worth something. The wrath in her had died with Kiev, and now? Now she had to figure out how to live again. How to be *Nyx* again when she didn't feel like her.

But she had to start somewhere, so she imitated, playing herself like it was a role in a film. She cleaned and re-bandaged her wounds according to the meticulously written instructions Griff had left on her nightstand. At the insistent beating of the soul shard against their glass jar when she tried to leave without them, Nyx placed them into her pocket before heading downstairs to receive the morning's Arrival. It was only four people—a family—and once they exited the Station, Nyx wandered into the cafe.

In Kalvar's absence, a silver bell had been placed on the counter with instructions that said: "Ring for service." Being in this space, she was hit with the guilt of not having said goodbye to him, of having been oblivious to his departure. And being in this space, she was hit with a false memory a Mindwitch had conjured, of Seth cooking behind the counter, of two little girls who would never exist.

She gritted her teeth and banished the image, walked over to the silver bell and rang it. Morgen came in, followed by Evra. Nyx raised her eyebrows at the Amazon also answering the service ring. "Please tell me you didn't let Evra make the coffee while I was gone." Maybe Nyx had raised her eyebrows a beat late, and maybe her voice lacked full sarcastic conviction, but it was what she would have said before, so she said it. She was trying.

"Once," Morgen said. "And only the once."

"It wasn't *that* bad," Evra muttered.

"You steamed the milk hot enough to give a base Human third-degree burns."

"It wasn't *for* a base Human, it was for a Livkai. They light their food on fire and eat it while it's still burning. I thought they would appreciate the personalization and knowledge of their culture."

"They might like charred meat, but burned milk is appealing to no one."

"How was I supposed to know that?" Evra demanded.

Nyx found a smile working its way onto her face. It was a small one, but it was another start. She drank coffee. She ate breakfast even though she wasn't hungry, and if it was obvious that Evra and Morgen's continued bantering was a little over the top, well, she didn't mind that they were trying to make her smile.

And when Kaden came in as she was finishing and said, "Your father wants to see you," she valiantly restrained herself from asking if he was Jevryn's personal messenger now. He *had* helped her instead of dragging her back to Jevryn, so she figured he'd earned a short reprieve where the sharpness of her tongue was concerned.

She sank into the Station's senses until she located Jevryn, then went to the library. He sat at the end of a low-backed couch, and

Griff had abandoned his preferred lounging spot on the backless couch to stretch out beside him. They were both reading, but Griff was using Jevryn's thigh as a bookstand, and Jevryn's arm was draped along the back of the couch, his fingertips just brushing the edge of Griff's wing.

Yeah, they had definitely gotten a lot cozier with each other in the last six months. "You wanted to see me?"

Jevryn looked up. "How are you feeling?"

"Like I almost had my body eaten alive by baby death plants but was saved by amateur surgery instead?"

"Ah. Fine, then, if your sarcasm is any indication."

She shrugged. Was she okay? Yes. Fine? That word didn't feel like it fit her yet.

"I took care of the matter you expressed to Arradin last night. Your grandmother has been laid to rest. Along with the others."

The tension Nyx had carried since seeing Ilera A-Morridahn finally eased. "And Tira?"

"That matter is resolved."

Nyx didn't like the way that sounded. "What do you mean 'resolved'?"

"She took her own life."

"What?" Nyx didn't bother to hide her shock.

"A Shaman should never be held to healing one person exclusively, Nyx. Even as few as three healings on the same individual in too short a time can form a bond between the two that skews the Shaman's emotions and reason. Consistently healing the same individual for decades? For centuries?" He shook his head. "The moment Kiev died, it was only a matter of time before she followed."

Nyx closed her eyes, letting the knowledge of Tira's death pass through her. It was already done, and there was nothing she could do to change it. She opened her eyes. "Is that all you called me here for?" To tell her that a grandmother she'd never met had at last been offered dignity in death, and that Kiev had managed to take a final victim with him, even after his passing?

"No. I require your help with something. Arradin? Would you mind?"

Griff closed his book and sat up. Nyx felt him plucking through the threads of the Station, then the floor bubbled and Kiev's sword slid through. There was a chunk missing from the center of the crossguard, the kind of hollow left when a jewel had been pried free of a setting.

"I believe," Jevryn said, "from what Lethe-Alihana has shared with me of your time together, that you understand the importance of this?"

Nyx's gaze flicked to Griff, then back to Jevryn. "Yes."

"I cannot speak to them. Though I have spent the night discussing matters with Lethe-Alihana, they refuse to be reasoned with, and so it is not safe for me to attempt communication with their other half. I would like you to speak with them."

Nyx hesitated. What would this half of her planet's soul be like, after so much time spent only with Kiev?

She must have remained silent too long, because Griff said, "If you do not wish to, we have discussed the matter and I am willing to try."

"No," she said quickly. She didn't know this half of Lethe-Alihana, and she didn't trust the one she *did* know. Was this half more like Kiev? What might they say to Griff? What terrible things had they been privy to in Kiev's mind? "I'll do it."

Before she could back out, she closed her eyes and grasped the sword's hilt. Silence greeted her, as if she'd plunged into an icy lake, so still and deep that the sunlight couldn't penetrate.

Hello?

A ripple went through the lake. *Are you to be my next keeper then, Nyx A-Morridahn? How do you compare to the rest of your family, I wonder?*

I'm not here to control you.

You are lying to yourself, if you believe that to be true. You fear me, and everyone seeks to control that which they fear.

She took a deep breath. *I fear that you might hurt people I care about. Kiev did so many things. I don't want you to show those things to them. To Griff or Jevryn.*

No? And what if I were to show them to you? What if I were to hurt you?

They pulled forth a memory and she dropped into it, into *Kiev.*

Elena Kormadin stood before him, having just told him that his brother had sired a child. He would not have believed her had she not given him a very interesting name for that child: Nyx Fortuna.

That had been the name of the little upstart on Earth's Station, the one Jevryn had tried to protect. Kiev had assumed he'd done so for Arradin's benefit, but now...now he wondered. She had had something of Ilera A-Morridahn in her features, now that he thought to look. But...she also had something of this woman in her. And that was so very interesting.

"She is your get too, is she not?" The woman's eyes flared for the briefest moment, and he laughed. "Come now, you did not think you could reveal her and not yourself? I am curious though, as to how you managed it. You are—how shall I put this?—not of a type to be of my brother's liking."

He had never wondered overmuch about his brother's sexuality. There had never been much point, as Jevryn had expressed his interest precisely once in almost ten centuries of life. Jevryn was entirely obsessed with Arradin Thesrani and, near as Kiev could tell, had never once strayed from that obsession. Kiev very much doubted his brother had chosen to do so for this creature, of all the ones available in the universe.

He could see the calculations running in the woman's eyes, before she settled on the truth as the most expedient option. "Bloodshot will work wonders on a person."

Kiev laughed. Of all the things to be brought low by, his brother had allowed himself to be drugged. "You come to me to bargain with this information. Have you not considered what I might do to the girl?"

Elena Kormadin's eyes hardened. "What happens to her is no concern of mine."

Ah, so there was the real reason she was here. She wanted to be rid of her daughter, and she thought to use him to do it.

The memory dissolved, reformed into another, one Nyx was certain had occurred earlier in time than the one she'd just relived.

The screams coming from the corner of the room had grown quieter in the last hour, though Kiev marveled at the fact they continued at all. He'd been alive for so long, had seen so much in this universe, and yet he never ceased to be amazed by how much a creature would endure simply for the hope of some future in which they were not forced to endure.

The man recently admitted into the room stood before Kiev impassively, without ever having so much as glanced at the originator of those screams. Either the sounds didn't bother him—or they bothered him too much.

Kiev drummed his fingers on the arm of his chair. "Kaden Moor. My brother was foolish to send you to me. And you were twice the fool to come."

"I am here of my own accord."

Kiev laughed. "I very much doubt that. But I will let you attempt to convince me. Tell me, then. Why have you come, when I am certain Jevryn must have offered a great deal to keep you at his side."

Kaden shrugged. "He promised me something he couldn't deliver."

Now that was interesting. "Something," he asked, "or someone?"

No answer. Kaden Moor was sensible enough to keep his mouth shut, at least. Not that it mattered.

"What is it about that girl that obsesses everyone?" Kiev mused. She was nothing. She was less than nothing. And yet she seemed to be the epicenter of so many interesting events of late.

Kaden didn't answer.

"Do you want her?" Kiev asked. "The Guardian from Earth? I could give her to you." He wouldn't, of course. In the fallout after the creation of the Stations, Jevryn had ensured that Earth fell under his purview, and he guarded it ruthlessly. It was obvious Arradin was fond of the girl and, for that reason alone, Jevryn would never give approval for her Guardianship to be revoked. And Kiev had, as of yet, no compelling reason to cross his brother when it came to Earth and Arradin.

But Kaden didn't know any of that. And one of two things was certainly true: either Kaden was here to spy for Jevryn—in which case Kiev was about to put him through a great deal of unpleasantness for no gain to Jevryn—or Kaden was here because he truly believed a girl was worth a fool's bargain. In the end, it didn't matter which it was. Kiev had uses for him either way.

The memory dissolved again, Lethe-Alihana ending it before Kaden gave an answer. They were trying to unsettle her, and they thought showing her this moment, this terrible thing Kiev had offered, but not letting her see Kaden's response, would rattle her. But she didn't need to see it. Kaden Moor was far from a perfect person. But the kind of man who was so obviously haunted by the things Kiev had made him do was not the kind of man who would accept a *person* in trade.

Lethe-Alihana's irritation rose, and a new memory forced its way into her mind.

Kiev looked at the man on the floor. Arradin was slumped against the chains that held him. He'd rubbed his wrists raw on the manacles, and Kiev had had to cut his wing joints to prevent his more desperate struggles.

He'd underestimated just how much power those wings could generate, and Arradin had snapped one chain from the wall before Kiev had cut the wings. He walked to the prone form and nudged Arradin's face with the toe of his boot.

Those hated golden eyes snapped open, spitting with fury. Arradin lunged upward, but even if his hands had been free, after three days with minimal food, and multiple injuries, the man could barely stand.

"Have you reconsidered my offer?" Kiev asked.

"No."

Kiev sighed. "You really should. What has Jevryn done to inspire such loyalty? He abandoned you. So much time spent together, and when things became difficult, he tossed you aside. He left you vulnerable, and to me of all people." He stepped forward and cupped Arradin's face in his hand. Whatever Jevryn saw in the man was invisible to Kiev. Whatever spark lived between them when they touched was not there for him.

"Go back to him," he prodded gently. He could be gentle, when it was necessary. "He will take an audience with you, no matter what he claims to the contrary. Drive a knife through his heart and all this pain will be over. Your bruises healed, your wings restored. And I promise that you will never see me again."

Arradin's eyes bored into him. Kiev had always hated the way the man could look at him, the way he seemed to assess him and find him wanting. As if Arradin's opinion or his judgment mattered. He was nothing, and he would have lived and died in obscurity had Jevryn not plucked him from the cosmos.

And Kiev never could tell what he was thinking.

Arradin's head tilted slightly, leaning into his touch, but his eyes never left Kiev's. "You touch me, because you imagine it can remind me of him. Because you look like him. But do you know what I feel from you? Do you know what I feel when I do this?" Arradin turned his head, his lips pressing to the inside of Kiev's wrist. It was a slow kiss, sensual, his tongue licking across the delicate skin before he drew back, his eyes cold. "Nothing.

Because you are nothing. You are hollow, Kiev A-Morridahn, and you will always be hollow.

"So kill me if you wish. But I will not return to Jevryn in some foolish attempt to murder him so that he is forced to kill me instead. Because I know that that is the pain you want to cause him."

Kiev's anger rose and he jerked his hand away. But he restrained himself from ending the man's worthless life on the spot. "I will not kill you, Arradin Thesrani. Though I promise that some day soon, you will wish I had. Still, I am not entirely unkind, so I will tell you of your future, so that I may make you an offer. You are going to live for centuries, once I'm done with you. By the end of it you will not recognize yourself, and you will have no freedom and no peace. You will be a construct at the whim of others, a thing no one will ever view as a person. It will eat at you, century after century, until you can no longer stand it. So here is the offer: at any time in those long years to come, do what I have asked of you, and I will undo your suffering."

There was no love that could withstand that much time and pain. And Kiev would enjoy the day Jevryn was forced to kill his precious lover. The day he finally realized that Arradin Thesrani was nothing special. That he was unworthy of A-Morridahn attention.

The memory dissolved, began once more to reform, this time to a planetary surface Nyx was all too familiar with, to a moment in time she would give anything to undo.

"Stop," Nyx ordered. Miraculously, they did. The memory washed away and she opened her eyes, finding Griff's. She couldn't focus on what she'd almost had to relive, so she focused on the last thing she *had.*

Griff. All this time, he'd lived with the knowledge that he could be free at any moment—if he killed the man he loved. She thought she understood, now, why he'd chosen to lose his identity to the blank persona of the Station's Avatar. He'd been afraid that one day, Kiev's offer would tempt him. So he hadn't wanted to remember that offer existed.

She opened her mouth, but Griff must have had some inkling of what she'd seen, because he shook his head, and she clamped her mouth shut. Not her secret to tell.

"What did you see?" Jevryn asked.

"Not what I needed to." She closed her eyes again, and slipped once more into that icy lake. Silently, to Lethe-Alihana alone, she asked, *Why? Why show me these things?*

Why not show them to you? This is what I have lived with for centuries. You would like a piece of the knowledge I have gained from that experience, but you do not wish the wealth of that experience for yourself.

Should I? she countered. *I didn't do this to you. Jevryn and Griff didn't do this to you. Kiev did, and I killed him. I stopped you from dying with him. I stopped your other half from killing you. Maybe, instead of showing me terrible things, you could try a simple* thank you.

You did none of those things for me.

Yet you benefited from them. I am asking you for one simple thing in return—for you to show me how to free Griff.

And what becomes of me, daughter of Jevryn, when I have served the purpose you seek to use me for?

Nyx didn't answer for a moment. It wasn't something she'd given thought to, and she felt them laugh in her mind as she recognized as much. They couldn't remain with Jevryn—their other half would keep trying to kill them. Unless…

Can you be made whole again?

The better question is, if I could, would I even wish to be? Our two halves have been diverged for nearly a millennium.

Nyx nearly growled in frustration. *What is with the two of you? Do you honestly both believe that the other part of you isn't* you?

Did you not have the same concern? You were not physically split apart, but your mind was fragmented, and I can feel that you hesitated to repair it. Hesitated to discover whether the you *that you were familiar with would remain the same once it was melded with the* you *that you once were.*

So tell me, they continued, *are you not changed? Do you not regret your choice?*

Nyx shook her head. *No. I don't regret it. And yes, I am changed. But I was missing a part of myself. Was I worried reclaiming it would make me something I didn't recognize? Yes. But it didn't. Because that missing part of me was still* me. *Reclaiming it made me more, not less.*

A deep hum went through the icy waters of the lake in her mind. *Perhaps. But I am, for the first time in centuries, unbound. To merge with the other half of my soul would mean being bound once more. While Jevryn may be different from his brother, I will not willingly be bound to anyone ever again. But the wound Kiev dealt me is more recent, and it festers still. So I would accept the return of that which was carved from me.*

As if on cue, the soul shard in Nyx's pocket began to seek escape like a trapped firefly. She grasped it in her fist and pulled it from her pocket.

Daughter, they said happily. *You freed us once, free us again.*

She opened her fist. The soul shard flew to the sword like a metal shaving to a magnet. It fit perfectly in the hollow of the crossguard, the metal of the sword closing around it, until the shard looked like a glittering sapphire jewel that had always rested in precisely that spot.

Nyx didn't know how long it took half a soul to reacquaint itself with a missing soul shard, so she waited. The answer was a few minutes, or at least, that was all the time it took them to speak to her again. When they did, their tone was a little more polite, a little less tense, as if the return of the shard had mellowed them.

For the return of that which was taken from me, you have my thanks.

Any chance that appreciation extends to telling me what I need to know? Nyx asked hopefully.

A lengthy pause greeted her. Then: *I have said that I will not be bound to another being ever again. But if I show you what you wish to know, you will have within your possession everything needed to perform such a binding. Because to understand how to break the bond that holds Arradin and your Station, you must first understand how they were made. Given that, perhaps you can understand my reluctance, for what guarantee do I have that I will not find myself bound to you, as I was once bound to Kiev?*

Nyx, as she had an unfortunate habit of doing, blurted out the first response that came to mind. *Because I'm not a monster? Because I am already bound and I understand what that's like? Because I've already promised to undo every bond that's been created?*

They laughed. *Do you think monsters are born, Nyx A-Morridahn? A tendency toward capriciousness may be innate, but to become monstrous requires cultivation. That you are not a monster now does not mean you cannot become one, given the time and the inclination. And every promise can be broken. What guarantee do I have that given enough time, you will not do both?*

She could give them no guarantee, so she didn't. *You don't. I can't make you trust me. But ask yourself this: is your current existence one you want for yourself? Trapped in a sword for all eternity? Because I am your one and only chance at getting out of that.*

They were silent for so long that she thought they would still refuse. But in the end, they said, *Perhaps there is some wisdom in what you say. Very well. I will show you what you wish to know, and in return, I will remain with you until such time as your promise is fulfilled.*

And that didn't sound like a threat to keep an eye on her at all times. Not at all.

A threat should be of no concern if you intend to do as you have said. And it is not wholly for that reason that I remain with you. A planet should be with their people, after all. And you and Jevryn are all that are left of mine. Now, let me show you what you wish to know.

And so she slipped into another memory, one that began as Lethe-Alihana's alone. She felt their pain as they were ripped apart and bound, and so she knew, precisely, the pain Griff had felt as it had been done to him.

Her heart broke anew, and she wished that Kiev were not yet dead, so she could kill him all over again. But the pain that she experienced in the memory was long in the past, and now? Now she knew who they needed to talk to.

25

Nyx felt the weight of Jevryn's presence at her side as they entered the Warlock's shop. She realized she had never before been in his company in any public place. In his home and in her Station, he felt more like an ordinary person. But now, standing with him in public, it felt like carrying a nuclear weapon around while trying to reassure everyone who saw it that the bomb wasn't in danger of going off any time soon.

She wasn't even sure that anyone recognized him for who he actually was—near as she could tell, the councilors were invisible in the lives of ordinary citizens, who were far more concerned with the immediate governing bodies on their own planets and in their own cities than they were with the distant members of the All Council— but he could wear power and authority like a cloak and he did so now, radiating with his stance and cool gaze and the hum of magic beneath his skin that here was a man who should not be crossed.

The Warlock's shop emptied of customers within thirty seconds of them walking through the door. Nyx tried and failed not to look at the spot where she'd portaled to in a frenzy so many months before. Tried and failed not to feel the weight of the rock at her throat, the tickle of the feather earring against her neck. Her chest tightened, like the moment was as fresh as it had been then.

Jevryn followed her gaze. Then he put his hand on her back, guiding her forward, until the space was no longer in her vision. It took her a moment, with everything, to realize the Warlock stood behind the counter of her shop, and her face was bloodless.

"Councilor," she said stiffly. "I assure you I can think of no reason for your visit." Beneath the stiffness was fear.

Nyx looked between them, settling on Jevryn. "Please tell me you didn't threaten her." Until that moment, she hadn't taken the time to realize that her hasty portaling into the Warlock's shop so many months ago was something Jevryn would very much have wanted hushed up.

"Of course not," Jevryn said.

Nyx crossed her arms. "So you said nothing?"

"Ah. I do recall pointing out the numerous hazards of everyday life that may befall a person if they are unfortunate. And that I have found misfortune comes easily to those whose tongues are far too loose."

Okay, then. "I apologize for"—she stopped before saying "my father" and went with—"Councilor A-Morridahn. He doesn't socialize often."

The Warlock, who hadn't looked at Nyx once since she'd walked in, did so now. "What can I do for you, Guardian?"

The use of Nyx's title and the businesslike tone told her that any hope she'd had of repairing their relationship had died months ago with whatever Jevryn had said to the Warlock. She cleared her throat. "I'd like to talk to Tobi."

The Warlock's fingers dug into the countertop. "No."

"I am afraid," Jevryn said icily, "that you do not have the luxury of refusing."

Ankira's gaze whipped to Nyx. "Is this who you are now?"

Guilt bit into her. She'd never intended to threaten the Warlock. She hadn't had any idea that Jevryn already had. She'd just known they needed a Shaman and Tobi was conveniently nearby. She put her hand on Jevryn's arm. "We can go to someone else."

Jevryn looked at her. "Since your introduction to the wider universe, you have conveniently had a Shaman at hand whenever you might need one, so I suppose you may not understand how exceedingly rare they are. Most of them reside in healer units within the Enforcer ranks, and are therefore unsuitable for this task. Can I find another who is not? Yes. Will it take time? Again, yes. I am not willing to wait on answers where this matter is concerned."

Knowing Jevryn wouldn't let it go, Nyx turned back to Ankira. "We only want to talk to him. Please?"

The steel in the Warlock's eyes didn't soften. "I believe I was informed the choice was not mine."

"I won't make you."

"You are not the only person in this room."

"Jevryn?" Nyx said softly. "Don't force her to do this."

"You are still young, *na'tria*. Your heart has not yet learned to harden itself against the world, and while that speaks admirably of your character, I fear it does not bode well for your survival."

"Arradin wouldn't want this."

"Arradin would suffer a great many injustices to spare others mere discomfort." He didn't say it, but there was a heavily implied, *That is why he requires* me, at the end.

Nyx's Salyrian wasn't great. As in, she'd only picked up a handful of words and couldn't even speak an entire sentence. But she pulled out a few of those words now, speaking them carefully. The literal translation of what she said was "Do me this honor", but it was the Salyrian equivalent of "Please". She repeated the words, softer this time, and added one more: "Vasi". *Dad.*

He exhaled sharply. "Very well. Since you have interceded so eloquently on her behalf, I will not force her. However"—he narrowed his gaze on the Warlock—"before you refuse, I would ask you something. How long do you think you can continue to pass that boy off as a mere Warlock's apprentice? How long before he slips and heals on instinct, far surpassing a Warlock's ability, and someone understands his true nature?

"Once that happens—and make no mistake that it will—do you truly believe you can protect him? Do you truly believe you will be allowed to keep him? The universe is filled with powerful, wealthy people who would do anything to possess someone who can bring them back from the brink of death.

"They will kill you and take him. If you hide him before they come, they will tear through your life to find him. They will torture you. They will uncover your wife's true identity and sell her back to her family.

"You could go on the run, and perhaps you would even manage to do so successfully. But what kind of life would you be giving him? A new city every few months, a new planet every</p>

year? Even if he did not grow to hate you for it, he would be miserable."

Nyx could see in the Warlock's face that Jevryn had struck a nerve. That he was not saying anything she had not considered before. But he was saying things *Nyx* had not considered before. She hadn't realized, when she'd asked Ankira to take Tobi and Lauralyn, that taking them came with any risk greater than the knowledge of where they had come from. But Ankira had. The others—Evra, Morgen, Kaden—must have known. But at that time, there hadn't been any alternative options, and they must have hoped that the relative obscurity of Earth Between would be enough to keep Tobi from notice.

"There is a reason," Jevryn continued gently, "that when a Shaman manifests, if their family cares for them, they surrender them to the All Council. Within the protective corps of the Enforcers, they are guaranteed safety. I am aware of how the boy came to you, and why there may have been concerns about what might happen to anyone surrendering him. I can remove any such obstacles."

If the Warlock had been angry before, she was practically incandescent now. "I am not giving him over to your blood machine. He is not going to spend his life patching up your soldiers. He is a child. He is *my* child."

"Sometimes what is best for a child is letting them go."

Ankira gave him a look that would have withered a lesser man and said, clearly, "No. Your own laws require parental consent to take him. I do not consent."

Jevryn took this in stride, clearly having expected the refusal, regardless of his reasoning. "So you will keep him, then, despite the dangers. Despite knowing that keeping him means he will likely end up in a situation not terribly unlike the one he was recently rescued from.

"So here, then, is my true offer. Let us speak with the boy, and I will guarantee his safety, along with yours and your wife's. Here, on Earth. Should relocation become necessary at any point, I will facilitate it, both financially and logistically."

The Warlock was quiet.

Once the silence had gone on long enough, Jevryn said, "You should know that my generosity, once rejected, is never extended again."

"Your word," Ankira gritted out, "that it is only a conversation."

"I will not force his hand to any action."

That wasn't quite the guarantee Ankira had asked for, and the look on her face said she recognized the evasion. But in the end, she relented.

Nyx and Jevryn followed when she motioned them around the counter. She did not lead them upstairs, to her family's home where she had once taken Nyx and Evra, but to a workshop in the back of the store. Shelves, filled with meticulously labeled jars of dried herbs, lined the walls, and a long, rectangular wooden table occupied the center of the room.

Ankira offered them the stools dotted around the table—Nyx took one, Jevryn did not—and turned to Nyx. "Be kind to him," she said, and then left to retrieve Tobi.

Be kind. Nyx frowned. Why wouldn't she be kind?

Nyx and Jevryn did not speak in the Warlock's absence. She suspected that, with the one thing he wanted above all else finally within reach, Jevryn was too keyed up for idle conversation. Though you wouldn't know it to look at him. Nyx wondered if *she* would ever be that guarded. Maybe, if she also lived a few centuries. But if this conversation went the way they hoped, she wouldn't have to to find out.

Ankira came back with Tobi in tow. He had the misshapen lump of fabric in his hands that he'd carried on Arkadia as a homemade stuffed animal. He'd quit carrying it everywhere a few months after he'd moved in with Ankira and Diana, but he squeezed it to him now as if it were a lifeline.

He looked at Nyx and tears welled in his eyes. "I'm sorry I couldn't help."

Oh, shit. The last time she'd seen Tobi, she'd wanted him to bring her dead lover back to life. "Hey, it's okay." She sprang off the chair and dropped to her knees, opening her arms in invitation. Tobi ran into the hug and she squeezed him tight. "It wasn't your fault," she said softly.

"I couldn't help," he said again. "He was my friend and I couldn't help. If I was stronger—"

"There was nothing you could have done." She closed her eyes, her own tears falling. "If I hadn't been so desperate, I would have realized that. I wish I could undo coming here, because you should never have seen that."

Tobi had looked up to Seth. It wasn't the kind of devotion that he felt for Kaden, but Seth was—had been—funny and clever and handsome, and Tobi had idolized him in a different way.

"You're not mad?"

"No, I'm not mad. And Tobi?" She squeezed him again and leaned back, so she could look him in the eye. "Anyone who was mad at you in that situation would be wrong. What you can do is wonderful. But it can't solve everything, and even if it could, no one has a right to your magic but you."

He looked like he wanted to believe her, but didn't quite. "You didn't come by, after."

"I know," she said softly. "The thing about people? We aren't perfect. And sometimes, when something hurts us badly enough, we don't know how to deal with it. I didn't know how to deal with it. I just wanted to be alone." *I wanted to not exist,* she thought, but he didn't need to hear that. "I'm sorry that made you think I blamed you. I don't. I never did."

He thought about it, then nodded. "Okay." It wasn't quite forgiveness, and that was all right. He had a right to feel how he felt. "So what did you want?"

Nyx looked up at Jevryn. They'd discussed how best to approach this, and fortunately for Nyx, Jevryn's knowledge of the Shamanic entity known as the Congregation was much deeper than her own.

He said, "We seek counsel from the Congregation on several workings performed by a Shaman some time ago. We wish to understand if the workings can be reversed."

Tobi frowned, the grave expression far too serious for such a young face. "Shamanic workings heal. Why would you want to undo them?"

"Under ordinary circumstances, they do," Jevryn agreed. "But in this case, they did not. I would like to understand why and how they were performed, and the method of their undoing. May we speak to the Congregation?"

"Yes." Tobi's voice was already growing distant, more adult, the way it did when he was slipping into the Congregation. "We too are curious. Ask your questions, Councilor."

"First, I request that what is discussed today remain within the confines of the Congregation. It shall not be repeated to anyone outside of it."

A moment of silence as the Congregation deliberated, then: "Agreed."

"This sword and I have a bond." Jevryn pulled Lethe-Alihana from their scabbard and held it out to Tobi. "Can you feel it?"

At Nyx's hip, in a scabbard Kaliaris had made for her, Kiev's sword—*her* sword now—pulsed uneasily. She placed her hand on the hilt, letting them see what she saw, though neither of them spoke to the other.

Tobi stretched out his hand, resting his small fingers atop of Jevryn's. "Yes, we recognize the bond."

"Does the Congregation remember the Shaman that created it?"

"We remember."

"And you know the other bonds they made?"

Tobi shuddered. "Yes."

"Can the bonds be severed without causing the death of either party? Can a Shaman return both members of the bond to their original states?"

"Yes." For a brief moment, hope flared in Nyx's chest. Then Tobi spoke again. "But you will not find a Shaman willing to do so."

"Why?" Nyx blurted out. They couldn't be this close to freeing Griff, to freeing the Stations, only to be told that no one with the magic to do so would help them.

"The first Shamanic duty is to healing, to making something whole once more. What you are requesting is a breaking, a severing."

Jevryn's words cut across the air like shards of glass. "What was done in the first place was a breaking."

"We understand how you might feel that way. We do not entirely disagree, from a philosophical perspective. But the magic itself is concerned only with the physical, and it is to the magic that we answer."

"So your *magic* would champion the eternal enslavement of two beings who want no part in it rather than do what they both desire?"

Tobi sighed. "The magic has no morality. It has no nuance. It is what it was created to be, and therefore must work within the confines of its creation, as must the Shamans who bear it. We understand your frustration and, were we capable of helping you, we would do so."

"You *are* capable," Jevryn said. "You have already stated that the act is within the ability of a Shaman."

"Within the ability, yes. But any Shaman who does as you ask will be acting against the foundations of our creation. The punishment for doing so is immediate excision from the Congregation.

"You must understand—that connection to the Congregation is what keeps us sane. Every healing a Shaman performs risks our sanity. We delve into another person to cure their ailments and to do so we must become them for a short time. We see the darkness and the light, the selfishness and the care, that resides within all beings. We absorb it into ourselves, and if we were forced to keep it, we would fill up with the lives of others until nothing of *us* remained.

"So the Congregation accepts that which the individual cannot hold. We are a memory of every Shamanic working, a repository of knowledge and thoughts. We are the voice that holds each Shaman to themself. When a Shaman loses that connection, they lose themself. They go mad. Most die seconds later. Some linger for hours, some days, but all fade in the end.

"Understand that the decision to exile a Shaman is not under our control. It is fundamental to our creation. We do not have the freedom to choose to be lenient. We cannot show mercy, and because we cannot, we will not condemn our Shamans to death to perform your request."

Jevryn's hands were white-knuckled fists. "This is an atrocity of your own making."

"Yes," the Congregation agreed. "And because it is so, we would offer you the one path you might walk to rectify it. We have said that Shamans exiled from the Congregation do not survive, and this is true. But there *is* one that yet lives. One who could do what you ask without risk because he has already survived condemnation."

"How did he do that?" Nyx asked.

"We believe the unique environment he was in at the time of his excommunication provided the necessary buffer for him to come to terms with the lack of inclusion. To…adapt, if you will."

"What did he do?"

"He killed someone under his care."

Nyx recoiled. Something Evra had said came back to her: *Shamans can be exceptionally dangerous. You think someone who can heal a broken ankle in a blink can't break it just as fast?*

"And you expect us to trust him?" Nyx asked.

"We expect nothing of you. We are simply providing you with the only option you might utilize. If it eases your mind, we understand what led to his action, and we are not without sympathy for it."

"And what led to the action?"

Tobi shook his head. "That is not our story to tell. It is his, should you seek him out and he decide to tell it. You must make the decision whether to trust or not."

Nyx blew out a breath and reminded herself that the Congregation wasn't *exactly* a person, and being frustrated with them wouldn't do her any good. "Okay. Where do we find him?"

"That we cannot answer. When a Shaman is exiled, as they lose touch with the Congregation, so do we lose touch with them."

Frustration bit at her. "Then how do you even know he's still alive?"

"Because even exiled Shamans rejoin the Congregation in death. It is why most choose to end their lives so soon. Tristen Veld has not yet returned to our fold. We know that when his tie to the Congregation was severed, he was in your Dead Earth and had been for some time. It is, we believe, why he survived the excommunication. Magic is blunted, in that place. His connection to us had already been tenuous long before then, and he was forced to adapt to a more limited access."

What the hell had a Shaman been doing in Dead Earth? *How* had he ended up in Dead Earth? "When was he exiled?"

Tobi's eyes went even more distant than usual before he said, "A little over fifteen of your Earth years."

Nyx blinked. "Fifteen *years*? If losing access to the Congregation screws with a Shaman's sense of self, what makes you think he's even rational after fifteen years?"

"We did not say that he was. We have no way of knowing. We would like to know. We would like you to find him."

Even setting aside the danger that came with tracking down and opening negotiations with someone who had, essentially, broken the sacred vow of his people and killed a person—for "reasons"—

someone who very well might not be in his rational mind, there was the further complication that she had nothing to negotiate with. "What makes you think he would even do this? You exiled him for going against your moral code and I'm supposed to walk up and say, what? 'Hi, so convenient for me that you've been cast out by your people, could you possibly do *more* things your people find objectionable because that would really benefit me?'"

Tobi gave her a look that had no business being on an eight-year-old's face. It was a look that said "We are not amused by your sarcasm". "You will tell him that the Congregation mourns his loss. You will tell him that we wish to speak with him, and that there may yet be a path for his readmission to our number, should he decide to help you."

Nyx shook her head. Fifteen fucking years. If *she* were Tristen Veld, and she'd been cast out and left to die or go mad, she knew exactly what she would say to someone who showed up and made her that offer. And it wouldn't be "Thank you so much for your generosity, I completely understand why what happened had to happen, I'm happy to do a lot of work for this woman I just met, please take me back."

Then there was another problem. Namely, Nyx's own skepticism. "You have no control over his excision, but I'm supposed to convince him you can choose to readmit him?"

"As we explained, his excision is necessarily built into our creation. What was *not* built into our creation were any laws regarding returning an exiled Shaman to our number. We will be truthful—we do not know if it can be done."

"Why haven't you tried it before?" This couldn't be the only case in which a Shaman had killed someone and the Congregation thought it might have been justified. Shamanic ability was magic, like any other, and if a person's life was in danger, they reached for their magic as they would any weapon.

"Because, if it *is* possible, it will require the Shaman to perform acts of penance. We cannot allow darkness into our Congregation— it would be poison the well, would shatter our consciousness. But if Veld is willing to balance the scales, we have hope of his return."

Great. So she wasn't even going into this with "Hey, trust me, that Congregation that exiled you will totally take you back if you do a bunch of stuff for me." No, she was going into it with "Hey, trust me, that Congregation that exiled you will totally *try* to take you back if you do a bunch of stuff for me."

"And if he's not interested in your offer?"

Tobi shrugged. "We advise you to be convincing."

"Is there no way to insulate a current Shaman against the repercussions? To reinterpret your moral code, or—"

"This is the only path forward," the Congregation said, cutting her off. "Take it or do not. The choice is yours."

Nyx's hands tightened into fists. The Congregation said they didn't know where Tristen was now. But they'd known he was in Dead Earth at the time of his exile. "Do you know where in Dead Earth he was?"

"A place called New York." They enunciated the last two words with careful precision.

"New York the city, or New York the state?"

Tobi tilted his head slightly. "Your people would name two places the same thing?"

She restrained a groan of frustration. "When Tristen was still in the Congregation, did you by chance see what the landscape around him was like?"

"He was indoors for nearly the entirety of his time there."

Perfect.

"But there was one occasion—he was quite young, and the memories are colored by that youth—where he was taken outside."

Nyx did not particularly like the implication of his being "taken" outside as opposed to him "going" outside.

"But it was a chaotic place, the structures so high it was if the builders sought to blot out the sun. Tristen was born in a more gentle, open place. The experience terrified him."

New York City, then. Wonderful. Of all the fucking places to try and find someone. *How* was she going to find him? How was she going to track someone who— Wait a minute. "Would you be able to give a Hound Tristen's scent?"

Tobi inclined his head. "This we can and will do. Send us your Hound, and we will share with him what he requires."

Nyx took a deep breath. She had come here hoping for a solution and been met with another stumbling block. This wasn't the answer she had wanted. But she couldn't logic and reason against an entity that had no room to act with empathy.

She'd wanted one thing—*one* fucking thing—to go right, to be easy. Had wanted some sign that there was some fairness in the universe, because thus far she hadn't seen any proof. Instead, she had been given this. And, like usual, *this* left her with two choices: give up, or deal with it.

She would deal with it. "Thank you for your time."

She waited while Tobi blinked away the Congregation, though his eyes remained a little unfocused. When he spoke next, his voice was shy and small again. "I'm sorry."

Nyx was tired. She was tired of the world being difficult for everyone, tired of systems that had been created long ago that exposed children to more than they should be expected to bear. She was tired of herself for having come here, knowing that. "You have nothing to be sorry for, Tobi. *I* am sorry that I had to come to you for this."

He blinked again, his eyes focusing a little more. "I didn't help." He looked down at his hands. "Maybe I can. If Tristen survived in Dead—"

"No," Ankira and Nyx said in unison.

Tobi's eyes filled with tears, and it punched Nyx right in the gut as he said, "I want to help. Like you helped me."

"You already have," she said. "You told us what we needed to know."

He shook his head. "It's not enough. I couldn't help you last time and—"

"*No one* could help me last time. And what you have done today is more than enough. Tobi…only a monster would ask you to do what needs to be done now. You understand the scope of it, intellectually"—his connection to the Congregation guaranteed that—"but you don't have the breadth of experience necessary to understand what you would be risking. What it would do to your future, even if you did survive it.

"You understand what it means to be severed from the Congregation, but you have not felt it, and you view the risk as trivial because you have proof of someone who has survived. A person cannot consent to something they cannot fully comprehend, and you should be wary of anyone who pressures you to. Do you understand?"

He nodded, then he shook his head. "You were gone, and Mom

wouldn't let me go to the Station, and Kaden said you hurt too much to go outside and that's why you wouldn't visit." His eyes welled up with tears. "If I'd fixed Seth you wouldn't hurt."

Nyx's own tears pricked at the backs of her eyes. She opened her arms in invitation, and Tobi walked into the hug. She squeezed him tight. "I am so sorry I couldn't visit. I am so sorry that you blamed yourself." She had never realized that she meant very much to the kid. She'd known he liked her, but Tobi seemed to like everyone. "But you know the truth, through the Congregation. When I came to you, was there anything that could have been done?"

He sniffled. "No."

"Then nothing is your fault. Okay?"

He nodded against her shoulder. "I miss him." There was so much vulnerability in that statement.

"I miss him too. It won't be the same without—" Her voice broke, and she had to collect herself to finish the sentence. "Without him at the Station. But if you want to visit, I'd love to see you there."

"I want to come."

Ankira shot Nyx a glare that indicated she didn't appreciate this invitation being given. Nyx didn't care. If the Warlock didn't want Tobi anywhere near Nyx, *she* could have that argument with her son.

Nyx gave Tobi a final squeeze and let him go. "You're very special," she told him, standing. "And desperate people like to use special people. So live your life for *you*, Tobi. It's yours and no one else's."

Jevryn remained seated for several more seconds, and for a moment she feared her father was going to contradict everything she'd just said to Tobi about his right to his own autonomy. The Warlock feared it too, if the way she stepped forward, her hands landing protectively on Tobi's shoulders, was any indication.

Jevryn rose, inclined his head to both Tobi and Ankira, and walked out. Nyx followed, exiting the Warlock's shop a step behind him. His face was inscrutable and she guessed that, as much frustration as was biting at her insides right now, he was feeling a thousand times more. And it made her worry. Jevryn was…complicated. Her feelings about him were complicated. She was, she realized, actually beginning to think of him as a father. Maybe not the same way she would have had she spent time with him as a child, but it was something.

He'd been there for her when she'd needed him, even if she hadn't wanted him. He cared, and that made it difficult not to care in return. The problem was, all those inconvenient feelings made her want to give him the benefit of the doubt. To believe him to be a better person than he probably was. To think he wouldn't do terrible things.

But…she thought she finally understood what his moral code was, and it was quite simple: do whatever was necessary to protect those he loved. The fact she was now included in that code didn't make her any less worried about what he would view as permissible under it. If anything, it made her *more* worried.

So she stopped walking. When he stopped with her, lifting an eyebrow in question, she said, "Promise me you aren't going to go back there and try to force Tobi into this later."

Jevryn sighed. "Of course I will not. He is a child."

Nyx relaxed. Then Jevryn started talking again.

"Even with his access to the Congregation, and the gaps in learning and knowledge that such a connection bridges, he is still in an eight-year old's body. It would tire quickly. He would be fussy. He would miss his mothers and cry often, in addition to being a vulnerability in need of constant protection."

And that line of logic right there was precisely why Nyx had worried. He hadn't discarded the idea because Tobi shouldn't be tricked into doing this, he'd discarded it because children were irksome liabilities. Still, it worked. "And you're going to be okay with it even if I can't find this exiled Shaman and convince them to help us?"

Jevryn shrugged. "Time is a thing we yet have, now that we have the answers we need. And if enough of it goes by, the boy *will* be old enough to consent. Given his history, I believe the devotion he feels toward Kaden, and his awe of you, would be sufficient to convince him to do it. Around seventeen, or so, would be the ideal time. Boys, at that age—well, anyone at that age truly, though societies often condition the males for it more—feel a pressing need to imagine they will leave some great mark upon the world, while simultaneously fearing they will be trapped in a boring existence that prevents them from seeking the glory they are certain should be theirs. And at that age, the sense of risk has not yet fully formed in the brain, so even if he recognizes the recklessness of his actions, he will ultimately fail to heed his cautionary thoughts.

"I can wait a decade, if I must. It is no great amount of time, in the scheme of my life."

"You know what the problem with you is?" Nyx said.

He resumed walking. "I am certain you will tell me."

"I can never tell if you're joking or not," Nyx said, falling into step beside him.

"Ah. An individual of my age must maintain a certain mystique. The easily understood appear weak. Do remember that, *na'tria.* Never reveal your intentions, your reasons, your hopes or your desires, unless absolutely necessary. And sometimes, not even then. To your enemies, they will be cracks in your armor through which to thrust a blade. To your friends, they will be promises with which to chain you. And that is if your friends do not *become* your enemies, as friends so often do."

Nyx chewed on that for a few seconds before saying, "Not that I'm criticizing, mind you, but whenever you decide to dispense fatherly advice, it's always…bleak."

"Existence is bleak, *na'tria.* Existence with no end in sight is a punishment. Were it not for Arradin's eternal captivity, I would have left this universe to burn, and gone on to wander the paths of old age long ago, that I might find rest in the natural ceasing of my existence.

"So if you wish to know my true advice, it is this: do everything you can to fulfill the promises you have made within a natural life-span. And if you wish to know my greatest hope for you, I will tell you that as well. I hope that you will fulfill those promises and, having done so, find peace in an ordinary existence. Strive for obscurity, my daughter, for it will treat you far more kindly than fame."

$$26$$

Back at the Station, Nyx made her way to the Arrival Room while Jevryn went to find Griff. It felt like a cop-out, letting Jevryn deliver the bad news, but she suspected he would prefer the privacy, and she had something else to take care of.

Something that, if she was going to move forward, had to be done. As she walked into the Arrival Room, she looked at the tattoo on her hand, the solitary "one" inked in elegant black. She would use that final number, if she had to. But she hoped Kaliaris could be reasoned with.

The portal bay floor was not entirely repaired, but it was healing. It laid flat again, and the three crude gashes had knitted back together, so they were thick scars rather than openings.

Nyx pressed the palm of her hand to floor. "Can I talk to you?"

The floor opened, Kaliaris inviting her in, and she stepped into the empty space, floating down to the Heart beneath. The new vine growth that covered the floor was thinner than what Kiev had destroyed, but it was regrowing.

"How are you?" she asked.

<We will heal.>

"Laiveran escaped."

<Yes.>

"How?"

<I am not entirely certain, though I believe it had something to

do with these.> A vine dropped several bottles at her feet. <He hid them, folded up in the shirt he wore when you brought him in. The shirt is not of me, so I could not feel its contents. I discovered them in the tumult, when the room's contents were upended.>

Nyx crouched, looking at the bottles. There were fifteen in total, small, the size eyedrops might be sold in in Dead Earth. Each one of them was meticulously labeled in Morgen's careful hand.

That damn cat you brought home is a kleptomaniac, he'd said.

Only four of the vials had been used. She had a feeling that, when she took them to Morgen, he would tell her the contents of those four specific vials, combined together, would have the ability to damage Laiveran's binding bracelets.

"Fangs is missing, isn't she?"

<Yes.>

Of course she was. Of all things—the fucking *cat* did it. *Soulsinger,* Lethe-Alihana had called Laiveran. Even with the binding bracelets, he must have had enough ability to influence Fangs. If Jevryn had had any idea that Laiveran could get a bloody housecat, of all things, to do his bidding, her father would never have suggested she get the cat for him in the first place. He was going to be livid when she told him.

"We'll find him," she promised Kaliaris. She didn't have a great deal of conviction on that point, but she would try. More likely— and more unfortunate—was Laiveran finding *her* first. But that was a problem for another day. For Calista's sake, Nyx hoped Laiveran hadn't returned to them. Was it too much to wish for? That, having escaped prison, he would decide to live out his days in peaceful obscurity, reflecting on his sins?

Probably.

<This is not what you came to speak with me about.>

"No."

<You wish to leave. Again.>

"There are things I need to put to rest. If I have to use this"—she tapped the tattoo on her hand—"I will. But I am asking you not to make me. You gave me space to recover, where I needed to. You trusted that I would come back. I am asking you to do so again."

For a long moment, they did not answer, and she was afraid they were going to say *no.* Then a vine lifted her hand, holding it up. <You are different than I believed you to be when you came here,

Nyx Fortuna. So perhaps it is time for a deeper extension of trust. I will not dissolve this bargain, but I will suspend it.>

A break appeared midway through the tattooed *one.* "Thank you."

Kaliaris dropped her hand. <It sounds as if you will need it, if I understand what Jevryn is telling Arradin. So go where you need to. Lay to rest what you must lay to rest. And when you return, you will work to keep your promise to us.>

They bore her up from the Heart. In the Arrival Room, she hesitated. Part of her didn't want to tell anyone where she was going, afraid that if she did, she would back out. But she couldn't disappear on them again, even for a short while, and leaving a note felt... rude. So she knocked on Griff's door. Jevryn was with him, and when she told them where she was going, she half-expected Jevryn to insist on going with her. He looked like he was about to, but then, with the air of a Dead Earth parent bravely letting their teenager climb behind the wheel without adult supervision for the first time, he unclipped a portal magic bracelet from his wrist, handed it to her, and said only, "Please be cautious. Though you should have no need of protective gear. It is not the right season."

That was something, she supposed. She took the bracelet and went to find Evra. The Amazon was on the back porch, reweaving pieces of wicker on the couch. It looked like one of the legs of the couch had given way, been glued back together, and now Evra was attempting to fix the wicker weave. "Attempting" being the key part.

"Do not ask," Evra said when Nyx's shadow fell over her.

"I wouldn't dream of asking why you're attempting to reassemble a couch Kaliaris made and could therefore fix in about two seconds."

Evra grunted. "Good."

A shadow of a smile curved Nyx's lips, and she realized she didn't want to do this alone. "Does this task require your undivided focus, or could I borrow you?"

"What did you have in mind?"

"There's somewhere I need to go. Something I need to do. And I was kind of hoping my best friend would go with me."

Evra let go of the long, loose piece of wicker she'd been weaving and stood, dusting off her hands. "Consider me available."

"Do you think we could take Morgen, too?" He would want to go. Though Griff hadn't said as much, she'd seen in his eyes that this was a journey he would want to make as well. But, since Nyx and Griff couldn't leave the Station at the same time, Jevryn would have to take him.

So she waited while Evra found Morgen, and while she waited, Temerex approached. The unicorn-dragon stopped ten feet away from her and pawed at the ground.

"Hey girl," Nyx said softly.

Temerex stopped pawing and tossed her head. Images came into Nyx's mind. Temerex with Jevryn, with Morgen, with Evra, with Griff. The unicorn-dragon was showing her the absence of Nyx.

"I'm sorry. I was…" Nyx sent her an image of darkness, infinite and fathomless. Then she showed her a light in the darkness, and Nyx crawling her way to it.

Temerex snorted, walked forward, and dropped her head onto Nyx's shoulder. Nyx hugged her neck. "I didn't mean to leave you. I promise not to again, okay?" She showed Tem an image of Nyx at the Station, sunset after sunset, and the unicorn-dragon huffed out a soft breath.

Morgen and Evra walked into the backyard, and an idea came to Nyx. "You want to go on an adventure?" she asked Tem, showing her an image of Nyx astride her, the two of them and Morgen and Evra walking through a portal.

Temerex's head shot straight up. She squealed and half-reared. The second her front hooves hit the ground she bucked, then took off in excitement, bucking and running back and forth across the Station grounds.

"Yes," Nyx muttered, "get *all* of that out before I get on your back, please."

"You're bringing Tem?" Morgen asked.

"As soon as she stops having the zoomies," Nyx confirmed. "I… think I owe her an outing."

Temerex zipped back, barreling toward Nyx, and skidded to a halt in front of her. "Ready?" Nyx asked. The unicorn-dragon let out a half-whicker of agreement. Nyx took two running steps and vaulted onto her back.

The four of them crossed over the Station's boundary. Nyx reached for the magic in the bracelet Jevryn had given her but, after a moment's hesitation, she instead gripped Lethe-Alihana's hilt.

May I? she asked. She wasn't bonded to them, as Kiev had been. They were not obligated to do as she said. But if they were going to be joined at the hip anyway, they might as well develop a working relationship.

Their answer was a flow of magic, free and pure. She spun a portal to Kyvren and nudged Temerex through it, Evra and Morgen following. Nyx had brought them to the base of Vorex Mountain, and their sudden arrival caused a stir. Because there were Meerkin *everywhere.* And not Meerkin alone, but Dwarves as well. The two peoples were fairly integrated, working and socializing in mixed groups, rather than each keeping to themselves.

Maybe he didn't die for nothing, a voice whispered in the back of her mind. *Maybe he died for this. For this hope for a better world.*

It didn't make it hurt any less. But it did make it feel a little less…ugly.

As everyone noticed their arrival and took varying turns stopping what they were doing and staring, it occurred to Nyx that maybe she ought to have done the equivalent of calling ahead to let them know she was coming. Though realistically, with Kyvren's Station still shut down, she didn't know how she would have done so.

Nyx slid off Temerex, keeping her hand on the mare's neck, as a single Meerkin bounded toward them. As the Meerkin neared, Nyx realized she recognized him. "Jori."

He dipped his head. "Hello, Nyx Fortuna." He turned slightly. "Evra al'Daemon, Morgen Drahl." He turned to Temerex. "I do not believe we have met. I am Jori."

Temerex whickered softly, and sent Nyx an image of Tem and Jori nose-to-nose. "Her communication doesn't translate, I'm afraid, but this is Temerex. She would like to say hello in her way."

"Of course," Jori said. Nyx sent the image of Jori and Temerex nose-to-nose back to the mare, who immediately stretched out her neck. She breathed in and out, in and out, nostrils flaring as she took in the Meerkin's scent. Apparently finding him acceptable—and by extension the rest of the Meerkin—she lifted her head and sent Nyx back an image of Temerex running with the Meerkin.

Nyx didn't know how the Meerkin, who had never seen a horse, much less a unicorn-dragon, would take to Temerex rampaging in their midst, even if it was all in good fun. She had a feeling the adults would herd the cubs into the den, and who could blame them? It was hard to tell from the outside that Temerex was, at heart, an oversized puppy.

Nyx sent Tem an image of her staying at Nyx's side, and the unicorn-dragon blew out a long-suffering breath that fluttered her lips. Nyx patted her neck. "I'm sorry to come here with no warning," she told Jori.

"You are welcome any time. Jevryn spoke to Vorex, after your... departure. He thought you would want to return, at some point. And while I suspect I know why you are here, and would not interfere with your purpose, Vorex would extend an invitation to speak with you, if you are willing."

She nodded. She had come here to do something that needed to be done, but that didn't mean she was ready. It didn't mean she wasn't happy to delay it even a short while longer.

Jori dipped his head and led them through the throngs of Meerkin and Dwarves, around an outcropping of rocks and to a small grassy area where Vorex lounged with three other Meerkin. He saw Nyx, and his eyes were at once welcoming and somber.

"Kin who is not of my kin," he rumbled.

She managed a shadow of a smile. "Hi, Vorex."

He nodded to the three Meerkin with him. They rose and departed, each one offering her a small nod as they passed. He motioned to Jori, who came forward, listened to whatever Vorex whispered in his ear, then trotted off.

"I am sorry," Vorex said, once they were alone. "For your loss, and that it came because of us."

Nyx shook her head. "I don't blame you. I never blamed you. Only Kiev." *And myself,* but she didn't say that last part out loud. "He's dead," she added, realizing her uncle's end had a relevance for the Meerkin, as well. "Kiev, I mean."

Vorex was quiet a moment, then asked, "By your own claw?"

"Yes."

"And has his death ended your pain?"

She considered the question before answering it, because he asked it like someone who wanted to know, rather than someone who asked it because they thought they should. "No. It has ended my wrath. But the pain?" She shook her head. "That might be worse, now."

Because she didn't have the purpose of Kiev's death to drive and distract her from it. Because she had to start over now, to pick up the shattered pieces of her life and figure out how to put them back together again. To rebuild a puzzle that would be forever missing its most important piece.

"I understand that feeling well," Vorex said softly. "My own wrath, which built for centuries, has also recently come to an end. And while my own deep losses are much farther behind me than yours, the reclamation of my home and the newly returned peace here drives them to the forefront of my mind again.

"It is easy enough to think, when things are difficult and dark, that perhaps it is not so bad that those you loved most are not with you. Because at least they do not have to suffer in that difficult dark alongside you. But when the struggle is past and the dawn comes, and everything is once more beautiful and full of promise, that is when your heart longs most for what you have lost."

Vorex's words wrapped around Nyx's heart, clenching like a vise. It was a sweet kind of pain, born from how completely he understood how she felt in that moment. "Yes," she whispered.

"Would you walk with me, kin who is not of my kin?" Vorex rose. His movements were stiff and slow, and she refused to let herself wonder how much time he had left. She could not bring herself to think of the potential of his loss, of another puzzle piece missing. "There is something I would show you. Something I believe it is important to remember, in times like these."

She assented and followed as he led her out, into the cleared area before the den.

"When last you were here, this space was a battlefield. The soil here will forever be painted with the blood shed that day, but if that stain can never be washed away, it can be remembered, and by remembering our history, we can work to ensure it is never again repeated.

"At the time I met you on Arkadia, I had no room in my heart for lenience or forgiveness. Perhaps I still have none of the latter, but the former, I have seen the wisdom of. I did not think I would suffer a single Dwarf to remain on Kyvren. But one cannot blame an individual for the sins of their people, just as the sins of a single person ought not be used to condemn an entire group.

"I realized this, as I spoke with the Dwarves who chose to risk their own lives, to go against the edicts of their own leaders, because they understood that what had been done to we Meerkin was wrong. For them—for their decency—I have granted lenience to those of their kind who did not possess such bravery, but who took no active role in my people's persecution, so long as they were willing to swear an oath of their intention to live in harmony with us.

"It is a concession that was difficult for me to make, and that is why it was not mine alone to make, but my people's as well. But while no place is perfect or without strife, I urge you to look around you at the community that has been returned to this land."

Nyx looked. She had been struck with it earlier—the difference between the Kyvren before her now, and the one she had encountered so many months ago. Part of that was simply that they were not in the season for fire rains, and so no one needed to make the choice of either remaining safe inside, or donning full armor to be outside. Families lounged in the sun. Meerkin played games or crafted or simply shared conversation. Dwarves lost themselves to metalwork or storytelling. All around her, Nyx saw a planet finally at peace with itself.

"All communities have difficulties," Vorex continued. "There will be disagreement and dissent, and the first time a significant issue arises, there will be those whose first accusation will be that it is either the Dwarves' fault or the Meerkin's, no matter what the evidence shows. But we have a strong foundation, and so long as we do not allow history to become lost or twisted with each new generation, there is no reason we cannot work toward an even better future with the passage of time."

"What happened to the others?" At Vorex's inquiring glance, Nyx said, "The other Dwarves. The ones you did not allow to stay."

"You do not know?"

She frowned. "Why would I?"

"Because it was Jevryn who facilitated their exodus from Kyvren. We spilled all the blood we were willing to spill on the battlefield. My people have no interest in cold executions, so we exiled from our planet those who could not coexist. Perhaps we could have sent them through our Station—I do not know—but we did not have to. Jevryn found places for them, and saw that they made their way there."

They walked in silence for a time as Nyx took this information in. She didn't understand her father. She had once thought him a terrible person, and he himself professed to be one. He had done things—was *still* doing things—she could not condone. But the more she learned about him, the more she realized there was a complexity to Jevryn A-Morridahn that she had barely scratched the surface of.

And maybe, if she wanted to understand the things he had done and why he did them, she would have to swallow her anger and *ask* about them. Motion caught her attention, and she saw Jori loping up to them. To Vorex, he said, "She will see us."

Vorex nodded and looked at Nyx. "There is someone I would like you to meet."

Nyx followed him to a small group of Meerkin. As they got close, she realized one of the Meerkin had a cub with her, a small bundle of black fur, curled into a ball, paws twitching. The cub woke when Vorex's shadow fell over them, sleepy brown eyes blinking open. Something painful squeezed in Nyx's chest.

"This is Amina," Vorex said, nodding to the mother. "Amina, Nyx Fortuna."

"You probably do not recall me, though we have met," Amina said. The cub tottered to his feet, and Amina steadied him with a paw. "When you held the portals open for the evacuations, I was among those who went through. I was near to giving birth, at the time, and the rooms I would have been in had I stayed were destroyed in the battle."

"I'm sorry," Nyx said.

"Do not be," Vorex said, taking up the thread of the conversation once more. "That is not why I brought you to meet Amina." He nodded at the cub. "Black is an unusual fur color among Meerkin. And we believe in signs, just as we believe in honoring sacrifice. In ensuring that those who have fought for us are not lost to the emptiness of time."

"My son was born a mere hour after the Dwarves surrendered," Amina said, softly. "And I heard of your loss, and I saw the physical similarities between my cub and your mate."

Black hair, brown eyes. Tiny needles stung at the backs of Nyx's eyes.

"This is my son, Seth," Amina said, nudging the cub toward Nyx. "I would be honored if you held him. For he has a name to live up to that will forever be remembered among our people."

Nyx swallowed and knelt, stretching a trembling hand toward the cub. He padded forward, making small cat sounds in the back of his throat. She didn't know what the development stages for Meerkin were, but, given that the noises were not made intelligible to her via her translator spell, she guessed that they developed more along a human timeline than a housecat one, and the sounds were only baby sounds.

He sniffed her hand and then put his front paws on her lap. Carefully, gently, she scooped him up. He blinked sleepily at her, warm brown eyes curious, and batted at her face. Once, twice, three times, and then the soft paw pad came to rest against her cheek.

"You have a good name," she told him. Her voice was a hoarse whisper that had to fight against the constriction in her throat in order to make words. "A strong name." She gently scratched behind his ear and a purr rumbled to life in the small body. "I can't tell you your future. That is not my gift. But I can tell you of your namesake. I can tell you that if you are anything like him, you will grow up to be kind, but also mischievous. Sweet, but also stubborn. You will be clever, and vibrant, and funny, and everyone who knows you will love you. And you will try their patience, at times, but you will bring them so much joy.

"And I wish—" Her voice broke. A tear spilled over her cheek, falling onto the silky black fur, and she wiped it away. "I wish that you will grow up safe and adored. That you will know only peace and love, and never war or hate. I wish that you are able to do all that you want. You have his name, but your life is your own to forge as you will. Live it well."

She pressed a kiss to the soft fur between his ears, then gently returned him to his mother, placing the cub in front of Amina. "Thank you." She stood, the necessity of what she'd come here to do urging her up, no longer able to be put off.

Vorex clearly understood the look on her face, the feeling that drove her, because when she turned, scanning the landscape, he raised one paw and pointed to a small sapling, no more than a foot tall, that grew in that space. "We planted it as a marker."

She nodded and walked. To the growing tree. To the place where it had happened. To the place where she'd lost him.

Now, as she had then, she dropped to her knees. The moment replayed in her mind. It had all happened so fast, her world forever altered between one breath and the next. She could still feel the heaviness of him in her arms, the weight telling her what her heart would not accept for some time after.

For a while she only sat there, staring at the young tree, the tiny budding leaves, and thinking about how, across species, it seemed common to attempt to replace death with new life. Seth was gone. Someone else now bore his name. This tree would grow every year that he was gone, as would the cub.

For some reason, she was reminded of that film with the retired assassin, the one where his wife died and, knowing she was dying, left him a dog because she knew that he would need something to care for once she was gone. Knew he would need something else to love. But then the dog was taken from him too, and he had been left with only the feeling that had driven Nyx these last months.

Wasn't that the problem with naming cubs and planting trees? These fragile new lives could end as unexpectedly as Seth's had, and then she would be left with this feeling again. Maybe it was best to be like Jevryn—to love so sparingly that the chances of a death ever again affecting her the way this one had were slim. But she was already too far gone for that. All her life, Nyx had wanted a family to love, and as Evra had reminded her, she had built one for herself.

But she hadn't truly come here to debate the merits of loving people. She hadn't even come here because she'd needed to find something else to live for. She had come here because she needed to find a way to let go, and she didn't know how to do that.

"I killed him for you," she told Seth's absence. "Kiev." But that wasn't exactly true, was it? "I killed him for *me*. For us. It helped. A little." Her fingers went to the stone nestled in the hollow of her throat. "But not enough. I loved you. *So much.* And I still can't believe you're gone. It doesn't feel real, it doesn't feel *right*. It hurts, and I don't think it's ever going to stop." It would be one of those ailments she simply grew accustomed to, like an ever-present ache that subsided at times and flared up at others to remind her of its existence.

"For a long time, I wanted to join you. I don't even know if there's a *there* that you're at, if there's anything after this, but I didn't care. Because either there is and I could find you, or there's nothing and at least in nothing I wouldn't be feeling *this* anymore.

"But...someone reminded me recently that I feel other things too. That I love other people, too. Evra. Morgen. Griff. And I hurt them and that hurts and just...everything fucking *hurts*. And I don't know what to do because you were the person who made everything hurt less.

"And I know you wouldn't want this for me. I know you'd want me to move on. I know that. So why does it feel like anything less than misery is a betrayal of you? Why does it feel like living is a betrayal when if you were here you'd tell me I'm being stupid?"

He didn't answer her, not even in her mind. She wished he would. She wished he'd haunt her, that she could see him in her mind's eye, hear his voice whisper in her ears like she had when the Mindwitch had summoned his image. Did she not love him enough to be haunted? Or did she just not have the kind of mind that could summon him as easily as he'd once summoned illusions?

"I don't know how to let you go. I don't think I *can*." She brushed her fingers over the rock at her throat. "I should leave this here. I should leave *you* here. But I can't. We were going to see the universe together." Tears poured down her face. "And if I can't have you with me, everywhere I have left to go, I at least want to have this piece of you. Maybe it's macabre. Maybe it's fucked up, to keep this. But we all turn to dust in the end, don't we? The dirt we walk on was once a person someone else loved. Is it any different to carry what I have left of you with me?"

A breeze, gently rustling the leaves of the sapling, was her only answer. "I can't let you go," she whispered, "but I'll try to leave the pain here."

She stood and turned. Evra, Morgen, and Temerex waited, far enough off that they couldn't hear what she'd spoken. She walked to them, waited with Temerex while Evra and Morgen approached the tree and said their own goodbyes.

And when it was finished, they all went home. Together.

EPILOGUE

One Week Later…

Nyx stood just inside the Station, looking through the French doors that let out onto the back patio. Her arms were crossed over her stomach, and she squeezed them tighter as she watched Morgen and Evra setting platters of food on the patio bar.

That should be Seth. She couldn't stop the thought, the feeling of wrongness that he wasn't here. That they were doing this without him—doing anything they'd done before without him. But that was all of living, wasn't it? There was no part of her life he hadn't touched. No part of her life that wouldn't always feel like it was missing him. She'd promised to try and leave her pain on Kyvren, and she *was* trying, but fuck did it still hurt more often than it didn't.

She squeezed her stomach tighter still, as if she could compress the feelings in on themselves, and watched as Griff and Jevryn walked up from the clearing, Temerex pacing them. Nyx swore Tem was more canine than unicorn-dragon, the way she devoted herself to Jevryn and, to a lesser extent, Nyx. Jevryn had been absent most of the last week, searching for Laiveran with no success. Nyx was surprised Laiveran hadn't gone back to Calista, but when she'd gone with Jevryn to check—because Calista had refused to acknowledge Jevryn when he'd gone alone—she'd found no evidence of Laiveran there.

While he was gone, Jevryn had left Kaden at the Station. She wasn't sure why. Kaden didn't seem to be under orders to watch her constantly, anymore, which was a relief, because now that she was in her home and not Jevryn's, she had no intention of being under constant guard. She didn't know how she felt about Kaden being at the Station, but there was no getting around the fact that she would need him when they started looking for Tristen Veld, so he might as well be here. And he was, for all intents and purposes, Morgen's brother, so she was glad for her friend's sake that he was here and putting actual effort into repairing their relationship.

But…it was hard to see them together and not remember that after Kaden had left in the Shadow Market, Morgen and Seth had been the ones thick as thieves at the Station. It was hard not to feel like Kaden was somehow replacing him, slipping into all the parts of life that Seth's absence had left with gaping holes. Rationally, she understood that was how Kaden must have felt when she'd first found Seth, and it wasn't any more true now than it had been then. People weren't replaceable, weren't interchangeable.

Still, she mostly avoided Kaden while trying to come to terms with everything. With accepting that Seth wasn't here anymore. It was why Jevryn and Griff were settling onto one of the outdoor couches while Morgen and Evra continued to argue pointlessly over the arrangement of food trays on the bar. It was why she needed to go out there, because she had someone else she needed to go get, but making her feet move wasn't going so well.

She didn't hear Kaden come into the room, but she felt him through the Station's senses. He stopped a few feet from her, to the side. He was in Dead Earth clothing again, a plain white t-shirt and jeans so faded and worn that the holes in the knees were onehundred-percent of natural origin. Where had he even found something that old? The reject bin outside the thrift store? She opened her mouth to ask, changed her mind and didn't.

His presence should have been enough to drive her outside, to make her finally get on with everything, but she remained where she was, that twisting feeling still snaking through her guts. She was sure, once *he* went outside, that someone would notice she was just standing here, staring, and come to get her. Until then, she'd keep on standing and staring.

Except he didn't go outside. He just stood there with her. Then, quietly, he said, "You don't have to do this today. You don't have to be ready for it."

She blew out a breath. "Yeah, I do." Because she was *never* going to be ready. So she was just going to have to do it anyway. She pushed the door open and walked out, just as Evra slapped Morgen's hand away from a tray full of cupcakes.

Spotting her, Morgen said, "Little Guardian, thank the stars someone of reason is here. Please tell her that the cupcakes cannot go next to the cake."

Umm, what? "But desserts go together."

Evra shot Morgen a triumphant look. "Thank you. As he said, I'm so glad someone of *reason* is here."

Morgen looked stricken. "Cupcakes are essentially miniature cakes. Given that they are superior to actual cake in almost all ways, if placed directly beside the cake, everyone will just take the easily picked up cupcake."

"Then maybe we should have just had cupcakes?" Nyx offered.

Evra snorted.

"Why is everyone against me?" Morgen asked.

Evra patted him on the shoulder. "How do they say it in Dead Earth? *There, there.*" She turned to Nyx. "Are you going to get her?'

Nyx nodded.

Jevryn cleared his throat. "If you could kindly refrain from creating a diplomatic incident, I would not be unappreciative."

"Have you ever considered that instead of being 'not unappreciative' you should try just being appreciative?"

Griff choked off a laugh and Jevryn's eyes narrowed. "No," was her father's succinct reply.

Nyx sighed. "There will be no diplomatic incident. No one's going to know."

"I sincerely hope that is the case."

"You could always forbid me from doing this," Nyx said lightly. She was surprised he hadn't already, considering where she was going and who she was bringing back.

"I could, but you would do it anyway when I am not here. The resultant mess would be more difficult to clean up, as I would not immediately be aware of it." He made a go-on motion with his hand.

She rolled her eyes. "Don't forget to hide your face before we get back." Quietly, to Evra, she asked, "Have you heard from…?"

A hint of sadness crossed Evra's face, and she shook her head.

"I'm sorry," Nyx said.

"It is fine. I am not surprised."

She squeezed Evra's arm and walked to the edge of the Station, crossing over the boundary. Portal magic spilled from the sword at her hip to her fingertips. She reached out, grasped her anchor on Endalna and pulled herself into her sister's room.

Serenity sat on her bed. Given the focus with which she stared at Nyx, Nyx guessed she must have been watching that spot for the last ten minutes, waiting for Nyx to appear. Her little sister slid off the bed, smoothing the skirts of a very formal gown that looked like it belonged on an adult. Resting atop her hair was something that was not *quite* a tiara, though close, gold metal and tiny gemstones glinting in the room's soft light.

Oh boy. Maybe she hadn't changed yet from…whatever formal event she'd obviously just come from? Except Nyx had coordinated this day with Serenity specifically because Elena and Emerik were gone, and Serenity did not attend public *anything* without Elena there to make sure she kept Serenity's Hidden nature from being discovered. Plus, Nyx and Serenity had chosen this specific time because it was after dinner on Serenity's planet and, according to her, if her parents were gone she was given the day off from tutoring, and only disturbed for meals, so long as none of the wards on her doors or windows were tripped. Or, as Nyx was pretty sure she was correctly interpreting the situation, Elena and Emerik put their daughter under suite arrest whenever they were gone, so no one discovered what she was.

All of which meant Serenity had picked this outfit for herself. "Are you…ready to go?" Nyx asked.

Serenity nodded.

"Do you maybe want to change into something more comfortable?"

Serenity frowned. "This is my best dress. Mommy says first impressions are important."

"They are," Nyx said carefully, "but you have to think about what *kind* of first impression you want to make. No one is supposed to know who you are, remember? So you want everyone to look at you and think you're just like them."

Yes, *most* people would already know who she was, but two or three invitees to that afternoon's movie viewing did not. And regardless, she didn't want Serenity to feel out of place, when no one else would be wearing anything even remotely close to formal clothing.

Serenity, persuaded, changed into what Nyx supposed would count as an everyday dress—Nyx wouldn't know, considering she'd worn a dress precisely never in her life—and reluctantly lost the tiara. But when Nyx held her hand out, Serenity picked at the cuff of her sleeve rather than take it. "What if the other kids don't like me?"

"It's just one other kid," Nyx reminded her. One was all Nyx could produce on short notice—well, on any notice, probably—and she was shocked she'd managed to get that one. Truthfully, *she* hadn't gotten them. Kaden had. How he'd convinced Ankira and Diana to let Tobi come to the Station for a few hours Nyx did not know and had not asked. "And if you're nice to him, he'll be nice to you."

Nyx held out her hand as she spun the portal to Earth open. Serenity put her hand in Nyx's and they stepped through. They crossed the Station border and the grounds to the back patio. "Serenity, you remember Morgen and Evra, right?"

Serenity nodded.

Nyx pointed to Griff, "This is Griff, the Avatar of the Station, and this is—" She cut off when she pointed at Jevryn. He had conde-scended to wear an illusion since, even though Nyx was relatively certain Serenity *wouldn't* tell anyone about this visit, because she wanted to visit again, it wouldn't be good if Serenity slipped and told someone that Councilor A-Morridahn was hanging out with the Guardian of Earth's Station.

However, Nyx hadn't thought to ask him what he'd like to be called in lieu of his actual name, so she chose the first nickname she could come up with, hastily finishing, "Ryn. He's Griff's… boyfriend."

Jevryn lifted a single eyebrow while Griff made a choking sound. The latter managed to compose himself and said, "It's a pleasure to meet you, Serenity."

Serenity inclined her head with more regality than a five-year-old should be capable of mustering. At the same time, she was trying—and failing—to be covert in her scans of the patio. She had been promised she was going to get to spend time with another kid close to her own age, and she wasn't seeing one.

Nyx squeezed Serenity's hand. "They're almost here." She could feel Kaden and Tobi moving through the Station, and soon enough they exited the building onto the back patio. "You've met Kaden, and this is Tobi. Tobi, this is Serenity."

"Hi," Tobi said shyly.

Serenity did not answer immediately, then blurted out, "Nyx said if I'm nice to you that you'll be nice to me, will you?"

Nyx winced. Yep, that level of blunt awkwardness alone would have proved Serenity was her sister. She didn't think their mother had ever been remotely like this, so it must have skipped a generation on the Fortuna side of the family.

Tobi blinked, then nodded.

"Good. Then I'll be nice," Serenity declared.

Nyx handed the two of them plates and set them loose on the dessert end of the bar, under the operating theory that they were not *her* children, and she therefore didn't have to feel guilty about how much sugar they ingested. The adults spent half an hour idly chatting while Tobi and Serenity grew cautiously acquainted, but what the adults were really doing was delaying.

Yet they could only wait so long, and eventually Morgen said, "Should we get started?"

Nyx had really, *really* been hoping that at least one of the other two people they'd invited would show up. "I guess—"

A ripple went through the Station as someone crossed over the boundary. "Sorry I'm late," Kalvar said as he walked up. "My History of the Connected Worlds assignment gave me a migraine. What kind of professor assigns an entire essay on trade policy? You know what I know about trade policy now? It's boring, it's vital, and no one wants to be the person who has to create, maintain, or understand it."

Nyx ran at Kalvar, pulling up just short of barreling into him.

His face took on a look of heroic suffering and he said, "It's fine, go ahead."

She hit him with a bone-crushing hug. "I'm sorry I wasn't there to see you off," she whispered. "I'm sorry I didn't say goodbye."

Kalvar squeezed her back. "I understood why. And you already said sorry like ten times in your letter."

"I know."

"Are you okay?" he asked.

What was the right answer to that? To lie, because despite being a newly minted adult, Kalvar was still so young and he'd already been through so much and she didn't want to dump more on him? To tell the truth, because he *had* been through so much that she didn't think he'd felt young for a very long time? She settled on a compromise. "I will be."

It was what she hoped for. And for the first time since Seth had died, surrounded by the people she cared about again, she thought it might actually be true. She gave Kalvar a final squeeze, let him go, and found Serenity staring up at them. Or rather, at Kalvar.

"Serenity, this is my friend, Kalvar. Kalvar, this is my sister, Serenity."

He raised an eyebrow at the "sister" part, but only said, "Nice to meet you."

"I've never met a Tiagren before," Serenity said. "Are they all as pretty as you?"

Nyx winced. "Serenity, it isn't polite to refer to someone that way." The Station's senses rippled as another person crossed over the threshold. Well, what would you know? A certain someone *had* decided to show up.

Serenity frowned. "As pretty?"

"As their race. How would you feel if I referred to you as 'the Endalnian'?"

"I don't know," Serenity said, in a tone that said she absolutely did know. "That's how Mommy talks about people."

"Mom is"—An elitist snob? A raging bitch? A sociopathic blight upon the universe?—"not the best role model for how to treat people if you want those people to like and respect you."

Serenity heaved a great sigh and looked at Kalvar. "I apologize. Is there a polite way to ask if all of your people are as pretty as you?"

"Did you run out of admirers at the academy and have to go hunting in younger forests, Zurin?" Tamrin asked, halting at the edge of the patio. The taunt, which could have been goodnatured, sounded as though it wasn't. And hearing anyone refer to Kalvar by his last name was just...weird. He was so thoroughly *Kalvar* it almost felt like he shouldn't even have a last name.

Kalvar's eyes narrowed as his gaze flicked to Tamrin. "No. Did Bryn finally run out of patience for you and send you crawling home?"

Tamrin tossed her hair back. "No." She glared at him. He glared back.

Well, that was...interesting.

Serenity cleared her throat, and Kalvar turned back to her. "No," he said, "not all Tiagren are as pretty as me."

Tamrin snorted. She hadn't looked at Evra yet, and Evra was pretending she didn't care that Tamrin was here.

"Well," Nyx said, "we should probably get started." Surely two hours of a movie would give everyone enough time to sort through their own emotions.

"What is it we are watching?" Jevryn inquired, in a voice that suggested he expected to be subjected to a particularly heinous form of torture, but had resigned himself to its occurring.

"It's called *Onward.* And I haven't seen it before." It had been time for something new. For something she didn't have prior thoughts and memories about. For an experience she could share with all of them. And a movie about a quest felt like something everyone in her group would enjoy.

She hit play and curled up on the couch next to Griff, his wing draped gently over her. Kalvar, Morgen, and Kaden took the wicker sofa opposite them, while Evra and Tamrin sat on the smaller couch between them, studiously ignoring each other with identical expressions of al'Daemon stubbornness. Serenity and Tobi ended up sprawled on the plush patio rug, surrounded by inadvisable amounts of cake.

Nyx watched the movie, and she watched the faces of her friends and her family, and she felt the cracks in her heart start to mend. It was a small mending—a small progress—but it was something, and she would take it.

BONUS SCENES

I have three bonus scenes for this book—one from Jevryn's POV, and two from Kaden's.

They are available exclusively to my newsletter subscribers, and you can get them by signing up for my newsletter at:

https://michellemanus.com/newsletter/

If you enjoyed the book, it would be beyond super awesome of you to leave a rating and/or review at your retailer of choice. Reviews really are one of the best ways you can help support authors.

Thanks so much for reading!

ABOUT THE AUTHOR

Michelle has recently escaped a desolate land, fleeing to the freezing north with her dark wizard, her unicorn, and her feline overlord. Despite certain stereotypes you may be familiar with, the dark wizard is not holding her captive, nor does the unicorn require virgin riders. The feline overlord, however, may well be evil.

You can find Michelle on her website: Michellemanus.com or join her newsletter by going to https://michellemanus.com/newsletter/ to get updates on new releases, and to receive exclusive bonus content.

ALSO BY MICHELLE MANUS

The Song Duology

A Song to Wake a Thousand Sorrows

A Song to End the World (Forthcoming)

The Aspect Society Trilogy

Siren's Song

Valkyrie's Call

Truthfinder's Promise

The Nyx Fortuna Series

Guardian of Chaos

Guardian of Shadows

Guardian of Madness

Guardian of Torment

Guardian of Defiance

Guardian of Wrath

Guardian of Exile